MW00778874

YOU ARE MY SUNSHINE

All My Love, Detrick
BOOK TWO

ROBERTA KAGAN

2nd Edition

ISBN (eBook): 978-1-957207-38-4
ISBN (Paperback): 978-1-957207-39-1
ISBN (Hardcover): 978-1-957207-40-7

Title Production by The Book Whisperer

FOREWORD

Due to falling birth rates and a desire to promote Nazi eugenics, it became evident that Germany had to implement programs to increase the population of pure Aryan children. In 1936, Heinrich Himmler built homes where women of acceptable bloodlines were to be bred with SS officers. These homes were called *Homes for the Lebensborn*.

Women who became pregnant out of wedlock could go to one of these establishments and receive the finest foods and care during their pregnancies, with no stigma attached. In fact, they were honored because they were bearing a child for Hitler, for the Fatherland. There was only one stipulation. Once the child was born, if the father was unwilling to raise it, it must be given to the Home for the Lebensborn. When a woman entered the home, she signed papers to this effect, and the policy forbade mothers from taking their children without marriage to an SS officer.

These breeding farms were created in the hopes of repopulating the world with a perfect Aryan race once the Nazis had cleared out all the undesirables, such as Jews, Gypsies, Jehovah's Witnesses, homosexuals, the physically or mentally handicapped, and anyone else Hitler saw fit to destroy.

PROLOGUE

Steinhöring, Home for the Lebensborn,
The Highlands of Munich, Germany, 1939

At first, she barely noticed the quickening. It came with just a slight flutter deep in the magical cavern of her uterus. Ever so insignificant, but Helga knew. The time had arrived. In just a few hours, the baby would enter the world.

With God's help, the child would be perfect because defective babies never leave the birthing room alive. Helga didn't know of euthanasia until she was too far into the program to escape. A shudder traveled down her back as she thought about the consequences of her actions. When she'd signed the papers and entered this place, she'd been wild with desperation. Eric, the dashing young SS officer with whom she'd fallen deeply in love, had seduced and abandoned her.

Pregnant, alone, and too ashamed to go to her family, she'd clung to the hope of a way out of her situation when the doctor suggested the Lebensborn Institute. It had seemed the perfect solution, the only solution. At the time, it had seemed easy. She'd agreed to give the child to the Lebensborn nursery as soon as it was born.

In turn, she would have a place to stay until the birth, and when she left, no one would ever know what had happened. The doctor had assured her that the child would receive the finest care until a loving family chose to adopt it. Of course, the family must meet the rigid specifications of the Third Reich.

Then, in the blink of an eye, everything changed the second she felt the tiny life stir within her. At that moment, she realized how much she had already come to love her unborn child. She found herself rubbing her belly and talking to the child that nuzzled inside.

Panic set in. Soon, they would take her baby, and she would never see it again, hold it when it cried, or comfort it in sickness. She would not be there to see the little one as it took its first steps or on the first day of school. Who would hold and love her child? *Dear God, what have I done?* She rubbed her belly and gazed out the window from her bed, watching for the light of the sunrise, but a shroud of darkness covered the lush countryside. Tears burned the backs of her eyes. *Forgive me, little one. I was young and foolish. Now it is you who will pay the price for my mistakes. If I could, I would trade my life for your safety.*

Just like the runaway train she'd boarded, her destiny raced before her at a full clip now, and she could not disembark. The Nazis did not understand a mother's love, needs, or mistakes. *Dear God, it was a mother's terrible mistake.* She prayed silently.

She'd tried to go back on the contract she'd signed, begged them, even. "Please, let me go. Please let me take my child. I will give you anything I have, anything at all. I will work and pay back the money that it cost you to keep me here all this time, but please, I am begging you, don't take my baby."

She went to the highest authorities, but they refused to listen. When Himmler visited the institute, as he did most months, she pleaded for an audience. He agreed to see her alone. She'd grasped his hand in hers, gripped it tightly, fell to her knees, and tried to make him understand how she felt. Her heart hammered in her throat as she begged, choking on the words, "Please, take pity on me." She gazed up at him, her eyes glistening with tears and hope, her body trembling as she waited for his answer.

Himmler listened. He smiled as if he were a father explaining to a young child why too much candy would give someone a tummy ache, and then patted her shoulder as she wept with her head hung down. "There is no need to cry, Helga. You are having this baby for our cause. For the Fatherland," he said, his voice gentle. "You did a good and noble thing. Now, after your child is born, if you want to raise the baby, leave here and find yourself an SS officer, get married, and then the two of you can come back and adopt your child.

“You’re a lovely Aryan girl. You should have no problem finding a good man who would be honored to be your husband. Otherwise, you must do what is best for the child. You see, your baby will have the finest home and family. The child will be adopted by a couple who will raise it properly to understand our Aryan ways and our doctrine. That will ensure that your little one will be a perfect leader in the new Germany and take his or her rightful place as a member of the superior race. You should be very proud, Helga Haswell. You should be joyful, not in tears.” He smiled and patted her head.

She released her grip on his hand, still on her knees. Then she fell flat on the floor and wept as he walked out the door.

Bastards, all of them. Helga would never have anything to do with another SS officer. She’d made that mistake before she knew who the Nazis were and realized what a price she would pay.

Good for Germany. That’s what everyone said about Hitler and his band of murderous monsters. True, he’d returned Germany’s pride, but at what price? It came at the cost of human sacrifice.

This brought back thoughts of her brother, Detrick. How he suffered. Helga knew. Everyone knew. Detrick loved the Jewish girl, Leah. When Detrick was very young, Leah’s father, Jacob, employed Detrick and offered him friendship, like a surrogate father.

The love her brother felt for the girl and her father was painful to witness because Helga knew her brother suffered every day for his feelings. Every hour, he was at risk. She hoped for Detrick’s sake that he’d broken off the relationship. Things would be easier for him. But she knew Detrick, and she knew how he loved. He could never walk away. Not her brother, not Detrick.

This time, the pain shot through her back, and Helga had to get up and sit in the rocking chair. She might be in labor for hours. It was hard to say. This was her first pregnancy, and the other girls had warned that it could be long and difficult. Perhaps she would die. Many women died in childbirth.

She felt she deserved to die, but how much pain would that bring Kurt? He loved her. They had found each other right here in Hitler's breeding lair. Kurt's sister, Hermina, was her roommate. Over time, the country girl won Helga's friendship with her honest approach. And then, one Sunday afternoon, Hermina's family came to have lunch with her. Sunday meals were when their families could come and spend time with the girls.

At first, Helga had no interest in Kurt, a mere farmer. But as she came to know him, his gentle sincerity won her over. They both knew the rules. The baby she carried would be left behind.

When Kurt saw the hurt inside of Helga, he'd urged her to try to see if they could make the adoption. "Promise them anything," he told her. "Tell them we'll raise the baby as a Nazi. Tell them we'll follow their doctrine. Tell them anything." That was a stretch for Kurt. Helga knew because Kurt hated Hitler and the entire Third Reich. Oh, how he'd tried, but in the end, all Kurt could offer Helga was a life filled with love and children she could keep, their children.

This baby, the one that lay breathing gently under her heart, this child must be sacrificed to Hitler's madness. Who was this baby? Was it a girl or a boy? What kind of man or woman would they grow up to be? Would they be kind, loving, happy—or mean and filled with hatred like all Nazis? Would it grow up to hate its mother? Helga felt she deserved to be hated, but would her baby be loved? Would it be happy? Would someone be there to bandage a skinned knee and kiss a scraped elbow? God, if only she could change what she had done. A signature so small and insignificant that was all it took to change her life forever.

It was early morning when the labor began in earnest, a little after four. Her new roommate slept soundly. Once again, Helga thought of running away. But she knew she didn't have the courage. If she were going to run, it would have had to have been much sooner than now. In a few hours, the baby would be born.

By six a.m., the pains grew more regular, still not too strong. They shot through her back and then gripped her lower abdomen. At first, the pains were at least a half-hour apart, but now they seemed to be coming every twenty minutes. She watched the sun begin to rise as a dusting of snow, like tiny bits of cotton, fell from the sky. *My baby's birthday is on January 4. No matter where life takes me, on this day every year until I die, I will think of my child. I will remember, calculate its age, and wonder where life has taken it. God, please protect my baby. Please watch over my baby. Please.*

The housemother found Helga awake at five minutes to seven.

"You are in labor?"

"Yes."

"How long, this labor?"

"About three hours."

"And your pains? When are they coming?"

"Every fifteen minutes now."

"Stay here. I get a bed, and we wheel you to the delivery room."

She labored for another five hours until the pains seemed unbearable, wishing her mother and Kurt could be with her. Then Helga felt a warm liquid running down her legs.

"Her water is broken," the housemother said as she looked under Helga's nightdress. "The baby is crowning."

Helga lay under a hot, white light. She felt the sweat dripping down her face. The pains were intense now.

"Don't push yet," a nurse said. "Wait. Not yet."

Another nurse put Helga's feet up in stirrups. The cold metal made her shiver, and the depth of the pain, along with her nerves, brought on nausea. She gagged.

"Wait… wait… wait. Okay, now, push as hard as you can."

Helga pushed. The cords in her neck and forehead stood at attention as every muscle in her body contracted, trying to force new life into the world.

"Wait… wait… All right. Now, again."

And this went on for nearly an hour before her body ripped as the tiny infant sprung from her loins, covered with mucus and blood.

The nurse caught the baby. She slapped the bottom, and a hearty cry filled the room.

"It's a little girl. She's perfect and beautiful."

Helga breathed a sigh of relief. Her child was perfect. It would be allowed to live.

"Can I hold her, please?"

"It is against the rules."

"Please, just for a moment. Please."

"Yes, okay, just for a moment."

The naked infant lay in Helga's trembling arms. Helga was exhausted, but as she looked at the tiny perfect face, the small ears, the little hands, and feet, she felt such overwhelming love and a desire to protect the child that she feared she might get up and run out of the institution in her nightgown. The stirring she felt within her breast was like none she'd ever known. Tears streamed down her sweaty cheeks.

"I love you, little one, and I am so sorry."

The nurse saw the bonding begin and reached for the baby.

"It is best I take her. It will be easier for you if you spend less time with her."

"Please let me take her home. Please. Please let me go from here and take her with me. She is only one small child. How much can one small little girl mean to Hitler? Please, I beg you, please…" Helga felt the sweat dripping down her face.

"Now you know better, Helga," the nurse said, firm but sympathetic, and she pried the infant from Helga's arms.

"No!" Helga screamed as the nurse handed the baby to the housemother. The housemother carried the child out of the room. As Helga watched, it felt like a knife had torn a hole in her heart. She hung her head and wept.

Before she knew what was happening, Helga received a shot that made her sleep, and she slept deeply. The housemother delivered the infant to the Lebensborn nursery, a room that was locked behind a heavy steel door. Although she pleaded, Helga would not see the child again.

In a week's time, Helga Haswell would be on her way to her fiancé's farm in Munich. For months to come, she cried, unable to eat or sleep, and Kurt held and comforted her, trying to ease her pain and loss. Kurt and Helga married. He was a good man and a good husband. But her arms continued to ache with emptiness for the small bundle of life she'd held for just a brief moment, an emptiness that would haunt her for the rest of her life. But somehow, Helga found the strength to go forward and build a family.

After spending the first year of her life in the Lebensborn nursery, Helga's daughter was christened in a Nazi ceremony where she would be given the name Katja and be declared ready for adoption by a suitable Nazi family.

Without the help of his Minister of Propaganda, Dr. Joseph Goebbels, Adolf Hitler could never have gained the popularity he needed to achieve absolute power. Goebbels was a master of lies, so convincing that he was able to fool an entire nation. At least, in the beginning…

CHAPTER ONE

Berlin 1936

Manfred Blau watched as Christa Henkener walked out the double doors of the high school. He could not help but notice that she had the attention of all the boys who stood on the concrete stairs smoking cigarettes. Her wavy, golden locks bounced as she descended the staircase and glittered in the sunshine.

Manfred knew better than to believe that a girl as popular and lovely as Christa would ever notice him when she could have her choice of athletes. He was nothing but a skinny, artistic boy with a bad complexion. And worse yet, his family was poor, while hers was wealthy. Everyone knew Christa's father was a famous doctor. No, she would never want any part of him. Still, he continued to gaze at her as she walked down the sidewalk on her way home.

"What are you looking at?" Alexander, a tall, muscular soccer player, asked.

"Nothing," Manfred replied and began walking away. He knew if he stuck around, Alexander's friends would be along soon, and his humiliation would be their entertainment for the next hour.

"What's your hurry?" Alexander asked.

But Manfred did not answer. Instead, he moved quickly toward home. He hated himself for the fear he felt when the others tormented him. It was not in his nature to stand up to them, and he despised that weak part of himself. If only he were stronger, more athletic, better looking, more popular. If only. Then he might have a girlfriend as lovely as Christa.

That night, he lay in bed and thought of Christa. He would do anything, anything at all, to win her heart. Soon, they would graduate, in just a month, in fact, and she would be gone from his life. If only there was a way to make an impression on her. If only.

Then Manfred got an idea. Although he had been a failure in the Hitler youth, he still planned to join the Nazi Party. He hoped to apply for a position working in propaganda under Dr. Goebbels. Of course, he knew this was a pipe dream, but his drawings were good.

It made him feel good to think that he might be someone important someday. Even his art teacher touted the excellence of his work. Perhaps his skills could be put to use. If not, he was not above making coffee or cleaning. Anything at all to find his way into the Party. From there, he just might make something of himself.

What a glorious fantasy—and then…perhaps…he could look Christa up, and she might agree to have coffee with him. Was he dreaming? He was a dreamer, but nothing can ever be accomplished without it first being a dream.

All night, he stayed awake and contemplated the situation. The more he gave it thought, the stronger the idea became. Now he had a plan.

For the next month, Manfred spent every free moment working. He illustrated and wrote children's books, stories that he knew the Party would embrace—stories about Jewish child molesters and Jewish businessmen who stole from innocent Germans—stories of Jews with tails that sacrificed Aryan infants and drank their blood. To him, the stories were silly. He knew many Jews, and they weren't really like this. In fact, he'd had a Jewish physician he had grown up with that he liked a lot, but it didn't matter. This was what the Party wanted. This was what he would give them.

Having grown up poor and unpopular, in order to survive,

Manfred had become wise in that he knew instinctively what it would take to win someone's favor. He used this knowledge sparingly, but when he did, it always worked.

The pictures were only pictures, after all, and the stories, well, just stories. How could they cause any real harm? And besides, if this little endeavor got him a decent job, he would have the money to build a life for himself and, hopefully, the woman he longed to be with, Christa. So he drew pictures of distorted-looking Jewish men with massive noses, very much resembling the pictures he'd been shown at the meetings of the *Hitlerjugend*, Hitler Youth. But in his stories, he'd added some frightening aspects. The old Jew was offering candy to beautiful blond Aryan children. On the next page, the story continued as it became clear the Jew was luring the unsuspecting children to their death. The message was clear: beware of the Jewish child molesters.

Another book explained how, on the Jewish *Shabbat*, Jews cooked and drank the blood of Christian babies. It featured a large, fat, Jewish woman, again with an oversized nose, standing over a kettle, a tail protruding from the back of her dress while she held the body of a tiny blonde infant over the cauldron, blood flowing from the child's breast into the pot.

Manfred drew pictures of Gypsies, filthy and ridden with vermin, stealing from local markets, laughing as they ran away. He wrote each story to accompany the illustrations, acting as a grim and terrifying warning to children. He made sure to fill them with the propaganda that had become popular with the Nazi Party. On the other hand, he also created books that praised the *Führer*, showing how he'd saved the German people from the devastation they'd suffered after the Great War, the loss of which he made sure to blame on the Jewish bankers.

Knowing that Dr. Joseph Goebbels was Minister of Propaganda and hoping that the time would come when Goebbels might see his work, Manfred drew a picture of a smiling Goebbels looking loyal and righteous, standing beside Hitler. Hitler's arm was around his shoulder, and at each of their sides stood a blond Aryan boy and girl, strong, athletic, and healthy. The caption Manfred wrote beneath the picture was, "The Future of our Fatherland, a land where the Aryan race can take their rightful place as rulers of the world, a land without Jews, Gypsies, and other sub-humans." And so, this was how he built a portfolio filled with children's books, all of them perfect examples of the Nazi doctrine.

Once he'd graduated from *gymnasium*, high school, Manfred would take these drawings to Goebbels himself. There, he would explain how important it was to begin educating the master race at a young age. Manfred didn't care one way or another about Jews, Gypsies, or other enemies of the Reich. What he cared about was making the right impression. This was what they wanted to hear. So this is what he would tell them. And hopefully, he would be rewarded with a job, even a small job, to get his foot in the door.

All through the graduation ceremony, Manfred kept his eyes on Christa. She moved with such grace, and her smile was so captivating. He wanted her more than anything in the entire world.

His family was poor, his father hadn't worked in a decade, and they lived on the money from his mother's sewing jobs. But if someone had offered him a choice between a million dollars and a kiss from Christa, he would have chosen the latter. She was unaware of him, and yet she was with him in his mind every moment of every day.

Manfred would make good. He would prove that he was worthy. He had to—he refused to live without her.

And so, on the first Monday after graduation, Manfred took the streetcar to downtown Berlin. The sun burned brightly in a silver-blue sky on that fateful day in June that would change his life forever. He got off at Wilhelmstrasse Street and walked along the well-manicured streets until he got to a beautiful old building known as the Leopold Palace, which housed the offices of the Propaganda Ministry. His hands trembled as he held the portfolio, and for a minute, he thought about turning back. But then, Christa's face appeared before him, and he knew he had to go forward.

People filled the palace, running this way and hurrying like bees working a springtime hive. Manfred's voice cracked as he asked a guard where he might find the offices of the Propaganda Ministry. A cute, blonde-haired receptionist directed him to go up a flight of stairs and turn left.

A dark-brown wooden door stood before him. It took all the courage he could muster to raise his hand and knock.

"Come in," said a female voice from within.

When he entered, he saw a woman sitting at a desk. She had a pleasant smile, not at all intimidating.

"Can I help you?" she asked, looking him up and down.

"I would like to speak with someone about a job."

"I don't think we need any help right now."

"Please, I need to see someone. I have some unique ideas here."

She was a middle-aged, heavyset woman with a ruddy complexion and a bun of red, wiry hair specked with gray sitting at the base of her neck. He thought that she was looking at him with a twinge of pity in her eyes.

"All right. Have a seat and wait here. I will get someone to help you."

He sat down and rubbed his hand over the leather of his portfolio. They might laugh him out of here. There was a good chance they would think him a fool. Manfred considered leaving, but before he could get up and go, a man stood before him. He was young and attractive, dressed in the neatly pressed black uniform of the SS. He reminded Manfred of the boys in the Hitler Jugend who teased him for being a poor athlete.

"Heil Hitler."

"Heil Hitler," Manfred answered.

"How can I help you?" the man asked, obviously already bored by the conversation.

"I am looking for work. I have a portfolio that I think you might be interested in looking at."

"I'm sorry. We don't need any help right now. You might want to check back with us in a few months." The SS officer turned to leave. He'd seen hundreds of these pathetic job seekers come through his doors.

"I see. But I am about to graduate from *gymnasium*. I will do anything, any type of work at all. I am a quick learner. Please, is there any work that I might qualify for?"

"I am truly sorry, but I cannot help you."

Just then, a gaunt man with dark wells forming deep eggplant-colored crevices beneath his hawk-like eyes came walking by. The skeletal man missed nothing, his eyes shifting around the room, surveying. He turned to look at Manfred. Their eyes locked, and a shudder ran through Manfred.

Hawk-Eyes stopped. He stood, listening to the conversation.

"Fritz, who is this boy?" His face was a death mask, but his tone of voice signified authority.

"He is applying for work, sir. I told him we have no work right now."

"I am Dr. Joseph Goebbels," the man said, turning to Manfred.

Oh! I never expected to meet Goebbels! I should have run out of here while I had the chance!

"My name is Manfred Blau. It is a real pleasure to meet you, sir."

"What kind of work did you have in mind?"

"Well, sir, I would do anything, anything at all. But I think I have some rather unique ideas, and I believe they could help our cause. I mean, I think it might strengthen the Fatherland."

"Hmmm, are you a party member?" Dr. Goebbels watched Manfred as he answered.

"Not yet, sir. I just graduated from *gymnasium*. I plan to join immediately. I want to be a part of this great movement. I can see Germany rising to her rightful place under the direction of our wonderful Führer."

"Of course, you were in the *Jugend*?" Goebbels asked. Although he was a twig of a man, he had an intimidating presence. Goebbels could see the eagerness in Manfred that he'd once seen in himself.

"Yes, sir. I was. And it would be my greatest wish to work for the Party in any way possible. I want to devote my life to bringing Germany back to the greatness it deserves." Manfred enthusiastically repeated the phrase he'd heard so often in the Jugend.

"Sounds to me like you are on the right track. You and I

certainly share a common goal." Goebbels studied Manfred. "I have a little time today. So I will take a moment to indulge a youth so intent on helping the Party." He smiled. "Come, follow me to my office, and let's have a look at your ideas," Goebbels said.

Goebbels limped along, dragging his leg toward the back of the building, and Manfred followed.

Once they were in the office, Goebbels motioned for Manfred to sit.

"Now let me see what this idea is that you have."

Manfred handed him the portfolio. He could hear the clock ticking overhead as the doctor slowly leafed through his work.

"This is very good. You know our *Führer* is an artist. In fact, he is quite talented, but his true brilliance is shown as a leader. As a leader, he is a god."

"Yes, sir." Manfred looked around the office. Pictures of Hitler adorned the walls, and a Nazi flag flew from the ceiling.

"This is very good," Goebbels repeated, running his fingers over his lips, "effective, too. I'd like to include these in my publication. Have you ever seen my magazine, *Der Angriff*?

"Yes, sir. I have."

"And?"

"It's brilliant, sir," Manfred said, clearing his throat.

"I founded that periodical. It is like my baby, you know, my special creation."

"Yes, I am aware of this."

Goebbels liked the boy. In Manfred, Goebbels saw himself as a youth. They shared a willingness to work and an undeniable need to overcome the obstacles of being less athletic. Neither of them had ever fit in, nor had they been accepted by their peers.

Goebbels remembered how he'd suffered at the hands of his fellow students due to his crippled leg caused by infant paralysis. He wanted to help Manfred, not so much because of Manfred, but because Manfred's success would be another blow to those athletic boys who had been born perfect. It was ironic that the ideal he promoted so vigorously would itself disqualify him from being part of the 'master race.'

"Would you like to have your work in my magazine?"

"Oh yes. It would be a great honor, sir."

"Hmmm." Goebbels nodded as he studied Manfred. "Let me make you aware that it's highly unusual for me to hire a boy right off the street, to take him under my wing and bring him into the Party, especially directly into the SS. You do realize this? I mean, this is what you are asking of me."

Goebbels had the power to do this, to take a boy, an underachiever, and give him the uniform, but until now, it had been unheard of. It was a rigorous road that led to acceptance into the SS —one Goebbels knew Manfred could not achieve without his intervention. Well, why not? That's what power was for, wasn't it? He would take this boy and mold him into a superior being. He would mold him into his own image.

"Yes, sir." Manfred looked down at his hands and saw they were trembling. He felt the sweat trickle down the back of his shirt.

"But in many ways, Manfred, you remind me of myself, my old self. The way I was at your age. You see my leg? I am a cripple. I had infantile paralysis. So I know what you went through in the gymnasium. I can see that you are no athlete."

"No, sir, I'm not, and the others never let me forget it."

"Ahhh, don't I know how that can be? Those boys who are born with perfect bodies, they can be terribly cruel.

"But you are smart. I can see that in these drawings. You know just what the country needs right now and just how to give it to them. In so many ways, you are just like I was." Goebbels looked directly into Manfred's eyes. "So, since you don't have the body, you have something better. You have the brain."

"Yes, sir."

"And I can see by your cheap suit that you come from poverty. I, too, came from humble beginnings… However, I was fortunate. I was able to attend several universities. I graduated from Heidelberg University with a doctorate in philosophy. Can you just imagine the look on the faces of all those boys who'd taunted me when I returned home with 'Doctor' in front of my name?"

He laughed and then indicated the degree that hung on his wall beside the picture of Hitler. "It was the best feeling I've ever had in my life. Except, of course, when I joined the Party, and *Mein Führer* took me under his wing. In the same way, I am going to mentor you, Manfred." Joseph Goebbels reached over and patted Manfred's shoulder. "This, my boy, is your lucky day."

"Thank you, sir. I will never be able to thank you enough."

"However, if I do this, if I hire you and take you as my own special project, you must be sure never to disappoint me. Do you understand?" Goebbels asked, smiling.

"Yes, sir. I will never do anything to disappoint you."

"Good. I need someone very discreet. I not only have a wife and five children, but I keep company with actresses occasionally. You see, the movie industry is directly under the control of the Ministry of Enlightenment and Propaganda. I have the opportunity to influence the careers of actresses. It is in the best interest of an aspiring actress to make friends with me. If I am, shall we say, unavailable at the time, and Frau Goebbels calls, I am in a very important meeting, you understand?"

"Yes, sir, completely." Manfred was awestruck that a skinny man, barely five-foot-five, dragging a club foot, would keep the company of actresses. Surely he was in the right place.

CHAPTER TWO

It was hard to believe what had just happened. He, Manfred, the nobody, had actually met and spoken to the great Dr. Joseph Goebbels. And to further escalate his excitement, Goebbels had offered him a job.

It happened just like he'd imagined it in his daydreams when the other boys were making fun of him. It happened exactly the way he'd planned. Never before in Manfred's entire life had he been showered with such good fortune.

He left the Old Chancellery building that housed the Ministry of Enlightenment and Propaganda and beheld the New Reich's Chancellery Building, where the Führer had his office. It was a magnificent structure with a pair of Hitler's honor guards by the front entrance. Manfred was relieved he didn't have to go there looking for work. He would have fainted before he made it inside.

All the way home on the streetcar, Manfred was in shock. In fact, he was so awestruck he almost missed his stop.

That day, Manfred joined the Nazi Party.

On Monday morning, he arrived at the Ministry of Enlightenment and Propaganda, bubbling with excitement, wearing his Nazi Party pin on his lapel. Although he only had a small desk in the back of the secretarial pool near the coffeepot, he was thrilled to be a part of this large and important division of the Nazi Party.

After several days, Manfred realized he was little more than an errand boy. Still, he carried it out as if it were crucial to the survival of the Fatherland. For a month, he brought coffee and strudel to the high-ranking officials. He sat quietly in meetings, not voicing opinions, just supportive of whatever Goebbels found agreeable. It was through his constant perseverance, willingness to work late, and lack of complaint that he won the favor of the Minister of Propaganda. And in winning Goebbels's acceptance, Manfred found that Goebbels was willing to take another look at his portfolio, a more serious look.

When Goebbels ordered Manfred's ideas to be incorporated by other artists who were higher ranking in the Party to create new and innovative ways of reaching the Aryan youth in the country, Manfred was flattered. Although Goebbels did not credit Manfred openly with the achievement, Manfred still felt honored to have come as far as he had. His salary also improved, along with several perks for his loyalty to the Party and the SS.

Late that summer, Manfred's father had a heart attack and died instantly. The Party rallied behind Manfred. The money for the burial, along with all the necessary arrangements, was generously taken care of by the Party. Manfred was given two weeks off work, with pay, to relocate his mother to the new apartment the SS had given them. Although his mother was grief-stricken, she found the new flat more than luxurious.

They had lived in a tenement in the poorer part of Berlin, where children ran around outside the building hungry and dirty. Now they lived in a neighborhood where flowers lined the streets, and shady trees covered the well-maintained lawns. Their lavishly-furnished new home had a plush sofa, hand-carved oak table and chairs, and two bedrooms with large beds and dressers. Food had once been scarce, but not anymore. Manfred brought home a good salary, more than enough for his mother to stop sewing, and his skinny frame began to fill out.

Every night before Manfred fell asleep, his thoughts drifted to

Christa, his dream girl. Everything he did, he did for her. Soon, he would be ready to find, approach, and win her, but not yet.

By December, Manfred was more than well-liked. He was a part of the inner circle. Goebbels often lunched with him just to talk and get things off his chest. It became known that Manfred kept to himself and never gossiped, so secrets were safe with him.

"Manfred, will you go down to the street vendor and get me a pack of cigarettes?" Dr. Goebbels asked him one cold winter morning.

"Yes, Doctor."

"And, Manfred, get me a copy of today's *Der Angriff*. I want to check the print quality."

"Yes, Doctor."

Manfred put on his SS winter coat, hat, and snow boots and, breathing out vapor with chattering teeth, trudged through the snow to the street vendor booth down the street from their office in the Ordenspalais, the old Chancellery building. The street vendor, a rotund, red-faced man with a Bavarian mustache and bundled up against the cold, greeted Manfred.

"Hello, Manfred, how is Dr. Goebbels?"

"Fine, Herr Arndt."

"And what can I do for the SS this fine, cold morning," he said, genuinely pleased to be of assistance.

"A pack of cigarettes, please." Then, considering how cold it was and that he was the office gopher, he quickly changed his mind. "Make it three packs instead—and a copy of *Der Angriff*."

"I will only charge you for the cigarettes—the paper is free. For why should Dr. Goebbels pay for his own paper?" he asked, smiling broadly.

"Thank you." Manfred counted out the Reichsmarks for the cigarettes and turned to hurry back to his warm office. He suddenly came face-to-face with an old, heavyset woman bundled up in a hat, a heavy gray wool coat, a red scarf, gray woolen stockings, and a pair of black, buckle-up goulashes over her shoes.

"Young man, do you know how to get to the Gestapo Office?" she inquired.

Recovering from the shock of suddenly seeing her when he turned around, he was curious about what this old woman would want with the Gestapo on such a cold day. *The Gestapo? Could this be an opportunity for me?*

"It is a long walk from here, and I don't have a car. What is this about?" he asked.

"I have news about a plot to assassinate our beloved Führer."

What she was saying was incredible! She could be a crackpot, and if he reported this, he could become a laughingstock. If it were true, his career might be advanced. Manfred gazed into her eyes to read her. Was she some crazy old woman with twenty-nine cats that talked to her dead husband and was having hallucinations? No, her eyes revealed a woman of clarity and reason. Manfred wanted to know more.

"And your name?"

"Kohler, Gertrude Kohler."

"Frau Kohler, let's go to the café down the street and get a hot cup of chocolate, and you can tell me your story."

"You mean I don't have to walk to the Gestapo Office?"

"No, of course not. I will help you myself."

Manfred took the old lady by the arm and guided her down the slippery sidewalk to the nearest restaurant. He helped her take off her coat and put hers and his on a coat rack by the door. Signaling the waiter, he said, "Two hot chocolates, please. And put a shot of schnapps in mine."

"Anything for our SS friends, Herr Blau," he said as he hurried to make the drinks.

The older woman took off her hat and scarf and laid them on the empty chair next to her. Her face was plump but showed lines around the eyes and mouth. Her hair was silver, but her bright blue eyes were clear. Manfred noticed age spots on the back of her hands as she removed her gloves.

"Frau Kohler—"

"Call me Gertie, please." He smiled. His black, neatly pressed SS uniform seemed to be working its magic.

"Gertie, tell me all about this plot."

"Well, I am a widow, you see. My Wilhelm passed away two years ago. Come next month, God rest his soul. I have a large house and empty rooms, and only my cat, Adolf, keeps me company. I named him after our beloved Führer. You know, I voted for Hitler."

Manfred nodded and patiently waited for the story to unfold so he could determine if any action would be needed. The waiter set two steaming mugs of hot chocolate before them and asked if they needed anything else. Manfred dismissed him with a wave of the hand. Frau Kohler took a sip of the steaming-hot, sweet, dark mixture and smiled. Considering how cold she had been, it was delicious and hit the spot.

"Anyway, where was I? Ah, yes, the plot. You see, I have an extra room in the basement I rent out to strong-looking men of the trusting sort. I am seventy-two years old, and it is good to have a man around to protect me and to fix a few things around the house." Manfred nodded, taking a sip of his chocolate schnapps mixture.

"Go on."

"Well, I rented Herr Schmidt my basement, which has a door to the outside. This is perfect for him. He can go as he pleases, and we both have our privacy."

The story was beginning to interest Manfred.

"You know how sometimes in a house with heating ductwork, you can hear it in another if someone talks in one room?"

Manfred's ears perked up, and he studied her intently.

"Well, I was listening to the radio, having a cup of coffee, petting Adolf, you know, my cat, and minding my own business when I heard two men talking. You see, my heating vent is on the floor right next to my favorite chair, the red velvet one my Wilhelm bought for me, and I could hear them talking, plain as day." She paused to take another sip of chocolate.

"What did they say?"

"They were discussing in detail how they were going to kill our beloved Führer."

"When and where?" Manfred asked, completely forgetting his chocolate and schnapps.

"Why, here in Berlin, when he delivers a speech next week. I don't know where the speech is being given, but I know it is soon."

Manfred studied her, considering what would happen if she was right and he didn't tell someone, or wrong, and he did. *If Hitler is killed, what would become of Germany? What would become of Manfred?* He decided that if this were an old lady's fantasy, the Gestapo would figure it out. It was his duty to report any possible threat to the Reich.

They talked some more and finished their chocolates.

"Gertie, would you like to meet Dr. Goebbels?"

"Dr. Goebbels? You wouldn't be teasing an old lady, would you?"

"No, Gertie, I certainly am not. Let me pay the tab, and we'll grab our coats and go there right now." He threw some Reichsmarks on the table, helped Frau Kohler put her coat on, and bundled up. They walked the three blocks to the Ministry of Enlightenment and Propaganda Office.

"Gertie, sit right here while I speak with Dr. Goebbels."

Manfred knocked on the doctor's door.

"Yes, come in. Ah, Manfred. Where have you been? I sent you for cigarettes and a paper an hour ago." Manfred handed a pack of cigarettes and the paper to his boss.

"Sorry, sir, but I ran into this civilian with this incredible story about a plot to assassinate Hitler." Goebbels's eyes widened. "I had to check the story's credibility."

"Certainly, my boy. You did right. Where are they?"

"She is just outside the door, sir."

"Bring her in."

Manfred brought Frau Kohler, and Dr. Goebbels rose to meet her, shaking her hand warmly. "Frau Kohler, this is Dr. Joseph Goebbels."

"I am honored, Dr. Goebbels."

"The honor is all mine, Frau Kohler."

"Call me Gertie," she said.

"Gertie," he said, turning on the charm. "Manfred says you have something to tell us."

Frau Kohler related the entire story while the doctor took notes, nodding at times, saying 'hmmm' at others and 'uh huh,' at others.

"Gertie, is this man still living there?"

"Why, yes, Doctor, he comes and goes daily."

"Gertie, go home and act as if nothing has happened. We will take care of this for you. Do not tell this man anything. What is his name?"

"Johann Schmidt."

"An assumed name, no doubt. In any case, let this be our secret, just between us."

She rose, and he took her hand. "Gertie, you have done a great service to our Fatherland and our beloved Führer."

"It has been a privilege to help you, Herr Doctor." Manfred walked her to the door at the front of the building. When he returned, Dr. Goebbels called him.

"Close the door, Manfred." Manfred did as he was instructed. "I know people, and that woman is telling the truth. You did the right thing, bringing her here. Yes, Manfred, you are a diamond and a true asset to the Party. Now, don't tell anyone about this. I will inform the Gestapo and send a letter to Hitler's office. If the account is credible, we will protect Germany from its enemies. If not, we did our duty anyway."

"Yes, sir."

"And Manfred?"

"Sir?"

"Any time you want to save the Fatherland, I can wait on my smokes," he said, smiling broadly.

Manfred smiled in return and went back to his desk by the coffeepot.

Three days later, the Gestapo arrested a German citizen, whose name wasn't Johann Schmidt, and two others for treason against the Reich, and all were executed. Manfred was called into Goebbels's office.

"Manfred, sit down," the doctor motioned, "and close the door."

"Yes, sir."

"Manfred, remember Frau Kohler?" How could he forget? It was all he had thought about since last week.

"Yes, Doctor. I heard the Gestapo arrested three men."

"Yes, the ringleader was half-Jewish. He influenced two German Aryans to join him in his filthy plot. That is why we enacted the Nuremberg Race Laws. A little leaven leaveneth the whole lump, eh, Manfred?"

"Yes, sir."

"I am happy to say that you will be receiving a commendation from our beloved Führer himself. And effective immediately, you are hereby promoted to *Scharführer*, sergeant."

A promotion—a promotion! Manfred would finally have found a place for himself in the world. Perhaps he would be in a position worthy of a man proposing marriage to a woman like Christa. His heart skipped a beat as he walked toward home, his mind racing. She didn't know who he was back in school. It was not as if he could just appear at her door and say, "Hello, would you like to have dinner with me?" even though he already knew where she lived. How was he to ever approach her?

All night he contemplated ideas but came to no logical conclusion. Then the following day, and without any plan at all, he took the streetcar to the neighborhood where she lived. For most of the day, he sat on a bench in the park across the street from her house. He had a book with him and held it open, but he never read a word. Instead, he waited to see if she would come outside. She didn't. Manfred waited until the sun had fallen and darkness descended upon the streets before heading home.

"Where have you been? I've been worried," Manfred's mother said, even before he took his jacket off.

"I was out with some friends from work."

She nodded. "I don't mind you going. It's good for you to get out with people your own age, but please let me know so I don't worry about you, alright?" She was glad he had finally made some friends. It was hard to watch him grow up as such a lonely child. But even though she was pleased, she was also a little jealous. After all, since her husband died, he was her sole companion.

Again, on Sunday, he went to the park across the street from Christa's house, watching, waiting, and hoping. He did not know what he might do or say if he saw her but was unable to leave as if held down by an invisible force. She did not appear.

Manfred was caught up in the preparations for the Führer's visit. He must see to the orders of the special food and handmade white tablecloths with the swastika insignia embroidered into their fine linen fabric. Manfred shellacked the wood of the podium that Hitler would use for his speech until it shined like brushed gold. A brand new Nazi flag was purchased and hung on a brass pole while he carefully placed an oil painting of the Führer behind the podium. It was ironic because Manfred was decorating and cleaning up for his own awards ceremony.

On the eve of Adolf Hitler's arrival, Manfred and Goebbels surveyed the conference room.

"Once again, you did not let me down, Manfred. You're a diamond, and because you have been such a help, I would like to introduce you to our leader."

Manfred gasped. He could hardly speak. "Me? Introduce me to Hitler? Thank you. Truly, thank you."

"Be here early tomorrow. I want to be sure everything is perfect. He wants to meet the man who saved his life."

"Of course."

The excitement spread through the office like smoke after a wildfire. It was unavoidable and strong enough to penetrate the lungs, polluting any clean air that might remain.

When Hitler arrived and entered the office surrounded by his entourage, a roar of enthusiasm shook the room. Although Hitler was not a large man, he commanded attention. It took five minutes of him raising his hands to quiet the crowd before he was able to speak.

Despite his small stature, Hitler's voice was anything but small. In fact, it was so loud that it rang throughout the hall with a power that could not be rivaled, even by an entire marching band. Manfred glanced around to see that the entire group was spell-bound, their faces open, receiving and internalizing everything the

Führer said. It felt good to see a man who was not athletic and, in many ways, very much like himself, so powerful and adored.

The women looked at him with such strong desire that Manfred was stunned. A smile crept over Manfred's face. This was what he longed for. He would rise in the Party. He would be a voice to be reckoned with. Hitler concluded his speech by awarding both Manfred and Frau Kohler *The Knight's Cross of the War Merit Cross.*

After his speech, Hitler's bodyguards escorted him into the private conference room of the Minister of Propaganda. Manfred was among one of the few employees invited. As the diners took their places, Hitler stopped for a moment to admire the lovely tablecloth, ordered and designed by Manfred, who beamed at the compliment, even though it was directed at Dr. Goebbels and not at him.

"You've done well, Goebbels."

"Thank you, *Mein Führer.*"

"And I finally get to meet the courageous young man who foiled the evil Jewish plot! Scharführer Blau, the Fatherland owes you a debt of gratitude."

"Thank you, Mein Führer," Manfred said.

"Manfred Blau, Joseph tells me that you are quite a help to him. In fact, he mentioned that you did some outstanding children's books to further our cause. The young people are the most important citizens of the Third Reich. They are the future of our Aryan race. Correct?"

"Yes, Mein Führer."

"Excellent! I saw some of your work. Being an art student myself, I must say it was quite impressive."

"Thank you. Thank you, sir."

"We'll have to keep an eye on you, Manfred Blau, now, won't we?" Hitler placed a firm hand on Manfred's shoulder. Manfred's star was on the rise, and everyone knew it.

The food was delicious, but Manfred could hardly eat. He was too enthralled. He met and spoke to Hitler himself, and Hitler was keeping an eye on him. Manfred was on his way. He was moving up in the world.

On Saturday, Manfred went to the park across the street from the Henkeners' home. He took his seat on the bench and opened the small paper bag he'd packed. Taking a bite of the pastry inside, he licked his lips. Life was sweet. He was no longer an outcast. He was on his way to becoming an important man.

His eyes were fixed on the large cherry wood door of Christa's house. Even from where he sat, he could see the thick gold knocker. Manfred took a deep breath. It took all the courage he could muster. Then he stood up and tossed the bag and its contents into a trash can. Wiping his hands together to be sure that there was no trace of powdered sugar, he straightened his suit and tie and walked over to the house where the woman of his desires lived.

Once Manfred knocked on the door, he was sorry he had. His nerves and feelings of inferiority returned. He wanted to run away and wished he'd brought flowers. A million thoughts ran through his mind. But before he could turn and bolt, the door opened. A maid in a navy-blue uniform with white lapels and a crisp white apron stood before him.

"Can I help you, sir?" the woman asked.

This was his only chance. If he left now, he could never come back. His heart beat so hard that it seemed to want to leap out of his chest. And then, there she was—Christa, beautiful Christa.

"Who is it, Mary?" Christa asked the maid.

"I don't know. Are you selling something?" the maid called Mary asked him.

"No, I'm here to see you." He could not believe his own words. "Christa."

"Do I know you?"

"Probably not. I was in your class in school, and I was wondering if you would like to have dinner or coffee with me." *How clumsy I am, how awkward,* he thought. He stood trembling—waiting for her answer, wishing the concrete beneath his feet would swallow him.

It took a moment, but to Manfred, it seemed like centuries. Then a smile came over her lovely face. Her bright blue eyes danced.

"Yes," she said. "A coffee would be nice. How about tomorrow afternoon?"

"Yes, yes, that would be fine. I will be here to pick you up at two. Would that be all right?"

"Yes, perfect." She nodded.

"Well, then…"

"I'll see you tomorrow."

She closed the door, and he walked back toward the bus, his feet on the ground but his head dancing in the clouds with the fairy king and his entire court.

By a quarter to two the next day, Manfred was pacing the sidewalks in front of the Henkener home. In his hands, he carried a bouquet of red roses and a box of cream-filled chocolates, which had been quite difficult to acquire.

He felt dizzy in a kind of dream-like state. It was hard to believe that he would be spending time with Christa, the woman he'd wanted as long as he could remember, a woman far above his class. Until now, this had been only a fantasy. But soon, he would sit across the table from her, and they would sip coffee. She would speak to him while he gazed into her crystal-blue eyes.

Manfred knocked on the door and waited. Christa answered instead of the servant girl.

"Would you like to come in?" She wore a pale blue dress that brought out the rich, sky-blue of her eyes. As she opened the door, he saw her pale-pink nail polish, and his heart fluttered. He missed nothing. From her slender ankles to her wavy golden hair, Christa was truly lovely.

"Yes, of course," he said, but he was frightened. He'd never dated a woman before, and he'd certainly never been inside a potential girlfriend's home, meeting her parents.

Manfred was glad that he was wearing the impressive black uniform of the SS. It gave him an air of sophistication and importance. Importance he did not feel. After all, until just a few months ago, he had been an unpopular boy at school, shunned by the more attractive athletic students and forced to spend his time alone, drawing pictures in the art lab. Well, he bore no resemblance to that boy anymore, at least not on the outside.

Christa showed him into a small sitting room with a plush love seat and two chairs upholstered in deep-gold velvet interlaid with hunter's green needlework. The walls were lined with books, their leather jackets bringing warmth to the room.

He handed her the gifts. "I brought you some things," he said, feeling clumsy and awkward again.

"Thank you. The flowers look and smell lovely. And the chocolates, well, they are my favorite kind. How did you know? And how did you ever get them?"

He smiled. She had such poise, such grace.

"I didn't realize that you were in the SS. You weren't wearing your uniform yesterday when you arrived."

"No, it was my day off, and I was just taking a walk."

"So you just decided to come by?"

"I… Yes, I just decided to come by…"

"How did you know where I live? I'm afraid I don't even remember you from school." She placed the flowers in a vase but did not yet go to the kitchen to water them.

"I… Well, I-I've always known," he stammered, almost wishing he could get up and run out the door. "I guess you could say I've had a crush on you for years." There, he'd said it. Now he felt even more foolish and vulnerable. His hands trembled as they gripped the sides of the chair. He looked down and noticed that his knuckles had turned white. Then quickly, he released them, hoping she didn't see how nervous he was.

"I'm flattered." She smiled. Her teeth were like snow on Christmas morning against her light red lipstick.

She sat down in the chair beside him. From where he sat, he could catch whiffs of her perfume. Not overpowering, just enough to be enticing.

"Well, Manfred. Tell me a little about yourself."

"I am an artist. I work under Dr. Goebbels."

"Really? That's rather impressive for one so young. Have you ever met him?"

"I have. I speak to him all the time."

"Do you really?" He saw that she was impressed. It gave him strength. "He scares me. He looks so serious and stark."

"I suppose he can be, but he has always been very kind to me." Manfred began to relax.

"Why don't we have coffee here? I can have Mary bring us a tray, and we can just sit and talk."

"If you prefer," Manfred said.

"Yes, and then perhaps I will allow you to take me to dinner." She smiled. "Mary!" she called, and within seconds, the woman appeared.

"Yes, ma'am?"

"Can you bring us a tray of coffee and some sweets?"

"Of course, ma'am."

"So, I suppose you have seen Hitler?"

"I've dined with him."

"My goodness, you really have made a name for yourself."

He smiled.

"My father doesn't like the Party. He doesn't like Hitler or, as he calls them, 'his goons.'" She laughed, and it sounded like the ringing of tiny bells to him.

Manfred knew this was treason, but he would keep his mouth shut. With any luck, this man would be his future father-in-law.

They sipped black coffee. The pastries were small and bland. Christa apologized for the lack of sugar. "It's hard to come by, as you must know."

"Yes, I know." He said and made a mental note to bring some sugar the next time he visited. Provisions were easier to acquire for party members.

The sun began to set, casting a golden light on the trees and grass.

"May I be so honored as to take you to dinner?" Manfred asked, not looking directly at her.

"Yes," she answered. "Let me go and get my purse."

He had plenty of cash, and that felt good for a boy who'd been raised in poverty. The Nazi Party was surely good to him.

As they walked toward the main street, he realized that he didn't know the area. It would have been wise to do some planning, to learn the area, so that he could suggest a restaurant.

"I'm sorry. I'm not familiar with this neighborhood. Do you have a favorite place to dine?"

"It just so happens, I do." She winked at him.

When he walked her home that night, they stood under the light over her front door. Manfred had never been out with a girl before. He didn't know what to do. He just stood with his hands in his pockets, staring at the ground, feeling foolish.

"Well, goodnight, and thank you for a wonderful evening," he said.

"Wait." She took his hand in hers and looked up into his eyes. "Would you like to kiss me goodnight?" she asked.

Would he? Would he? Of course he would, but he'd never kissed a woman before and didn't know what to do. *Just do what you've seen in movies*, he told himself. Taking her into his arms, he pressed his lips to hers. Every nerve in his body and his senses came alive in a divine dance of heightened awareness. He took in the sweet fragrance of her perfume, the taste of her lips. The softness of her cheek as it brushed against his. *I must be the luckiest man in the world*, he decided.

Every Saturday night, from that day on, he took her to dinner, followed by long walks. They discussed everything, their favorite foods, how much they both enjoyed swimming on a hot summer day and their love for children and animals.

"Someday, when I marry, I want to have lots of children," Christa said.

"Yes. It would be wonderful to sit at the table on Sunday nights and have a big dinner, like a real family."

"Yes, that would be wonderful. When I was little, I used to plead with my parents for a brother or sister. But I was born sick, and my father, being a doctor and all, didn't want to risk having it happen again."

"Are you all right?"

"Yes, I'm fine now."

"I'm glad. I wouldn't want to think you were not well."

She squeezed his upper arm. "I'm just fine. I still wish I had a brother or sister, though."

"I felt the same growing up. It was lonely growing up an only child," Manfred said. It was hard to admit how vulnerable he'd been in his youth. But he found himself opening up in ways he never thought possible.

"It's very strange that we are both only children."

"Yes, it is. It is another thing we share in common, and there are so many," he said.

She smiled at him. "Yes, there are…"

They walked through the zoo in the park, holding hands. It was enough just to be together.

Often when we fall in love with someone from afar, we find that when we meet them and spend time with them, they do not live up to the fantasy we have created of them. This was not the case with Christa. Christa, the woman, was every bit the dream realized.

What began as a regular Saturday night date grew to include a twice-a-week luncheon. Every Tuesday and Thursday, Christa took the streetcar into town to meet Manfred for lunch. Often they dined at outdoor cafés on bratwurst and beer. They sat under an umbrella, laughing, talking, and smiling at the locals who walked by with their dogs on leashes. Whenever the flower girls came by selling flowers on the street, Manfred always bought a bouquet for Christa.

It was mid-March, and though winter was soon to yield to spring, winter had not yet gotten the message. Snow covered the trees and lawns when Christa invited Manfred to Sunday dinner with her parents.

"I would like my parents to meet you. They have begun to wonder where I am going all the time and just what I've been up to. It's time they knew." She gazed at him, her eyes as warm as honey butter. "But Manfred…" she hesitated. "I have to ask you to please not be offended, but you mustn't wear that uniform when you come. I think I've mentioned it before, but I have to tell you again, my father is a little skeptical about the Party."

Her eyes told him that she was unsure of how he might respond.

She needn't have worried. No matter what, he would not turn on anyone from her family. He would never alert the Gestapo. If need be, he would cover for her father himself if it meant that her father would give his blessing to the relationship.

"I will wear street clothes," he said. "Does your father know what I do for a living?"

"No, I've just told him that I am keeping company with someone. He was rather angry that I have not yet invited you to the house."

"I am glad to be invited to meet your family."

"You know I would have invited you sooner, but I was afraid of what you might say when you found out how strongly my father disapproved of the Party."

He was quiet for a moment. Then he gingerly took her hand in his. The skin was softer than anything he'd ever felt. She turned to face him.

"I believe in the Party, Christa. I believe we are doing the right thing for Germany and the German people. But well…" He sighed and took a deep breath. Her eyes were locked on his. "I love you." There—he'd said it. His voice cracked, but he'd said it. Manfred cleared his throat. "And so I will respect your father and his beliefs. I will keep the secret of how he feels to ensure his safety and, most of all, yours."

On the Friday night before Manfred met Christa's family, Christa agreed to meet Manfred in the city. She was to arrive at his office just as they were closing.

"When you come to town on Friday night, I would like to take you to a fancy dinner and then out dancing. Would you like that?" he'd asked.

"Yes, I would, very much," she'd said.

During the week, as they sat having lunch in the lunchroom, Manfred had asked all of his coworkers for a recommendation for where to take Christa. Everyone piped up with a suggestion. This was an important night. Manfred wanted to be sure that everything was perfect.

"Oh, the café at the corner is nice."

"No, that's not fancy enough," Manfred said.

"How about the nightclub with the big statues in front?"

"No, that's not elegant at all." Manfred shook his head.

Finally, one of the women suggested, and Manfred agreed upon an expensive restaurant with a dance floor and complete band right in the center.

"Can you waltz, Manfred?" a secretary in the office asked. Manfred had become friendly with Lydia. She was an older woman, kind and understanding, and always willing to lend an ear when Manfred wanted to talk, especially about Christa.

"Actually, I can. My mother taught me," he said. "I am a little nervous, however, because I am going to ask Christa to be my wife tonight."

"Oh, how special! Well, she should love the restaurant."

"I hope so." Manfred's fingers caressed the box in his jacket pocket. "Would you like to see the ring I bought?"

"Yes, of course."

He took the box from his pocket and pulled the top back to reveal the ring. It was diamond, over a carat, so much more than a poor boy like Manfred would ever have been able to afford. Before he became a part of the New Germany—before he claimed his rightful place in the world.

"Oh, my goodness! This is a beautiful ring, magnificent, really," Lydia said.

"Thank you. She is more than deserving," Manfred said.

And so Christa came into the city to meet Manfred at his office after work. He saw the admiration shining in her eyes as he showed her his desk. But when he introduced her to Goebbels, she beamed. It was then that he knew that she would accept his proposal. Christa Henkener would be his wife.

She linked her arm to his as they walked a few blocks to the restaurant. They entered to find a large room with white-tablecloth-adorned tables and a dance floor in the center. The waiters wore white gloves, and the centerpieces were made up of wildflowers surrounding a thick, ivory-colored candle. Manfred had telephoned the restaurant earlier in the day and arranged for the band to play a song and dedicate it to Christa after dinner.

"I will pass a note through the waiter when I am ready. Then you will announce that the song you are about to play is from Manfred to Christa," Manfred had told the restaurant host. Of course, the request had been received without a question once Manfred told the host that he was an SS officer working directly under Dr. Goebbels.

Christa looked lovely. She wore a dove-gray skirt with a blouse that matched her eyes perfectly. In her ears, she wore small diamonds, and her golden hair waved back away from her face just enough to show off their sparkle.

"You are breathtakingly beautiful," Manfred said.

"Thank you." She smiled, her eyes catching the light from the candles' glow.

Although the food was scrumptious, neither could eat. There was tension between them. Him because he knew and her because she sensed something. Once the dinner plates had been cleared, Manfred took Christa's hand and led her to the dance floor. She moved like a butterfly, delicate and agile in his arms. They danced through two songs before he escorted her back to the table.

He sat across from her for several moments. He didn't speak, couldn't look at her. His face flushed, and his fingers felt as if they were being pricked by tiny pins. In his pocket, he grasped the small box.

"Christa..." he stammered, "I... I..." Then he got down on the floor on one knee. "Will you marry me?"

She took his hand in hers. With her other hand, she lifted his face until their eyes were locked.

"Yes, Manfred, I will marry you," she said. A tear fell from her eye and lingered on her cheek. Manfred stood, lifted Christa, took her into his arms, and kissed her.

He brought the ring from his pocket. "I hope you like it."

"Oh, my! It's lovely," she said. He put it on her finger.

"Tomorrow, we must talk to your parents."

"Yes, tomorrow."

Manfred gave the signal, and the bandleader introduced the song.

"This is for Christa, from Manfred," he said over the microphone. "It's called, 'I Will Love You Forever.'"

"Oh, Manfred, I am so touched," Christa said, her eyes shining.

"I will love you forever, Christa," he said. "I will."

That night, Manfred hardly slept. He'd won the woman of his dreams. Christa would be his wife, and she would bear his children. And together with their offspring, they would go through life in a state of incredible bliss. The Party would help him to buy a home. He would become well-known as a man of power and be respected. Life was good, and it was in the process of getting better. What more could a poor boy from the wrong side of Berlin ever ask for? He smiled in the darkness. Manfred had made this all happen.

That was until the Sunday when Manfred arrived, toting a bottle of fine wine for Dr. Henkener, a box of chocolates for Frau Henkener, and a large bouquet of red roses for Christa. He had never been beyond the sitting room right off the front door in the Henkener home.

When he rang the bell, Mary opened the door and showed him into the living room, where Christa waited with her parents. He'd been careful to wear a civilian suit, as Christa had requested. It was made of dark-gray wool, well-tailored, and had cost him nearly a week's salary. However, he didn't care. Christa was worth every penny. Manfred presented them with his gifts. Christa's mother smiled and glanced at Christa as he gave her the chocolates, but Dr. Henkener just glared at him. When Manfred handed the physician the wine, he didn't even thank him. Instead, he placed the bottle on the coffee table as if it were a mere afterthought.

"Mother, Father," Christa said, "This is Manfred Blau. We have been keeping company for several months." She looked down at the floor. "He has asked for my hand in marriage, and I have accepted. We would like your blessing."

"Oh? You would, would you?" Her father said. "You know how I feel about the Nazis and how they have ruined Germany."

"Father, please."

"You think you can fool me by wearing that suit? I know who you are and, more importantly, what you are. You are one of them, one of the murderers. I don't bless this marriage, Christa. Not at all. He is not a man I want to have in my family. You work for Goebbels, don't you?"

Manfred knew he had to confess. "Yes, sir. I do."

"Why? Why do you want to be part of a hate squad, son?"

"How did you know I work for Goebbels?"

"I'm a doctor in this town. I see and hear everything. My patients tell me everything. You and your cohorts are responsible for making many people miserable. Do you have any idea how the propaganda you spread affects people? The Nazis made it illegal for ethnic Germans to patronize Jewish businesses or work for Jews.

"The propaganda taught in schools is spreading racial hatred. Have you heard of the nonsense the Party teaches the children in school? Young man, I suppose since you work for Goebbels, you are involved in spreading these lies. It has been reported that the Hitler Youth have been beating Jews who stray out of the Jewish sector. This is not Christian, and this is not right in the sight of God."

"Father…" Christa raised her voice.

"I am not afraid to speak my mind. Take me, arrest me. Go ahead. Send me off to one of your work camps if you wish. But I will tell you this. These crimes you are committing, you and your Nazi friends, will not go unpunished. There is a God, and I have news for you; it is not Adolf Hitler."

Dr. Henkener walked out of the room. Christa burst into tears. Her mother went to her and took her in her arms. Manfred sat on the edge of the sofa, feeling awkward and uncomfortable. Dr. Henkener had hurt his feelings and forced him to think too much. If the man were not Christa's father, he would turn him in to the Gestapo today for his comments against the mighty Führer, who Manfred had come to believe had saved Germany. But a little voice in Manfred's head said, "If not Germany, well, at least he saved me."

"Excuse me…" Manfred said. "I must be going." He got up to leave, and Christa rushed to his arms.

"Wait. Please, let me go for a walk with you."

If he was correct, he saw a glint of fear in her eyes. Did his beloved believe he might turn her father in for treason? Was she that unsure of his feelings for her?

"All right," he said.

A fresh blanket of snow covered the sidewalk. Manfred held Christa's arm so she would not slip and also because he loved touching and being close to her.

"My father didn't mean what he said," she said as they walked toward the park. "He thinks he knows so much, but he doesn't really understand. Please forgive him."

"It doesn't matter what he thinks. If you will still be my wife, we will marry without his blessing."

"Of course I will," she said. "Manfred..." She cleared her throat against the cold. "You won't report my father, will you?"

"No, darling, I would never do that to you. But you and your mother must speak with him. He is far too outspoken for his own good and for the good of his family. If he continues to voice his negative opinions, he will surely be arrested. There are spies everywhere. He must learn to be quiet. I love you, Christa, and I would do whatever I could for you and your family, but if he is caught, I may not be in a position to help him."

"I'm afraid for him, Manfred. I'm terribly afraid."

"I know, darling. You must go to your mother, and the two of you must make him understand. He is not only hurting himself, but he is also hurting both of you. Silence him—you must."

She nodded, wondering how she would ever reach her strong-willed father.

"Now, on a happier note, let's plan a wedding," he said, gently squeezing her arm.

"I don't know if my father will pay for a wedding."

"We don't need him. We'll have a small ceremony, something I can afford."

"Are you sure?"

"Absolutely." He gently pinched her cheek. "Your father will come around. He'll see I'm not such a bad guy after all."

"I hope so. He can be so stubborn sometimes, but he is a good man. It hurts my heart to think he might not attend my wedding."

"I know. We will do what we can to try to convince him. Yes?"

"Yes." She sniffled, and he knew she was close to crying again.

"I love you, Christa. I am going to do everything I can to give you a good life and make sure you are happy. I think perhaps I loved you from the first time I saw you. Give me a chance. Don't let this thing with your father discourage you. Please."

"I won't. I will still marry you," she said. But he saw that a dark spot of doubt had covered the sunny glow in her eyes.

"Trust me. When he sees how much being on the right side of the Party can do for him, he will surely change his mind. They are generous and good to their own. I promise you this."

She nodded.

CHAPTER THREE

"I'M GETTING MARRIED," Manfred told Goebbels the following day as they ate their lunch in Goebbels' office.

"Oh, is it the girl who was here the other night?"

"Yes, it's her. Christa Henkener."

"She's a real beauty."

"Thank you, sir."

"You should be proud."

"I am," Manfred said. He thought about talking to Goebbels about his future father-in-law. Perhaps his mentor could help. But then again, he might alert Goebbels to an enemy of the Reich, and the doctor could be arrested. That would be a big problem with Christa right before the wedding. It was best not to mention anything.

"Where are you going on your honeymoon?"

"I don't know. We haven't decided."

"How about the highlands? It's a beautiful country up there in Munich. I've always loved Munich. Once, long ago, I wanted to live there. Have you ever been there?"

"No, sir. My family never had enough money to travel."

"Ah well, I could arrange for the Party to pay for a lovely honeymoon for you and your bride in Munich. Would you like that?"

"Oh yes, sir. That would be wonderful. And my future wife would appreciate it as well. "

"I will take care of it right away."

"When do you plan to marry?"

"As soon as possible."

"Well, this is rather good news. Hitler will be coming to visit again in early May. Perhaps you might want to invite him to the wedding. Of course, only if that gives you enough time to plan everything."

Manfred thought of his father-in-law. He worried that the old man might say the wrong thing. Still, Adolf Hitler, attending his wedding! What a compliment—what an honor. He would surely go places in the Party with a credit like that under his belt.

"Of course. I would be honored, sir. And we will make sure to book the reception when our Führer will be here in Berlin. Do you think he actually might attend?"

"He might. You never know with him. Sometimes he will do something so wonderful and unexpected. There is no telling."

"I will send an invitation to his secretary as soon as we book the banquet room."

"No need to book anything, son. Would you like to have the wedding at that lovely restaurant where you proposed?"

"You know where I proposed?" Manfred didn't remember telling him.

"Of course, I know. I know everything that goes on around here. That's why I am the Minister of Propaganda."

Manfred felt a pang of concern. Perhaps Goebbels knew about Dr. Henkener as well. "I would love to have it there, but I am afraid it might be too expensive."

"Your future in-laws have plenty of money, don't they?"

"Yes, but they are not as generous with it as we would like."

"Well, don't worry. The Party will cover the wedding as well. You just tell your future wife to get her guest list together. And let's get started planning this wedding. And perhaps, just perhaps, I might play a song on the piano at your wedding."

"You play piano, Doctor?"

"In fact, I do. I love music."

"So do I," Manfred said.

"So, Manfred, what do you say? Shall we begin wedding preparations? "

"Oh yes, sir. Thank you, sir. Thank you so much," Manfred stammered. The Party was good to him—very good.

CHAPTER FOUR

With only a few months to plan the wedding, the couple was caught in a whirlwind of excitement. They sent invitations to relatives on both sides. Manfred, escorted by Goebbels, went to see the proprietor of the restaurant. The owner and manager of the restaurant personally greeted them like royalty. They offered tastings of the food until they selected the menu to be served on the special day. The band that had played the night of Manfred's engagement agreed to play at the wedding.

The hall would be decorated with Nazi flags and pictures to honor the Führer and the Fatherland. Goebbels ordered that the tablecloths Manfred designed, those with the embroidered swastikas, be used. Manfred agreed whole-heartedly. The silverware was plated with 14-karat gold, and the ivory dishes made of fine German China had tiny gold swastika emblems around their perimeters.

Christa quickly took her mother's gown to the dressmaker for alterations, which took time, but Frau Strum had known the Henkeners for over ten years, so she agreed to put the job in front of any others she might have in her queue. Of course, part of that decision was made when she was told that Christa's future husband was working for the SS directly under Goebbels.

Together, Manfred and Christa visited a florist that was highly recommended by Dr. Goebbels. Goebbels made a phone call before the couple arrived, and the florist agreed to do the tables, boutonnieres, and bouquets, all in pink tea roses, at no charge. The florist said it was a gift for a fellow citizen who was working so hard for their cause.

As a wedding gift, Manfred gave Christa a necklace of ivory-white pearls. He gave them to her early so she would be able to wear them on their wedding day. When she received his gift, she cried joyfully and put her arms around his neck.

"Manfred, you have made me the happiest woman in the world!"

"And you have made me the happiest man."

One evening, Manfred and Christa were invited to have dinner with Goebbels and his wife, Magda. They met at a favorite restaurant a few blocks from the New Reich's Chancellery.

"Heil Hitler." The group had exchanged greetings before the host ushered them to a table by the window.

"This is my wife, Magda. Magda, this is Manfred Blau. I've told you a little about him. And this is his future wife, Christa Henkener."

"A pleasure to meet you both," Frau Goebbels said, smiling.

"My pleasure," Christa said.

The dinner went well. The women talked about weddings and children while Manfred and Joseph looked on.

But even in the midst of all of his joy, and even with all that Joseph Goebbels had done for him, when Manfred looked at the doctor, he still looked like the death-head symbol.

It was mid-April when Manfred found the letter waiting on his desk. It was stamped with Hitler's insignia. His hand trembled with excitement, but he wanted to keep this letter in mint condition to serve as a keepsake. He resisted the impulse to tear into it. He took the letter opener with the Nazi symbol on it from his desk drawer and slit the envelope open.

"The Führer will be honored to attend the wedding of Manfred Blau and Christa Henkener."

Manfred read the letter over twice. He could not believe it. Hitler himself would be at the wedding! Carefully, Manfred placed the letter in the drawer in his desk, where he kept his most special Nazi memorabilia. Later, he would buy an expensive picture frame and display it prominently on his wall.

CHAPTER FIVE

THOMAS HENKENER SAT beside his wife, Heidi, at their kitchen table. Christa was not yet awake.

"Manfred brought Christa some butter. If you would like, you can have some of it on your toast. I'm sure she won't mind."

"I mind. I mind very much. I don't want anything from that boy or his Nazi friends. He is nothing more than a hoodlum."

"Perhaps, Thomas, but Christa is fond of him, fond enough of him to agree to be his wife. We don't want to lose our daughter over this, do we?"

"I cannot understand how a child of mine could be seduced by the lies of the Nazi Party. Not only is this boy a Nazi, but he is a member of the SS, the worst kind of Nazi, the cruelest."

"Maybe not. He only works in an office."

"Yes, he works slandering and ruining good people. Why? Because he feels superior? Somehow, in his distorted brain, he has decided that he is part of some imagined Aryan race, an insane notion. That is for sure. I hope you know that most of these SS men couldn't be compared to a doctor like Dr. Shulman in knowledge or character."

"I understand. I know you think of Dr. Shulman as a friend, a colleague who has earned your respect over the years. But Thomas, please remember, Dr. Shulman is a Jew, and we live in dangerous times."

"Do you think I am afraid? How can you forget how sick little Christa was with that terrible heart problem? It was Dr. Shulman that helped her and, in truth, saved her life. Without him, we wouldn't have a daughter. You must remember how we prayed. I can still see Shulman walking into the room, taking your hand, then telling you it would all be all right. How can you forget this, Heidi? He is a brilliant doctor. Besides, do you think these boys, with their fancy uniforms and ridiculous notions, scare me?"

"You should be afraid. You should take care of what you say. It not only affects you, but it also affects Christa and me, not to mention your sister and her family. Be more careful, Thomas. Think before you speak and before you act. I know you see these stormtroopers as mindless thugs, but they have power, Thomas, real power. The power to make our lives a living hell, even to kill us."

"Can't you see? How can I turn on the men I have worked beside at the hospital for the last twenty-five years, men like Shulman, Kahn, and Schultz? They are all Jews, but each of them, in his own right, is a brilliant doctor. I've gone to them for help with consultations. They have stood beside me in surgeries. I know these men. I know their hearts and minds. What is going on here is a dirty shame, an embarrassment to good German people. When Germany persecutes its citizens for no valid reason, we, the German people, lose."

"I know all of this. I've heard it a dozen times. You have told me and told me. But you must not forget for a minute that the Nazis are in control. They have the power to send you to a work camp or worse. That would kill me. So please, I am begging you, for my sake, if for nobody else, try to be quiet. Try, Thomas, please. Try to ignore them." Her eyes fixed on his, and he could see the lines deepening in her brow.

Thomas Henkener sat in silence, staring at the bread and the large bowl of butter, his fingers running up and down the handle of the sterling silver knife. He could not eat the butter, for it would turn his stomach. He stood and got up from the table.

Heidi, poor Heidi, she was afraid. He looked at her slumping shoulders. Age had given her back a slight hump. Looking at it made him feel sad and tender toward her. He walked over and gently squeezed her shoulder.

"I will try. For you, I will try," he said. She looked up at him, her eyes glistening as if she might cry. Thomas managed a smile and reached down to stroke her cheek.

"We must attend the wedding, or there will be problems…suspicions." Heidi took his hand in hers and held it for a moment.

"Yes, I suppose we must," he said, nodding. He'd thought about this day since Christa was young, the day he would give her away. And now, look at her choice of men. It turned his stomach. Poor Heidi, she would do anything, say anything for the safety of her loved ones. She'd always been a good, devoted wife and mother. He patted her shoulder again. But he believed a man's character was more important than his safety or even his life. Thomas walked to his bedroom at the back of the house. Locking the door behind him, he picked up the phone.

"This is Dr. Thomas Henkener," he said, his voice low, almost a whisper.

"Yes. I've been waiting for your call since you came to see me," a gravely male voice answered.

"I have given the matter that we discussed last week a great deal of thought. I have decided that I would like to volunteer to help the underground. I want to do what I can to help as many Jews as possible leave Germany. I will give money to those who do not have enough to leave."

"I must ask you because I must be sure. Are you aware of the danger?"

"Yes."

"And you still choose to do this?"

"I do. I must," Dr. Henkener said.

CHAPTER SIX

WARSAW, POLAND. NOVEMBER 1938

SEVENTEEN-YEAR-OLD ZOFIA WEISS braided her thick black hair. She was getting ready to leave for school. Her deep-burgundy dress was made of coarse wool, and she wore heavy, black stockings. Soon her best friend Lena would arrive, and they would walk the two miles together. She had looked in the mirror, and being satisfied with her appearance, Zofia put on her heavy coat, wool scarf, and hat. November in Warsaw was bitterly cold.

A single knock on the door to not awaken Zofia's mother, who had been ill, and Zofia stepped outside to greet Lena.

"I baked these last night. I brought you one." Zofia handed Lena a roll wrapped in brown paper.

"Thanks. How did you know I was hungry?" Lena asked. She was a heavyset girl with a warm smile. The two had been best friends since they were toddlers.

"You're always hungry," she said, and they both laughed.

"It's freezing," Lena said as she pulled her scarf tighter around her neck.

"Yes, it certainly is."

"Zofia, is that lipstick you're wearing?"

"No," Zofia answered, turning her face away.

"Yes, it is. Where did you get that?"

"I'm not wearing lipstick."

"Don't lie to me. I know you better than anyone."

They both laughed. "All right, so maybe I am."

"Don't tell me. You're still crushing on Mr. Taylor?"

"I never said I was crushing on him."

"You didn't have to. Every time we are in music class, and he plays that crazy American jazz, your face turns as red as a ripe apple."

"I just like the jazz."

"And the way he looks when his long hair falls over his forehead as he sits at the piano, I look over, and your eyes light up like the candles on my mama's menorah."

"Well, you do have to admit he's wildly attractive."

"And American."

"Yes," Zofia said, "and American."

"But he is too old for you. And besides, he is our teacher. Nothing good can come of this. I hate to see you get hurt."

"Perhaps you're right." Zofia stretched her fingers. They were uncomfortably cold as she held her books. "But he is still fun to look at."

"Yes, he certainly is," Lena said as she finished the last crumb of her roll.

CHAPTER SEVEN

Donald Taylor sat at the piano in front of his class, playing a wild rendition of a popular American song. As his voice crooned the seductive blues melody, he gazed out at the students. There was no doubt that the girls were swooning over him. Their glazed-over eyes and sensuous smiles brought him to heights of ecstasy. And that was why he'd come here to Poland.

In America, he'd been little more than a mediocre music teacher. But here, in Europe, in his small classroom, he felt like a superstar, a musical version of Clark Gable. The girls were young, that was true, and he knew better than to take them to his bed, but he'd done it against his better judgment. Not regularly, but often enough. How could a man resist when these young girls, tender, just on the brink of womanhood, offered themselves to him? They were like delectable chocolate morsels, irresistible. Still, if you ate too many, you might find your health in jeopardy or, in his case, your job.

Lately, he'd been watching one of his students, Zofia, with her slender but voluptuous figure, dark, alluring eyes, and long, wavy hair. She stared at him as he sat at the piano, licking her lips that sparkled in the overhead light, deep, dark red, like ripe berries.

There was no doubt he wanted her. Who wouldn't? No man could resist a woman like that twitching around his classroom, even if he were her teacher.

He was on his way to the lunchroom when he saw Zofia. She was sitting by herself on the bench beneath the tree, reading a book. Her lunch was spread on a white cloth napkin beside her.

"Hello," he said as he approached.

"Hello, Mr. Taylor," she said, looking up.

"May I sit here?" he asked, indicating the empty seat on the other side of her picnic.

"Of course." She began to gather her food together to put it away.

"No, please eat. I didn't mean to disturb you."

"You aren't disturbing me at all."

"Well, I wouldn't feel right if you didn't finish your lunch."

"I'm all done. I was just reading for a bit."

"What are you reading?"

"Nothing, a novel."

"A romance novel?"

She blushed. "I suppose you could call it that." She giggled.

He let out a laugh. "Don't be embarrassed. I like them, too."

She smiled and looked away.

"I really enjoy your class. I love the American music, especially the big band stuff."

"Yes, so do I. I suppose you can tell."

"Yes, I can."

"I wish I had a turntable so that I could play some of the records at home," Zofia said. Before her father died, there had been very little money, but she might have gotten one. However, with her mother ill, it was impossible.

"You could borrow mine."

"Really? You would allow me to do that?"

"But, of course. I mean my personal one, not the one that belongs to the school. Would you like that?"

"Oh yes, I really would. But I don't have any records."

"Of course, you don't. Why would you have records if you don't have anything to play them on, silly? I would lend you some of my personal collection."

"That would be wonderful."

"Why don't you come by my apartment on Saturday, and I can give them to you?"

"Oh, I can't come on Saturday. I'm Jewish, and it is our

"Shabbat," or "Sabbath, as you Americans say."

"Ahh, I see. Well, Sunday, then?"

"Yes. Sunday would be fine."

"Here, let me jot down the address for you."

CHAPTER EIGHT

Zofia decided to save streetcar fare and walk the mile to Mr. Taylor's apartment. Even though she was working, her mother was not, and every penny she earned counted. The turntable would be heavy, and she would rather spend the money to take the streetcar home when carrying it. Although the icy wind blew, Zofia did not feel the cold because she was too excited.

All last night she'd thought about Mr. Taylor, how he looked when he sang with enough passion to reach out and touch something deep inside her. He caused stirrings that she'd never felt for anyone before. Puckering her lips together, she giggled. The red lipstick she wore made her look older, more mature.

Because she'd grown up in Warsaw, she knew the area fairly well and had no trouble finding the building where he lived. Before she rang the bell, she looked in the compact mirror in her handbag. Zofia applied a fresh layer of lipstick and a spritz of the toilet water that had been her mother's. Then she pressed the button and waited, and her heart skipped a beat.

"Who is it?" Mr. Taylor asked.

"It's Zofia."

"I'm on the third floor."

"I'll be right up."

A loud buzzer went off, and she grabbed the door handle. It seemed like a long walk up. But when she got to the third floor, Mr. Taylor was waiting in the doorway to his apartment.

"I'm so glad you made it. Come on in. It's not much, but it's home."

She entered his apartment and surveyed it with her eyes. It was sparsely furnished, with just a small table and chairs in the kitchen attached to a living area. In the living room, there was a sofa upholstered in dark blue fabric and a matching chair. But on the walls hung pictures of American musicians, Benny Goodman and his band, Count Basie, Duke Ellington, and Cab Calloway.

"Here, let me take your coat."

She removed her coat, hat, and scarf and handed them to him. He hung them on a wooden coat rack by the door.

"Please sit," Mr. Taylor said, indicating the sofa.

Zofia sat down.

"Would you like me to play a record?"

"Yes, Mr. Taylor. I'd enjoy that very much."

He smiled and began shuffling through a pile of vinyl records. "Call me Don."

"Are you sure?"

"Well, yes, of course I am, but only when we are not in school."

"Don, then."

"Would you like to hear a song, a special song? I think you will enjoy this. It's real American music, not jazz, something different. In fact, it was released in America."

"I would love to hear it."

He placed a record on the turntable. A group began singing.

"You are my little Mary Sunshine. Good morning, Mary Sunshine. You wake the stars…"

"I love this. It sounds just the way I think that America would look, not in the cities, but in the country."

"You're right. This is American folk music. Would you like to learn the words?"

"I would."

"Then we can sing along with the record."

He taught her the words in English and explained what they meant in Polish. Once she'd mastered the song, they sang it together.

After the record finished playing, he smiled at her, his eyes liquid, like hot oil.

"How did I do?" she asked.

"You did wonderfully. Can I get you something to eat or drink?"

"No, thank you. I've already eaten."

Don sat down on the couch beside Zofia. She'd never had a man sit so close to her. It was exciting and uncomfortable at the same time. Of course, he could not be interested in her other than as a student. But her mind raced, and her fantasies of him kept surfacing so much that she could not meet his eyes. Zofia felt like a small animal huddled in the corner of the sofa, trembling.

"So tell me all about you, Zofia. I like to know about my students."

"There really isn't much to tell. I'm not terribly interesting."

"I'll be the judge of that." He smiled, and she noticed a slight cleft in his chin. Just looking directly at him made her stomach weak.

"Well, I live a couple of miles south of the school with my mother. Last year, my father passed away from a terrible bout of influenza. Since then, my mother has been very lethargic. She doesn't get out of bed much. After school, I work for the diamond seller."

"Oh, I am sorry. How do you do it all?"

"It's all right. I manage. I don't really have any choice. Between what my father left us and the money I earn, we survive."

"Please, if I can help in any way, you must not hesitate to ask."

"That is very kind of you, but we're fine."

"Here, let me get you some tea. I have some lovely biscuits as well, and it is not so often that I have company. Will you please share them with me? I would enjoy that so much."

"Then yes, of course, I will." She wasn't hungry, but it didn't matter. Here she was, alone with Mr. Taylor. He'd asked her to call him Don. He liked her. He wanted her to be his girlfriend. She was so excited and nervous that she could hardly contain herself.

Don Taylor got up, put the teakettle on the stove, and then took a swig from a bottle of vodka on the counter. Zofia studied the pictures on the walls and wondered what life might be like in America.

When Don returned, he put another record on the turntable. He wound the crank and carefully placed the needle on the edge of the black vinyl.

"*Bei mir bist du sheon…*" a sultry female voice sang in German.

"You like it?" Mr. Taylor asked.

"Oh yes, very much."

"Come, dance with me."

"I don't know how," Zofia said, blushing, feeling awkward and inferior. She'd never learned to dance. There had been no one to teach her.

"Come on." He took her hand. "I'll show you. You'll get this quickly. You have a great sense of rhythm."

At first, she was clumsy, but the smooth beat of the swing music took hold, and she began to loosen up. She giggled as he spun and flipped her.

"I love this." She laughed. "I can't remember when I had so much fun."

"I'm glad." He smiled, his eyes twinkling.

He is so attractive. He would make the perfect husband. I don't care if he is Jewish or not. I like him so much. I could see us living happily together in this apartment. I would decorate it a little bit and add a few touches here and there.

The piercing whistle of the teakettle brought her back to reality.

"I'll be right back." Donald winked at her.

In a few minutes, Donald returned with a plate of shortbread biscuits, a pot of tea, a small bowl of sugar, and two cups on a tray.

"I am so glad you came today. I don't know if I should tell you this. It is certainly out of line, and I hope you will not take it the wrong way, but, well… I think you are the prettiest girl in my class."

Zofia quickly glanced at Donald and then turned away. She

knew her face was crimson red, but she was flattered. Perhaps it was true. Perhaps he really did like her. Perhaps they would marry.

"You really think so?" Zofia asked, her voice small and cracked.

"Undoubtedly. I thought so from the first time I saw you."

Involuntarily, she sat up a little straighter. "No one has ever told me that I was pretty before." She bit her lower lip.

"That's because the boys in your grade are just that, boys. Any man who is a man would tell you that you are gorgeous."

"Oh…" The word caught in her throat.

He laughed. "And you're even lovelier when you blush."

She cast her eyes down. Looking desperately for something to do to cover the awkwardness she felt, Zofia poured the tea. A small puddle formed on the tray.

"I'm sorry, I've spilled it," she said. Putting the teapot down, she picked up the linen napkin and began to clean the mess.

He took her small, soft hand gently into his. "No need to clean up," he said. "I'll take care of that later." She dropped the cloth.

"Your hand. The skin is so soft." He caressed her hand. She did not pull away.

Then he opened her hand and brought her palm to his lips. *He is in love with me, too, the same as I have been with him all these months.* Her eyes glazed over with passion and joy.

"You are very special to me, Zofia," he whispered in a husky voice.

Without another word, he took her into his arms and kissed her. It was the first time any man had kissed Zofia. She shivered in his arms, but her body went limp as she yielded to the warmth. It had been years since anyone had touched her, and she was starved for affection. At first, she was timid, but when he kissed her again, her arms went around him. His kiss became more demanding. She didn't back away. Instead, she found that her desire matched his. Donald leaned her back on the sofa. He gazed into her eyes.

"Zofia…" He whispered. But that was not what Zofia heard. What she heard was, "I love you," even though he never said it.

Everything happened very fast. Nature, youth, and hormones

took over. Before Zofia realized how far things had gone, she and Don had consummated their friendship and become lovers.

Once he'd finished, he stood up, clearly sobered by his actions.

"I'm sorry, Zofia. I don't know what got into me." He brushed the hair out of his eyes, quickly pulled his pants on, and zipped them up.

She didn't answer. Why was he sorry? She wasn't sorry.

"Please, forgive me. Let's pretend that this never happened."

"Why? I am not sorry it happened," she said.

"Zofia, I am too old for you, and besides, I am your teacher. I didn't mean to take liberties with you. My goodness, you were just so lovely and so willing… What was I to do? You must promise to keep this a secret because if anyone finds out, I will be fired from the school."

"I would never tell anyone. It is our special secret. But," she hesitated, her heart breaking a little, "you are not too old for me. I am very mature for my age." She sat up, pulling her clothes back around her body, suddenly ashamed of her nakedness.

"That you are. But you deserve better than me. I am nothing more than an old, alcoholic schoolteacher. You have your whole life ahead of you. There will be many men, better men than me." He spoke fast, his hand continually running through his long hair.

Then, even though the sofa was dark, he saw the spot of blood.

"Oh!" he said as if he'd been hit by a train. "I had no idea. You were a virgin?"

"Yes." She hung her head and could not look directly at him.

"I'm sorry. I really am." He walked over to the kitchen counter and poured himself a shot of vodka. After he'd drunk it in a single gulp, he poured another.

"Do you want me to leave?"

"I think it's best that you do." Donald was flushed. "Here, take the record player and this pile of records. They are a gift, no need to return them," he said, handing her the coat and hat she'd worn to his apartment and loading the heavy pile of records and player onto the table in front of her.

She trembled and held back the tears as she put her coat on.

There should be something she could say, but she could think of nothing. She wanted to say, “I thought you loved me,” but the words would not come. Instead, Donald ushered her out, and before she knew it, Zofia was walking home, carrying a heavy load.

After he had closed the door, Donald threw his vodka glass at the wall, his face burning with anger. Why couldn’t he stop seducing these young students? This was dangerous. He could lose his job and maybe worse.

CHAPTER NINE

When Lena arrived at Zofia's house on Monday morning, Zofia was still in bed, but she got up to answer the door.

"Are you sick?" Lena asked.

"I'm not going to school today."

"I can see that. What's wrong?"

"Nothing. I think I am going to quit."

"Are you crazy? You love school. Why would you leave?"

"I am going to work full time. My mother and I need the money."

"It's only a few months to graduation. Why don't you just stick it out?"

"I can't. We need the money now. I am going to talk to my boss and see if he will give me more hours."

"Are you sure, Zof?"

"Yes, I'm sure."

"Then I guess I should go. I'll see you later, after school, maybe?"

"Maybe… I don't know what hours Mr. Budowsky will want me to work."

"I'll try to drop by and see if you're here."

"All right."

Zofia did not go to work that day. She stayed in bed. When Lena knocked at the door after school, she didn't answer. How could she have been such an idiot? How could she have made such a fool of herself?

Her mother's demands continued. She had been ill for so long now that she did not get out of bed unless she had to go to the bathroom. Zofia realized that her mother's illness was more mental than physical. She had died inside when she lost her husband, and now she just lay in bed waiting for the time she would join him.

Usually, Zofia brought her trays of food and tried her best to engage her in light conversation. But today, Zofia had her own bundle of emotions to contend with, so she just got out of bed to bring her mother a slice of bread with a bit of butter and some tea. Then she sat on the chair in the living room, gazing out at nothing and wondering where she could go from here. Determined not to face Mr. Taylor Donald, she decided that she was going to find full-time work and leave school forever. She would miss her friends and had always done well in her studies, but seeing him and reliving her humiliation was far too much to bear.

Tomorrow, she would ask Mr. Budowsky to teach her more about the diamond business. Until now, she'd done little more than keep the store clean and occasionally help a customer. Perhaps he might hire her to learn the trade.

Lena came by again the following morning. Zofia ached to get dressed and go to school. She felt empty inside, as if a part of her life had ended and ended abruptly. But she could not bring herself to face him. So she bid Lena farewell, dressed, and walked to Budowsky's Jewelry Store.

"Zofia, what brings you here so early in the morning?" Frau Budowsky asked.

"I have a problem. I need to talk to you and Mr. Budowsky."

"Yes, dear. Of course. Come in. You want some tea, maybe a little something to eat?"

"No, thank you."

"Sammie, Zofia is here. She needs to talk to us. Come, take a minute."

The Budowskys lived behind the store in a small apartment. Zofia followed Frau Budowsky back to the small kitchen, where they both sat down at the table.

Frau Budowsky took a small glass jug of milk out of the icebox.

"Here, you'll have a little milk?"

"No, thank you. I'm fine."

"I insist. You can't come to my house and not have a little bit of something," Frau Budowsky said, smiling. She poured a glass of milk and gave Zofia a thick slice of bread. "You should eat a little bit. You're too skinny." She smiled at Zofia and then called out again. "Sam? Come on. What are you doing?"

"All right, give me a minute. I'm coming."

When they were all seated, Zofia looked at the kind faces of her boss and his wife. *God forgive me for lying…*

"Mr. and Frau Budowsky, my mother and I have fallen on hard times. As you know, my mother, Selda, is ill—bedridden. It seems that the money my father left us is running out. I must leave school and find full-time work. Can you extend my hours? I am willing to learn the business so that I can help you even more efficiently."

Mr. Budowsky ran his hand over his beard. "I don't know if I can afford to give you any more hours. My son George is finishing school and will need a job."

"What can we do to help her?" Frau Budowsky asked. She was a heavyset woman with a round face, soft blue eyes, and a warm smile.

"I can give you a little bit of money. Perhaps that will help."

"No, I don't want to take your money. I am looking for a trade. Something for the future," she said.

"You don't want to finish school?" Frau Budowsky asked.

"I can't. I need to find work."

The older woman nodded.

"You know, I heard that the seamstress, Frau Kowalsky, is looking for a girl to apprentice. She is only a few blocks from here. Do you sew?" Frau Budowsky asked.

"I haven't, but I could learn. I'm a quick learner."

"She is a friend of mine. Well, not exactly a friend, but I know her. She has done alterations for me, plenty." Frau Budowsky laughed, and her large tummy shook. "Give me a few minutes. I have some things to do, but then I will go with you and talk to her. How will that be, Zofia?"

"That's so kind of you, Frau Budowsky."

"Oy, it's nothing." She smiled.

"I am glad we can help." Mr. Budowsky said. "I hope the seamstress will be able to give you work."

"Yes, so do I."

After she had bundled up against the cold, Frau Budowsky put her arm through Zofia's, and together they walked the two blocks to the storefront of the seamstress.

"Good morning, Frau Budowsky."

"Good morning, Fruma. This is Zofia."

"Good morning, Zofia. Sit down, ladies. What can I do for you? Let me guess, maybe this is George's bashert? Are we going to be making a wedding dress?"

Zofia blushed. Esther Budowsky cleared her throat. "No, nothing like that, not that I would be opposed." She smiled at Zofia. "But that's not it at all. Zofia is our part-time employee. Last year her father passed away, God rest his soul, and her mother is ill. She needs full-time work, but we don't have the work for her. I heard from some of the ladies I play cards with that you might be looking for an apprentice. I can tell you that she is reliable and an excellent worker. Maybe you would consider giving her a job."

Frau Kowalsky scrutinized Zofia. Her eyes traveled over the girl until Zofia looked away.

"She looks capable," Frau Kowalsky said. "If you want the job, I will give you a try. You are going to find, however, that sometimes we will have to work long hours into the night if we have a special event like sometimes a wedding dress needs to be finished. You understand this? And I cannot afford to pay you seamstress wages while you learn. It will be much less until you know what you are doing. But if you do well, then you will make a decent salary."

"Yes, ma'am, I am grateful for the opportunity."

"All right, then. You come tomorrow morning at eight o'clock. Don't be late."

"Yes, ma'am, and thank you."

After Zofia and Frau Budowsky had left, they walked to the end of the block, where they would separate. Zofia was going north toward her home, and Frau Budowsky headed south.

"I cannot thank you enough for doing this for me," Zofia said, squeezing the older woman's arm.

"I am glad it worked out the way that it did."

"Yes, so am I."

"Listen, maybe sometime you are going to come to my house? You'll have some cake and meet my George? He is a good boy, a Jewish boy from a good family. It's hard to find a nice Jewish girl these days."

Zofia smiled, but inside, her heart was breaking. She wasn't a nice Jewish girl anymore. She'd done something bad. She'd sinned. Zofia believed herself undeserving of a boy like George.

The following day, Zofia arrived fifteen minutes early at *Perfect Stitches*, Fruma Kowalsky's dressmaking shop. She sat outside, waiting for Frau Kowalsky to open the door.

"Good morning, you are early. That is a good thing. It shows me that you care about your job."

"I care very much, Frau Kowalsky."

"You and I will be working very closely together, so you might as well call me Fruma."

"Thank you. I will."

"All right then, let's get started."

Zofia followed Fruma's directions, but it seemed as if her stitches were always crooked or in some way displeasing to Frau Kowalsky.

"Remove this line and try again. I cannot have such sloppy work. You will learn to do this perfectly before you work on my clients' orders."

Zofia resented Frau Kowalsky. She was demanding and overbearing. Every stitch had to be perfect. She gave no slack.

"Slave driver," Zofia whispered as another customer came in, and Fruma was busy helping her.

Zofia worked from early in the morning until well past sundown. Every day she stitched, removed, cut, and measured patterns to Frau Kowalsky's standards of perfection.

November passed to January, then to February, and still, Zofia was only an apprentice. Her back ached from sitting at the sewing machine for hours.

But she had something even greater to worry about. Zofia had not seen her menstrual blood since the month before her moment of indiscretion with Donald Taylor. She tried to deny it to herself. Perhaps I am just late because I have been going through so many changes in my life. But she knew better. She was nauseous and could not eat. She was very tired, and her belly was growing. Zofia was pregnant.

On a brisk morning in March, Helen Sobczak came in. Zofia looked up from her machine to see a lovely woman just a few years older than herself, with curly blonde hair and soft blue eyes. Fruma had left to go to the bakery, where she would purchase some rolls to share with Zofia.

"May I help you?" Zofia asked the beautiful blonde.

"Hello, my name is Helen. My mother and I have been coming here since I was just a little girl. Is Frau Kowalsky here?"

"No, she just went to Zuckerman's bakery. When that Frau Zuckerman bakes, the smell is so wonderful that everyone who works on this street lines up to buy the bread. I am Zofia, her apprentice."

"Hello, Zofia. It's so nice to meet you. Well, let me get to the point of why I am here. I am getting married this summer. I would like to have a dress made for my wedding."

"I am sure we can help you. But I have a feeling that Fruma will probably want to take your measurements herself."

"Yes, probably so, but if you want to try and then compare them to hers, I don't mind." She smiled. Zofia liked her right away.

"I would like that. It would help me to see how accurate I am."

When Fruma returned with the bread, Zofia was taking Helen's measurements.

"What are you doing?" she asked.

"Nothing," Zofia said, putting the tape measure on the table.

"It's all right. I asked her to do it."

"But she isn't ready to measure you properly."

"I don't mind, even if it's just for practice," Helen said.

Fruma smiled. "All right then, Zofia, you can go ahead, and let's see how you do."

After Zofia had finished, her boss checked her work.

"Very good. I am happy to say you are getting the hang of this."

Zofia and Helen smiled at the compliment.

Helen spent hours sifting through bolts of fabric. She finally decided upon an ivory satin with a lace overlay.

"She is a nice girl," Fruma said after Helen left. "I've known her and her mother for a very long time. Her mother is a midwife. She is a good woman, though not a Jew. But she's never shown any disdain for us, either."

"Oh," Zofia said. She turned away. *A midwife. She would need a midwife, but she was an unmarried woman. Nobody in their right mind would want to become involved in such a scandal.* She was worried. How would she tell Fruma that she was pregnant? What if she lost her job? But before Zofia had a chance, Fruma decided to talk to her.

"Here, eat. I brought some rolls and a hunk of cheese. Are you hungry?"

"Yes, a little..." Zofia was ravenous.

"Zofia, sit down here. I want to talk to you." Fruma Kowalsky put the grainy bread on a plate. "I have fitted women longer than you have been on this earth. That would come to about thirty-five years. I know the female body very well. And, well, I am not going to beat around the bush here. Zofia, you are with child. I can see it."

Zofia dropped her thin slice of cheese.

"It's all right. I am not going to let you go. You have a job here. I might seem harsh sometimes, but I understand more than you know. I am going to help you. That's why I told you that Helen's mother was a midwife. We will talk to her, and perhaps she will deliver the baby here in my apartment right above the shop."

Zofia realized that she knew very little about her boss's personal life. But the kindness Frau Kowalsky was showing her brought tears to her eyes.

"It's going to be fine."

"Will your husband be angry if I give birth in your apartment?"

"I have no husband. I have never been married. I live with a lady friend. She is kind and understanding. You will like her. She will be fine with us using the apartment."

"Are you sure?"

"I am sure. Gitel and I have lived on the edge of society for a very long time. So we have learned long ago not to worry too much about what people say."

"I don't understand."

"I know, you don't. Gitel is my husband."

"But you said she is a woman."

"Yes. Now you understand?"

Zofia nodded.

"Close your mouth before you swallow a fly." Fruma laughed.

"But your title is Frau.?"

"Yes, I use that. Like I said, Gitel and I are married, if not in the synagogue, then in our hearts, for sure."

"I've never met anyone who…"

"And so, there is a first time for everything. By the way, you did very well with your fitting today. You are going to be a good dressmaker, Zofia. I know I have been hard on you sometimes, but that is the only to make you excel at your work. And I must say, I am very proud of you."

"How can I ever thank you?"

"Ach, I don't need thanks. I need an apprentice. I need your help. So if you are in agreement, once the baby comes, we are going to set up a playpen here so that you can continue to work. Gitel already knows about this, and she has agreed to help. Between the three of us, we will care for the child."

Tears flowed down Zofia's face. Fruma had known all along! "You are so good to me…"

"Ach, stop. You make me embarrassed," Fruma laughed. "Come on now, eat. You must eat. The baby must be healthy and strong."

Zofia felt unburdened. It was as if a thousand-pound weight had been lifted from her shoulders. Since the incident with Mr. Taylor, she'd borne the fear of her pregnancy alone. She could not discuss her predicament with Lena, who she rarely saw these days, or with her mother, who was wrapped up in her own depression. But now she had a friend, an ally, who would help her get through this. And Fruma was right. She was becoming a good seamstress.

Zofia still loved American swing music and sang it to herself while she worked.

One afternoon, Gitel arrived at the dress shop carrying a large package.

"I'm Gitel. Fruma said she told you about me?" Gitel asked.

"Yes, she did. I'm Zofia."

"Fruma asked me to bring this for the two of you. She says she is sick of your singing." Gitel laughed, and she put the box down on the counter. "Go on, open it."

Zofia opened the box. Inside, she found a turntable with four American swing records. She gasped with delight. "Oh, my gosh, thank you. Thank you, both."

When Zofia returned from Donald's apartment, she put the turntable and records into the closet. It had been unbearable to look at them. Now she thought she might bring some of the records into the shop.

When it wasn't busy, and no customers were around, Zofia would get up and coax Fruma to dance with her. She taught Fruma the steps she'd learned from Donald, and Fruma learned to appreciate American music as much as Zofia did. Sometimes they would splurge and buy a new record.

When Zofia entered her sixth month, there was no longer any hiding her extended belly. The baby would arrive soon, and she knew she must tell her mother.

After work on a Friday evening, Zofia picked up her usual challah and chicken on the way home from work. It was *Shabbat*, so she got off early to prepare. She arrived home, put the chicken up to roast, and then went into her mother's room. As always, the room was dark. Her mother lay facing the wall, eyes open.

"Good Shabbat, Mama," Zofia said as she smoothed her mother's thinning hair back from her troubled face.

"How do you feel?"

"Oy, not so good, Zofia."

"What hurts you?"

"Everything. My whole body aches. I am so tired, but I cannot sleep. I don't know. I am just not well."

"I'm sorry, Mama. Can I get you anything?"

"No, nothing. You do enough already."

"Mama," Zofia hesitated. Her mother did not look at her. She continued to stare at the wall. Zofia wished she didn't have to tell her. But soon, the cries of an infant would echo through the house. She had to be made aware of what was to come.

"I have something to tell you."

Her mother did not answer.

"I am pregnant. I think the baby will be born in October." Zofia swallowed hard.

Her mother found a burst of angry energy. Zofia had not seen her so enraged in years.

"A *Shanda*, scandal! You will never marry a decent boy. How could you let something like this happen? Did someone force himself on you?"

"No, Mama. I am sorry."

"Get out of my room. I am sick when I look at you. As if we didn't suffer enough, now you have brought shame upon us. How could you do this to me? How?" Frau Weiss asked.

That night, Zofia's mother refused to eat. The next day, she refused again. She would not speak to her daughter at all. Instead, she just lay there, staring at the wall and shaking her head. Zofia was filled with guilt, but she hoped that once her mother saw the child, her heart would soften. Eventually, she would get hungry, and she had to eat.

On Monday, Zofia went to work. When she returned that evening, her mother had slit her wrist. She was dead.

CHAPTER TEN

Dr. Goebbels leaned back in the chair behind his desk, smiling.

"So, Manfred, since the Führer was coming to Berlin to see me, anyway, he has agreed to come to the wedding. You are a very lucky man. He is bringing *Reichsführer* Himmler with him. Do you realize what an honor this is? Your bride will be overcome with excitement. However, since our leaders will be attending, we must change the venue. I am sure your bride will understand. The wedding will take place at the Nazi Headquarters. There, we should be able to follow the traditions properly, and that will make our Führer proud."

"Of course, whatever you think should be done. I am so indebted to you, Dr. Goebbels. I can never thank you enough for all you have done for me." Manfred was a little concerned. Christa would have to make a lot of concessions.

Goebbels smiled. His teeth were large and protruding, and his bone structure jutted through his delicate skin. Manfred was, once again, taken aback at how much he resembled the death-head symbol.

"You tell your lovely bride that we are all looking forward to her bringing us plenty of Aryan children. She and her parents must be very excited about the wedding and, of course, for our honored guests."

"Oh yes, they are, sir." Manfred thought about his future father-in-law. Somehow, he would have to find a way to win the old man over. It was essential that Dr. Henkener not cause any problems for the couple. If things continued as they were going now, Manfred would rise in the Party. He and Christa would have a big family, plenty of money, and a life he could never have dreamed of before Hitler's rise to power.

CHAPTER ELEVEN

It was almost five o'clock, but Thomas Henkener had waited for a particular patient to arrive.

"Hershel, come in, please," Dr. Henkener said. "How are you? How have you been? And the family?"

"All right, they are all right, Thomas."

"I brought you Dr. Shulman's chart. Do you need anything else?" Hilde, Dr. Henkener's nurse, and oldest friend, entered.

"No, thank you, Hilde," Dr. Henkener said. "That will be all, Hilde. Thank you."

After the nurse had closed the door, Dr. Henkener spoke in a whisper. "I called you to come here because I want to talk to you."

"Yes, of course, Thomas. What is it?"

"I want to help you, you, and your family."

"Thomas, I couldn't let you do that. I shouldn't even be here now. It is dangerous for both of us."

"You are in worse danger than I am. Have you thought about leaving Germany?"

"I have thought about it, but I am a doctor. My patients are here. They need me," Dr. Shulman said.

"Persecution is intensifying, and I am afraid that things are only going to get worse here for Jews. Look at the laws going into effect. Things are happening around us all the time, horrifying things."

"I agree with you. Things are bad, but how can I leave? How can I leave all the patients who need me? Don't you think that this fire under Hitler will burn out? I have always had faith in the German people. They are smart and cultured. It is just a matter of time before this whole thing blows over, but you are a good friend to offer me your advice. I will keep it in mind."

"You have always been there for my family and me. I will never forget what you did for Christa. She was such a sick child with a bad heart. We knew it as soon as we saw the blue lips when she was born. You helped her."

"Yes, well, that is what we doctors do, isn't it, Thomas?"

"It is. We heal, and when we can, we save lives. I am here if you should need me, anytime at all."

"It is probably best that I stop coming to your office, and you stop coming to mine. It will only bring us trouble," Dr. Shulman said.

"I don't care, Hershel. I will not deny our friendship."

"Do it for my sake. Do it for the sake of my family if you won't do it for yourself."

"If you ask, I will stay away from you."

"Just until this is all over with the Nazis. I tell you, it's only temporary. People are frightened, but such a fanatical dictator cannot last in a civilized country like ours. Soon everyone will have had enough, and then everything will be as it was before. I will come back to the hospital, and we will work together again. You'll see." Dr. Shulman smiled. He patted his old friend's back. Then he left the office and headed as quickly as he could out of the Gentile sector of town.

CHAPTER TWELVE

Everything for the wedding was planned to coincide with the visit that Hitler and Himmler would make to the Ministry of Propaganda's Office. Goebbels had involved the entire office to ensure every detail would be perfect. In fact, to show how much affection he felt for Manfred, Dr. Goebbels planned to preside over the wedding himself.

And so it was on a morning in early May that Manfred awoke, his stomach tight with nerves and excitement. Although he'd dreamed of this day, he, an awkward, unattractive boy from a poor family, could hardly have expected a life like this ever to become a reality. But here he was, Manfred Blau, about to marry the girl of his dreams in a ceremony attended by the highest, most revered men in the land.

He was awestruck, delighted beyond his wildest dreams, but secretly he fought against a nagging fear. A part of him whispered in the night: *I am a fraud. What if they find out I am not as talented an artist as they believe me to be? What if they find out I am not as strong as they are and I don't really fit in? Or worse, what if they realize that I am nothing but the poorest specimen of an Aryan and hardly worth the position I've been awarded?*

It was hard to forget how clumsy he'd been in the Hitler Jugend, how the other boys had made fun of him, and how the girls had giggled behind their hands, watching him as he failed. No doubt, Manfred was the slowest runner, and he was never chosen by anyone to be on a team when they played football or any other sport.

Fencing and archery took far more physical strength and agility than he possessed. However, because of Dr. Goebbels, he was far above all of them, those mindless athletes who stood around in groups taunting him, so sure they were his superiors. If only he could silence that annoying voice. If only, somehow, he could believe in Manfred, in his own worth.

Manfred took his black dress uniform out of the closet and put it on. The night before, he'd spent an hour polishing his shoes to a high shine. He combed his blond hair back from his face with a little water and hair cream. When he looked in the mirror, a handsome man stared back at him. His features were chiseled, and although he was small and slender, the uniform gave him presence.

With Hitler attending the wedding, all the plans that Christa and Manfred had originally made as a couple had to be changed to create the Führer's ideal wedding. Manfred knew by the look on her face that the changes disappointed Christa, but when he'd explained the necessity of his actions as an important career move, she'd agreed. It was hard to believe that Christa was as easygoing as she was beautiful. Fortune indeed had smiled upon him.

The building at the Nazi Headquarters was decked out for the occasion, with Nazi flags suspended from the ceiling, life runes laid out on the altar, and pictures of Adolf Hitler hung in expensive wood frames on the walls.

All the flowers had been changed from roses to golden sunflowers because these were the flowers Hitler had chosen to represent the Third Reich. The bride would carry a simple bouquet of sunflowers adorned with fir twigs. This gnawed at Manfred because he knew how much Christa loved roses.

But Manfred dared not disappoint Goebbels. So, he decided that he would make this up to Christa. He vowed to himself to see to it that every week of their lives together as husband and wife, he would bring her roses to make up for her sacrifice. A red runner with a swastika in the center had been placed on the aisle for the couple to walk down. At the end of the aisle stood the altar and a large brass urn, burning brightly with the eternal flame.

And so it began...

The band played a simple German folk song.

Manfred walked down the aisle alone and stood at the front of the altar, waiting as Dr. Henkener escorted his daughter to her new husband's side.

When he saw Christa, Manfred felt a pang of guilt for a moment because, under Dr. Goebbels's insistence, he requested that Christa wear a traditional German folk dress instead of her mother's gown. Again, she had made the concession. To make it up to her, Manfred had purchased the finest fabric he could find for the dressmaker to design the wedding dress. Now as she walked toward him in her colorful full skirt, with the golden threads and puffy-sleeved blouse, she looked like the most stunning example of German womanhood.

Christa came closer. Manfred stood staring at her in awe at how beautiful she truly was. Her golden hair caught the glow from the eternal fire, illuminating it until it looked like a halo of sunshine caressing her head. She smiled at him, and her tender, blue eyes melted his heart like snow on the first warm spring morning.

Dr. Henkener placed his daughter's hand in Manfred's. Then he went to sit in the front row of the audience.

Manfred and Christa turned to face the altar.

Together they stood before Dr. Goebbels and swore their oaths of loyalty to each other and the Party. Manfred had purchased gold bands with tiny swastikas engraved all around them. They exchanged the rings. There were tears in Christa's eyes.

"I love you," Manfred mouthed. He could not speak the words out loud because Goebbels was handing him the bread he would share with his bride.

"This bread is a symbol of the earth's fruitfulness and purity," Goebbels said.

Manfred broke a piece and handed it to Christa. Together, they took a bite.

Next, an officer brought a heavy oak box carved with runes. Goebbels opened the box and took a book from inside.

"This is a gift to you from the Reich." Goebbels handed Manfred a copy of Hitler's book, *Mein Kampf*.

"Thank you, sir," Manfred said.

"You're welcome. You are now man and wife. And may you both be very fruitful and produce many Aryan children for our fatherland."

Manfred smiled at Goebbels and then at Christa. He took her hand and kissed it. Then he led her through a crowd of saluting SS men, his heart pounding with joy. These were his people. Here he was loved and accepted. Here he was at home.

CHAPTER THIRTEEN

Once the ceremony was over, the wedding party and their guests were escorted into a large banquet hall. Overhead, crystal chandeliers twinkled, casting a soft glow over the embossed China and crystal. In the center of the tables were large arrangements of dazzling yellow sunflowers, their heads dipping over their sparkling vases.

The entire party was seated, including Manfred and Christa, before Dr. Goebbels and Himmler entered. The two stood behind their chairs, and the band played a marching song as Adolf Hitler entered the room. He wore a smile and greeted the guests as he walked by, shaking their hands and patting their children's cheeks. When he arrived at his seat, he turned to the crowd and raised his hand in a salute. Everyone stood, returning the salute and calling out "Heil Hitler," except Dr. Henkener.

Once everyone was seated, Himmler gave Christa a strange look.

"Your father did not salute?"

"No, he has been having trouble with his leg. It was very difficult for him to walk me down the aisle. He must be in pain again," she lied.

"I see," Himmler said, with a twinkle in his eye and a smile spreading across his face.

Manfred and Christa sat at a long head table with Dr. Goebbels, Hitler, and Himmler. They were surrounded by Hitler's bodyguards, who stood behind them quietly and unobtrusively. At the first table to the left of the couple, Manfred's mother sat, accompanied by Dr. and Frau Henkener.

Once the excitement of Hitler's arrival began to die down, a group of white-gloved waiters carrying trays of food paraded through the door. They offered overflowing platters of roasted meats and fresh vegetables, cheesy potatoes, and fresh bread. Girls with their hair in braids, wearing traditional German costumes similar to the bride's but not as exquisite, carried pitchers of dark German beer.

After everyone had eaten, Hitler stood. A roar of applause followed. He smiled and gave a short speech honoring the couple. Reiterating his constant message to Germany that it must be the responsibility of all good German citizens to marry and have lots of Aryan babies. These children, he said, would be the future of the Reich. Everyone cheered when he finished, and their hands went up in the Nazi salute. Hitler smiled like a benevolent father. Then Hitler, Himmler, Goebbels, and the bodyguards left the celebration. But as he left, Heinrich Himmler took a longer-than-usual glance at Christa's father.

Then a band began to play traditional German folk music, and everyone danced the polka. Manfred led his new wife to the dance floor. Pride swelled in his heart as he took her hand, and together they danced their first dance as man and wife.

"I will spend every day of my life doing everything in my power to make you happy," he said. "I know how much you wanted roses at the wedding, and so every week from this day forward, you shall have roses in our home."

"Oh, Manfred, I am happy. I am so happy," she said as they whirled around the dance floor under the large Nazi flag and the picture of Adolf Hitler.

That night, the couple stayed in a hotel in downtown Berlin.

Even though Manfred was a virgin and had no idea what to do, Christa was not, so she helped him learn. Because he loved her so much, his lack of experience made little difference. The depth of his feelings came through every time he touched her, and she responded to his tenderness.

When they finally drifted off to sleep in each other's arms, Manfred felt sure that every day of his life from this day forward would be joyous. *I am blessed.*

CHAPTER FOURTEEN

In the morning, the couple took the train out of the city to Munich. They sat together, holding hands and watching the countryside roll by out the window until they arrived in Munich, a fairy-tale wonderland with storybook cobblestone streets. Around every corner lay another enchanted castle. The Reich had arranged for them to stay on the outskirts of town in a small chalet overlooking the Alps.

Manfred had never been out of Berlin. His family had been too poor to even think of traveling. Now here he was, with his beautiful young wife, walking the streets in the quaint Bavarian city of Munich. They walked for over an hour, stopping briefly to buy a sausage from a street vendor. Neither of them wanted to miss anything this magnificent city had to offer. He took a deep breath and sighed. Then he reached for Christa's hand and brought it to his lips. She smiled at him, and he kissed her hand again. The clouds gathered overhead, and it began to rain.

The shower quickly turned into a downpour, like the tears of all angels in Heaven combined. Manfred and Christa stood under the awning of a tall building and held hands. They'd both gotten wet, but it didn't matter. They were young and in love and together. Soon the car that Goebbels had arranged would arrive to take them to the little chalet where they were staying on the city's outskirts.

As planned, the driver arrived. The automobile edged through traffic, navigating out of the city and toward the mountains.

Manfred stared out the window, mesmerized by the beauty of Munich. He'd fallen instantly in love with the old buildings, the massive towering clock in the center of town, the museums, the restaurants, and even the opera house. As they left the congestion in the city and began to enter the rural area near the mountains, the rolling landscape turned every imaginable shade of green, from forest to emerald, and shimmered in the drying rain.

Christa laid her head on Manfred's chest, his arm protectively around her as they gazed out the window at the farms with sprawling green hills scattered across the countryside, with cows and horses grazing. *This was the real Germany… Beautiful, untouched…*

After the driver had let them off in front of a small chalet that looked like it had been in a Hans Christian Andersen novel, the two were eager to be alone.

Christa ran inside the cottage and sat down on the bed. She bounced up and down, reveling in its soft, pillow-like quality. Manfred joined her, and they both bounced on the bed. Then Christa got a pillow and swung it across Manfred's body. He returned with a pillow of his own, and they began pillow fighting, like two children, until they fell into each other's arms, laughing.

After they made love on the feather bed, they lay together, gazing out the large picture window at a breathtaking view of the mighty Alps. The icebox had been filled with food, so there was no need to leave the chalet that day. Instead, they ate and made love again. It was enough just to be together.

That night they slept holding hands, and in the morning, they awoke, eyes glossed over with love.

"Let's take a hike through the mountains today," Christa said.

"I've never been much for hiking," Manfred admitted.

"Please? We won't go far…"

He smiled. "For you…I would walk all the way to France and back."

She laughed.

They hiked up into the mountains under a sun so bright that it looked silver.

"Look, a waterfall! Oh, Manfred, how beautiful!"

"It is. Very, but not as lovely as you."

She began to remove her clothes.

"What are you doing?"

"There's no one around. Come and swim with me."

"I couldn't."

"You could." She giggled, and before he could protest, she was naked and running toward the water.

He took off his clothes, feeling pale and clumsy in the light of day.

"Come on. The water is nice."

He followed her, his body tensed with shock as his naked body met the frigid water. "It's freezing."

The sound of her laughter was like the sound of ripples of joy. "I knew if I told you that, you'd never come in."

They embraced. Christa took Manfred's hand and led him under the waterfall. He held her tightly as the spray from the falls drifted into their young faces.

"I love you so much."

"And I love you too, my wonderful, kind husband. I am so happy to have found you."

They kissed, their lips warm as they pressed together.

"Look, Manfred. A rainbow."

"Yes, darling. I see it."

Over the next two weeks, Manfred and Christa explored the quaint Bavarian town of Munich at the same time as they reveled in exploring each other.

They went into town and had breakfast at small outdoor cafes, laughing and talking for hours. They held hands, eating ice cream cones as they walked along the lake in a park so green it could have been a painting. An entire afternoon was spent admiring the treasures in the art museum, followed by an evening at the opera house, enjoying the music and elaborate costumes of an opera by Wagner.

In what Manfred referred to as his former life, he meant his life before he swore allegiance to the Nazi Party and Adolf Hitler. He would never have dreamed of attending an opera. In fact, he could only imagine a life like this, a life that the Reich had made possible for a poor, lonely boy like him.

Everywhere they went, Manfred wore his uniform. Because of this, he was shown the utmost respect by everyone, from wait staff in restaurants, who insisted on serving the couple free drinks, to shop owners, who were happy to present gifts to Christa at no charge. All of this was astonishing, but when he saw the pride in his wife's eyes, Manfred began to feel like a very successful man indeed.

Long, lazy afternoons drinking dark beer and making love made Manfred wish he could stay in Munich forever, but he knew better. Soon he must return, and when he did, he must prove himself worthy of all the Party had given him.

CHAPTER FIFTEEN

WITHOUT HER MOTHER, Zofia was alone, and even worse, she blamed herself for her mother's suicide. She still made it a point to come to work each day and do a good job, but she'd stopped singing and had grown quiet.

"You might as well move in with Gitel and me. There is no sense in you staying in that big house by yourself. And being pregnant, well, it will be good to have someone around in case you need help," Fruma said matter-of-factly.

Zofia nodded. "Are you sure you would want that?"

"Yes, if I didn't, I wouldn't have suggested it, now would I?" Fruma smiled. "Besides, Gitel likes you, too. It will be good for us to have some young people around. We're becoming like two boring old ladies."

Zofia liked Gitel, who had come to the shop whenever she had time off from her job at the fishmonger.

The funeral for Zofia's mother had taken a toll on her. She wore a black mourning dress with a piece of fabric torn at the lapel. When she looked in the mirror, the darkness of the dress against her face added to the somberness she felt.

It was true that since the loss of her father, her mother had been little more than a shell, but she was still a presence, sometimes a burden, often an extra job, but always a presence. For a very long time, her mother's depression had affected Zofia's entire life. But still, she was there, giving Zofia a purpose, if not in mind, at least in the body. Now Zofia was an orphan. She had no one.

"I understand if you are ashamed. People will talk because of how Gitel and I are together. They talk anyway, but the talk will now include you," Fruma said, folding a square of lace.

"People should mind their own business. I am not ashamed of you and Gitel. You are entitled to live your life any way you choose. Besides, how about me? I am pregnant without the benefit of marriage. What are people going to say about that?"

Fruma smiled. "Yes, it looks like we are the perfect band of misfits: two old lesbian lovers and a young, unmarried woman with a baby on the way."

Fruma and Zofia laughed.

Living with Fruma and Gitel was more fun than Zofia could remember having in a long time. Gitel loved to sing, and she strolled through the house, filling it with song, her voice a deep, resonant alto. Most days, the three prepared meals together while Gitel sang.

Zofia continued to work with Fruma at the dressmaking shop. But she grew larger. The larger she grew, the more tired she became. The older woman saw the difficulty Zofia was having with her heavy belly and the sewing machine. Once Zofia's belly became too big to sit at the machine, Fruma insisted that she relax on the sofa.

Zofia did as she was told, but she began taking on all the embroidery work. It was tedious, but Zofia had a natural talent for the tiny stitches. So, the demand for her embroidery grew quickly.

In exchange for Maria, Helen's mother's midwife services, Zofia had sewn over a hundred tiny pearls into Helen's wedding dress. She also embroidered cabbage rose bouquets into the white satin. Even Fruma, as particular as she was, had to admit it was stunning.

At least twice a week, Helen and her mother came into the shop to see how the dress was coming along. Sometimes they brought kolacky, and Fruma and Zofia would take a break to share the apricot-filled cookies with their clients.

Often Helen stayed to chat with Zofia while she worked. Maria didn't look down on Zofia for being pregnant and not married. In fact, she was surprisingly supportive of her daughter's newfound friend.

Although Zofia tried hard to hide her feelings, it was painful for her to listen to all the wedding plans while she planned for life raising a child alone. All she wanted was to find love, get married, and have children. *Stupid girl.* She chastised herself continually, but secretly, over her mistake.

She'd believed that Don Taylor would be the man to fulfill her dreams. Well, be damned if she'd ever let anyone into her heart like that again. But even though she envied Helen, she was happy for her, too. It was hard not to be caught up in the excitement, and it was fun to watch the beautiful blonde dance around the room in her wedding gown while Fruma yelled, "Stay still! I can't pin this right with you moving all over the place."

Zofia and Helen would look at each other and burst into fits of laughter.

In just a month, Helen would marry the boy she had been in love with since she was only fourteen. They were childhood friends and neighbors who had grown into sweethearts. Once, Helen's fiancé had picked her up for dinner after a fitting. When Zofia saw them together, their affection for each other made her feel empty. It seemed to Zofia that, unlike her own, their lives would be wrapped up in a perfect package. But Zofia was young, and how was she to know that sometimes what appears to be perfect can be destroyed in a second?

The first time Zofia felt the baby move, she and Fruma were at the market, shopping for food for the Shabbat dinner. As Fruma smelled an apple for ripeness, she noticed that Zofia had stopped moving and stood still, with her hand clutching her belly and a strange expression.

"Are you all right?" Fruma asked, her voice betraying alarm.

"Feel this," Zofia whispered. She took Fruma's hand and placed it on her swollen abdomen.

As the baby twirled about, the two women looked at each other in awe.

One night, the three sat together, drinking cups of dark, bitter coffee after dinner. The sun had just begun to set, and it looked like a large red ball in the western sky.

"Zofia, you have brought lots of joy to our home," Gitel said. "We've always been a happy couple, but we used to talk and say how much we missed having a child of our own. You are like our daughter."

"Thank you. It warms my heart to know that I am not a burden to you."

"You have never been a burden to us. Not even when you first started working at the dress shop, and you made so many mistakes," Fruma said, laughing. "It was still a delight to have you here."

Zofia smiled.

"Zofia, can I be so bold as to ask you a question?"

"Yes, of course, Fruma."

"The baby's father? He knows that a child is coming?"

"No, he has no idea."

"You think about him?"

"Not anymore. He was a mistake. I did a foolish thing, and I never want to speak to him again."

"But if he knew about the baby, maybe he would help you. It is his responsibility too, and maybe he would give you some money."

"I don't want anything from him. I never want to see him again."

"Do you ever worry about passing him on the street?"

"No, not here. He's not Jewish. He would never be in this part of town."

Fruma nodded. "Can I get you anything?" she asked. "Either of you?"

"No," both Gitel and Zofia said.

"Zofia, it is your choice. If you don't want the father involved, then that is the way it will be, and I think I can speak for both Fruma and me. We will stand behind you no matter what happens. Together, the three of us will find the money to raise the baby. Isn't that right, Fruma?"

"Of course it is."

Zofia's water broke on a lazy sun-kissed afternoon late in the autumn, as the smell of burning leaves filled the city streets. It happened as she stood in the kitchen helping to clean up after supper. There was no pain, just a stream of warm water running down her legs.

Fruma saw it first. She knew a little about babies, so she was very concerned when she saw the water was green. But she didn't want to alarm Zofia or Gitel. The best thing was to get the midwife as quickly as possible. She would know what to do.

"Gitel, hurry up and go get Maria. The baby is coming. I'll stay with Zofia," Fruma said.

"Yes, all right. You stay here with Zofia. I'll go."

The two fumbled like two nervous mothers.

"Here, come on now. You should get right into bed and wait for Maria." Fruma took Zofia by the arm and carried her to her small bedroom.

Fruma grabbed a pile of folded towels and put them under Zofia's buttocks to catch the flow of water.

Gitel dressed quickly and ran all the way into the non-Jewish sector to Maria's house.

As soon as Gitel and Maria returned, Maria examined Zofia.

"Well, it looks like she is going to have a dry birth."

When Fruma was able, she pulled Maria out of the bedroom and into the kitchen, where Zofia could not hear.

"When her water broke, it was green. I think that maybe that is a sign of some sort of evil spirit."

"No, but it is a sign that we have to do what we can to get this baby out as soon as possible. The baby has had a bowel movement. If we are not careful, when it comes, it could inhale the nasty material and die instantly."

"*Oy vey*, what should I do?"

"You and Gitel get me a bowl of hot water and some towels, and then leave the rest to me."

The pains grew stronger and more frequent as the hours passed. Zofia lay in her tiny cot, sweat pouring out of her body as her two surrogate mothers waited, filled with angst, outside the closed door. Hours passed, and the sun set and rose again. Zofia grew tired from the intensity of the pain.

"I don't think I can do this. I am afraid I am dying."

"You will not die. This is your first child. It is always a hard labor with the first baby," Maria said, but she was worried. The baby was not crowning. In fact, it was coming feet first, if it came at all. She knew she would have to reach inside Zofia and turn the baby so that it could come forward into the world.

As Maria reached up through Zofia's vaginal cavity to turn the baby, Zofia's screams filled the room. The old midwife was covered in sweat, her hair stuck to her forehead as the skilled hands moved inside Zofia's body. One mistake and the mother would be lost. She would bleed to death. It was a tedious and painful process.

Finally, she was ready.

"Push now," Maria said, out of breath from the stress and exertion.

Zofia had never before been this tired. It took all the strength in her body to push.

"Again."

The cords stood out in Zofia's neck as the beads of sweat ran from her face, into her hair, and down onto her flushed neck and chest.

"Again, push. You must push."

"I can't!" Zofia cried.

"Again, now… Push!" Maria demanded. "Push, I said, push…"

Zofia did not respond. Maria slapped her face to bring her back to reality. Zofia must use all the force left within her to bring this child into the world. "Push…" Maria growled. "Push, I said, push…" If she stopped now, Zofia would die.

Zofia cried out, tears falling on her face. "I'm so tired. Please…"

"Push!"

Zofia pushed with all the strength that was left in her body.

Once the walls of Zofia's body tore open, the tiny slippery infant left the safety of its mother's womb and poured into the world in a river of blood, water, and feces.

Immediately Maria grabbed the child. Her thick, knowing hands cleaned the infant's air pipes, and then she held the baby high in the air by its feet and slapped the child hard on its buttocks. A hearty cry echoed through the rooms.

Maria took a deep breath and sighed. She laid the baby beside her mother. With her forearm, she pushed the hair off her sweat-laden brow. Her work was done. "You have a daughter, Zofia."

Zofia smiled, cradling the baby gently in her arms.

Maria took the little girl and gently laid her in the dresser drawer that had been made into a makeshift cradle. "One more push. You have to get the afterbirth out. Then I will give you the baby."

Zofia looked at her daughter, who whimpered, waiting, and felt a burst of energy. She pushed hard. Her body gave way to more blood and water, and then the rush of a large slimy mass came forth, and she knew it was over.

Not yet washed, the child lay contented in her mother's arms as the midwife cleaned the mess. Then she took the baby and tenderly washed her clean.

"She's a beauty," Maria said, handing the baby back to Zofia. "What are you going to call her?"

"Eidel. It means gentle."

"That's a lovely name. Let me go and get Fruma and Gitel. They will want to see the baby.

Fruma and Gitel came storming in like two protective wildcats.

"Are you all right?" Gitel asked.

"Yes," Zofia said and then moved the blanket away so they could see the baby. "This is Eidel."

The two women looked on in amazement at the tiny hands, feet, and ears.

"*Oy*, she is really *shane*, beautiful."

"So *shane*."

They cooed and giggled like young girls, gently fondling the soft skin of the baby's cheek.

Zofia was happy, content even. But she could not help thinking of her parents. A pang of sadness shot through her. She wondered how they had felt the day she was born. It must have been something like this. They must have felt this extreme love and need to protect her, as she now felt toward the bundle that slept softly in her arms. She was sure they had been in awe at the wonder of a new and precious life. Zofia missed them.

She realized she'd done wrong and had brought shame to her family's name, but she wished they were here. She wished they could see their grandchild. Surely if they saw this little wonder, God's perfect creation, all would be forgiven. A tear escaped from the side of her left eye, but no one noticed. It trickled away quietly and mingled with the sweat that was beginning to dry on her face.

Zofia was tired. Fruma took the baby, and Zofia slept.

Over the next week, Zofia regained her strength, but she was still in bed. The tearing of her delicate parts was taking time to heal. Fruma and Gitel did not mind. They enjoyed being helpful.

Having an infant in the house changed the lives of all three women immensely. They fussed over the baby and took turns getting up to bring her to Zofia's side. They then watched as the little lips grasped Zofia's nipple and sucked vigorously.

"She is a healthy baby," Fruma said. "Thanks be to God."

"Yes, thanks be to God," Gitel said, taking Fruma's hand and smiling at her.

As the baby grew, so did the responsibilities that Fruma and Gitel took on with relish. They had been so long alone that they enjoyed the role of grandparents. At first, Fruma insisted that Zofia stay home and take care of the child, but as the child grew sturdier, they set up a playpen in the dressmaking shop. All day, Zofia and Fruma worked while Eidel slept in her playpen. Many times, they had to put work aside to comfort a fussy baby, but it was all right. After all, it was Eidel.

When Helen returned from her honeymoon, she and her mother, Maria, visited the dressmakers.

"Oh, look at her. She is beautiful," Helen said about Eidel as she smiled at Zofia. "She has such light hair. I think she will be a blonde."

Helen had never asked who the baby's father was, but Zofia could see by the way that she looked at the child that she wondered. After all, how had a woman with hair the color of a raven's wing produced a child with a full head of hair as light as a field of wheat? It was apparent to Zofia that Eidel, with her striking sapphire eyes, looked a lot like her father.

"I really like her name. It's lovely."

"Oh, thank you. It means gentle. But so far, she's more feisty than gentle. As a matter of fact, when she nurses, I feel like a whale is pulling at my nipple."

Helen laughed. "I can't wait to have a child. I've always wanted children. Fritz says we should start immediately."

They both laughed.

"How was your honeymoon?"

"It was very nice. We didn't have much money, so we were limited to what we could do, but we enjoyed it," Helen said. Then she gently ran her finger along Eidel's cheek, trying to make the baby smile.

"Can I hold her?" Helen asked.

"Yes, be careful. Remember to hold her head."

"Of course," Helen said, reaching down to lift the baby. At first, little Eidel's lower lip went out, and she looked like she might cry. "Shhhh," Helen whispered, stroking the baby's soft cheek. She walked around the room, gently rocking the child and holding her against her chest. After a while, instead of crying, Eidel sucked her fingers, curled into Helen, and fell asleep.

"She is a wonder."

"I know. Sometimes I cannot believe I have a child. It's almost inconceivable. I have to pinch myself," Zofia laughed.

"This little girl is special. I can tell."

"Can you?"

"Of course," Helen smiled as she gingerly touched the small head that rested on her shoulder.

"I wonder what she will be like when she grows up."

"Oh, I think she will be very smart."

"And pretty?"

"Not pretty, beautiful," Helen said. Then she whispered, "Won't you, Eidel?"

CHAPTER SIXTEEN

"AT LEAST HITLER is going to leave us alone. He promised to stay away from Poland. Thanks be to God," Gitel said, "He is most surely a madman."

"Yes, it's true, he has promised to leave Poland alone, and that is good," Fruma said as she washed the cereal off Eidel's chin. "But do you trust him? Really trust him?"

"Of course not. Who could trust him? But if he stays away from here, that is all we should be concerned with."

Zofia came into the kitchen. "Who is this Hitler, anyway?"

"The leader of Germany—a real conqueror, I think," Gitel said. "But don't you worry about him. He is far away from us, and we have too much to do with our tiny package to worry about such a disturbing man."

"I have a cousin in Germany," Fruma said. "I am concerned for her. Although we have not spoken in years, I think I will send her a letter."

"You want to ask her to come here?" Gitel said. "We don't have so much room, but if need be, we can manage."

"Yes and no. I don't even know her, really. We met once when I was just a little girl. If I saw her on the street, I wouldn't recognize her. But I hear it is bad for Jews in Germany. I don't know what to do. Do you think all of this will pass?"

"You mean this anti-Semitism? Of course, it will pass. It always does. I wouldn't worry too much. Besides, this Hitler is so busy conquering the world that he probably has very little time to concern himself with the Jews in Poland."

CHAPTER SEVENTEEN

"MANFRED, Dr. Goebbels would like to see you in his office," Dr. Goebbels's secretary announced when he walked into work on that day in early November.

"Thank you," Manfred said and rushed to put his things on his desk. Then he went immediately to the doctor's large corner office in the back of the room.

"Dr. Goebbels, sir. You asked for me?"

"Yes, I did. Sit down, please. I want to discuss something with you. I need someone I can trust to talk to about a pressing matter in order to gather my thoughts. You see, something interesting has happened. Something I believe we can use to our advantage. What I have heard is that a Jew in Paris, his name is Herschel Grynszpan, went to the German embassy and shot a German official. The official was really nobody of importance. His name is Ernst vom Rath. But, if this Ernst should die, we have an excellent case to start a program against the Jews here in Germany.

"It will bring the people together, strengthening their love for Hitler and all he has done to rebuild the Fatherland. And because of how we will present this situation as a terrible crime that was committed against us, the rest of the world will understand. We will show them how the Jews sabotage our country and make them see our side. This is an opportunity for us. The more we can unite the German people against a common enemy, the stronger our nation will become."

"Yes, sir, as always, you are right. This is a bad situation, turned into an opportunity by your brilliant mind. I am just curious. Does anyone know why this Jew did such a thing?" Manfred asked.

"From what I understand, his family was forced out of their home in Germany, and all their possessions were confiscated. Apparently, they were forced over the border into Poland. Their son, this Herschel, had some nerve. He was living in Paris when he got the news, and this Jew had the balls to go into the German embassy and shoot a German official.

"This sort of behavior must be nipped in the bud. It cannot be tolerated. If we should overlook something like this, then the Jews will inevitably begin to act out more and more until they are out of control. We must deal with them in such a manner that the Jews begin to know their place. We must show them who is boss right now with such a strong demonstration that they will never even consider acting up again. They must be terrified of us. That way, we can keep them where we want them.

"So you see, if this works out the way I am planning, we will have achieved three things. We will show the world that the Jews are the enemy, show the Jews who is the boss, and unite and strengthen our Aryan brotherhood."

"You are truly a genius, Dr. Goebbels. No one else could take such an unfortunate incident and turn it into a victory for the Fatherland."

Goebbels smiled, and Manfred knew he'd said the right things. He could see in the doctor's eyes just how much his boss enjoyed having him around. They made a good team.

For several days, Manfred and Goebbels waited. Then on November 7th, Ernst vom Rath died.

It was like any other day in November 1938, except that when it was finally over, it would go down in history as the date when Hitler openly waged war on the Jews of Germany. And so, on the ninth of

November in 1938, everything began its rapid descent in a downward spiral.

For two blood-splattered nights under Goebbels's direction, with Hitler's approval, the Jewish communities throughout Germany were ravaged by gangs of hoodlums intent on revenge for the death of an unknown German diplomat at the hands of a young Jewish man.

The cries of victims and perpetrators echoed through the streets as synagogues were set on fire, windows, storefronts demolished, people beaten, dragged from their homes, and murdered. That night, the genocide began. It would last until the end of the war. November 9, 1938, would go down in history, in infamy, to be known forever as *Kristallnacht*, The Night of the Broken Glass.

On November 9th, unsuspecting Jews all over Germany and Austria went about their lives as they always had. The growing anti-Semitism had not, as of yet, turned violent. Some Jews had been forced from their homes. But those still living the way they did before Hitler rationalized this by telling themselves that those evicted must have committed a crime. Jewish businesses were boycotted, but then again, the Jews had lived through this sort of thing before.

Although the Nuremberg laws had been passed, declaring that it was illegal for Jews and Gentiles to marry, again, they rationalized this as just a part of Hitler's campaign. They told each other and themselves that it would pass. When neighbors saw each other at the butcher shop or the bakery, there were whispers of concentration camps and work camps being built. Still, most people believed that only those guilty of crimes would ever see the inside of these prisons. In short, the Jews believed that if they remained quiet and endured the insults, all of this would soon pass.

They could not have been more wrong.

That night on November 9th, truckloads of German youths were brought into the Jewish parts of town all over Germany and Austria. They carried clubs, were told to destroy the businesses and beat anyone they saw on the streets.

"You may do as you wish, but do not steal anything. Only

destroy it," the leaders told the young men. For it was to be a demonstration, not a robbery. The Germans must be exacting revenge for acts committed against their fatherland. If they took any valuables, the entire act would lose its ideals.

Besides, there would be plenty of time to confiscate Jewish property later.

The sound of crashing glass echoed for miles, combined with the wild hollering of the youths as they ran through the towns bent on destruction. The smell of burning permeated the air as the hundred-year-old synagogues burst into roaring flames. Blood covered the sidewalks as men and women were torn from their homes and crushed under the clubs and boots of the raging attackers. By morning, the Jewish sectors of the towns were nearly destroyed.

Thirty thousand choice, healthy, strong young Jewish men were arrested and transported to the Dachau, Buchenwald, and Sachsenhausen camps. Still, most of the Jews were paralyzed by fear and did nothing.

CHAPTER EIGHTEEN

On January 22, 1942, Goebbels laid the letter on his desk and rubbed his eyes. It was the minutes of the Wannsee Conference, and he still burned at the slight of not being invited. There had been a bad harvest this year, and food supplies were growing short. There were too many mouths to feed, and who better to eliminate than the Jewish menace? Hitler decided that *the Final Solution* to the Jewish problem would have to be initiated immediately instead of after the war.

The conference had been driven by *Obergruppenführer* Reinhard Heydrich and *Reichsführer* Hermann Göring. Goebbels felt that with such an important decision, he should have been invited.

He sighed as he remembered how, at Hitler's command, he had returned to Berlin while the Nazi Party was about to collapse in the face of the communists proclaiming Red Berlin to help save, reorganize, and rebuild the Nazi Party. It was an uphill battle. He fought the communists, the middle-class newspapers, and the speakers in the parliament.

Opposing him was easy. No newspaper had been banned as many times as his *Der Angriff*. He smiled, then the smile evaporated like a vapor as he recalled how he used propaganda as a weapon until the Party had seized power.

He alone had been responsible for using his propaganda to transform the struggling politician Hitler into the messiah-redeemer persona of the Führer. Then why was he excluded from the conference? There was always someone jockeying for power within the Party, trying to get their star to rise while pushing someone else's down. Leopold Gutterer had been invited instead but, for some reason, did not attend.

Hitler had no wife, so Magda, with her beauty and popularity, became known as "The First Lady of the Reich." It backfired when Goebbels was found having various affairs and embarrassing the *First Lady* and, therefore, the Reich. Hitler had to intervene more than once by ordering Goebbels to break off the affairs. Goebbels's enemies were using this against him, and he was not in favor at the time.

Part of the trouble was that Himmler disliked Goebbels and was critical of him to the Führer, referring to *Kristallnacht* as a result of Goebbels's 'megalomania and stupidity.' Whether he simply disagreed with his methods or he was jealous of Goebbels, he did not know.

He sat down at his desk and gazed out the window. He needed to talk. Desperate for someone with whom to discuss what he'd heard and seen, Dr. Goebbels sent for Manfred. Manfred had proven to him time and again that he was a good friend and a competent understudy. Joseph Goebbels enjoyed the admiration he saw in Manfred's eyes, and he believed that he could trust and confide in this young apprentice who reminded him so much of himself. After the others had left for the day, Goebbels called Manfred into his office.

"Would you like a beer?" Dr. Goebbels asked as he opened a bottle for himself.

"I would, yes."

"Nothing on this earth is like a good German beer."

"I couldn't agree more."

"How is your lovely wife?"

"She is doing very well, thank you."

"Soon, we can expect a child?" Goebbels asked.

"We are trying..."

"That's the good part, huh?" Goebbels laughed, and Manfred laughed, too.

"I received a letter today, the minutes of a conference ordered by the Führer himself."

Goebbels lit a cigar and placed it into his pelvis ashtray.

"Anyway, this business with the Jews is getting out of hand. I received a notice that we are to begin the *Final Solution*."

"I'm sorry. I don't know what that is."

"Nasty business..."

"I don't doubt it. Everything having to do with Jews is a nasty business."

"Yes, that is true." Goebbels hesitated for a moment. After taking a long puff on his cigar and a sip of beer, he looked Manfred straight in the eye. "It is the elimination of all the Jews in Germany."

"Elimination? You mean murder?"

"I mean... elimination. You do understand."

"We have to kill them?"

"I suppose that is the only way to eliminate them."

Manfred nodded. He felt a thickening in his throat as if he might vomit. It was best to remain quiet and regain composure. He would not be directly involved, so why worry? This would take place far from his tidy office.

"We should be arresting them soon enough and shipping them off to the camps we've been building for this purpose. There we will deal with them," Goebbels said.

Manfred nodded again.

For several minutes, the room was quiet. The only sound was the irritating ticking of the clock on the wall.

"Nasty but necessary business," Goebbels said. "It is barbaric, but thoroughly deserved." He blew a cloud of cigar smoke into the air and drained the last of his beer bottle.

"Would you like to join me for dinner down the street at the café? Or do you want to get on home to that pretty wife of yours?" He patted Manfred's shoulder. "I would really like it if you joined me."

"Then, of course, I would be happy to accompany you to dinner. Just give me a moment to call Christa and let her know I am going to be late."

"Of course, we would not want her to worry," Goebbels said, smiling.

CHAPTER NINETEEN

Try as they might, Christa could not become pregnant. After dinner the following evening, they sat at the table, having their strudel and coffee. Manfred looked worried.

"What is it? You look upset."

"No, darling, nothing is wrong," he said.

"Are you upset that I cannot conceive?"

"No, I am sure you will soon enough. We are probably trying too hard."

"Perhaps we should go and see my father. He can test us to see what is wrong. It might be something simple."

"Yes, all right. If you would like, we will go," he said, patting her hand.

Manfred was worried. He was worried about many things. The inability to conceive was certainly on his mind, but covert operations that he had become privy to at the office greatly concerned him, and his workload was continually increasing.

Most troubling of all was the fact that he had stood by and watched as an old friend had been arrested. He could not erase the scene from his mind. It was the man who owned the delicatessen right down the street from the apartment where he'd grown up. The man was a Jew, which should have been nothing to him.

But one incident that occurred when he was just a boy stuck out in his mind. It was a terrible winter when he and his mother were so poor that they went for days without food. Manfred had gone down to the butcher and begged for credit, only to be turned away.

On his way home, he'd stopped at the delicatessen, hoping to ask for the crumbs of bread that diners had left on their plates. At the time, the deli owner was much younger than he was today. Manfred recalled walking up to the counter, his head hung in shame, and asking for anything edible that might be in the trash can. The Jew had looked at him and refused to let him look in the trash. Instead, this man had given him two sandwiches to take home to his mother.

That night he'd slept on a full belly for the first time in a long time. He had never forgotten it, yet, when this man lay on the cobblestones just a few feet in front of him, beaten and bleeding, speaking in a voice barely audible…

"Manfred," he'd said his name as he stared at him through eyes crusted shut with blood. "Manfred Blau? Is that you?" The old man squinted against the bright sunlight.

"Manfred?" Again, he said it in a voice that cracked, like the dried blood in the old Jew's white hair. "Help me, please, Manfred. Help me… you've always been a good boy. Please, don't let them do this to me…"

Manfred turned his head. He could not bear to look at the old man lying on the pavement, surrounded by a pool of dark blood.

Why did he have to see this? He was only here because Dr. Goebbels had sent him on this mission with the Gestapo to see how things were being handled.

For Joseph's sake, he must show leadership qualities. He needed to convince them that he was strong and would not become squeamish performing the tasks the Fatherland demanded of him. He wanted to be heartless, ruthless, and single-minded: a perfect soldier and Nazi, the man the Party expected him to be.

But now, here he was, in the middle of the street with the

Gestapo agents standing right beside him, so close that he could smell their cologne, and all he wanted to do was help the old Jew. He dared not acknowledge this man or, worse, tell him to run. He wanted to—he wanted to scream—to vomit at the sight of the battered man covered in blood.

He could still taste the sandwiches. If he closed his eyes, he remembered his mother's smile when he'd handed her the food wrapped in white butcher paper. This was madness. It was suicide. He must look the other way. Any feelings of sympathy would mark him as either too weak to be an officer or, worse, as a traitor. It would put him and Christa in terrible danger. For just a second, his eyes connected with the rheumy, pleading eyes of the old Jew. *Stop accusing me, stop begging me*, Manfred said in his mind. "There is nothing I can do to help you."

Then he turned and walked away to the sound of his heels clicking against the cobblestone walk. Manfred told himself over and over that the man was a Jew and Jews were enemies of Germany. It must be this way if the Fatherland was to be saved. Still, he kept thinking of how kind the man had been to him when he was just a boy.

And now, Manfred knew that same man was to be taken to a camp. And unlike so many others, Manfred already knew about the *Final Solution*. The old Jew was to be murdered. Every night since the incident, Manfred found it hard to sleep. He would fall asleep in exhaustion as soon as his head hit the pillow, but within an hour or two, he was awake. He'd get up and walk around, the demons in his mind taunting him.

He'd taken a liking to drinking shots of whiskey to quieten those demons. As the alcohol burned his throat, it also clouded his feelings, making it easier to conduct the necessary business. *For Germany to take its rightful place as the world power, all the undesirable elements must be eliminated. This is the way it must be,* Manfred thought. He poured another shot.

CHAPTER TWENTY

For several months, Dr. Goebbels released propaganda-filled films to the German population, showing how the Polish people were taking advantage of their German neighbors. But even though Hitler had promised to protect and never invade Poland, these movies made it clear that Germany must defend herself.

On a cool day, the first of September in 1939, Hitler broke his promise to Poland. Because Germany had vowed to protect and never invade their Polish neighbors, Poland did not see any need to strengthen their army. Instead, they relied on the integrity of the word of the great Führer. Therefore, when the German army invaded Poland, the Polish were no match for the powerful Third Reich. Germany conquered Poland within two weeks, and the Nazi occupation began.

CHAPTER TWENTY-ONE

Eidel crawled across the floor of the apartment. She went straight to Gitel's waiting arms. Gitel lifted the baby into the air as the child's giggles filled the room. Fruma was in the kitchen preparing pancakes, and Zofia was washing diapers.

"Can you believe she is almost a year old?" Fruma asked.

"Well, not quite, but yes, almost," Zofia said.

"Eh, you just don't want to get old, so you want her to stay a baby forever," Gitel said.

"Don't you?" Zofia took a moment to walk away from the wash-basin and marvel at Eidel.

"I do, actually. She is the most wonderful treasure we have ever had here."

"That she is," Fruma said. "I think we should try to buy a used rug. I hate that she is crawling around on the cold floor. The winter is coming. It will be too cold for her to be doing that."

"Yes, let's see what kind of rug we can get," Gitel said.

"Oh, Zofia, I forgot to tell you, when you were buying milk yesterday, Helen came by the shop. She brought you a little present for Eidel. And she brought news, too. She would probably want to tell you herself."

"Oh, come on, Fruma. You can't do this to me. I can't stand the suspense. What news?"

"Well…"

"Come on…"

"She's pregnant."

"Oh, that's wonderful."

"Yes, isn't it? The babies will be close in age. That will be nice for them as they grow up."

"It will."

"Here is the gift Helen brought for Eidel. It's a small toy, a little yellow duck." Fruma handed the toy to Zofia.

"She is so kind. Her mother is, too."

"Yes. I like them both very much."

"You know, I've noticed that Szmul has taken quite an interest in you," Fruma said.

"Szmul? Who is Szmul?" Zofia asked.

"You know who that is. It's the boy who brings the fabric samples. He always watches you work. I see how he looks at you."

"Oh, Fruma, I'm not looking for a husband. I don't have time for such things."

"What do you mean you have no time? Only a stone should be all alone. You need someone in your life. I have Gitel, but who do you have?"

"Well, I have you and Gitel, and of course, I have Eidel."

"But one day, Eidel will go off to live her own life. Gitel and I are much older than you. What will happen when we die?"

"Don't talk about dying, please."

"Well, at least you could give this Szmul a chance."

"Perhaps, I don't know."

"Why don't you invite him for a Shabbat dinner? You'll see how you like each other. If you like him, fine. If not, well, nothing is lost, right?"

"Oh, Fruma, I don't know. I'll have to wait and see."

"Fruma, leave her alone. She has to decide this kind of thing by herself. She'll know when she's ready."

"Oy, Gitel, you know she won't be young forever. Youth and

beauty fade. One day, her youth will be gone. If she's going to find a partner, now is the time."

"You're no longer young, but to me, you're still and always will be beautiful."

"Gitel, you are a dear," Fruma laughed.

It was two weeks before Szmul came to the shop with his trunk filled with fabrics and odds and ends. As always, he laid the trunk open in the middle of the floor, where Fruma and Zofia could look through it to see what they might need.

"So Szmul, you're married?" Fruma asked. She avoided looking at Zofia, who was giving her a dirty look.

"No, I've never been married," Szmul said to Fruma, but he was looking at Zofia.

Zofia felt her face burn with embarrassment.

"Do you have a special girl?"

"No, not really. I see a few girls on occasion."

"You know that Zofia is not married."

"Fruma!"

"Well, you aren't."

"So what does that have to do with buying fabric?"

"Nothing, nothing to do with buying fabric."

"I think your boss is trying to arrange a date for us," Szmul said.

"Yes, I can certainly see that." Zofia glared at Fruma, who turned away, putting all her focus on the pile of fabrics.

"I would like to take you for dinner, or maybe we could go for a walk," Szmul said.

"You do realize that Eidel is my daughter."

"Yes, I know. I remember when you were pregnant."

Zofia nodded.

"And you still want to take me to dinner?"

"Yes, I do. Would you like to go?"

Zofia looked up at him. If he wasn't exactly nice-looking, at least he was very well-dressed. Szmul wore a very well-tailored gray suit and black tie. His shirt was white cotton, and he wore beautiful, shiny gold cuff links.

"All right," Zofia said. Now Fruma looked up from the pile of fabric. "You and Gitel will watch Eidel for me?"

"Of course. Did you doubt it?" Fruma smiled.

"No."

"Maybe tomorrow night?" Szmul asked.

"Yes, all right, tomorrow night after work."

"Is seven too early?"

"Seven is fine. She can leave a little bit early," Fruma said.

"I'll meet you here?" Szmul asked.

"Yes, here at the shop," Zofia said.

After Fruma had picked several bolts of material and a small bag of pearls from Szmul's trunk, he left.

"Why did you do that?" Zofia asked. "I told you I am not interested in looking for a husband."

"So you'll have a nice dinner. What's so wrong with that?"

"Oh, Fruma, I don't know what to say."

"Then, say thank you."

Zofia shook her head and then laughed. "Thank you," she said.

Szmul took Zofia to the small kosher restaurant three blocks from the shop. He ordered crispy-skinned roasted chicken, *kishka*, and potato pancakes with applesauce.

"If I keep eating like this, I'll get as fat as a cow," Zofia smiled.

"Do you like it?"

"Yes, of course. It's delicious."

"You have probably heard this before, but I wanted to say that you are beautiful."

"Oh, thank you," Zofia said, turning away, embarrassed.

"You are so closed up, though. Why?"

"I'm not closed up."

"Sure, you are. You won't even give me a chance. I'm a pretty nice guy."

"Yes, well, the truth is, I'm not ready to get involved with anyone. I have Eidel to think of, and quite frankly, she is my main focus."

"I understand. I'm not looking for anything serious, like

marriage. But I know you must get lonely, and having someone to have dinner with is not such a bad thing."

"No, it isn't," Zofia said. "I am sure you've heard the rumors about me, a woman bearing a child without a husband."

"Yes, I have."

"And I suppose that makes you feel I am easy?"

"I'm sorry, but I don't know what you mean."

"I mean that you know that I am not a virgin, and so you assume taking another man into my bed would be nothing for me."

"Well, yes. I do feel that way. Women make too much of this sort of thing. It would be nice if it could be more casual."

"Well, let me say this. I do not plan to sleep with you. Do you understand?"

"Yes, and no. I mean, why not? Don't you get lonely? And isn't it true that once a woman has been with a man, she needs to have it again? Sort of like an itch that needs to be scratched?"

"Oh, Szmul," Zofia shook her head. "This was a mistake. I knew it was. Fruma meant well, but I am not looking for something like this," Zofia said, removing the napkin from her lap and placing it on the table. "Goodnight," she said and stood up to leave the restaurant.

"Zofia, what are you looking for? Do you want to spend the rest of your life alone, or worse, living with two lesbians? A little time with a man would do you good. Or maybe you are living with two lesbians because you are one?"

Szmul was still talking as Zofia walked out the door.

The following day, Gitel went to work, and Fruma and Zofia took Eidel to the shop. Eidel fussed most of the morning, wanting to be picked up and carried, but both women were busy, so all they could manage was a few minutes between seams.

"She's very fussy today."

"Yes, does her head feel hot?" Zofia asked.

"No, I checked a few minutes ago. Maybe she's cutting a tooth."

"Yes, perhaps that's it. Here, give her to me for a minute." Fruma handed Eidel to her mother. Zofia rocked the baby in her arms and tried to look in her mouth.

"I think her gums are swelling. Do you have any whiskey?"

"I do, but it's back at the apartment. We don't have any here."

"Then she'll have to wait until tonight," Zofia said.

"By the way, how was your date with Szmul?"

"Terrible, like I thought it would be. I know that no man is going to have respect for me because of what I have done, having a child without the benefit of marriage. They think that since I've already been with a man, I would think nothing of doing it again. They look at me as an easy mark. I'm not."

"Of course, you're not. Did he try to take you to bed?"

"Yes, and no. I mean, he didn't touch me. He asked, and he let me know that he felt that I would be easy, so I walked out of the restaurant."

"Oh, sweetie, I am so sorry. I never meant for you to get hurt. It's my fault. I meant well; I really did."

"I know you did, Fruma. But I think that part of my life is over. No more love affairs for me. From now on, I need to focus on my child."

"Over? You are so young. Were you so in love with Eidel's father that you can't look at another man?"

"I thought I was. I was just a silly young girl. I wanted a storybook romance, complete with a prince, to sweep me off my feet. Instead, I got a frog. I got pregnant by my teacher, who wanted nothing to do with me after he got his way."

"Oh, you never told me before."

"I know. I wasn't ready. But yes, he was my teacher, an American, not Jewish, and very dapper. I was a fool. I won't be a fool for any man ever again."

By lunchtime, Eidel's whining had begun to grate on both of their nerves. Between the humming of the machines and the noise from outside, Zofia was getting a headache.

"Oh, Eidel, please be quiet already," Zofia said, but of course, she knew the baby did not understand. Her hands were shaking, and she felt like she might cry. "She is really getting to me today, Fruma."

"Maybe you should take her out for a walk in the buggy for a little while. The fresh air will do you both good," Fruma suggested. "Besides, Eidel always calms down and takes a nap after she goes for a walk outside."

"That's a good idea. I'll feed her first and then walk her to the park. By then, she should be ready to nap."

The fishmonger Gitel worked for had given them a carriage for the baby. His children were all grown, and the grandchildren had long since left the infant stage. So, he no longer had any use for the buggy. In the afternoons, sometimes, when the weather was nice and if they had time between jobs, Fruma and Zofia took turns pushing the baby through the park. Fruma knitted two thick blankets, a hat, mittens, and a sweater for Eidel. And now that the weather was changing, they would be put to good use.

Zofia took Eidel to the back of the store and offered her the breast, but Eidel was too fussy to eat. With her little fist, she kept pushing Zofia's breast away. After several tries, Zofia decided to wait until later. Instead, she changed the baby's diaper and dressed her for the walk outside.

When they left, Fruma sighed. It was hard but enjoyable to have a little one around. She stretched her back and shoulders. As she was getting older, the long days hunched over the sewing machine had taken their toll, and she'd begun to have aches in her upper back.

It was unusual for Fruma to stop working, even to eat, unless it was with Zofia, but she was tired today. The baby had been up a lot the night before. Fruma looked out the window as Zofia pushed Eidel's carriage down the busy street. Then she set aside the dress she'd been working on to have a quiet, uninterrupted lunch.

The sky sparkled silver-blue, like a crystal. A cool but not yet cold breeze brushed through the autumn-colored leaves of the trees like a young girl brushes her long hair, and a blindingly bright sun dominated the sky.

"Look over there, Eidel. That's a squirrel," Zofia said as a squirrel scampered through the long golden grass. Eidel giggled and pointed her finger.

"Yes, sweetheart. It's a squirrel," Zofia cooed. *Eidel is such a beau-*

tiful baby, she thought. "If someone had told me that I would ever love anyone or anything as much as I love her, I would have told them that they were crazy," she said aloud to no one but herself.

Zofia decided to walk over to the bakery and pick up a strudel for Fruma. She knew how much Fruma loved the vinegar raisin strudel that Frau Zuckerman, the baker on the corner, made. If she hurried, perhaps they would not be all gone, and what a delight it would be to serve it after dinner tonight.

She pushed the carriage slowly along the cobblestone walk toward the bakery. It was necessary to go slow because the stones made the buggy rock, disturbing Eidel. As she crossed the street, she ran right into her old friend Lena. There was no avoiding the confrontation. The two women were face to face. Zofia had heard that Lena's parents forbade their daughter from having any contact with Zofia because Zofia bore a child out of wedlock. From the way that Lena looked, her face as red as a ripe pomegranate, her eyes averted, Zofia knew it was true.

"Hello, Lena. I haven't seen you in months."

Zofia, pregnant and big-bellied, had gone to Lena's home twice, trying to see her, but her mother had always said that Lena was not at home.

"Yes, I know. I'm sorry, I've been busy."

"I left word with your mother that I was living with the seamstress, Fruma. You could have come by anytime."

"Yes, I knew where you were," Lena said, biting her lower lip, her eyes darting around to see who was watching this conversation.

"You knew? But you never came by. We used to be best friends. You do remember?"

"I have to go. I'm sorry, Zofia. I can't stay and talk. I must hurry and get home."

"You're ashamed to be seen talking to me, aren't you?" Zofia's face dropped.

"What do you want me to say, Zofia? You've done a terrible thing. You've shamed yourself. Now you want to drag me into your embarrassment. If I'm seen keeping company with you, I'll never find a decent husband.

"You've always been this way, doing just what you want and never thinking about the consequences. I'm sorry, but I don't have that luxury. I want to get married and have a family. I'm not like you. I don't want to live on the outskirts of society. I need friends. I want to be accepted. I'm sorry, Zofia. Now please, move out of my way. I have to leave."

Lena practically ran down the street. Zofia stood there, watching Lena's full skirt flutter around her legs as she left, her heart breaking. She knew that whatever friendship they'd shared was over. It had been over for a while, but she'd always hoped that somehow, when they saw each other, Lena would remember how close they'd been and would want that closeness again. But it would not be so, and it would never be so again.

Zofia's mouth sagged a little, and she felt the tears burning at the back of her eyes. Yes, sleeping with Mr. Taylor had been a mistake, but now, she wouldn't trade Eidel for anything. She was not sorry that she'd given her daughter life, even if it meant that she was to be an outcast forever. Zofia looked down at Eidel's little hand holding on to her blanket. The tiny fingers fisted on the pink knitted cover as the baby smiled at her.

It's all worth it. God works in strange ways. I don't care at all about the baby's father anymore. In fact, I don't know what I ever saw in him. It's strange that I thought I was in love with him. However, he gave me Eidel, and I am forever grateful for that. I love this child so fiercely that I would give anything I have for her, even my life.

And then, without warning, breaking through the sameness of the early afternoon, of the vendors hawking, the customers quibbling, all the sights and sounds of the city, she saw them marching. German soldiers in uniform, toting guns, marched right through the center of town.

Zofia could not move. Her feet felt like they weighed a thousand pounds and were glued to the sidewalk. In a few moments, the soldiers would turn the corner right in front of where she stood. Instinctively, Eidel picked up her mother's angst and began to cry. Usually, Zofia would lift the baby into her arms and cuddle her. The crying was just the catalyst Zofia needed to free her from her trance.

With her heart pounding to the rhythm of the marching soldiers, she began to run toward the shop. She must get off the street before the soldiers get any closer. As mother and baby raced down the sidewalk, the carriage hit a cobblestone and almost toppled over. Zofia cringed and trembled with nervous fear. If the buggy had turned over, Eidel could have been hurt. She could have hit her head. Zofia shivered. *Stop thinking and keep moving*, she told herself. Get back to the safety of the shop and lock the doors.

When she arrived at the shop, Zofia's mouth was so dry that she could hardly speak. Her heart pounded like a steel drum. As quickly as she could, she locked the door. Then she pulled the curtains tightly closed over the window.

"What's the matter? You're as white as a ghost," Fruma said, putting down the thick wool fabric she was working with. She'd finished the dress for Frau Balinski and had begun working on a coat for Frau Kleinstein, the banker's wife.

"The Germans are here, right here in Warsaw," Zofia said, and she began coughing, choking.

"Where? What are you talking about?" Fruma got up and handed her a glass of water that had been sitting beside Zofia's sewing machine. "Drink this."

Eidel let out loud, hysterical wails. She sensed the tension in the room. Her face had turned crimson.

"Here, look. Come, they are right outside. Get down low. We don't want them to see us. I don't know what is happening, but I thought Hitler had agreed to leave Poland alone. I heard that. I know he said that. Come, come, and peek out the window," Zofia was almost hysterical. Her voice was high-pitched, and she was shaking. Fruma rubbed her back for a moment.

"Shhh," she said, "It's all right. You are upsetting the baby," Fruma said.

Eidel's incessant crying filled the room. Fruma took the baby into her arms. She rocked her back and forth, and Eidel began to quiet down. Next, the two women got down on their knees and parted the curtain a crack, just enough to see the street outside.

People stood watching as the soldiers marched through. Some

were blank-faced, staring out of unseeing eyes. Others cried or covered their mouths with their hands in shock, horror, or both.

The news of the plight of the Jews in Germany had reached Poland. There was no doubt as to the anti-Semitism of the Nazi regime. For months, many Polish Jews, Fruma among them, had sent word to their German relatives, inviting them to leave Germany and come across the border to safety in Poland. Gitel's only living relatives were in Hungary.

Gitel had tried to convince her aunt but to no avail. Often at night, when everyone had gone to sleep, Gitel sat up, unable to rest. Zofia would hear her in the living room. She knew that Gitel worried that perhaps her family refused because she lived a life they did not approve of.

It grieved Zofia to think that such hatred and misunderstanding could keep people from their best interest. Well, at least you tried. Zofia would hear Fruma tell Gitel when they discussed the matter.

German marching music came thundering in from outside.

The Third Reich had come to Poland. The terrifying Nazi flag flew at the front of the legion. A chill ran down Fruma's back.

Since she was a little girl, she'd always had a gift for seeing the future, but she'd never had control of the gift. It came whenever it chose to. Once, as a child, she'd gone to the hospital to see a friend of her mother's. The friend had minor surgery and was expected to leave the hospital in a few days. However, as soon as Fruma saw her, she knew the woman would never leave alive. That night, her mother's friend developed an infection. By the end of the week, she was dead.

Incidents like these had occurred throughout Fruma's life. Now Fruma stared out the window, her eyes blurring as mental pictures came to her. Horrible visions of mountains of corpses, their bones jutting from emaciated bodies. Fruma collapsed.

Zofia saw that she had fainted. Carefully she put Eidel down on a thick square of fabric and took Fruma into her arms, laying her down gently on the floor.

"Fruma," Zofia said. Fruma did not answer, although her eyes were wide open.

Zofia got the glass of water she had been drinking from and brought it to Fruma's lips, but Fruma did not drink.

"A dark day is upon us," Fruma said, her voice distant, deep, and frightening.

The tone of Fruma's voice made Eidel begin to fuss again.

"Shhh, it will be all right," Zofia said, her finger gently rubbing Eidel's cheek, but even she didn't believe her words.

"I wish Gitel were here with us," Fruma said.

"Yes, so do I. Shall I go over to the fishmonger and fetch her?"

"No, no, don't leave here. Stay. Keep the drapes closed. Let them pass like the Angel of Death on Passover," Fruma said. "We will see Gitel tonight."

Once the troops passed, the streets began to clear, and everything seemed to return to normal. The vendors haggled with customers, the old orthodox men walked, huddling together, wearing their black coats and high hats, and women hurried along in fashionable dresses, but even with all the regularity, for Fruma and Zofia, everything in their world had changed.

Zofia hand-sewed the buttons on the winter coat while Fruma rocked Eidel. But instead of the usual conversation and gossip, they worked in silence, neither knowing how today's events might change their lives.

CHAPTER TWENTY-TWO

"MAYBE NOTHING WILL CHANGE. Maybe the Germans will be too busy conquering the world to bother with us Jews," Gitel said.

"Always the optimist, my love," Fruma answered.

"Well, who knows? It can't be that bad. So the *goyim*, non-Jews, stop shopping in our stores. Business might be hurt a bit, and money might be tight, but we'll survive. We always have. I'll get a second job if need be. I am not going to let us starve," Gitel answered.

Zofia sat quietly, listening. She had heard about the Nuremberg laws and was concerned because Eidel was half-Jewish and half-Gentile.

"Do you think that Eidel will be in trouble? I can't remember if I ever told you two this, but her father was not Jewish."

"What? She's a baby. Nobody is going to bother with a baby," Fruma said. "Don't be so silly."

"I am worried. You know that it is illegal for Jews and Gentiles to have children."

"Who knows that her father was a *goy*? Only you, only us, and we certainly aren't going to say anything. So, stop worrying."

Eidel started fussing, and Gitel lifted her out of her playpen.

"Come here, *shayna maidel*, you beautiful girl," Fruma cooed, smiling until the wrinkles around her eyes were deep crevices. "Nobody would ever hurt such a *shayna maidel*."

Gitel reached for the baby, and Fruma handed Eidel to her. She lifted Eidel high above her head, and Eidel giggled. Then she drooled onto Gitel's shirt.

Zofia had a memory of how strict she'd thought Fruma was when she'd first begun working for her. How wrong she'd been. Fruma only seemed hard on the outside. Underneath, her heart was as warm as a cozy blanket.

"You deserved that," Fruma said, laughing as Gitel wiped the drool from her. "You lift her so high up. Of course, when she drools, it will land on your shirt. You're lucky it doesn't land in your eye."

"I guess I do lift her high up, but I love it when she laughs."

"We all do," Fruma said. "So, you'll just have to cope with the drooling."

"That I can do," Gitel smiled. Fruma returned her smile.

"Oy, my Fruma, you've made my life complete."

"And you mine."

Zofia prepared dinner while the two surrogate grandmothers played with Eidel. They whispered their worries to each other, not wanting to alarm Zofia, but Zofia was young, and her hearing was exceptional.

"Whatever happens, at least we are together," Gitel said.

"I am so afraid." Fruma looked at Gitel, her eyes cast dark with shadows.

"I know. I know. So am I."

CHAPTER TWENTY-THREE

CHRISTA AND MANFRED were seated in a private room in her father's office. The results of the fertility tests were back, and Dr. Henkener's nurse called them in to discuss what the doctor had found. Manfred got up to look out the window onto the street. So many things were happening so fast in his life. Hitler was moving forward in his conquest to make Germany the most powerful nation in the world.

At the last rally Manfred had attended in Nuremberg, Hitler explained how he planned for the Reich to last a thousand years and for Germany to take its rightful place as ruler of the world. Since then, things have been moving at an alarming rate. Manfred tried not to think about the extermination of the Jews, gypsies, homosexuals, and other inferior classes. He understood the necessity. It was just the actual act of murder that left him sick and speechless.

How far would Hitler take all of this? It was hard to say. Could entire races of people be annihilated? And how would such things be carried out? What would they do with all the bodies? Manfred hoped that he would be able to avoid seeing any of what was to be done. With any luck, he would never leave his work at the office or be subjected to a field trip to the camps where it would take place.

The theories worked just fine for him. It was the acts, the blood, and the death that frightened him.

"Manfred, do you hear me?" Christa asked.

"I'm sorry. I was lost in thought…"

"I know you were. I was asking if you wanted to have dinner with your mother on Sunday. She called."

"My mother, on Sunday? Yes, if you would like to…"

"You seem distracted."

"I'm sorry, darling. It's work. I was thinking about some things I had left undone at the office."

She nodded. "Well, let's go out for a nice lunch when this appointment is over. I never see you anymore. You are always at work. This is my time." She smiled. "So, just for a few hours, please put the office out of your mind. All right?"

"Yes, of course, and you choose the place for lunch. How does that sound?"

He thought about how neglectful he'd been lately and decided that he would bring her a dozen roses on his way home from work tonight. This job of his consumed him. It demanded everything: all of his time and all of his attention. He wondered if his being overworked might have something to do with their inability to conceive.

Many nights he would go to bed exhausted, only to wake in a few hours, unable to sleep. It would then take him half the night to fall back asleep again, and by the time he did, the alarm was sounding, telling him it was time to return to the office.

Perhaps this was how it was for all men attempting to better themselves through their careers. It seemed to be a never-ending struggle up the invisible ladder of success.

Dr. Henkener opened the door carrying a manila file. He walked over to Christa and kissed her cheek.

"Hello, Manfred." Dr. Henkener reached out to shake his hand.

Manfred saluted him with the Heil Hitler salute. Dr. Henkener followed with a less enthusiastic salute. Then walked behind his desk and sat down. Manfred sat beside Christa, reached over, and took her hand.

"I have the results of your physical exams right here. From what

I can see, both of you are healthy, and there is no reason you should be unable to conceive a child. I will say this: sometimes, if the man is overworked and tired, he has a more difficult time. Emotions can also have an effect. What I mean is that if you are so worried about getting pregnant, sometimes that can stop it from happening for you. Or it could be that your job is so overwhelming, Manfred, that it is taking a toll on you? But I think that if the two of you both try to relax and not rush things, Christa will become pregnant in a short time."

Manfred looked away. He did not want to meet Christa's eyes, so he dropped her hand. His old feelings of inadequacy peeked out from under the carefully placed rug in his mind. He was sure it was him. It sounded as if Christa's father blamed him and his job. His face flushed as he got up and walked toward the window again.

"You forget who I am, sir. I am *Scharführer* Blau, a successful member of the German SS, and I don't have any problems." *I am not tired or emotionally upset.* Manfred tried desperately to regain his self-confidence. "Do you have problems with infertility in your family history, Dr. Henkener?"

"No, Manfred, we don't. But it may not be a problem at all. You both might just be trying too hard. Sometimes that can be a sort of block for conception."

"That's absurd. It must be Christa."

Christa's head snapped as she turned her head to gaze at him. Never had he said anything like this before. Her lips parted, and she almost said something, but then she closed them again.

"Manfred," Dr. Henkener locked his eyes on him, "It may be nothing at all, and then again, it may just be you."

Manfred's face turned the color of fresh blood. He clenched and unclenched his fist. Dr. Henkener had touched a nerve. Christa got up to walk toward Manfred. He glared at her, and she did not move.

"Let's go now," Manfred said to Christa. "That is all you have to tell us, right?"

"I am afraid so. I'm sorry, Manfred. I think you might just be under great pressure from your work. But then again, who knows?" Dr. Henkener said.

"No need to be sorry. The tests are wrong. I am not an emotional weakling who can't work and produce a child at the same time. For God's sake, men do it all the time. I am afraid, Dr. Henkener, that you just don't want to admit that the problem might be your daughter. I can assure you that it is not me. Are you coming, Christa?" He opened the door and stood, waiting. "Well, are you coming?"

Christa looked from Manfred to her father. Hurt and unspoken apologies were all over her face. Her hands trembled as she gripped her handbag in front of her.

"Goodbye, Father," she said, her voice trembling, tears welling in her eyes.

Dr. Henkener watched Christa with sympathy.

Before Christa could kiss her father's cheek, Manfred was outside the door. He let it slam behind him.

Christa followed Manfred out into the street. He was well down the block, so she had to run to catch up with him.

Manfred walked so fast that Christa had to jog to keep up. The sound of his boot heels clicked on the pavement.

"Manfred, slow down. I can't keep up with you."

"I'm in a hurry. I have to get back to the office."

"But we were going to have lunch."

"I realized that I don't have time today."

"Manfred, please don't be this way. We love each other. It will be all right."

"I'll see you tonight," he said, walking away so fast that he left Christa behind. She stopped trying to keep pace with him. Instead, she stood still, watching the man she loved race away from her.

Only once did he turn back to see her standing alone on the street, watching him. He was too far away to see it, but he knew she was crying. Still, even though he wanted to, he could not go back and take her in his arms. Something inside of him—the need to be strong, to be powerful, and to be respected—stopped him.

When Manfred returned to the office, he went to his desk without saying a word to anyone. Dr. Goebbels saw him and walked over.

"Is everything all right? You went to the doctor, yes? You look upset."

"Yes, it's fine. We just need to try harder."

"Nothing wrong with that, right?"

"Yes, sir."

"Ach, don't feel bad. Before you know it, she'll be pregnant, and you'll have a beautiful child."

"Yes, that will be very nice."

Goebbels patted Manfred's back. "Have you had lunch?" he asked. He put down the latest copy of *Der Stumer*, the newspaper he had been leafing through when Manfred arrived. He was proud of the propaganda paper his office produced. It had proved helpful in swaying the hearts and minds of the German people against the subhuman and rallying them behind Hitler and his noble cause.

"No."

"I thought you might stop with the wife and grab something."

"She had to get home. Her lady friend was stopping by to drop off her child. Christa promised to watch her baby," Manfred lied.

"Well, then it's you and me. Why don't we take a walk down to the corner pub? We can have a couple of beers, a few brats, and an hour or two away from work?"

"Sounds good, sir."

When they got to the pub, there was a line of people waiting for a table. The proprietor, a rotund, little, red-faced man with a white apron and reddish-blond hair so thin his scalp shined through, walked over to them.

"Heil Hitler," the restaurateur said.

"Heil Hitler. Table for two," Goebbels answered.

Although they were the last to arrive, he seated them first. Once again, the black SS uniform had worked its magic.

They sat at a table in the corner by the window. The table was covered with a red and white checkered tablecloth.

"Bring us two beers," Goebbels told the young waiter, "and a plate of brats and some sauerkraut. Also, some fried potatoes and a green salad. Do you want anything else, Manfred?"

"No, sounds perfect, sir."

"Very well, then," turning back to the waiter, "keep the beers coming."

After the waiter left, Goebbels carefully placed his napkin on his lap.

"So, the invasion of Poland was a landslide success."

"I know, sir. It surely was."

"Our Führer is a genius. He told them not to form an army, that we would protect them, and would you believe they listened? The Poles are not very smart. Well, it's no wonder they are not the superior race. But at least the Poles aren't Jews or Gypsies. We can find a place for them as our worker slaves in the New World Order. You know, some of their children are beautiful. They look German: blond, blue-eyed, beautiful, Aryan-looking. Actually, the last time I saw Heinrich, he thought that perhaps we should take a few and send them off to be retrained as Germans. It's an idea, anyway. At least we could consider taking some of the pretty ones."

"You mean the *Reichsführer*, commander of the SS, special rank, sir?" Manfred looked at Goebbels and thought about Hitler and Himmler, whom he had met. None of them looked like the Aryans they professed to be. They proclaimed the German man tall, athletic, blond, and with blue eyes. And yet, Hitler had all the physical qualities of the Jews he hated. He had dark hair, was small in stature, and did not appear athletic.

Furthermore, the large nose he used as a symbol of the ugliness of Jewry sat right in the middle of his own face. *These are treasonous thoughts I am having. These thoughts must be kept under wraps at all costs.*

"Yes, of course, I mean *Reichsführer* Himmler. He has been setting up homes for the Lebensborn. It is an exciting idea. These are wonderful institutions to help increase the Aryan population through a mating process.

"He also thought we might take a few of the Polish children and put them in there. They are young, and the young are quick to forget. If they are away from their parents, they will forget their parents, and we could turn them into Aryans. Of course, we'd set up schools for retraining."

"It's a good idea," Manfred said, nodding and taking a swig of his dark German beer.

"You and your missus will have beautiful children."

"Yes, she is lovely, my wife."

"You are both blond. That should give you bright Aryan babies. By the way, have you ever seen photographs of my wife and children?" Goebbels asked.

"Only the one on your desk, sir."

"Oh, let me show you. You already know my beautiful wife. There she is, my Magda." He showed Manfred a picture of a slender woman with wavy hair, smiling at the camera, surrounded by a brood of light-haired, laughing children.

"I don't think you've ever seen my five beautiful children. I will tell you a secret. We haven't told anyone else yet, but we have another on the way." He smiled a sly smile. "My mistress is also pregnant. She will have the child in the Home for the Lebensborn and then return to the movies."

"Congratulations," Manfred said, trying to sound sincere and hide the jealousy. Goebbels had five, soon to be six, not counting the mistress. Manfred and Christa could not even produce one. Why?

"Yes, we are quite excited. The more Aryan babies we can bring into the world, the better things will be for the New Order of Germany. Our leader is doing a wonderful job of restructuring Germany. Soon, we will be the world leaders it was always meant to be. We will leave this world to our children, a world free of undesirable elements. It will be filled with the beauty, grace, and charm of the Aryan race. I've been meaning to tell you, Manfred, you should take a mistress. It is, after all, the duty of an Aryan of the SS to produce as many Aryan children as he can."

"I will look into it," Manfred said, not meaning it.

The food arrived. Manfred was relieved not to have to discuss having children anymore, at least for today. They ate and discussed food and beer. By the end of the meal, both men were full and tired. As they walked back to the office, Goebbels smiled at Manfred.

"I meant to tell you some good news. I am promoting you to *Oberscharführer*, master sergeant."

"Sir!" Manfred beamed. "Thank you."

"You deserve it, my boy. You are a wonderful employee and an excellent friend and confidant. Yes, Manfred, I chose you well. You are a true asset to the Party."

"Thank you. Thank you, sir."

CHAPTER TWENTY-FOUR

The Germans established ghettos in Poland. The arrests began even before the Nazis could build fences around them. At first, it was a small number of Jews, and so their neighbors, other Jews, were able to overlook what was taking place. People were able to deceive themselves by rationalizing that those arrested were criminals.

But no Jew was safe. The Nazis meant to kill them all: men, women, children, and infants.

And then, one day, without warning, those Jews who had carefully looked the other way in hopes that it would all disappear were seized at gunpoint from their homes, the streets, and jobs. They were torn from their lives, and all their possessions were confiscated. They were just ordinary people, guilty of no crime, yet they were often beaten or shot if they resisted.

They were taken to a small area set off from the rest of the population, the ghettos, where they again chose to deceive themselves that they would live and work until the war was over.

But unbeknownst to them, they were only in line for an even more sinister fate. The ghettos, rotting with filth and disease, were plagued by starvation and overpopulation. They were merely a stopgap measure.

Next, they would face the answer to the race contamination that the Third Reich had put into effect and named the *Final Solution.* Hitler planned to begin the annihilation of millions. It was not just the Jews. Oh no, the Nazis wanted to erase the Gypsies, homosexuals, the Jehovah's Witnesses, and many others from the face of the earth.

At first, large groups of people were shot and thrown into ravines, but this method was far too slow. Europe was filled with undesirables, and the Nazis decided they all must be eradicated. And so, next came the trains. Camps were set up close to the railways for the ease of transporting prisoners. The Nazis filled the trains with people like cattle and shipped them to the camps. The perverse logic of the Nazis was to use a poison gas called Zyklon B, which they had developed to exterminate pests to eliminate the Jews and other undesirables.

These houses of death were accompanied by the ever-operating crematoriums or crematory pits with pyres, which could never work fast enough in the effort to dispose of the dead bodies. The surrounding cities were subjected to constant rain that poured from the ovens made from the ashes of the dead.

CHAPTER TWENTY-FIVE

The sewing machines buzzed. Fruma and Zofia had a wedding gown to make for the Eisenstats' youngest daughter, Sarah. It had to be finished by the week's end. There were pearls to hand sew and hems to be finished. The women worked quickly as their skilled fingers flew across the fabric like tiny birds.

"Can you believe it? Next week is Eidel's first birthday already. How the time flies," Fruma said, shaking her head and smiling.

"I know. My figure tells me every day. I can't seem to get my old shape back," Zofia said.

"You look lovely. You're just not a girl anymore. You're a mother, a woman."

"Old and flabby, in other words."

"If you're old, then Gitel and I are ancient."

Zofia laughed and shook her head. "I want to make Eidel a new dress for her birthday party."

"I think that's a wonderful idea. How many children are coming?"

"Just Helen, the baby, and Esther from next door and her son."

"Oy, he is a wild little boy. I hope he doesn't tear up the apartment."

"Yes, I know he is out of control, but he's just a normal three-year-old."

"He is not refined, like our Eidel. Eidel is special."

"Of course not," Zofia laughed. "Nobody is as good as our Eidel."

The floor was littered with strings, dust, and small bits of fabric. Eidel slept quietly, lying on her stomach in her playpen with a pink knitted blanket over her.

"She looks like an angel."

"Doesn't she? You know, as much as I regret what I did with her father, I mean, having relations with a man who was so much older and all of that, I can't be entirely sorry because I was blessed to have her."

"I know. You know what my grandmother used to say?"

"What?" Zofia asked, both women staring at the sleeping child.

"She said every blessing is a curse, and every curse is a blessing. Yes, her father was a curse, but Eidel is such a blessing to all of us."

"That she is…" Zofia said.

CHAPTER TWENTY-SIX

The small apartment that Zofia shared with Fruma and Gitel was decorated with balloons and streamers. Gitel dragged herself out of bed that morning and went to the bakery nice and early. There, she bought a small birthday cake.

Fruma and Zofia had both made dolls out of fabric and stuffed them. They'd sewed on buttons for the eyes, nose, and mouth. Then Fruma made a few dresses to fit the dolls, giving them a wardrobe.

Zofia laughed. She knew it would be several years before Eidel would change the clothes, but the effort that Fruma and Gitel made to make things beautiful always touched her heart. She knew how fortunate she was. Regardless of what people said about them, her friends were the kindest women she had ever known.

A pot of thick, strong coffee was brewing on the stove, its fragrance filling the rooms. Soon, the guests would arrive. It was Eidel's first birthday. She wore a dress that was the color of the deep pink of a summer sunset. Her dark-blonde hair was caught up on top of her head in a bow to match the lacy ruffles on her dress. Zofia watched Eidel playing, and her heart swelled with joy, pride, and every emotion any mother had ever felt.

Helen knocked on the door. In her arms, she carried her son,

Lars, and a gaily wrapped gift for Eidel. The babies were born a few months apart, and the mothers hoped their children would grow up to be friends.

"Come in. Will you have some coffee or tea?" Fruma asked.

"Thank you, Fruma. I would love some tea. Hello, Zofia, Gitel." Helen smiled, and Zofia realized again how beautiful Helen was. She was tall and blonde. The pregnancy had done nothing to her slender, girlish figure. Not only was she lovely, but she was also kind. "And who do we have here?" Helen asked as she bent to tickle Eidel's cheek. "Why, it's the birthday girl." Eidel giggled.

"Here, let me take him for a minute so you can enjoy your tea," Gitel said.

"Are you sure?"

"Of course. I have lots of experience with Eidel," Gitel said, but as soon as she took Lars, he started crying.

"Ech, he's just used to his mother. I'm sorry, Gitel," Helen said, and Gitel handed the baby back to Helen.

"You look incredible. Zofia, you're glowing. Motherhood really agrees with you," Helen said.

"Oh, how I wish that were true. I can't seem to lose this baby weight."

"Well, you gained it in all the right places. You have a beautiful shape. I wish it had done the same for me."

"Oh, Helen, you still look like a young girl. You will always be lovely."

Eidel must have seen Lars being held, because she began fussing and reaching her arms toward Zofia to pick her up. Fruma saw Eidel reaching and lifted her. Then Gitel also reached for the baby, lifting her high. Eidel forgot what she was fussing about and giggled loudly.

Esther, the widow who lived next door, arrived with her four-year-old son, an active little boy with a mischievous smile. He immediately began grabbing Eidel's toys. He picked up a fat baby doll and began racing around the room.

"No, Manny, behave. We are not at home. This is Eidel's party." Esther pulled Manny by the arm and took the doll away. She held him close, and he began to cry in frustration. "Please, Manny, behave. We are going to have cake soon enough. You love cake. Now, if you don't act properly, I will not allow you to have a piece."

Fruma glanced at the boy and frowned. Little boys were such a pain in the neck. Best to get the cake out before the little monster got his destructive hands on something else.

Fruma put the cake on the table with a single candle in the center.

"Is everyone ready?" Fruma asked, and there were nods all around.

Zofia picked Eidel up and held her so that she could see as Fruma lit the candle. Eidel began to giggle as everyone sang a happy birthday song.

Zofia blew out the candle for Eidel, and she silently wished that her child would have a long and happy life. Everyone clapped, and Eidel tried to clap, too.

Fruma went into the kitchen to get a knife and the pile of plates she'd taken down for the cake.

There was a knock at the door. Fruma put the plates down and opened it. The entire festive mood changed in a single moment as the room seemed dwarfed by the presence of three tall, menacing men wearing long, black leather coats—the Gestapo.

Fruma's hands trembled, and her face turned white. She could not speak or hear. All she heard were two words: "Arrested" and "Jews."

"What's going on here?" Helen asked. "Why are you arresting these women?"

"It's none of your business. You don't look like a Jew. Why are you here?"

"I am not a Jew. I am a Christian, and my husband is a member of the Nazi Party. Now tell me, please, what is going on here?"

"You should not even be in this neighborhood. Get out now and be glad we don't arrest you, too." He pushed Helen against the wall, slamming her hard. The pain sobered her. She rubbed her shoulder. Helen watched the man. Her eyes were filled with fright. She glanced at Lars, suddenly afraid for him.

"*Mach schnell*, hurry up. You have five minutes to gather your things together. Let's go! Move!" he shouted at the three women.

Gitel looked at Fruma. Zofia stood glued to the floor. It felt as if her feet would not obey.

"Move, I said!" The Gestapo agent took a club from the side of his uniform and hit Gitel across the face. Blood flew across the room onto the wall, covering the birthday cake. Fruma ran to Gitel, but the man raised the club to hit them both again.

"Move, now!"

Gitel spit a tooth into her hand.

Everyone scampered. Helen took Lars and left as quickly as she could. Within minutes, Gitel, Fruma, Zofia, Eidel, Esther, and Manny were being driven away in the notorious black car that had taken so many of their neighbors. Gitel was holding a towel against the side of her face. As the car rounded the corner, Zofia saw Helen standing on the sidewalk with Lars in her arms. The baby was crying, and so was Helen.

CHAPTER TWENTY-SEVEN

EVERY DAY, more families arrived in the already overcrowded Warsaw Ghetto. The Jewish Council that ran the ghetto for the Nazis had negotiated to open several factories to produce things needed for the Nazi war effort in exchange for food. The Jewish Council, also called *Judenrats*, received the food payments and were in charge of the distribution.

The people fit enough to work long hours in the factories were issued ration cards, which provided each person three hundred calories worth of food per day. Soap was a luxury, and everything was filthy. Bouts of typhoid and plague erupted, seizing the healthy and ending in death within hours.

The ration cards did not provide enough food to avoid starving. So, out of need, women resorted to the only commodity they had to sell their bodies. Children begged for money or food. The black market flourished. At night, those who could escape over the wall and out of the ghetto to make deals with the Polish returned with food, medicines, and other necessities to sell. Those who were able survived. The sick or elderly perished within days.

The Judenrats were instructed to select a certain number of Jews to be taken to the trains each day. Everyone was led to believe that the trains led to work camps where the Jews would be employed in the Nazi war effort. At least, at first, everyone believed. Anyone not fit enough to work in the factories was selected for train transport to the "work camps." Starving people were lured to the trains with promises of food.

But where there is life, there is hope, and those who lived made the best of the situation. Schools were put together for the children, plays were performed, music and art thrived, and people still fell in love and married. All this continued with the hope that soon the nightmare would end.

Esther and Manny shared an apartment with a family of five on the other side of the ghetto.

Zofia, Gitel, Fruma, and the baby found housing in a crowded apartment building. They shared a small two-bedroom flat with another family, the Gursteins: a young mother whose wrinkled brow gave her a far older appearance than her thirty-five years, a consumptively thin father, and two daughters, one ten and the other eleven.

When it worked, the water was icy cold, making bathing an uncomfortable but necessary evil. Zofia noticed that the parents who lived in the other room gave most of their food to their children.

The two girls attended a makeshift school, where they learned music and drama in addition to the basics of reading, writing, and arithmetic. Mara, the older of the two daughters, would often come home singing an opera song. Her sister would join in, and even though the house was crowded, there was joy.

Little Eidel loved the girls who picked her up and played with her like a human doll. They carried her around the apartment, singing to her, or sat on the floor talking amongst themselves and playing with Eidel.

Between the two preteens, her mother and grandmothers, Eidel never lacked attention. She was a happy baby, laughing and smiling all the time. The child took her first steps in that tiny apartment in the Warsaw Ghetto. Everyone laughed and cheered as she toddled along, holding onto the worn, threadbare furniture.

Zofia and Fruma were employed in a textile factory, while Gitel worked in a munitions factory that produced explosives for the war effort. Even working full time, there was not enough food from the ration cards to stop the hunger pangs.

It came to Fruma's mind one afternoon as she walked home from the Judenrat market with a measly small bag of food for the entire family that her sewing services might be useful to those on the other side of the wall. After all, she was a master seamstress, and Zofia could embroider better than most.

Perhaps there was work they could do that would buy them more food on the black market. Everyone knew where to find the sellers who dealt in black market goods, except the Judenrats, who were kept in the dark because they were not to be trusted.

Fruma rounded the corner and ducked into the alleyway. There she saw the young man, who everyone knew as Karl Abendstern. He was making a deal with another man. She saw Karl pull a vial of something out of his pocket, which was exchanged for a few coins. Once the man took the vial and left, Fruma approached.

"You are Karl Abendstern?"

"Who wants to know?"

"My name is Fruma Kowalsky. I'm a seamstress, and so is my daughter, Zofia. We can do sewing and embroidery very well. We will work cheap, for anything is better than nothing. Is there any call for such things outside the ghetto?"

Karl looked at the woman. He felt sorry for her. Although he'd never looked into the sale of such services, he could do so the next time he went to the other side.

"I don't know. I can look into it," Karl said.

"You will? Please. Of course, I would expect you to take a cut. I understand that everyone must make a living," Fruma said.

"Where can I find you?" Karl asked.

"I will come back if you tell me when to be here."

"Come the day after tomorrow, and I will have some information for you."

"Thank you."

"Don't thank me yet. I'm not sure I can get you any work, but I will try," he said, his eyes scanning the old woman. She was painfully thin.

"I am grateful that you should even try," Fruma said.

Karl gazed at Fruma, who began to walk away. "Wait," he said, pulling a hard piece of bread out of his coat pocket. "Here, it's not much, but take this." Karl handed her the food.

"Are you sure?" Fruma asked.

"Yes, take it, please." Karl was suddenly embarrassed.

"Thank you. Thank you so much."

Karl nodded. "It's all right. I'll find out what I can."

Fruma nodded her head and left. As she walked home, she was excited. It was a large, heavy roll of dark, grainy bread. She would share it with Gitel and Zofia.

CHAPTER TWENTY-EIGHT

THERE WAS WORK! Karl said he would bring them work. The Polish with whom he traded were willing to use their services as long as the work was done cheaply, more cheaply than any seamstress would charge outside the wall. It was decided that Karl would focus on getting work that was easier to carry through the wall, embroidery, and other finely detailed work.

Zofia was thrilled. It was good to have work. She and Fruma were busy all evening, long after they got home from their factory jobs. Frau Gurstein took care of Eidel until the young girls returned from school, when they happily took over the job, and Fruma, Gitel, and Zofia shared their rations with the Gursteins. Frau Gurstein was able to work for a Judenrat business at home, sewing military patches on German uniforms, while Mr. Gurstein worked in a factory splitting mica.

Karl Abendstern brought fabrics to be embroidered, pearls to be sewn on carefully and individually, hems to be taken up, and various other tasks. The pay was not even half of what they earned when they had the shop, but it was enough to help buy some small extras, like a bar of soap, and some food, although there was barely enough for the four of them, things were better than they were before.

One evening, as Zofia returned from the bakery on the way home from work, Koppel Bergman, a well-known Judenrat, walked over to her. She had noticed that he had watched her come and go through the market for the past month. Zofia took him to be about thirty years old.

He was tall, with an arrogance about him, with pleasant, even features, dark, deep-set eyes, and straight dark hair combed away from his face. His clothes fit his slender frame, and it was obvious to Zofia that he thought himself a ladies' man. Most women probably fell at his feet, and why not? He was a Judenrat. That meant he had access to better food and he could offer safety. After all, he was one of those with the power to decide who was to be selected for the next train to the work camp.

"Hello," he said, smiling. "I'm Koppel Bergman. I don't think we've ever formally met."

"Hello," Zofia said, walking faster.

"Wait, what's your hurry? You haven't even told me your name. That's rude."

"I'm sorry. My name is Zofia, but I have to get home." She kept walking.

"I'm sure you could spare a few minutes. If you would like, I could offer a pastry and a cup of coffee if you would like to share them with me."

Dear God, she was hungry. The idea of a sweet pastry and a cup of coffee made her mouth water. But it was dangerous to become too involved with this man. Better to stay out of his way. "No, I'm sorry. I really must go."

"Wait, just a minute, slow down. You're practically running. I only want to talk to you," Koppel said.

Zofia was afraid. *Best not to anger him.* She stopped.

"There you go. Now we can talk. Would you like to go with me and have that pastry?"

"I'm sorry. I would like to, but I have to get home."

"It will only take a few minutes. I promise you. It is delicious."

"All right, then."

"I knew you would see reason. Come on, follow me," he said, smiling.

Even as she followed him, Zofia felt uncomfortable. She wanted to go home, but he would be angry if she did. Then who knew if he might decide to put her on the next list for the train to the work camp?

They walked for three blocks; he stomped confidently ahead of her, and she walked slowly behind him. When they arrived at his apartment, Zofia felt a sick twitch penetrate her stomach.

"Well, come in. I won't bite you," Koppel said, his smile charming as his eyes glanced at her.

She entered. The apartment was the nicest she'd ever entered inside the ghetto.

"I live here alone," he said, "so make yourself comfortable." Then Koppel put on a pot of boiling water. The aroma of the coffee filled the room. Zofia felt herself salivating in response. It had been so long since she'd even smelled good-quality coffee brewing. Koppel saw the look on her face and laughed.

"As you can see, I have access to the finer things of life."

He took a small plate with three white, doughy cookies out of the pantry. It was covered with a waxy, white paper. He removed the paper and set the dish in front of Zofia.

"Go ahead. Enjoy," Koppel said.

Zofia took one of the cookies and bit into it. It was as if she had never tasted sugar before. All of her senses came alive. She chewed slowly, savoring every morsel. But even as she enjoyed the incredible sensations, her thoughts turned to guilt as she thought of Eidel and her family.

"May I take the rest of these for my daughter?" She could easily have devoured the entire plate's contents in seconds, and it took every ounce of restraint for her not to.

"Of course. They are all for you," Koppel said.

Feeling like a thief, Zofia quickly wrapped the cookies in the paper and stuffed them into the pocket of her skirt. Powdered sugar fell onto her black skirt. If she'd been alone, she would have licked it off. Instead, as discreetly as she could, she rubbed her finger into the white powder and brought it to her lips. Closing her eyes, she delighted in the sweet pleasure.

"They are very good, yes?"

"Yes, thank you, very good."

"I'm glad you enjoyed them. I can always get more," he said, clearing his throat. "Now, Zofia, that is your name, correct? I have a little proposition for you."

She didn't answer. She sat there, listening, knowing how vulnerable she was here alone with him, in his apartment. She was constantly aware of his position and the power he had to decide who would stay in the ragged safety of the ghetto and who would be forced to the unknown destinations on the train.

"I can get you work, money, and plenty of food. I know that has to sound good to you," Koppel said.

Zofia nodded. "Yes, of course. I would appreciate any work." He must never find out about the work she and Fruma did through the black market.

"You're young and very pretty. That's in your favor. And may I be so bold as to say that I have been watching you, and I know that you have a child, so you are not unfamiliar with the ways of the world."

"I'm afraid I don't understand," Zofia said, her voice cracking like icicles falling from tree branches.

"Well, there are a lot of men here who would give up their food rations, money too, for an afternoon of badly needed release. Do you understand?"

She understood. Of course, she understood. Zofia coughed and cleared her throat, stifling the desire to slap his pretty face, to see her handprint on that perfectly chiseled cheek.

"I'm sorry. I couldn't. It's just not something I could ever do."

"So many women are doing what they have to do to survive. This would be an easy way for you to get the things you need, and what is the big problem? It's really nothing, just a few hours doing what you've done before."

"I'm sorry. I'm very sorry," Zofia said, getting up and heading for the door. It felt like a lump had formed in her throat, and she couldn't swallow.

"Wait..." he said again.

She stopped only because she knew she must. It was dangerous to offend him.

"I understand." he smiled at her. It was a wide-open smile, but she felt the hair on the back of her neck stand up. "I like you, Zofia. I'm not going to hold it against you that you have so arrogantly refused my kind offer. Instead, I am going to assume that you are a decent girl, and instead of being offended, I am going to ask you if you would like to see me again."

She would like never to see him again.

"Of course, I would, but I am so busy with my daughter that I don't have much time for socializing."

"Well, you realize that it could be arranged for your daughter to be on the next transport. Then you would have time, right?" He put his finger up to his lips.

She felt her knees buckle. He could do it. It was in his power. Here was a Jew as bad as a Nazi. Tears welled up in her eyes.

"Please, don't do that. I will see you again. I will arrange whatever must be arranged in order to see you. Just please leave my child alone," Zofia pleaded.

"I thought you would see reason. I know where you live. I will come by to get you tomorrow night. We can have a nice evening together," Koppel said.

Zofia nodded and left. A cold wind blew as she walked toward home. Without thinking, she put her hand in the breast pocket of her blouse and felt the cookies. She took them out and put them into the bag she'd gotten when she went to the bakery before her confrontation with Koppel.

Tears attacked her eyes. She could not tell Fruma or Gitel what was going on, or they would force her to refuse Koppel, and then what? Worse yet, if Karl, the man from the black market, found out that she was keeping company with a Judenrat, he would stay away from the whole family. Then she and Fruma would not have any work.

All the way home, she agonized until she decided that she must tell Fruma and Gitel everything. There was no other way. They, in turn, must explain to Karl. This was not her doing, but if she dared to refuse Koppel, the consequences were far more than she was willing to pay.

When Zofia arrived at the apartment, she put the bag on the kitchen table and took off her coat. Fruma was sitting in a chair working on some needlepoint, looking at her strangely.

"Where have you been? You've been gone for over an hour. We were afraid that something happened to you," Fruma said, her voice stern.

"I need to talk to you and Gitel privately."

"Certainly," Fruma answered. They all went into their bedroom in the apartment and closed the door shut.

"What is it, Zofia? You are as white as a winter storm."

"Fruma..." She burst into tears, realizing how vulnerable she was. "Do you know who Koppel is?"

"Stop crying. I can hardly understand you," Fruma said, her voice still stern but her eyes kind. Then Fruma walked over and put her arms around Zofia, leading her to the small cot at the side of the room. "Sit down and take a breath. I'll get you some water, and then we will talk, yes?"

Zofia nodded her head. The room was cold. There had been no heat for several days. Fruma took a long piece of wool from the bolts of fabric to be used for upcoming jobs and draped it around Zofia's shoulders like a shawl, then got her a glass of water. Zofia wiped her eyes with the back of her hand and sipped.

"Koppel, you know him. He is the Judenrat, the young one."

"Yes, I know who he is. He is a pimp," Fruma said with disgust.

"You know that?"

"Of course, I know that. Everyone knows that."

"I didn't. Maybe I just wasn't paying attention," Zofia said. "Anyway, he tried to recruit me for his prostitution ring. When I refused, he decided that he would like to see me socially."

Fruma shook her head. "No, don't do it."

"I have to. He threatened to have Eidel taken away. He has the power to do that. I have to do it. I can't put Eidel in danger. She is my child, my life. I love her." Zofia began to weep in powerful gusts of pain and anguish.

"I know. I love her, too," Fruma said, patting Zofia's back as if she were a little girl.

"I must do as he says. I must, or he will do something terrible to us. He can."

"And he is a Jew. He believes that the Nazis are his friends, the stupid fool. What he doesn't realize is that one day the Nazis will turn on him, and he will end up in worse shape than all the rest of us." Fruma's eyes had a glazed-over look. Zofia had seen this before. It happened when Fruma saw visions of the future.

Both women sat quietly for several minutes and watched Eidel, asleep in the dresser drawer that Gitel had made into a cradle.

"Do you think he would actually do it? Do you think he is really that cruel?" Zofia asked.

"Yes," Fruma said, her voice broken. "Zofia, we must do something. We cannot put Eidel's safety in Koppel's hands. If he should decide for any reason that he wants to take her, God forbid. Well, he will."

Zofia swallowed hard. She tried to speak, but at first, she couldn't. Then, whispering, she asked, "So what can we do? If we try to escape, they will find all of us, and Eidel will suffer anyway."

"My plan is not a pleasant one. I am sorry to suggest this, but I think we should have Karl, that man from the black market, find Helen and ask her to take Eidel, to keep her as her own until we can get out of here. She can tell everyone that Eidel is hers. Helen has a good heart. She will do it. She will help us. I know she will. Eidel is blonde, and she doesn't look Jewish. This may be our little one's only chance."

Zofia could not speak. Give Eidel up? Send her away? Dear God, my child, my precious child. But if Zofia refused, then she would put Eidel at risk. This way, no matter what happened, Eidel would be safe. Was there really any other choice?

Again, she looked at the baby, asleep, her tiny thumb in her mouth, the brush of her soft eyelashes against her pale skin, the sweet smell of her essence when Zofia held her close. Eidel will be gone for now, maybe forever. But at least Eidel would live. Zofia might not see her daughter grow up, get married, or have children, but Eidel would have this chance. She would live.

She would be away from the ghetto, with its constant threat of disease and starvation. In a Gentile home, Eidel would be safe from the cold, from the ghetto, and from Koppel. Eidel, my life, my child.

"Tell Karl to contact Helen the next time he goes outside the ghetto. Tell him to ask her if she is willing to take Eidel. We will pay him for his help," Zofia said.

CHAPTER TWENTY-NINE

Christa Blau had come to enjoy the lifestyle she and Manfred shared. Every week, he remembered to bring her roses. He scooped them up from the street vendor on his way home from the office. When he entered their home, he never forgot to kiss her and tell her how beautiful she looked.

The Nazi Party saw to it that they had a lovely two-story house made of sturdy white brick, with a flower garden surrounding the front entrance. In fact, the house was already exquisitely furnished when they moved in, with stylish pieces of well-made furniture and real artwork. She never questioned where these things came from.

When Goebbels offered gifts to the Blaus, Christa smiled and thanked him for his extreme generosity. She and Manfred had come to know the Goebbels family quite well after several dinners at their home. The Blaus reciprocated the invitation as soon as they moved into their home.

At least once a month, Manfred and Christa attended elegant parties where she was entertained with bright and witty conversations by some of Hitler's elite. These charming men in pressed black uniforms complimented her shimmering blond hair and athletic figure.

Twice, she had also been a dinner guest at an affair given to honor the Führer himself. In fact, she'd been introduced to Adolf Hitler, and he'd complimented her on her remarkable Aryan beauty. She'd blushed with pride. Everyone they met always told Manfred he had a perfect German wife. It was an ideal life of luxury, friendships, acceptance, and beauty.

However, there was one small glitch. No matter how hard the couple tried, Christa did not conceive. They increased the frequency of their attempts, but still, Christa's menstrual blood came on time every month. It was obvious that Goebbels was disappointed. He made occasional snide comments to Manfred and even mentioned it to Christa.

Then one night at dinner, when she spoke with Heinrich Himmler, he seemed surprised that she and Manfred had been married over a year, and she was still not with child. It happened at a gala, a rally of sorts, at the Nazi Headquarters in Nuremberg. Goebbels and his wife shared a hotel room down the hall from Manfred and Christa, whom Dr. Goebbels had invited as his guests.

The night they met Himmler, they attended a dinner in a room decorated with banners, flags, and photos of the Führer. Just by the décor, Manfred could see that Goebbels had a hand in the celebration. A crystal chandelier twinkled like stars in the dimly lit room. Each table had a centerpiece, a silver candelabra with a large swastika in its center.

The band played traditional German tunes and music from Wagner's operas. Since his association with Goebbels and the Party, Manfred had become a fair dancer. He'd developed a charming disposition, which he used when cavorting with his superiors. They liked him.

He—unlike some of the others who were ungrateful—showed a genuine love and respect for the Nazi Party and, even more importantly, a willingness to do whatever was necessary to bring the dream of a thousand-year Reich to reality. Manfred was clever. Any distaste he might have toward an idea or program was well-hidden. Whatever his superiors proposed was golden to him.

After several dances, the bandleader announced that dinner was served.

Manfred and Christa took their seats. Although they were not at the head table, they were close enough for Goebbels to wink and smile at Manfred, who returned the gesture. After dinner, the band began to play, and almost everyone got up to dance. Himmler walked over to the table where the Blaus had been sitting. Although he was not handsome, his black uniform fit him impeccably, and his shoes were shined, reflecting the light.

"May I be so bold as to request this dance with your wife, Manfred?"

"But of course, if Christa doesn't mind."

"I don't mind at all. I am honored, *Reichsführer*," Christa said to Himmler as her blue eyes glistened in the candlelight that illumined her ivory skin.

It was a waltz. As they whirled around the room, Himmler directed his complete attention to Christa.

"You dance beautifully," he said.

"Thank you." She blushed.

"I don't know how to address this with you, so please don't be offended."

She did not answer. She waited.

"Dr. Goebbels has spoken to me about you and Manfred wanting to have children. And, of course, we, the Party, want that more than anything because we need more good Aryan children. It is crucial to our growth as a nation."

"We can't seem to have children. I don't know why."

"Well, may I make a suggestion?" he asked. "Not to be bold or rude…"

"Yes, please do, *Reichsführer*."

"Have you considered adopting a child from the Lebensborn?" he asked.

"I've never thought about it."

"There are many beautiful blond-haired, blue-eyed children waiting to be adopted by a fine Aryan couple, just like you two."

"Really? What would we have to do to adopt?"

"Actually, nothing. The truth is that you and Manfred are perfect candidates. In fact, I would bet that you might even find one of the babies that looks so much like you. You would forget it was not your own."

"Oh, *Reichsführer*, my arms have ached for a child. I would be so grateful if you could help us," she said.

His hand moved a little lower on her back as he pulled her a little closer to him.

"I'm sure it can all be arranged. I'll speak to Dr. Goebbels about it, and we will send you and your husband to Munich, to Steinhöring, the home for the Lebensborn, where you can choose a child."

"I can never thank you enough."

"I'm sure we will think of something," Himmler smiled.

It was late when Manfred and Christa arrived back at the hotel room. He undressed and showered while she sat at the vanity, removing her makeup and combing her hair. When he came into the bedroom, she turned to look at him. He was still slender, but he'd filled out since their marriage.

In his black SS uniform, he appeared to be a man: strong, powerful, and daunting. But standing here wrapped in a towel, to her, he still looked like a young boy. That same young boy she'd taken to her bed on their wedding night. She couldn't help but compare him to Himmler. Himmler, a powerful man, not necessarily a looker, but the authority in his step, the confidence in his manner—well, it was very attractive.

She put the comb down on her dressing table. It was an ivory comb inlaid with mother-of-pearl. Manfred had given it to her as a gift for their first anniversary.

"Manfred…"

"Yes, dear."

"Please sit down. I want to speak to you about something."

"Yes."

"Well, tonight, when I was dancing with the *Reichsführer*, he mentioned something to me," she said, looking into his eyes, assessing his mood. This pregnancy issue sometimes brought out a dark side of him. Christa knew she must tread very gently.

"I hope you won't be angry, but he mentioned adoption. He said that we would qualify for a baby from the Lebensborn. He said that there is a home in Munich. I have heard of it, too. It is called Heim Hochland or Steinhöring. He also said that if we wanted it, we could receive a beautiful Aryan child in need of a home just like ours, a home with a father who is devoted to the Reich and a mother who will love and care for it."

Manfred sat on the edge of the four-poster bed. Perhaps this was the answer. It would take the stress off their marriage.

"I'm not angry. In fact, I think it might be good for us. We've both wanted a baby for so long now."

"Oh, Manfred, do you mean it?" She got up and wrapped her arms around his neck.

"Yes, I do. I will talk to Dr. Goebbels on Monday morning and see when he thinks it might be convenient for me to take a week off so that we can go up to the highlands and bring the child back with us."

She rubbed the back of his neck, and he pulled her closer.

"Come to bed," he whispered in her ear. "Even though we will adopt a child, there is no need to stop trying."

She kissed him and broke away for a moment to turn out the lights. Then she got in beside him, and they made love.

CHAPTER THIRTY

"Heil Hitler." Manfred walked into his office to find Dr. Goebbels waiting.

"Heil Hitler," Goebbels said.

"Can I have my secretary get you anything? Coffee? Tea, perhaps?" Manfred asked.

Goebbels shook his head. "No, thank you. I just finished breakfast," he said, smiling like a Cheshire cat. "Manfred, your beautiful, charming, little wife, made quite the impression on the *Reichsführer*. Do you know what he has done? Up until now, you've been a non-commissioned officer.

"The Führer himself has been watching your career closely since you foiled his assassination attempt. Typically, to become an SS officer, you have to go to an officer's training school. It's quite grueling physically. We both know, dear boy, that your worth to the party is your intellect, not to mention your loyalty. I assured *Reichsführer* Himmler that The Ministry of Enlightenment and Propaganda was the perfect place for officer training. He agreed, and so you have been made a commissioned officer. Congratulations, *Untersturmführer*, Lieutenant Blau."

"I am taken aback," Manfred said, and his face broke into a huge smile. "Untersturmführer?"

"Yes, yes," he said with a smile one has for a favorite son. "There's more. He has instructed me to present you with a car and a driver. You will have your own automobile."

"An auto? That's quite a gift."

"Well, Himmler said that you and Christa planned to adopt a child from the Lebensborn, and with a little one, you will need reliable transportation. Is this true about the adoption?"

"Yes, it is. In fact, I was going to ask you about taking a week off to go up to Munich and see the children so that we could select one."

"Of course. It will be arranged. Would next month be soon enough? I need you for a few things this month."

"Yes, that would be just fine."

"I think the spring should be a nice time to travel. By then, the weather should have broken, and you can have a few nice days to enjoy the country."

"Dr. Goebbels, you have always been so kind to me."

"Yes, you are a good employee, a dedicated member of the Party, and a good friend. I am proud to know you, Manfred."

"Sir, knowing you has been the greatest honor and most precious part of my life."

"I'm glad to hear it. In fact, I brought you a gift because you made such a good impression on the *Reichsführer*. Something for your office. The good impression you've made reflects on me; you know."

"I do, and I can never tell you how much it means to me to be someone you can be proud of."

Goebbels handed Manfred a large box. It was wrapped in white paper with a black bow.

"This gift I am giving you is unique, very unique," Goebbels said. "Go ahead, open it."

Manfred untied the ribbon. Then he tore the paper and took the top off. Inside, he saw the dried white bones of a human pelvis. Skeletal, bleached. He almost let out a scream. Looking up, his eyes met the doctor's eyes with confusion.

"It's an ashtray, a conversation piece. We have them made from the pelvises of dead Jews. Only top-ranking officers own them. I thought you might like it. Gives people something to look at when they come into your office." Dr. Goebbels smiled. "I have one."

"Thank you, sir. Thank you," Manfred said, trying to hide his revulsion. He put the box on the side of the desk. "It is a truly unique gift." Later, he would put the human ashtray on the other side of the room, where he might avoid looking at it. But the harder he tried to avert his eyes, the more drawn they were to the white, sloping pelvis.

CHAPTER THIRTY-ONE

Once he was sure his wife Heidi was asleep, Dr. Henkener left the bedroom and dressed quietly in the downstairs bathroom. It was best to keep Heidi from knowing anything. The less she knew, the better. It was not that he didn't trust her. Although she did not agree with his sympathies for the Jews, he knew she would never turn him in. But why subject her to this possible danger? If she remained ignorant, at least she remained safe. He dragged a wet comb through his thinning, white hair and looked in the mirror. Satisfied that even though his insides were churning, he appeared calm and normal. After quietly locking the door, he left the house.

Dr. Rosen, his wife, and his fifteen-year-old daughter were to meet him at his office. Thomas Henkener knew it was far more dangerous for them to be out after curfew than it was for him to be taking a stroll. Even if he were stopped by the police, he could always tell them he'd forgotten important papers at his office. After all, he was a doctor. Doctors worked all hours. His excuse was quite believable. Still, he felt the sweat trickle down his neck, even as the icy wind assaulted his face.

He arrived at the office and only lit a small lamp in the hallway, far away from any windows. The Rosens arrived almost immediately. As instructed by Dr. Henkener, the family carried no luggage, but Dr. Henkener could see that they wore several layers of clothing.

"I'm glad to see you, Zalman." Dr. Henkener reached out and shook Dr. Rosen's hand.

"Thank you for doing this for us, Thomas. I realize what a risk you are putting yourself at."

"How could I not do this? How can I forget *Kristallnacht*? People were beaten, tortured, and killed. The Jewish-owned businesses were taken away, and they could no longer make a living. You, my friends, and colleagues, decent and brilliant healers, are all forbidden to practice because you are Jews. Anyway, we must not loiter. Let me show you and your family to the attic."

Dr. Henkener lit a candle and turned off the lamp. It was best that they do as much without light as possible. Then he put another candle in his pocket.

"Follow me," he said.

Dr. Henkener led them through a dark, winding hallway, through the back of the building, where no one ever went as he fought the cobwebs in the way. Dust covered the floor, and Frau Rosen coughed. When they got to the end of the hall, Thomas Henkener pulled out a small footstool from under a hidden crawl space.

"Hold the candle for a moment, Zalman," Dr. Henkener said.

Then he climbed on the step stool and pushed hard on a heavy tile in the ceiling. It opened, pouring out a gust of dust and grime to reveal only darkness.

"Come, we have to go up here." Dr. Henkener said as he used his arms to pull his body up into the attic. Next, Dr. Rosen followed. Then they reached down and helped the women, who were not strong enough to pull themselves up.

Once everyone was inside the attic, they looked around. Although they only had the light of a small candle, it was evident that the room was covered in filth. A few wooden crates sat in a corner, but other than that, the room was bare. Minka Rosen, Dr. Rosen's daughter, screamed as a spider crawled across the floor.

Then she began to cry. Her mother cradled her. Dr. Rosen stepped on the insect and frowned at his daughter.

"Shh, shh, Minka," Dr. Rosen said. "We must be very quiet. If we are not quiet, we will be discovered. And that would be bad, not only for us, but for Dr. Henkener. So, you must never scream like that again. Do you understand? It is very important that you understand, *mein kind*, my child."

Minka nodded, wiping the tears from her face. "I'm sorry, Dr. Henkener. I didn't mean it. It was a reaction. I'm afraid of insects. It won't happen again, though. I promise," she said.

Minka began taking bits of food out of her clothing and laying them on the crates.

"Next time I come, I will bring blankets," Dr. Henkener said. "I'm sorry. I didn't think of it."

"We'll be fine. Don't worry about us," Dr. Rosen said. "We have plenty of clothes. Besides, you are doing enough."

"I'll bring as much food as I am able to secure, as well," Dr. Henkener said. He looked around the room. He could not imagine what staying in this grimy, cramped area would be like.

Years ago, before the country had gone mad, he'd been to a party at the Rosen's home. He remembered it was a lovely bungalow, stylishly furnished, immaculate. Dr. Henkener felt a deep sorrow as he watched his colleague and his family endure these horrendous conditions. Not only was he sorry, but he was ashamed to be German, to be part of a regime that treated people the way the Nazis treated the Jews.

CHAPTER THIRTY-TWO

Christa sat beside Manfred in the backseat of the shiny, black car. The rich smell of leather mingled with cigar smoke and expensive cologne. Manfred closed the privacy window between the couple and the driver. Then he took Christa's hand and held it between both of his.

"Would you prefer a boy or a girl?" Christa asked.

Manfred thought for a moment. "Oh, I don't know. Let's have a look and see what is available." It would be easier to raise a girl. So much less would be expected of her, leaving fewer opportunities for disappointment among Manfred's superiors. If he had a son who did not excel, it would be a bad reflection on him. He'd worked too hard to build a rapport with all of those who could further his career for him to allow a child to get in the way.

"I think a girl would be nice, a girl who looks like you," Manfred said, and he squeezed Christa's hand. She squeezed back and smiled at him.

It was warm for a day in early May, and the flowers had just begun to bud outside the Steinhöring home. The four-story country castle had been newly painted sugar white, with canary yellow trim the previous summer. Gorgeous green leaves had burst from the trees to celebrate the end of the long German winter, and emerald grass covered the lush, rolling hills.

"Such a quaint and lovely place," Christa said as the driver pulled up to the front of the Lebensborn home.

Manfred held Christa's hand as they walked in.

Women were everywhere, in all stages of pregnancy, all of them blonde, blue-eyed, tall, and with athletic builds. They were so similar that they seemed like living dolls, something created instead of real people. As Manfred and Christa walked by, the girls offered white-toothed smiles.

Then there were the others—nurses and helpers. These women, some blonde, but many brunettes, some young, some also older and well past childbearing age, were in the workforce. These, too, were Aryan women. Their bloodlines had been checked, but their looks did not reflect the qualities needed for breeding. These women were responsible for the well-being of the superior blonde, blue-eyed, perfect specimens of Aryan womanhood.

A large mahogany desk with intricate carvings of Teutonic Knights was centered a few feet from the door. Behind it sat a woman in her early forties. Her blonde hair was combed neatly into finger waves around her face. She had deep-set blue eyes and features so strong that they almost appeared masculine.

"May I help you?" the receptionist asked.

"Yes, my boss, Dr. Goebbels, arranged for us to see someone here about adoption," Manfred said.

"Of course, you must be *Oberscharführer* and Frau Blau." She smiled, showing off her slightly sharp teeth. "Please, make yourselves comfortable." She stood and walked them over to the living room area, where she motioned for them to sit on a plush white sofa. "May I offer you a coffee or a cold drink?"

"No, thank you, nothing for me," Christa said.

"No, thank you," Manfred answered.

"Wait here. I'll be right back," the woman said. Then she turned, her high heels clicking on the marble floor.

They sat together on the sofa and waited. Manfred held

Christa's hand, which was wet with perspiration. He knew how nervous she was and wanted this to go smoothly for her sake.

It was only a matter of a few minutes before an elderly woman, heavy-set, with a salt and pepper bun, limped into the room. Her hair frizzed around her face, and Manfred could not help noticing the three black hairs that sprung from a mole on the side of her cheek.

"Welcome, *Oberscharführer* and Frau Blau. I have heard so many nice things about you. My name is Beatrix, and I will be here to help you with anything that you might need."

"Thank you, Beatrix, but it is now *Untersturmführer* Blau."

"Oh, congratulations. You should be so proud," she said a little too loudly.

"Thank you," Manfred said, looking away, his face burning with embarrassment.

"Have you decided whether you would like a boy or a girl?"

"Actually, we have. We would like a little girl," Manfred said.

"As I am standing here looking at your wife, I can see we have the perfect child for you. In fact, there is such a resemblance. You're not going to believe it."

Christa smiled. "Can you tell us a little about her?"

"Of course, I would be more than happy to. The child is a little over a year old. Her naming ceremony, well, Himmler performed it himself. He gave her the name of Katja. A pretty name? Ja?"

"It is. May we see her?" Christa asked.

"Of course, you may. Wait until you see this beautiful little Aryan girl. She is so good—she hardly ever cries. Come on, follow me. I will take you to the waiting room outside the nursery, and then I'll have one of the nurses bring Katja out so you can see her."

The waiting room outside the nursery looked like a comfortable living room in a prosperous country estate. There were large, overstuffed chairs in a deep, hunter-green fabric embroidered with a gold thread design. On the white marble floor lay a large wool rug, mostly the same green color, with touches of gold and deep burgundy. Two lamps stood across the room from each other on similar mahogany coffee tables.

Manfred and Christa sat together. He reached for her hand, patted it, and she smiled. A half-hour passed before a nurse wearing a starched white cotton uniform and a small head cap entered, accompanied by Beatrix. The nurse carried a bundle swathed in blankets so white they looked brand new.

"This is Katja," Beatrix said, smiling, as the nurse turned the infant so that Manfred and Christa could see her face.

Christa stood to get a better look.

Katja's minuscule eyelashes brushed against her cheek as she slept. A dusting of golden hair covered her small head.

"She's beautiful," Christa said, tears glistening in her eyes.

"Would you like to hold her?" the nurse asked.

"Yes. Oh yes. May I?"

"Of course." The nurse placed the baby in Christa's arms, and Christa sat back down to hold her.

"You look radiant with that child in your arms," Manfred said. Once again, he was reminded of how fortunate he was to have won this beautiful woman as his wife. He remembered how he had watched her from afar, wishing, hoping, dreaming, and eventually scheming so she would someday be his.

And now, he was beside her, *Untersturmführer* Blau, her husband, Goebbels's friend, and the father of their soon-to-be child. *Untersturmführer* Blau, that was him, the man who'd dined at the same table as Adolf Hitler. *Manfred, you have so come far from the weak and uncoordinated boy who failed at every sport in the Hitler Jugend.*

A secret smile crept across his face. He had done it. He'd created the life he'd longed for as a child, and now things would only get better and better. In his mind's eye, he saw himself rise in the Party. Maybe someday, just maybe, he would replace Himmler as *Reichsführer*. Dare he dream so big? Why not? Look at where he'd started and where he was now. There was no telling how far he might go in his career.

Manfred watched Christa. She seemed to glow as she tenderly touched the infant's cheek.

"I love her already," Christa said, biting her lower lip.

"Are you going to want to see more of the children?" Beatrix asked.

"I don't. I am happy with Katja. But do you, Manfred?" Christa asked, sounding hopeful that he would agree with her decision.

He walked over and looked closely at the baby. She was lovely, and it was true. There was an uncanny resemblance to Christa: the light hair, the soft, blue eyes. Why look at any other babies? This child made Christa happy, and that was all that mattered. Little Katja was perfect.

"I don't need to see any others. She's a lovely child. I'd like to begin the adoption process for this one."

"Her name is Katja," Beatrix said.

"Yes," Manfred said. "Katja."

"Katja," Christa repeated as she looked at the perfect little face. "You are beautiful."

"Just look at how pretty that baby is. Why, she is the perfect Aryan child." Beatrix smiled. "Look at that light hair. It looks like an angel's halo around her head and those blue eyes. She will surely grow up to be a beauty and make you both very proud."

Manfred smiled. It would have been better to have their own, but this did make life easier. Now he could concentrate on his career.

Before they left Berlin, Manfred and Christa had set up a nursery for the baby they planned to bring home. It was painted yellow. Shelves lined the walls, covered with stuffed animals. There was a white bear with a pink and blue ribbon around its neck, a tall dog with an enormous black nose, and a fat, little pink pig. There was a brown teddy bear and a wooden rocking horse. The cradle was made of wood and painted white. Manfred had it suspended from the ceiling, enabling it to rock slowly back and forth. A white wooden dresser that matched the cradle stood beside the bed.

Now that they'd decided upon a little girl, they left the institute to wait for the papers to be processed. That afternoon, Manfred and Christa went into town, where they purchased a pretty blonde-haired doll. Her eyes were royal-blue, and she had full, red lips. The doll wore traditional German attire, similar to what Christa had worn at her wedding: a white blouse with puffed sleeves and a full, green skirt.

They purchased blankets in different shades of pink to be stacked in her closet on a shelf. Before the couple had gone to Steinhöring, they'd received gifts from all the people at Manfred's office for the new baby. But since no one knew if it would be a boy or girl, everything they received was yellow. There were little yellow undershirts, sleepers, and yellow socks. Christa mentioned this to Manfred, and he suggested that she go ahead and buy some frilly pink dresses for the baby because he knew it would make her happy.

The following day, they returned to Steinhöring to pick up the baby. All the papers had been signed and notarized. After placing an envelope filled with documents in Manfred's hand, the baby was placed in Christa's arms. Now she was officially a mother.

Katja slept off and on all the way home, waking only to take a few sips from her bottle and then falling back into a peaceful slumber. The motion of the automobile calmed the baby and kept her sleepy and quiet.

When they returned to Berlin, Manfred placed the manila envelope at the bottom of his desk.

Christa laid Katja in her crib. The baby fussed until Christa gently rocked the cradle, helping the child to drift off to sleep.

Manfred entered the room and stood beside his wife.

"Are you happy?" he asked, knowing the answer.

"I am. I am so happy."

"I am, too. When you're happy, I'm happy," he said.

She turned and kissed him. He hated to return to work. It was so lovely to spend time with his wife. Manfred decided to bring her a dozen roses the following day from the vendor outside his office.

CHAPTER THIRTY-THREE

A SHROUD OF darkness covered the street as Dr. Henkener walked, almost hugging the building, staying carefully out of the lamplight. It was nearly midnight as he hurried toward his office, carrying a small bundle of food for the Rosen family. Passing an alleyway, he thought he heard footsteps behind him. He shivered, imagining it might be the Gestapo. If he were caught with the food, there was no explanation.

From now on, he would bring lunches to work and save them, then bring them up when he was sure everyone had left. This method of carrying large quantities of food was far too dangerous. He whipped around quickly, but no one was there.

The wind whistled through the trees, and in the distance, he heard a crash of thunder. Thomas Henkener jumped. It was going to rain. He sped up, walking as fast as possible without running. Then he heard the footsteps again.

"Thomas." It was a whisper in the dark. "Thomas, it's me, Hershel Shulman."

"Hershel? Is that you?"

"Yes, it's my wife and me."

Out of the darkness, Dr. Shulman appeared. He wore a ragged, black wool overcoat and was accompanied by a tiny woman with long, dark hair pinned up into a messy bun.

"Come, follow me. Hurry," Dr. Henkener said. He glanced around. The street was bare. There was another crash of thunder, followed by lightning. The storm moved closer.

The Shulmans followed Dr. Henkener into his office building. "We must not turn on any lights. Come, I have a candle in my office."

They navigated the building by holding on to the walls until they found Dr. Henkener's office.

"Wait here," Dr. Henkener said.

Henkener went into his office, lit the candle, and returned.

"Follow me," he said.

Dr. Shulman and his wife followed Henkener into the attic, their way lit by the tiny flicker of light. Once they were upstairs, they saw the Rosens.

"Do you know Dr. Rosen?"

"I think we've met. I'm Hershel Shulman, and this is my wife, Perle."

Dr. Rosen nodded.

"Now, Hershel, what can I do for you?" Thomas asked.

"We need your help, my wife and me. We were in hiding. Our neighbors were trying to help us, but they became afraid. People began to suspect, and we were forced to leave."

"Where is Meyer?"

"Meyer, our son, God bless him… He is in America with his wife. He has been trying to get papers for us, but so far, he has been unable to do anything. We need help. Jews are being arrested every day. I have heard frightening things. I have heard that the camps are not work camps but death camps. The Nazis are murdering Jews at these concentration camps."

Hershel Shulman was covered in sweat. The perspiration from his brow was dripping into his eyes, and he wiped it away with the back of his hand. "I am sorry, Thomas, to come to you and burden you with my problem, but frankly, I have nowhere else to turn."

"There is not enough room here. We hardly have enough food

for ourselves. We cannot take on another two people, Thomas," Zalman Rosen said.

"We must and we will," Thomas Henkener said. "This man is my friend. He saved my daughter. Without his help, she would be dead. My Christa, my precious child, was born a blue baby. Dr. Shulman was the only one who could help her. He stays."

"How will we manage?"

"We will manage the best we can. These are bad times. I am doing what I can to help you, but selfishness isn't the answer," Thomas said. Then he turned to Hershel Shulman. "There is not much I can do for you. There is only this small room and whatever food I am able to bring. I wish it could be more. You deserve only the best, but I am afraid this is all I can give."

"It is everything. You are giving us our lives. What could be more than that?" Dr. Shulman said. Tears had begun to form in his eyes. He embraced Thomas Henkener. "You are a good man. God bless you, my friend."

Dr. Henkener turned away in embarrassment. Then he opened the package. "Here is food. Please share it among yourselves. I will bring more as soon as I am able. And Hershel…"

"Yes?" Hershel Shulman was gazing at him, his eyes illuminated by the flickering candlelight.

"I am glad, no honored, that you came to me. It is a privilege to be given this opportunity to help you," Thomas Henkener said.

CHAPTER THIRTY-FOUR

"It's all arranged. Karl Abendstern has found Helen. She said she would take Eidel until this was all over. At least, Eidel is a girl, and blonde, too. That is good. If she were a boy, we would have to worry about the Nazis seeing the circumcision. But with a girl, there is nothing to distinguish her as Jewish," Fruma said. Then she wrapped her arm around Zofia. "Zofia, it will be all right."

"I know. I know it will. I trust Helen, but I will miss Eidel terribly."

"We all will," Gitel said. "But it is in her best interest to get her out of here."

"Yes, it is." Fruma looked across the room at the baby in her playpen.

"Tonight? He is taking her so soon?" Zofia asked.

"Yes, the sooner, the better. Koppel is a pain in the ass. I don't trust him."

"I know. I've been holding him off, but soon he will insist that we sleep together, and I don't think I can bear it."

"Well, no matter what happens to us, at least Eidel will be safe," Fruma said.

"Yes. At least, Eidel will be safe," Zofia repeated.

Zofia could not eat. A crevice began to open in the pit of her belly, and as the day wore on, growing deeper until it felt like a canyon. She knew it was best for Eidel to be as far from the ghetto and her Jewish roots as possible. But the pain of separation was almost unbearable.

Every time Eidel smiled at her, she wept. But when the sun descended from the sky and the darkness covered the streets, Zofia dressed the baby as warmly as she could, layering her clothes because Karl had insisted that there be no luggage.

This, bringing a baby to the other side outside of the ghetto walls, Karl told the women, was the most dangerous mission he'd ever taken on. At any time, Eidel might cry and alert the guards. In fact, it was probable that she would because the baby did not know Karl and would be frantic for her mother.

He'd given Fruma a shot of whiskey to give the baby before the journey began, hoping she might sleep through the entire process. Once Eidel was dressed, Fruma gave her the whiskey through a dropper. Eidel made a face of dislike, but Fruma continued to force the alcohol into her mouth, and then she rocked the Eidel to sleep.

Together, Zofia, Fruma, and Gitel took Eidel to a crawl space under an apartment building, where they met Karl. He was waiting with his arms folded across his chest, eyes darting, keen and aware. There were only a few short seconds for Zofia to hold her child tightly to her breast. Then each of the women kissed Eidel's cheek as she slept. Karl reached out and took the baby. He was a big man, but even in the darkness, the women saw the gentleness in his touch.

"She will be all right," he promised, his dark eyes filled with sincerity.

"I will pay you money for doing this for us," Fruma said.

"It's all right. I will do it because I want to do it, not for the money, but so that another Jewish child might live and someday be a part of a Jewish state, the state that I see in my dreams, the state of Israel."

"You're a Zionist?" Gitel asked.

"Yes."

"I have Zionist leanings, although I've never shared that with anyone except Fruma. Without a Jewish state, the world is bound to keep on treating us like dirt. We need a homeland of our own."

"I agree with you, and so many others feel the same way. You see, we have meetings. They are secret meetings and must be kept quiet because of the Judenrats, but you're invited. I am inviting you. However, I don't want to stand here talking. It's far too dangerous and puts the child at too much risk. I must go now but come tomorrow morning to the alleyway where I sell my black-market goods. I might have some work for Zofia and Fruma, but I will also have time to give you more details about the meeting."

With that, Karl turned and ran, Eidel asleep in his arms. Zofia watched as he held the child with one hand and gripped the rail with the other. Then he nimbly climbed an iron ladder on the side of the building. Soon he was little more than a dark shadow as he sprinted like a panther across the rooftops and out the walls of the ghetto.

Zofia lay awake all night, staring out the window the entire time. It was hard to believe that Eidel would not be there waiting for her when she got out of bed. Somewhere outside, far from her arms and protection, her infant daughter was at the mercy of others, not necessarily strangers, but not her mother.

It was true that Helen had been a good friend. There was no doubt that Zofia liked her, but this was Eidel, her child, her only child. Helen would be the one to hear her speak her first words. When she reached up and said, "Mama," it would be Helen's arms she yearned for. Helen would be there to comfort her when she cried and, God forbid, care for her when she was sick. Helen would rock her to sleep and teach her the alphabet. But would Helen ever feel the same way about Eidel as Helen felt about her own son, her flesh and blood? Or would Eidel always be the second-best child?

It tore at Zofia's insides as she went over the answers again and again in her mind. If things had been reversed, she would surely have taken Helen's son. She would have cared for him, but would she ever have loved him as much as she loved Eidel?

If only the Nazis would disappear from the face of the earth, and she could go home to live a normal life, to raise her child. Why had the Jews been cursed to suffer like this? What had they done? Tears spilled upon her pillow. Eidel, dear, sweet, Eidel. Her tender, toothless smile, the sweet baby smell of her peach fuzz hair. Eidel, gone for now and perhaps forever.

CHAPTER THIRTY-FIVE

"You have to eat. It's essential that you eat," Gitel said to Zofia. "You haven't eaten a thing for almost a week. You are going to get very sick, and we have very little medicine here. If you should die, then who will claim Eidel when this is all over?"

"You. You and Fruma."

"Yes, but you are her mother. If you don't want to live for yourself, then at least live so that you can go back and get Eidel and raise her as soon as the Nazis lose the war."

"Maybe they'll win, and we will all be exterminated like rats," Zofia said.

"They will not win," Fruma said firmly. Her eyes glazed over again with that strange look indicating she was experiencing another vision. "But you are right. Many will be lost before the Nazis are defeated. But you mark my words, Hitler and his precious Third Reich will be defeated.

"Zofia, listen to me and hear me good. It is for that day when the Nazis are gone that you must stay strong. You must eat, and you must take care of yourself as best as you possibly can. Because there are great things that you have yet to do on this earth, and you're not done yet. You have a future. Don't throw it away. Keep believing.

You must, and most importantly, not lose the will to live. You must live. You must do this for Eidel."

Bright sunshine came pouring through the kitchen window.

"Where will Eidel be at the end of the war if you are dead? You cannot expect Helen to care for her forever. Every day, you must remember why you are living, for your child, and let that knowledge be the flicker of light that gives you the strength to stay alive. Do you understand me?" Gitel asked.

Zofia turned away. But Gitel grabbed her arm and shook her hard. "Listen to me. Look at me. You must not give up. You cannot give up. You brought that child into the world. You owe her. Live, Zofia. Chose to live," Gitel said.

Until now, Zofia felt as if she were already dead. She'd died as she watched Karl Abendstern carry her only child over the rooftops and away from her grasp. But Gitel's words penetrated through the darkness in her heart, shooting like a bolt of bright silver lightning. Gitel and Fruma were right. Even though she was far away from her daughter, her daughter needed her. She must live, she must survive, and she must be there at the end when the Nazis are defeated. She must be there for Eidel.

From that day forward, Zofia began to fight.

As the days passed, she grew stronger. Every day, she awakened with a new resolve that someday she would hold her daughter again. She fantasized about the day she would design Eidel's wedding dress and walk her to the canopy. The future would be filled with *Hanukkahs*, the Jewish festival of lights, where she prepared potato latkes with thick spoons full of sweet applesauce for her grand-children.

Zofia would live. She would choose to live no matter what the Nazis threw at her. She would not let them take this from her or her daughter. In her mind's eye, she watched Eidel grow every day, putting her trust in Helen to do what she could not, to be the mother she longed to be.

Meanwhile, Koppel was relentless in his empty pursuit to make her his conquest. He came to visit often, bringing gifts for Zofia. He was kind and affectionate, showing a side of himself that few had ever seen. Zofia began to feel sorry for him.

Then, to remind herself of who he really was, she got up early one morning and watched him as he directed his own people onto the boxcars at the trains. He didn't see her watching. He was unaware of her presence, so he showed the other side of his face. The side that he masked for Zofia. His eyes looked like glass when he spoke, his voice harsh and commanding as he ordered the old men, women, and children to form lines and walk quickly onto the trains. Zofia shivered.

Rumors flew through the ghetto as to what was actually taking place in the camps. Escapees had returned just to tell the others what they had seen and what had been done to them. It was hard to believe, but the news confirmed their greatest fear, that the camps were death camps.

They were not work camps at all. In fact, they were places where the Nazis killed Jews by the thousands and burned their bodies like old rubbish. Her eyes darted from Koppel to the old, feeble, helpless, and sick taking his direction without question. He had to know where he was sending them. The Nazis must have told him; if not, he must have heard all the gossip. But still, Koppel smiled and offered bread with jam to those too hungry to resist and too hopeful to believe that they were going to their deaths.

Her feelings of pity for Koppel disappeared like vapor as she watched him work.

Gitel had talked to Karl Abendstern, and since then, she'd begun to go to Zionist meetings that took place in secret at apartments all around the ghetto. She asked Fruma and Zofia to go with her.

They had refused, but Zofia felt the need to find an outlet as time passed, and this seemed a good one. So, she agreed to accompany Gitel one evening. They walked in the shadows until they arrived at a tall brick building. Then Gitel looked around, assuring herself they'd not been followed, and they slipped inside. There they climbed three flights of stairs up to a small room crammed with Jews. The air reeked of sweat. Gitel introduced Zofia to over a dozen people. It seemed she'd met so many that Zofia could not remember their names. They became faces that moved in front of her like a stream of players in a parade.

"This is Peter and Michael. This is Judith and Ruth," Gitel said.

Zofia nodded and smiled.

"This is Dovid Greenspan. Dovid, this is Zofia," Gitel said. "He is new here, like you. We met last time I was at a meeting. If I remember correctly, you told me that was your first time at a Zionist meeting?"

"Yes, it was," Dovid answered. He was slender of build and medium height. "It's nice to meet you, Zofia, and good to see you again, Gitel," he said, his voice refined. "So, Zofia, you, too, have come to join us in building our dream of a Jewish state?"

"Yes, I have."

"You are from Poland?"

"Yes, Warsaw. And you?"

"I was born in Austria, a little town outside of Vienna, a beautiful city."

"I have heard that Vienna was lovely before the Anschluss. Is your family still living there?"

"My parents and sisters were there when I left. God only knows where they are now. I've sent letters, but I never hear anything." He shook his head. "And you?"

"Gitel and Fruma are my family. My parents are dead, and I was an only child." She was afraid to mention Eidel. She wanted to assure Eidel's safety with silence.

"Did you have a trade? Or were you in school?"

"I am a seamstress. I worked with Fruma, one of the ladies I live with, Gitel's friend. Fruma and I worked together before the invasion. What was your trade?"

"I am a violinist. I played with the Vienna Concert Society. When news came that Hitler planned to invade Austria, I escaped the Anschluss with the help of many of my non-Jewish colleagues.

"It was decided that the best place for me to go was Poland. Then, as you know, it was not long before Hitler came here. I don't believe there is anywhere to escape the Nazis. They are everywhere, like an ant colony." He laughed a slightly bitter laugh. "That's why we need a Jewish state."

"I must agree with you," she said. "I'm sure every Jew would agree."

"Not so. I have many friends in the Hassidic community, and they have all but ostracized me for my support of the Zionist movement."

"Were you Hassidic?"

"No, but I knew many Hasidim from the neighborhood where I grew up. They are difficult to understand."

"I've seen a lot of them, even worked on wedding dresses for a few, but I don't know a great deal about the culture. Only that they dress strangely with little care for style or fashion."

"They don't care for modern styles. Their big concern is modesty. In fact, from what I understand, they wear their strange, outdated clothing and long sideburns to make them look different from non-Jews. I've heard they do this so that God will recognize them."

"God recognizes all of us, regardless of what we wear. Don't you think?"

"I would think so, yes. But they are a hard bunch to understand. They don't reveal a great deal about their culture."

"Do you know about them? I'm sort of curious?"

"A little. Perhaps a little more than you, but still not much."

There was a stirring amongst the crowd.

A young man got onto a wooden box used as a makeshift podium. He stomped his feet to get the crowd's attention and raised his hands to quiet them.

"Good evening and a very warm welcome to my fellow Jews in search of a homeland." Everyone cheered enthusiastically. "My name is Mordechai."

Zofia looked at the faces surrounding her, young, old, women and men, all brimming with determination. These people were not like the others. They would not go down without a fight.

There was a discussion of the escapees who'd come back from the camps with grim warnings of what lay ahead. Many people declared they would rather die fighting in the ghetto than be shot and thrown into a mass grave or gassed and burned.

Zofia longed to be like them, to be strong and unafraid. But the truth was that she was afraid. They talked about forming an uprising in the ghetto, building an armory, and fighting the Germans in the streets. "Kill Nazis!" they cried out. It all sounded fantastic as these Zionists proclaimed their loyalty to their dreams and each other.

But Zofia could not imagine herself taking up arms and shooting to kill. She'd never held a gun. In fact, she'd never even struck another person. Besides, maybe it was all lies. What if it was all exaggeration, and there were no shootings or gassings? It wasn't logical. Why would the Nazis kill the Jews if they could use them as free labor? Wouldn't it be wiser to have them working for the war effort? She would rather work at the camp until the end of this than go to battle in the middle of the street and probably die there, never to see Eidel again.

So many thoughts ran through her mind as the meeting ended.

Zofia headed for the door. Dovid was suddenly beside her.

"May I walk you home?"

"I was just waiting for Gitel."

"I'm sure she won't mind."

"Of course, I don't mind." Gitel came over. "I will see you at home, Zofia."

Dovid held the door, and he and Zofia walked out into the cool night air.

"Do you like to read? I love books. When I was not playing music, I was a volunteer librarian," Dovid said.

She laughed. "I do like to read, but what a change for you… From a musician and a librarian to a street fighter?"

"No, I don't think I would be able to be a part of the fight. I wish I could, but I don't know how to use a gun. Still, I admire those who would fight. It takes a lot of courage."

"Yes, and so do I, but I'm not sure I could do it. I've never even held a gun."

"I keep telling myself that perhaps this will all end before I am forced onto one of those trains," he said.

"The thought is paralyzing."

"I know. I agree with you, but what are we to do, run around with rifles? Someone would have to teach me, and I am afraid I would waste more ammunition than I'd put to good use just because I am not sure of my aim," he said, shaking his head. "I probably don't seem like much of a man to you. I'm sorry. I've always been a bit of a gentle soul: a violinist, a reader. I paint and draw and sometimes even write poems."

She smiled. "I find you manly. You are just not a violent man, not a warrior."

"That's terribly sweet of you to say. But the truth is, I'm a coward, not really much of a man at all, and certainly not a fighter."

"Well, every person is different, I suppose. Until all this stuff with the Nazis began, I don't think too many people realized that if they wanted to live, they would have to fight."

"I admire your strength. You seem to take it all in stride."

"It's an act. Inside, I am a nervous wreck most of the time. But what can I do? I just live from day to day like everyone else."

"You have a strength about you, a presence. You know what I mean?"

"Not exactly, but I try not to wear my heart where everyone can see it." She smiled in the darkness.

"Fair enough," Dovid answered, nodding. "So, Zofia, tell me… what are your dreams? What do you plan to do if, by some miracle, we should survive this mess?"

"Me? I don't know. I don't give dreams much thought. I would just like to be reunited with my family." She gave a bitter laugh. "You want to hear something silly? I can't believe I'm even remembering this now, but…" She hesitated for a moment and glanced over at him in the darkness. "You know… I always wanted to be a jazz musician when I was a young girl. It was a secret dream. Not something I ever really believed would come true, but it was a nice dream, if nothing else."

"Do you play an instrument?"

"Not really, a little piano, but nothing to speak of. I wanted to take lessons, but there was never enough money. Then all of this happened, and now I can't think of learning anything. I only think of survival. I wish I did play an instrument, though, now that you mention it. It would be wonderful to fill our apartment with beautiful music. I think it would lift everyone up. Perhaps it would take away some of the feelings of hopelessness."

"Yes, you're right, it does. Music is a fantastic release." He turned to her and smiled. Then he took her hand and squeezed it gently. "Believe it or not, I have my violin here in the ghetto. I managed to bring it with me. I could teach you to play. Would you like that?"

"I would, actually. I would like it very much." It wouldn't be lessons in the American swing that she loved, but still, it was music, and music was life.

"You know, sometimes I sit back, and I remember so much about my life, about the way things were before the Nazis came," he said.

"Yes, you know what's strange? I never realized how good life was until it wasn't anymore. I was never rich, but now we are practically starving."

"I understand how you feel. Whenever I paint, I paint my memories. I never paint or draw pictures of the ghettos, the trains, the starving, or the dying. Instead, I painstakingly force myself to remember, to remember: the beauty of a sunset, the snow falling on Vienna at Christmas time, a concert hall filled with people and glittering crystal chandeliers, the toothless smile of a baby, an old woman smelling a bunch of flowers…" He seemed lost in the tenderness of his memories until he glanced up to see that Zofia was crying.

"I'm sorry," he said. "I didn't mean to make you feel bad."

"I know you didn't. It's all right. I guess it just made me think. I, too, have so many memories. There is so much that haunts me from the past. Sometimes my longings for what used to be are so strong that I almost can't bear it."

They walked in silence until they reached the stairs to her apartment building. She stopped.

"This is where I live."

He reluctantly released her hand and gently squeezed her shoulder. "Would you like to come and see some of my artwork sometime? Perhaps we could even start your violin lessons."

"I would like that," she said.

"Maybe tomorrow?"

"Yes, tomorrow is fine."

"Shall I come and call for you tomorrow evening, about eight?" He was gazing into her eyes. She felt the heat of his desire, and it made her feel alive.

"Yes, come tomorrow at eight. I'll be waiting."

"Eight, then." His hand was still on her shoulder, massaging.

"I'll see you then." She said, breaking free from his eyes and turning to go.

"Zofia…"

"Yes?" She glanced back at him.

"Thank you."

"For what?"

"For making this night the most special one I have had in a very long time."

She looked away, embarrassed, and then went into her building, turning quickly, just once, to see him standing and watching her go.

The following night, Zofia went to Dovid's apartment.

"Does anyone live here with you?"

"No," he said, pointing to the paintings on the wall. "One of the Judenrats has a connection with the Polish Police. I paint the paintings. He takes them to his contact, and they sell them to an art dealer. There is a great demand for beautiful art from happier times, especially smiling children and unspoiled landscapes. In exchange, I get an apartment where I am not disturbed while I paint and enough ration cards to keep me alive. I'm not a starving artist, but I'm hungry most of the time."

"Then you are not a collaborator?"

"No, they use me for profit. If I could no longer paint, I would be on the next train to Treblinka."

His artwork covered the apartment walls. In each piece, she felt the power of his emotions and the yearning for the world before Hitler. A canvas over the living room sofa was filled with bright colors, joyful colors, surrounding a carousel at sunset. Another featured children playing in an emerald forest, and another of lovers drinking wine at an outdoor café with red and white tablecloths and matching umbrellas, their bodies leaning toward each other in intimate conversation.

Then she saw Dovid's self-portrait in the concert hall, where he sat in front of a blur of a thousand faces playing his violin. Overhead, the twinkling light of a chandelier, like a thousand diamond crystals, reflected in his eyes, his face fully enraptured. If she stared long enough, she felt as if she could almost see his fingers trembling and hear the haunting strains of melancholy notes as the bow reached its arm out to caress the strings.

"They're beautiful paintings," she said.

"Thank you. They tell the story of my life before Hitler."

"Is this your child?" she asked. It was a picture of a very young girl, perhaps two or three, smiling with only a single tooth.

"My niece, I was there when she was born. My sister's husband was my best friend. Their family lived a few blocks away from ours. When we were growing up, Yoseph and I played kickball and walked to school together.

"Then, as we became young adults, he and my sister began to notice each other. And before I knew it, he was more interested in her than he was in me," Dovid laughed. "Oh, at the time, I was angry at both of them. I felt so betrayed. Of course, I got over it by the time they got married. In fact, I was Joseph's best man. The night Issy was born, Yoseph and I sat smoking all the way until morning together in the waiting room."

She smiled.

"It was early in the morning that she came, just at the crack of dawn. We looked outside at the sunrise, and I remember confiding in Yoseph that I doubted my turn would ever come."

"Your turn?"

"Yes, my turn. My turn to find that special person who makes my heart beat just a little faster, and then to marry her, and if we are both very fortunate, to be blessed with a house filled with children. Well, I was right… I never did get married or have children of my own.

"Hitler had invaded before I had the chance, and everything changed. Now I wouldn't want to bring a child into this mess. So, I suppose that's why Issy is so special to me. She is like my own daughter."

"You may love her, and I have no doubt that you do. But Dovid, there is nothing in this world like your own child. The feelings that you have for a child of your own blood are indescribable." Zofia said, crossing her arms over her chest and fighting the urge to cry.

He looked at her sharply.

"I'm sorry. I didn't mean to offend you."

"I'm not offended. Just reminded of what has been stolen from me by the Nazis," he said.

"I'm sorry, Dovid. Sometimes I am so thoughtless. I should never have said that. I was selfishly thinking of my own problems."

"You wanted children, too?" he asked.

She considered telling him about Eidel but decided against it. She shrugged.

He saw the pain on her face and didn't ask anything more. Instead, he got up and took out his violin. "Would you like to hear me play?"

"Yes… Yes, I'd love to." It was a good way to change the subject; besides, she loved music.

"Here, sit down, and I will play for you," he said. They sat at a small kitchen table with two chairs.

She smiled at him. "I look forward to hearing you," she said.

"I'm sorry. I feel like a terrible host, but I'm afraid I don't have much to offer. I can make a pot of coffee if you would like."

"No, thank you. I don't want anything." She smiled.

Dovid took the violin out of its case. He held it like a man holds a woman he adores, fondling the glossy wood. Then he pulled the bow across the strings and began.

He played for a half hour. Painfully beautiful music filled the apartment. The tenderness in his hands and face moved her to tears. When he'd finished, he looked up from the instrument, and his eyes locked on hers.

He reached up and touched her face. She held his hand.

"Thank you for playing for me," she whispered, still in awe of the sounds that had just entranced her.

He nodded. "It's been quite a while since I've touched the violin. When I play, all of my feelings come to the surface. Sometimes, it's too painful."

"I know. I saw that."

He took her hand in his and squeezed. "I don't want to fall in love with you, Zofia. It's too dangerous to love anyone or anything right now. Everything can be taken away in an instant."

"Do you want me to leave?"

"Yes, and no.... No." His eyes were soft, like black oil. "I am only fooling myself. I am falling in love with you. Either it's love, or I'm just so damned lonely. I don't know if I can tell the difference."

"I know. I've been lonely for a very long time. But I have also been hurt, and I'm not ready for anything serious."

"I would never hurt you, Zofia. Never."

"Dovid, you are like a little boy. I can't take care of you. I have too much to worry about on my own."

"That was a cruel statement, Zofia. I am not a boy. Sensitive, yes, but I am a man in every sense of the word. I might not be as strong as some men, not the he-man every girl dreams of, but I would give my life for someone I care for."

"I'm sorry. That was terrible of me to say. I don't know what's wrong with me. I keep saying awful things. I didn't mean it the way it sounded. I'm just afraid, I guess. I just don't want to get hurt."

"And I suppose you don't find me attractive in that way?" he asked, looking down at his hands.

She studied him. He was nice-looking, kind, and gentle. It had been long since she'd felt a man's arms around her. Sometimes late at night, she'd hungered for the physical affection of a man. She'd only tasted it once, and it seemed so long ago, but somehow her body remembered and craved what it had once known.

And besides, since Eidel was gone, she'd not felt the warmth and the much-needed touch of another human being. She yearned for physical contact. Zofia ached to hold her child. She ached to hold a man and ached to be whole.

"Kiss me," she said. It had been so long since she'd felt the intimate touch of a man. Her body trembled in anticipation.

Dovid touched her face, his eyes brimming with need and disbelief. Slowly, he moved closer to her, taking her face in his hands. Gently, his lips brushed hers. She put her arms around him and held him close to her. The heat of his body sent shockwaves of need through hers. It was an awkward, clumsy embrace at first. Neither knew where to put their arms or their hands. As both were trying desperately not to look foolish, their heads bumped. Then they stopped for a moment, looked at each other, and laughed.

"Just kiss me, Dovid," she said. Unlike her relationship with Don Taylor, Zofia had no illusions this time. She was not searching for undying love, only momentary warmth and companionship.

This time, his arms draped around her, and hers reached up to embrace him. They kissed several times in a state of discovery. Then she took his hand and led him to his small cot. Lying back, she beckoned him to lie beside her. He did, and for a short hour, they forgot that they were Jews waiting for Hitler's decision on whether they were to live or die. For an hour, they were just a man and a woman entwined with each other on the precipice of love.

CHAPTER THIRTY-SIX

IT FELT good to have somewhere to go and something to do, if only for short periods. Dovid kept Zofia's mind occupied, helping her to forget how much she missed Eidel. He began teaching her to play the violin. Learning the instrument proved harder than she'd expected, and the more she worked with it, the greater her appreciation for Dovid's talent grew.

Sometimes, Dovid offered free concerts, gathering a large enough audience to force him to play outside in the open field so there would be room enough for everyone to come and listen. Zofia would sit in the front row, beaming with pride.

In the early evening, just at sunset, she and Dovid took long walks, talking, sharing, and daring to dream. He loaned her his favorite books, books he'd sacrificed food rations to purchase from the black market. Often, they sat in his apartment sipping coffee and discussing a book he'd given her to read. It was wonderful to share ideas. They even went to a theatrical play several other ghetto dwellers put on in one of the apartments.

Zofia had never played cards before. Dovid purchased a dog-eared deck from the black market, and he taught her. Often, she brought her sewing jobs to his apartment and worked while he played the violin.

The weeks passed by, and not a day passed that Zofia did not miss Eidel, but the pain had begun to lessen a bit, and she was grateful to Dovid for the distraction. She was not in love with him. For her, it was not the passionate, all-encompassing relationship that it was for him. She'd been hurt and could not give her heart as easily as he seemed to, but she enjoyed his company. Their conversations flowed freely and effortlessly, although she still did not feel secure enough to tell him about Eidel.

One night they lay together, talking and sipping wine that Dovid had purchased from the black market, his arms wrapped around her in the sweet afterglow of their lovemaking. In the darkness, lit only by the radiance of the streetlights shining through the window, Zofia could see his profile. Suddenly she was overcome by great sadness and felt sorry for him.

"Dovid, don't fall in love with me," she said.

"What? Why do you say that?" He reached for her hand.

"Because I'm damaged. I've been hurt, and I don't think I'm capable of love anymore."

"You're too late. I'm already falling in love with you. I think of you all the time. You're the only bright light in my life."

"Dovid... Dovid..." she said and got up to walk to the window. "I don't want to hurt you."

"I would rather you hurt me than push me away."

"I don't want to do either. Can't we just be friends? No promises, no future? I can't make any promises, Dovid."

"Oh, Zofia, I don't know if we have a future, anyway. It seems as if that is not for us to decide. But for now, can't we just be happy in what we've found in each other?"

"Of course, it is for us to decide. What do you mean?"

"Zofia..." He choked on the words and had to turn to the side table where he had a glass of water. "I mean, the Nazis plan to kill us all, and they will probably succeed."

"Only if we let them," she said, her chin firm, but she felt the tears welling up in her eyes.

"You're such a fighter. I wish I had half of your courage," he said. She turned to see him smile wryly in the darkness.

"Dovid, I'm not courageous, just stubborn. I refuse to let them win. If they kill me, then they do, but I won't stop trying."

"If you won't stop trying, let yourself love me, at least. It is the least you can do for yourself, Zofia. If you can have even a little happiness, it's worth the pain."

"Dovid… Dovid…" She shook her head. She had no answer.

CHAPTER THIRTY-SEVEN

Every Friday night, Koppel still came to Zofia's apartment to wish her a good Shabbat. He insisted that she accompany him on occasional walks when he backed her against the walls of the buildings, trying to kiss and touch her. She knew better than to complain. Instead, she fended him off as gently as possible. But he didn't seem at all discouraged. In fact, the more she pushed him away, the more he wanted her.

On one such Friday night, as the women were preparing for Shabbat, Koppel arrived bearing gifts of roasted chicken wrapped in white butcher paper and fresh bread, a small box of cookies, and three oranges. It was a feast in such hard times, more delicious food than the three women had seen since they had been taken to the ghetto.

"Good Shabbat," he said.

Gitel frowned at him, but she answered. "Good Shabbat."

"Good Shabbat," Fruma said as well.

"Hello, Koppel, and good Shabbat," Zofia said. She could not help but think that the food he brought was a gift to him from the Nazis in exchange for the lives of so many poor Jewish souls. He put the food on the table. It was already set for the Shabbat.

"It's only right that you should invite me to dinner," Koppel said. "After all, I did bring the meal."

"Yes, you did," Fruma said. She was stirring a pot of soup that contained a few beans and potatoes. If Koppel had not arrived, this would have been their Shabbat dinner.

Zofia looked at the kettle that simmered softly on the stove. *At least, it was not provided by the blood of the innocents. Hold your tongue,* she told herself. *He has the power to destroy you and these two women who you care so much about.* "Of course, you are invited, Koppel," Zofia said.

"Well then, let's have dinner…" he said.

Fruma covered her head with a shawl and began lighting the candles. Then she spoke the prayers as she closed her eyes and moved her hands, pulling the smoke toward her. With a voice soft but firm, she began, *"Barukh atah Adonai, Eloheinu, melekh ha'olam.* Blessed are you, Lord, our God, sovereign of the universe…"

At the end of the prayers, there was a chorus of "Amen."

Zofia could not help but wonder what God thought of a man like Koppel, who would sacrifice his own people to save himself.

"May I do the honors?" Koppel asked as he stood up and began to carve the chicken. Once he finished, he asked each of them, "Dark or white meat?" Then he served each of them.

Zofia was hungry. It had been months since she'd had meat, but as delicious as it tasted, it stuck in her throat. She could not swallow. She drank water, and it still felt like it would not go down. Koppel didn't seem to notice. He was busy talking, doing his best to charm Fruma by telling her how beautiful the embroidery was on her Shabbat tablecloth.

"Thank you, though I must confess my eyes are old, and it is getting harder and harder to do intricate embroidery work."

"You aren't old, Fruma. You're in your prime."

"Yes, of course, Koppel," she said with a smile, unconvinced by his flattery.

After dinner, the women cleared the table. Koppel sat on the cot in the adjoining room and waited for Zofia.

Zofia and Fruma went to the room where the other family who lived with them slept. They were there. Fruma knew that they had no dinner for the Shabbat. They'd run out of rations. She offered them some of the soup she'd made. They graciously accepted.

"I'll bet they had nothing left from their rations for dinner," Zofia said.

"I know, it's hardly enough, and with a man living with them, it must be even harder to make ends meet. Men have such big appetites. They can't help that."

Once they'd finished eating, Koppel asked Zofia if she would accompany him for a walk.

"Would you like to come to my apartment?" Koppel asked as they walked down the cobblestone street.

"I don't think so, Koppel."

"You don't? It's been a long time already that we have been seeing each other. It is time, don't you agree?"

"Koppel, I am just not ready…"

"You're ready when it comes to that sniveling little idiot."

She glanced over at him quickly. What did he know? He didn't look at her, but his face burned red despite the cool wind.

"You know exactly what I am talking about. Nothing happens in this ghetto that I don't know about. I have spies everywhere. You think you're fooling me? I know about you and Dovid. It shames me, Zofia, shames me."

Her breath caught in her throat. She swallowed and choked on her saliva. As hard as she tried to contain herself, she began coughing.

"So, admit it's true. I'm not a jealous man, but I won't be taken for a fool. Do you think you can sleep with him and deny me? I have given you and your dyke friends so much. I could force you, and you would have nothing to say about it. Worse, I could sell you to every man in the ghetto if I wanted to, and you would have no one to complain to. I am *the* authority, Zofia. I make the choices. I decide who stays and who goes and don't forget it. Remember, if you get me angry enough, I could put you and your perverted little family on the next train."

She trembled. "Koppel…"

"And don't think I couldn't alert the Gestapo about you sending

Eidel out of here. They'd find her out there. Don't think they wouldn't. And they would kill her. In a second, they would kill her."

"No!" Zofia screamed.

He grabbed her shoulder and swung her around hard to face him. "Then stop playing the innocent, self-righteous bitch with me and act like you appreciate all that I have done for you."

She hated him. She could hardly look at him. He was worse than any Nazi she'd ever seen. Worse, he was a Jew, just like her, and he was worse than the persecutors.

"So enough said. You will come to my apartment, and you'll make me feel like you are grateful. Do you understand what I'm telling you?" His voice was filled with warning.

She felt the bile rise in her throat, but she nodded and followed him as he walked several paces in front of her. The wind whipped her hair into her eyes, wetting it with her tears.

CHAPTER THIRTY-EIGHT

As SHE STUMBLED back on shaky legs to her apartment, Zofia turned into an alleyway and vomited. She could still smell Koppel on her skin, and the images of what had just happened would not leave her mind. She wanted to talk to Dovid, to feel his comforting arms around her, to hear the smooth, soft lilt of his voice. What had happened with Koppel would hurt him, but he would understand. Dovid knew what it was like to be too weak and too caught in the web to fight.

It was well after dark, and she knew she should hurry home as quickly as possible, but she could not. Careful to avoid the street-lights, she slipped through the alleyways all the way to Dovid's apartment. Before she knocked on the door, she looked around to be sure she had not been followed. Then she entered the building and climbed the familiar stairs.

When she got to the apartment, she rapped softly on the door. There was no answer. She knocked harder, and still, there was no answer. Fighting the reality that slowly seeped into her mind and heart, filtering through her blood like a lethal dose of poison, she pounded her fists on the door. "Dovid! Dovid!" she called out, knowing he would not answer. Still, she hoped and prayed she was wrong. Her voice louder than she intended, she called again, "Dovid!" Still no answer. "Dovid!"

A woman wearing a loose-fitting housedress came out of the apartment next door.

"Shhhh… Quiet. The man who lived here was taken away on the transport last night. I saw the Gestapo come and get him. They dragged him outside and herded him onto a train that was leaving. I'm sorry, but you should go away from here. It's not safe."

Zofia sunk to the floor, burying her face in her hands. "My God, Dovid, what have I done to you?" Tears flooded her face as she wept, her grief pouring from her in loud, gulping sounds.

"Come in. Please, I have some tea. You are welcome to a cup."

Zofia shook her head. "No, thank you."

She felt weak, so she held on to the handle of the door of Dovid's apartment that she had entered so often in the past and used it to help herself stand.

"I'm all right," she said. "Thank you."

Her hand gripped the railing, and her knuckles turned white as she descended the stairs into the street. Her legs felt like jelly beneath her, and she thought she might drop to the ground any minute. High in a tree, a black crow let out a scream. Zofia looked up to meet its eyes. A dull pain shot through her chest, and she reached up to touch her heart.

This was Koppel's way of punishing her. Koppel had done this.

CHAPTER THIRTY-NINE

CHRISTA CHANGED KATJA'S DIAPER. Then she carried her into the kitchen, humming softly. Manfred warmed a bottle on the stove and carefully tested it on his inner wrist to be sure it was not too hot.

"She's so pretty, isn't she?" Christa said.

"She looks just like you. She has your blonde curls and your lovely skin," Manfred said, leaning over to kiss his wife.

"I am so happy that we adopted her," Christa said.

They sat on the sofa, side-by-side, while Christa fed the baby.

"The doctor says she can have more table food now."

"Pretty soon, she won't be taking the bottle at all."

"I know. I will miss her being a baby. You know, I meant to tell you that she let go of the sofa for a few steps yesterday."

"I missed her first steps?" Manfred asked.

"I'm sorry, you were at work. She walked for almost two whole steps. Then she looked at me to make sure I was watching, and it distracted her. So, she sat back on her little bum."

They both laughed. "I wish I had seen it."

"Well, no doubt she will do it again."

"Yes, and then before you know it, she'll be running."

Manfred reached up and tenderly caressed his wife's hand as she held the bottle.

"It means everything to me to see you so happy," he said.

She reached over and brushed his lips with her own.

"She'll be asleep soon," she said, a smile finding its way onto her face. Any feelings of attraction she'd thought she had for Reichsführer Himmler were gone. Motherhood suited Christa Blau.

"Yes, and then I will have you all to myself."

"I can't wait," she said.

"Me either..." He tenderly touched her cheek.

She glanced over at the roses on the mantel over the fireplace and decided that she must be the luckiest woman in the world. How many wives could say that they received roses almost every week?

CHAPTER FORTY

On Katja's third birthday, Christa and Manfred gave a small house party for the family. The only attendees were his mother and Christa's parents. They had a scrumptious dinner and a small cake.

After they had finished, Dr. Henkener stood up and apologized. He said he had to leave early to check in on a patient at the hospital.

As he was gathering his coat, the family surrounded the baby grand piano. Manfred played as everyone sang well-known German folk tunes. Christa sat cross-legged on the floor, holding Katja at the waist to secure the child, who was attempting to stand while playing with the toys she'd just received. Baby giggles filled the room, interrupting the singing, but nobody seemed to mind. They'd just enjoyed a sweet apple birthday cake, and even now, the smell of an orchard lingered behind, blending with the hearty aroma of robust South American coffee.

The sun had just descended from the sky, and the night was enfolding the city in the mysteries of her dark arms. Dr. Henkener took a last look around at his family. They were beautiful. If only Hitler had never risen to power, he would have been a happy man. But as things stood, he could not turn a blind eye. His sense of right and wrong would not allow it.

And so, Thomas Henkener left the party and made his way to his office, watching behind him with every step, careful to ensure he was not followed. A light blanket of snow covered the sidewalks, and a cold wind began to blow out of the north, freezing the snow and turning it hard. But to Thomas Henkener, the winter was a blessing. It enabled him to hide the food he carried inside the lining of his wool coat.

He'd stayed up late one-night making pockets inside the garment, secure enough to hold the packages he planned to take. Tiny particles of snow danced in the streetlamps as he hurried along. A slippery undercoat of ice was hidden beneath the powdery cover, causing the doctor to lose his footing several times. His hand clutched the building as he moved closer to his office, taking great care to stay on his feet.

Because his mind was so fixated on not falling, he never heard the soft footsteps falling behind him. When he arrived at the heavy doors to his office building, he looked around to assure himself that he was alone and then slipped inside. He wiped his shoes on the rug by the door and then turned to lock it.

Without flipping the light on, he headed toward the attic with the food he'd brought for his Jewish friends still hidden inside his coat. When he got to the end of the hall, he looked around again. In the silence, he could hear his own breathing. It was ragged and nervous. Dr. Henkener was getting older.

The flirtation with danger was too taxing for him. And yet, he must do this. The doctor removed the ladder from its secret hiding place and climbed into the attic. Then he pushed the tile out of the way and entered the attic where his friends waited. It brought a tear to his eye to see how badly in need they all were of the food he had brought.

They greeted him warmly, hugging him, thanking him, blessing him.

These were good people. Competent doctors who'd spent their entire careers saving lives. They had been reduced to this.

CHAPTER FORTY-ONE

Outside Dr. Henkener's place of work, Gestapo officers Schweissguth and Girtz watched and waited. They had been following the doctor for several weeks on a tip from one of the other tenants in his office building.

Because of the doctor's relationship with Manfred Blau, that little ass-kissing puppy of Dr. Goebbels, they had to be careful before apprehending him. If Henkener proved innocent, there would be hell to pay. Goebbels would see to that. So, they'd taken extra time, followed the doctor, and observed his every move. And now, they were pretty sure he was up to no good.

The tenant who'd called them in the first place, a dentist working only a few doors to the left of Dr. Henkener, had shown them around the building, including the location of the hidden attic, but they had not gone up yet. They could not break their cover until they could catch Dr. Henkener in the act. If they did, the old man could always claim he knew nothing about the Jews there. And because of Goebbels, he'd get away with it. They weren't going to let that happen.

Girtz knew Manfred personally. They'd gone to school together.

In Girtz's mind, Manfred was nothing but a weakling, undeserving of the position he held. Girtz despised him even more for how quickly he'd earned the favor of Goebbels. Most of the men had to go through the army and rigorous training to be accepted into the SS, but not Manfred. Somehow, he'd weaseled his way in with Goebbels.

When the news of Manfred's father-in-law possibly hiding Jews came to Girtz's attention, he wanted to make sure to trap Manfred. The task of surveillance was top secret. Girtz had been told by his superior, who was also jealous of the snot-nosed kid who'd gotten into the SS and Goebbels's office without working for it, that he must catch the doctor red-handed. Otherwise, no arrest was to be made.

If all of this worked out the way Girtz and his superior officer planned, shame would surely fall back on Manfred, who did not deserve to work beside such a high-ranking officer. Not to mention that he, Girtz, might just receive a promotion for his hard work. It was also dangerous to mess with Manfred because of his favor with Hitler himself after the failed assassination plot. Yes, it was dangerous, but even the Führer himself would not excuse the doctor for hiding Jews.

Schweissguth was Girtz's best friend. They spent time together outside work, drinking beer and dreaming of success. Just recently, Schweissguth had married. Girtz trusted Schweissguth and told him about Dr. Henkener. Schweissguth volunteered to accompany his friend on the arrest, telling Girtz that he too desperately needed a promotion since his marriage.

Now the two stood outside in the darkness, shivering with cold and anticipation with the old dentist's key to the building snug in Girtz's right pocket. His fingers fondled the key. This could be the key to his future. Girtz and Schweissguth had made arrests before, but nothing as big as this. By tomorrow morning, the entire Party, possibly Hitler himself, would know what had happened. The arrest of his father-in-law would cast doubt on Manfred's loyalty. Manfred… Goebbels's right-hand man.

They waited in the darkness for a quarter of an hour to be sure that Dr. Henkener had already gone to the attic.

Girtz and Schweissguth turned to each other. "You think it's enough time?"

"Yes. I'm sure he is there right now. If we are quick, we can catch him in that attic with those Jews."

Girtz nodded. His hand shook as he put the key in the lock, turning it and changing everything in Manfred's life forever.

The two Gestapo agents quietly made their way into the building. They dragged their feet to prevent the marble floor from clicking beneath their shoes. When they got to the secret door that opened into the attic, Schweissguth climbed the ladder and pushed the ceiling tile.

Perle Shulman saw them first. She screamed, and her hand went to her lips. *"OY! Got in Himmel!"* she cried. God in heaven!

"Gestapo!" Girtz bellowed.

With guns drawn, the two SS officers entered the attic. Perle Shulman clutched her husband, who turned toward her, taking her into his arms. When he saw the two men, Dr. Shulman gasped softly. "*Oy*, dear God."

Zalman Rosen stood gripping the small table, his knuckles white, his face a pale mask. Bluma, his wife, began to cry.

Thomas Henkener stood paralyzed, staring at the two young men in long, black leather coats.

"You are under arrest, all of you. That goes for you, also, Dr. Henkener. I am sure you knew that it was a crime against the Reich, treason, to hide Jews," Girtz said.

The loaf of bread and hunk of cheese that Dr. Henkener brought stood in the middle of the table, untouched. Henkener looked at the food, then his eyes drifted to the two men.

"You boys should be ashamed of yourselves," Dr. Henkener said.

Girtz took his gun and cracked it across Dr. Henkener's face. Blood spurted from the doctor's nose, landing on the opposite wall.

Thomas Henkener winced.

"That should shut you up. Now let's go, quickly."

The Gestapo loaded all five people into a waiting automobile. The Jews would be transported to Gestapo Headquarters and then to a camp for extermination. Henkener would face a worse fate. Before they were slaughtered, Girtz and Schweissguth would see to it that Manfred was knocked off his pedestal and brought to his knees.

CHAPTER FORTY-TWO

THE PHONE RANG AT HALF past midnight. Christa jumped out of bed. A late-night call could only mean one of her parents was ill. As she picked up the receiver, Manfred appeared at her side, pushing the hair out of his face.

"Hello," she said.

"I need to speak to Manfred. This is Dr. Goebbels."

"One moment, please..." she said to the caller, then turning to Manfred, she handed him the phone. "It's Dr. Goebbels."

Goebbels? At this time of night? "Hello, Doctor," he said into the receiver. "This is Manfred."

"You must meet me at the office immediately. There is a serious problem."

"I will be right there."

Manfred hung up the phone.

"What did he want at this time of night?" Christa asked.

"I don't know," Manfred said as he dressed quickly.

"Be careful, my darling. Don't drive too fast."

He leaned over and kissed her. "Go back to bed. I will be home as soon as I can," he said. Then he left, quietly closing the door.

Manfred's hands trembled as he drove through the sleeping city. Almost no cars were on the road, and only a few people walked the sidewalks. For the most part, darkness surrounded him, save only small illuminations from the streetlamps.

His mind raced. Why would Goebbels be calling him at this time of night? What could be happening that could not wait until morning? Perhaps it was a personal problem. Lately, Dr. Goebbels had begun to discuss his personal problems with Manfred. Would he call at this time of night for something of that nature? Or perhaps Hitler was making a surprise visit, and the doctor wanted everything to go well. Maybe something had happened to Hitler. That would be terrible. Manfred pressed the gas, moving the automobile faster down the road.

Manfred parked his car in front of the door and went inside. The entire structure was dark except for one dim light in Goebbels's office. Manfred entered.

"Dr. Goebbels, you wanted to see me?"

"Yes. Your father-in-law was arrested tonight for hiding Jews in the attic of his office building. The Gestapo are on their way to arrest your mother-in-law. They would have come for you and your wife if not for my intervention. This is serious, Manfred. This is treason."

Manfred sunk into the chair opposite Goebbels. "I had no idea, none."

"I knew that. That's why I intervened. But things are going to get very ugly."

My wife? My career? Manfred was in a state of panic. "I had nothing to do with this, Doctor. I swear it, on my life, on my wife's life. Neither of us knew."

Goebbels lit a cigarette. "Your father-in-law has done a terrible thing. He's broken the Nuremberg laws. I won't be able to keep you here at the office. If it had not been for your part in uncovering the assassination attempt on the Führer, I might not have been able to keep you from being arrested. Because of this, you must prove your loyalty to the Fatherland."

"But you know me, sir. You know I am devoted heart and soul to Hitler and the cause."

"I do know this. Still, there is much that is not under my control. The chances are good that you will be taken in for questioning."

"What can I do? Help me, sir, please help me."

Dr. Goebbels rubbed his chin. The minister of propaganda was lost in thought. He got up and looked out the window. For several moments, he was silent. Manfred felt like his heart would jump out of his chest and lie bleeding on the floor.

Finally, Joseph Goebbels turned to Manfred. "I have an idea."

"Sir?" Manfred said. Hope rose with his heartbeat.

"I will stand by you, but sadly, I think I must ask you to do something that will be very difficult for you," Goebbels said, taking a long drag on his cigarette.

"Anything, anything at all. Just ask."

"You must show your devotion to the Party by executing Dr. Henkener. You will be the one to fire the shot. Your wife must be present to witness the execution of the traitor. Manfred, you must kill your wife's father. He must die at your hand. This and only this will prove your loyalty."

Manfred gasped. He hung his head. He did not care much for Thomas Henkener, but he knew Christa would be devastated. Would she ever forgive him? He put his hands to his temples and squeezed.

"My wife… She will never forgive me."

"She should be thankful that she is not being arrested and sent to a camp. She must be made to understand the seriousness of all of this. Her father is a traitor. Either way, he will be destroyed. If you are the one to complete the task, things will be better for both of you. You realize that you, too, are at risk here. If it is somehow suspected that you are a traitor, you could easily face execution yourself. Now I've come up with an idea that I believe will work. But you must do as I say."

Manfred's head was spinning. He felt himself falling, plummeting from his high position to a slave in a concentration camp. Damn his father-in-law. Damn him to hell for this.

"I'll do it," Manfred said. He'd never killed anyone. Just the idea was horrifying. And now, he had to kill his wife's father. There was simply no refusing.

CHAPTER FORTY-THREE

CHRISTA WAS awake when Manfred turned the key in the door and walked into the house. She was sitting on the edge of an overstuffed chair in the living room. When he entered, she jumped to her feet.

"Manfred, what is going on here? My mother just called. My father went to the office earlier, and he has not returned. She is frantic."

"Yes," Manfred said, but he could not meet her eyes. Instead, he walked to the window and faced away from her.

"What is happening? Please tell me." Christa ran to him and put her arm around his waist. "Manfred, talk to me. Please…"

He took a deep breath and then turned to face her. She looked at him pleading, her eyes swollen from crying.

"Has my father been in an accident? Is he…?"

"Christa." He cleared his throat. "Your father has been arrested by the Gestapo for hiding Jews in the attic of his office building. When did you last speak to your mother?"

"Over an hour ago, I told her I would call her back as soon as you came home."

"She has probably been arrested. She is most likely already at headquarters for questioning."

"Mama? For what?"

"It is really your father they are after. They know he committed this crime. But I believe your mother will probably be released after questioning."

"Can you help Papa? Please? You must, Manfred. You have lots of important friends. Do something…" She began shaking him, tears threatening to fall from her eyes. Her face was blotchy, and he could see that she was terrified.

He shook his head. His shoulders slumped. "I can't do anything. I tried. The only thing I can do now, at this point, is to try to save your mother, you, and myself."

"And Papa?"

"I'm sorry." He looked away.

"Sorry?" she raised her voice in pitch and volume. "Manfred, please! Manfred, he is my father."

"He is a traitor. Look what he has done to me, to us? How dare he put all of us in this position! Whatever happens to him, he deserves it."

"And what will that be, Manfred?" she asked, her voice cracking. "What will that be?" She grabbed him, spinning him toward her.

"I don't know," he said, turning away again. "But whatever it is, he deserves it."

For the first time since they were married, Manfred and Christa slept apart. He went to the guest room, where he sat up trying to devise a plan, and she lay in their bed staring at the ceiling until the sun rose.

By morning, Manfred felt as if he might collapse with exhaustion. He walked slowly to the kitchen. With every step, his heavy heart was torn with grief for his wife.

The baby was in her highchair, playing with a toy. Christa did not turn to look at him as he entered. She filled a pot with water for coffee and then cut two thick slices of bread for his toast. Watching her do this daily, a common act, almost brought tears to his eyes. He wanted to get up, take her into his arms, and beg her forgiveness.

The last person on this earth he would ever want to hurt was his beloved Christa. Everything he did, he had done for her to woo, win, and build their lives together. But now, should he refuse to carry out the dreadful task Goebbels demanded of him, they would all be sent to a camp. Even Christa, delicate Christa… She would die if exposed to a work camp's harsh conditions. He must do as Goebbels asked. But how could he ever make her understand?

Gingerly, he walked up behind her and put his arms around her small waist. "I'm sorry," he said.

She turned around. "Me, too." There were tears in her eyes.

He kissed her.

"Then you will help Papa?" she asked.

"Christa, if I could help him, I would, but I can't. He has destroyed himself, and if we don't turn away from him, he will take all of us right down with him. I can't bear the thought of you in a camp."

"They would do that to us? To you, after you have been such a loyal party member?"

"The Nazi Party is hard to explain. It is filled with treachery. Goebbels is my friend, yes, but I must still be careful. Everyone is always a suspect. If they can prove that I knew about your father's activities, we are all doomed."

"But you didn't."

"That doesn't matter, Christa. If they think I am taking his side in any way, all of us will be finished."

"I don't care if they fire you. I would rather that you cleaned the streets than worked for a man who would not stand by you when you need him."

"Silly girl, I wish that was all there was to it. The Nazi officials will do far more than that. They may even execute all of us. You don't realize what they are capable of," he said, wanting to shake her until she saw the truth.

"So, what will they do to Mama and Papa? Dear God, Manfred, did you know they were so terrible?"

"What difference does it make what I knew or what I didn't know? All I know is that your father has proven himself a traitor to the Party, and now we must all pay a dear price."

She struggled away from him. "Who were the Jews he was hiding?"

"I don't have any idea. What difference does it make? A Jew is a Jew; you don't hide Jews from the government. It's against the law. Your father broke the law."

"I think I know who it was. Dr. Shulman."

"So, what difference does that make to us? Why should I give a damn about Dr. Shulman? He's a Jew, and that makes him a problem."

"Because he saved my life when I was just a little girl. I have a heart condition. I would have been dead long ago if it weren't for him."

She picked up a dish towel and began wiping the counter. "Christa, I am sorry. I understand why your father did what he did. But you must understand that if we don't turn away from him, there will be no way out for us. If he must go down, then at least you and your mother will be saved. It is better than nothing."

She hung her head and wept.

Manfred grabbed his coat off the coatrack. He couldn't bear to be in that house any longer. He'd get something to eat at the restaurant next to his office.

"Please, Christa, try to understand. I am going to work now. Let me do what I can. I will check on your mother and call you as soon as I know anything."

"Don't let them hurt her, Manfred. Please. Oh, dear God!" she cried. "My Papa! My sweet, gentle Papa!"

Manfred left as quickly as possible, closing the door behind him.

CHAPTER FORTY-FOUR

WHEN HE ARRIVED at the office, his co-workers, usually so eager to win his friendship, were cool but polite. But more importantly, Joseph Goebbels did not extend his usual luncheon invitation.

Manfred sat in his office working quietly, feeling disconnected from the world where he'd grown comfortable. He could muster no appetite for his afternoon meal.

As the day progressed, his resentment toward Dr. Henkener grew. All that he'd built and strived for seemed to be sifting through his fingertips like sand at the ocean and through no fault of his own. Damn his father-in-law. No matter what Manfred tried to do, this crack in the foundation of his character would strangle his rise to success.

He'd been drawing with a charcoal pencil and didn't realize he'd broken it in two. Right then, he could kill Dr. Henkener with his bare hands. Everything was gone in a single, careless moment. What a fool Henkener had proven to be. If not for Christa, it would be a pleasure to make him pay for what he'd done. Manfred imagined standing over his father-in-law and kicking him, then choking the very life from the man.

At the end of the day, Manfred waited, hoping Joseph Goebbels would call him into his office for an after-hours sip of schnapps, a common occurrence, but Goebbels never asked.

Manfred walked into his house to find his mother-in-law and wife huddled together, waiting for him. The baby sat on a blanket in the middle of the floor, playing with a stuffed rabbit. Christa ran to him as soon as he put his briefcase on the dining room table. She threw her arms around him.

"Have you heard any news about Papa?"

He stood staring at her, his arms at his side. "I told you. We won't hear anything about your father. He is dead to us."

"Manfred, please. You have so many friends. You must do something to help him. I'm begging you."

"Christa, I can't help him. And furthermore, now we are all in trouble. I will be lucky if I can save the three of us. Your father was selfish and inconsiderate. What he did has put our entire family in jeopardy." Manfred's voice was harsh and unforgiving.

Katja began to cry. Frau Henkener reached down and lifted the child into her arms. Still, Katja cried.

"Manfred, you mean to say that we will never see Thomas again?" Frau Henkener asked.

"Yes, that is exactly what I am telling you."

"Oh, God! My husband!" Heidi Henkener got up from the sofa and handed the baby to her daughter. She walked toward her son-in-law, her arms outstretched and pleading. "Manfred, is there nothing at all…?"

"No, there is nothing to be done. I'm sorry," he said and walked into his bedroom. Then he sat down on the bed and put his head in his hands, squeezing his temples forcefully as he listened to the weeping coming from the living room.

CHAPTER FORTY-FIVE

Dr. Henkener looked like an old man. His body was bent, with a mass of gray, unshaven hair covering his face as he stood against the wall awaiting the shot that would end his life. His eyes met his daughter's, who stood with her arm around her mother. He gave her a wink and a reassuring smile.

Then an armed guard escorted Manfred outside. From where Christa stood, she could see her husband's hands shaking. Goebbels stood on the other side of the field, wearing a grave expression. She saw him look at Manfred and nod. Manfred raised the pistol, his hands trembling so badly he almost dropped it.

Heidi Henkener reached for her daughter's hand and held it so tight that her nails began to penetrate Christa's flesh. For a moment, Christa thought Manfred would refuse to fire the shot. Not that it would save her father, she knew. He would die today, by either her husband's hand or that of another SS officer. Dr. Henkener would not leave this field alive. Christa longed to see Manfred's eyes, but he would not look at her. Instead, he kept his gaze forward, firm with the task at hand.

The shot rang out. Manfred had missed his target. He looked around frantically until his eyes met Goebbels's. Goebbels nodded, and Manfred took aim. He used two hands to steady himself. Then he fired. The second bullet found Thomas Henkener. He crumpled to the ground, blood flowing from his chest. Christa and her mother ran to him as Manfred was led away, the pistol still hot in his hand.

When Manfred arrived home that night, Christa could not bear to look at her husband. He'd explained why he had no choice but to do what he did that day. He'd told her over and over that if he did not follow through with the execution, it would not have saved her father. He would have still been shot, but then Manfred's loyalty would have been questioned, and the rest of them would suffer as well. He did it for her, he said. Christa held Katja close to her heart. The warmth of the baby against her body gave her comfort. Katja reached up, her tiny fingers tangling in Christa's hair as the tears flowed down Christa's cheeks.

There was no dinner prepared. She had forgotten. Manfred said nothing. He looked around, assessing the situation: mother, child, and the room in shambles. There was nothing left to say. He went to his bed and lay down. Christa sat holding Katja until well into the dark of night. The baby slept in her arms. Had she forgotten to feed her? She could not remember. Several hours later, Katja stirred. Christa put her down on a blanket, and with unsteady hands, she began to warm the bottle.

CHAPTER FORTY-SIX

For over an hour past curfew, Zofia walked the forbidden streets. Dovid's love for her would destroy him, all because of Koppel's jealousy. Her feelings for Dovid were not love, but he was a good friend, and she could not help but be touched by his gentle soul. In fact, she might have married him. It amazed her that he loved her as much as he did. Now it broke her heart to know that he sat imprisoned on a train on the way to some horrific destination because he'd given her his heart and soul.

She felt physically ill. Because of Dovid's fragile nature, it was doubtful he could endure what awaited him. She was angry at Koppel, so angry she could kill him. She was also angry at herself and the world. Helpless, she wrapped her arms around herself and looked up at the sky. If only she could do something to save Dovid. But what? She wished she could go to Koppel and plunge a knife deep into his chest. A shiver ran down her spine, and she trembled. What had she become? A murderess?

At least Eidel was safe, far away from the ghetto. Thank God for Helen taking her and Karl Abendstern for getting her out. At least her child would know peace, even if she would not.

To go home and try to rest was futile. Even though he had the power to destroy her, she must confront Koppel.

The cold air rushed at her as she ran to the building where Koppel lived. Her cheeks were stained with tears, her face windburned, and her nose was running from the chill.

Koppel answered the door to his apartment in his undershorts and white undershirt. With his disheveled hair, it appeared as if he'd been asleep.

"To what do I owe this pleasure?" he said, half-smiling.

Zofia burst through the door. "What did you do?"

"Hold on a minute, you little spitfire. What do you mean? What did I do?" His mood instantly changed.

"You know what I mean. Where is Dovid?"

"Oh, your boyfriend?" he asked, closing the door behind her and sitting on a chair. "You mean the weakling who you were unfaithful to me with? You little ingrate, I got rid of him. I suppose you thought his Jewish Council contact who sold his paintings would protect him?"

He retrieved a switchblade knife from the counter, switched it open, and stabbed it into the table. "His contact, Joel Günzburg, was found with this knife in his back early this morning. One of your Zionist Jews murdered him. The Polish Police had already arrested the killer and turned them over to the Gestapo. Anyway, your sissy little boyfriend is gone."

"Koppel, did you think we were in a serious relationship, that I was not keeping company with anyone else? Nothing I ever said could have made you believe that. Now just look at what you have done, Koppel. You've sentenced an innocent man to God only knows what kind of torture." Her voice cracked as she watched him sitting there, unmoved. "But then again, I should have expected as much from a weasel like you. You're a coward, Koppel, nothing but a coward. How can you call yourself a man when you can easily sell your people to save yourself? You disgust me."

Something she said touched a nerve. He stood up, grabbed her arm, squeezing hard, and jerked her in front of him. Then he pointed his finger right in her face and said, "Listen to me, you are lucky I like you or your sweet little ass would be on the next transport. Don't push me, Zofia. I'm warning you."

"And what do you think, Koppel? Do you think that you're different from the rest of us? You're a Jew, nothing but a Jew, just like all the rest of us. When the Nazis are done with you, you'll go to the same place you're sending all the rest. The only difference is that you won't be able to turn to God for help."

"There is no God, Zofia. Haven't you realized that yet? Look around you. The starvation, the sickness, the death… and the Jews are supposed to be God's chosen people. Chosen for what? If you consider everything around you, you can't continue to believe in God. You can't believe in anything but yourself."

"You're a cruel and terrible man, Koppel, but you'll see. You will be cursed. I know it. You will pay for your actions, for your treatment of others."

"Shut up, Zofia. Shut up, now!" He slammed her against the wall. She hit the side of her face on a shelf, and her teeth felt as if they had loosened in her gums.

"Are you afraid my words have a ring of truth to them?" she asked, glaring at him.

He looked into her eyes, which burned with hatred and accusation. Zofia reached to grab the knife stuck in the table, and Koppel backhanded her with all his body weight, causing her to fall to the floor like a rag doll.

"You test me, bitch. Get up. Get out right now and never come back. I never want to see you again."

She arose, wiping the blood from her mouth. He grabbed her arm again, and she winced at the pain. Then he opened the door and threw her out into the street. She fell on the sidewalk, skinning her knee and elbow.

"Never come near me again. You hear me? Never!" He slammed the door. He removed the knife stuck on the table and folded it back up. He never liked Joel Günzburg anyway. It had been easy to kill him and blame it on the Jewish boyfriend of one of his working girls. His angry expression changed to one of smug satisfaction.

Zofia lay on the sidewalk, trembling. Her arm and her knee hurt, and her mouth was bleeding. She reached up and touched her cheek. It was tender and aching. There would be a dark-purple bruise by morning.

She got to her feet and realized her stockings had torn when she fell. Straightening her clothes, she began to walk home. Guilt haunted her. If Dovid died, she would never forgive herself, not that she would ever know. How would she know? People got on those transports and were never heard from again. Knowing Koppel's cruel streak and abuse of power, she should have kept her distance from Dovid. Was she so stupid that she'd not known it must end this way?

Zofia was grateful to find Fruma and Gitel asleep when she got home. Quietly, she cleaned the blood from her injuries and lay down on her cot. Although her body ached with exhaustion, she could not sleep. Her mind continued to race.

It came as no surprise to Zofia. In fact, she was expecting it: the knock on the door in the middle of the night and the deep voice bellowing, "Gestapo! Open the door!"

What did come as a surprise was that Zofia expected they would only come for her. She was wrong. Again, she must shoulder the burden of guilt. Those who loved her would suffer for her harsh words to Koppel. Zofia felt the tears rain down upon her cheeks, but it was not for herself that she cried. Again, she'd brought suffering to those who loved her.

Zofia went first. Then she watched Gitel and Fruma as the men pushed them into the backseat of the waiting automobile. Once they were inside, with the doors locked, the three women sat in silence as the car headed toward the transport station. The dawn broke just as they arrived at the cattle cars.

Nazi SS stood around the lines of people. They carried guns, pointed and ready to kill. Women holding babies, men bent with age, young and old, male and female, some crying, others stone-faced. They all just stood, waiting, hoping, praying, and wondering where they were headed.

Zofia looked around her, sickened at the scene. Two women sat at a table, handing out single slices of bread with jam to placate the people as they entered the cattle car. Hordes of those nearly starving waited in line for food. They then followed like sheep as they were pushed into the closed cattle cars.

In the corner sat Koppel, eating and watching. When Zofia's eyes met his, he smiled, and she swore she had come face-to-face with the Devil. Because he'd touched her in that way, her body now repulsed her. Never before had she felt such hatred for another living thing. If she had another night alone with him in his bed, she would wait until he fell asleep, and then she would take a kitchen knife and plunge it deep into his black heart.

"*Mach schnell!*" a guard yelled at Zofia, causing her to realize she'd been standing and staring. He gave her a shove, and she fell forward into the line. Fruma put her hand out and took Zofia into the fold of her arm. Gitel held up on the other side, and the three friends entered the boxcar.

Once the cattle car was filled wall-to-wall, standing room only, so tightly that the prisoners were pressed into one another, with wretched, frightened people, a guard slammed the door, obliterating all light. Darkness hovered over them like a shroud. The smell of fear, mingled with vomit, filled the air as the train rattled into motion. A baby wailed in its mother's arms. Its piercing cries sent shivers through Zofia as she tried not to think of Eidel. The train chugged along the track. It was known in the ghetto that the Warsaw Jews were all transported to Treblinka, only fifty-five miles away. *At least the trip would not be long*, Zofia thought. Zofia didn't know how long she could endure the stuffy, overcrowded cattle car.

Thirty minutes into the trip, an explosion from the engine car rocked the entire train. The brakeman stopped the train, which came to an ear-splitting, screeching halt. Inside Zofia's car, the passengers, already frightened and on edge, began inquiring of each other about what had happened.

The German guards bailed out of the train and investigated the damage. "Keep watch over the prisoners," Unterscharführer Kaufman said as he raced to the engine car with his machine gun ready, expecting possible Jewish sabotage. He arrived to see the devastation.

The steam boiler had exploded, destroying the entire engine car. He peered inside and saw what was left of the burned bodies of the engineer and the laborer who shoveled coal to the burner. The smell of burning flesh was all-too familiar to an SS soldier who had seen action in the invasion of Poland. *You never quite get used to that smell*, he thought. The fire from the explosion caught fire to some of the coal in the coal tender car. He jumped into the car and kicked the coal out on the ground to keep the fire from spreading. He immediately assessed the threat situation.

The Jews must be secured at any cost, and he must radio back to Warsaw. He was not going to make a mistake. His career was riding on thin ice. He had been caught raping a young Jewish woman by his commander when they invaded Poland. His commander was willing to forgive his indiscretion—if he killed her. After buttoning up his pants, he put a bullet into her head. Still, it was a black mark on his record, and he got this crap detail as soon as the camp was opened. He found his four men outside the cattle cars with weapons drawn and the Jews locked up tightly.

"*Sturmmann* Schröder, continue to secure the Jews. It was apparently a mechanical failure. It does not appear to be sabotage but keep alert in case it is a clever Jewish trick. I will call Warsaw to get further orders," the sergeant said.

"Yes, sir."

Since the radio had been destroyed in the explosion, the sergeant went to a farmhouse close by and called the SS train station in Warsaw.

"Heil Hitler," the lieutenant answered in a detached and rather bothered tone.

"Heil Hitler. This is *Unterscharführer* Kaufman on the train to Treblinka that left this morning," responded the sergeant.

"This is *Untersturmführer* Klausen. What is the problem?"

"The steam boiler exploded, and the train is completely stopped. The engineer and his helper were killed. We have secured the Jews. What are our orders?"

"Are there dual or switching tracks where you have broken down?"

"No, sir."

"Is the coal tender car damaged, too?"

"Yes, sir."

"First, we will send a crane to remove the two cars from the track, probably late today. Then we will send a new engine car and tender car with an engineer and helper. Unfortunately, that will be a couple of days. All available engine cars are being used right now to move weapons, fuel, and food for military purposes, and they take priority over your miserable Jews."

"We do not have food or water for the prisoners. It was supposed to be an hour-long trip."

The lieutenant's laugh was cold as ice and hard as obsidian. "What does it matter if they die in your train or if they die at Treblinka? Jews are Jews, and they will all die soon enough. Do not let a single one escape. There will be hell to pay if you do!"

"Yes, sir, *Untersturmführer.*"

The lieutenant hung up the phone, ran his fingers through his dark-brown hair, and decided that the Jews suffering in the hot train without food or water was a bonus. He put his hat back on and smiled. *Most of the Jews will be dead by the time they arrive. There really was a silver lining to every cloud.*

The soldiers rationed what little food or water they had among themselves, keeping vigilant guard in shifts while the Jews were left with nothing, crammed as tightly as sardines in the hot cattle cars.

One of the Jews in the second car who spoke German had overheard the sergeant explaining what happened to his corporal. He passed the word in Polish, which was shouted from car to car until everyone knew the situation.

Just before two o'clock, three trucks with a crane in pieces on flatbeds arrived.

"I can hear the men talking. The crew of the big machine is Polish." one prisoner said. "They are moving the damaged cars off of the track."

"We will get water soon, maybe?" a woman asked. Most of

them remained silent, dejected by what seemed to be a hopeless situation.

A crew of fifteen men put the crane together, and the crane removed the damaged engine car from the track and the coal tender car.

There had been a pail in the front of the car to use as a makeshift bathroom and a water bucket, but the prisoners were packed so tightly that none could access them. Men, women, and children urinated on themselves and soiled their clothing. By the next day, the smell of human excrement overpowered Zofia.

It caused many prisoners to vomit, which only added to the stench. Others vomited because of the smell of the first. Several times Zofia felt as if she might faint.

No fresh air entered the stifling hot train car that felt like an already-buried casket. Bathed in sweat, she had never been so thirsty. Her throat felt sore and gravelly, like sandpaper. How long had it been since they left Warsaw? Two days? That was the last time she'd had a sip of water.

After a time, the baby who had been crying grew silent. Zofia knew it was dead. Thank God Eidel was not there. At least, somewhere, Eidel was safe.

She fell asleep on occasion, and the days passed from night to day again. The sick, old, and very young started dying. Unable to fall, their bodies were held upright in a tight press. The smell of decaying flesh only added to the misery of the smells of vomit, feces, urine, and sweat.

When she felt as though she might die from the heat and thirst, Zofia heard a train coming. Then she heard the sound of an engine car with its coal tender car moving up to the rear of the train, then coupling up with it. The steam engine hissed for a couple of minutes, and then the engineer blew the whistle, and the sound of choo-choo-choo hissing as the train took on a rhythmic beat as it headed to Hell, their new destination. In less than an hour, they arrived at the Treblinka Work Camp. Thrown forward, the passengers fell upon each other as their hearts trembled with the terror of what might be waiting outside the door.

A voice on a loudspeaker greeted them before the cattle car doors were opened. "This is a work camp. You Jews may want to die, but you will work." The Nazis used a mixture of hope and fear to control the prisoners.

From inside, Zofia saw the Nazi guards yelling and commanding as they opened each train car. Then came a loud clanging as the lock released and the train door opened. After over two days in near darkness, the light hurt Zofia's eyes. Her limbs felt numb from lack of movement, and she was filthy from urinating in and soiling her clothes. She stood, paralyzed, dizzy, and looked around her. As the prisoners left the car, the pressure holding the bodies upright was lessened, and the dead dropped, and Zofia stepped over the bodies and left the car.

As she exited the car, she saw a doctor lifting a right or left thumb as each prisoner passed, and the guards pushed them in the direction the doctor indicated. She had no idea what it meant to go right or left.

Zofia inhaled deeply of the first fresh air she had breathed in days. *But what was that stench?*

Once the train was unloaded of its living passengers, the doors were closed again, and the train continued east of the camp and stopped next to a stinking, smoldering pit.

The new *Arbeitsführer* was scheduled to arrive at any time. The ranking SS officer at the camp nodded to the sergeant and ordered a head count and roll taken. The live head count would be added to the dead count and compared to the head count that left Warsaw.

She never saw the guard as he came up behind her, hitting her across the back with a club.

"Move! *Schnell*! Get in line."

The pain shot through her as she fell forward. He raised the club to strike her again, and she quickly got into the line. Fruma came up behind her with Gitel. Fruma appeared pale and weak.

"My God, there you are. We've been looking everywhere for you. I was frantic."

"I'm sorry. I was…"

"Shut up, Jew. No talking," a guard said in broken Polish.

Taking the queue from the doctor, a tall, white-haired man said in Polish, "Left, right, left, right," directing the prisoners.

"What does this mean? Some go left and others, right?" Zofia asked no one in particular.

"It means that some live, and some die," a middle-aged woman with a red rash on her face answered. "Look like you are strong and like you can work. If they think you are too weak to work, they will send you directly to the gas chamber. You see that line? They tell everyone in the line that they must take a shower. That line leads to the shower. It is a huge room. Everyone is forced to go in at once. Then, just as you think they are going to turn on the water, water isn't what comes out. It's gas, and everyone that is inside is murdered."

Zofia looked at Fruma and Gitel. Both were pale, but Fruma vomited while they were in line to be viewed by the doctor. She was suffering from severe dehydration.

"Where did you hear such a thing? Would they really kill us, just like that?" Fruma asked, looking pale.

Zofia found it hard to believe.

"Don't ask questions. I heard it in the ghetto from someone who escaped this place. For now, just look strong and healthy. Your life depends upon it."

"Shut up, I told you. Keep moving," the guard said as he cracked the club across the middle-aged woman's shoulder. She winced and then fell silent.

"Right," he said to Gitel.

"Right," he said to Zofia.

"Left," he said to Fruma.

"No!" Gitel yelled. "No! We must stay together!" She grabbed Fruma's arm and held on to it. "Please, have mercy," Gitel said to the guard. The guard clubbed her elbow, and her hand released. Another SS officer pushed Fruma forward into the line to the left. "I can't let her go, not all alone. We lived together. It's only right we should go to wherever this line leads together. Goodbye, Zofia. If my Fruma must die, then I, too, must die," Gitel said, and she ran after Fruma, taking her hand. Zofia watched as they were forced, at gunpoint, to stay in the line to the left.

"Fruma! Gitel!" Zofia shouted as loud as she could. Then Zofia felt a deep jab in her stomach. Clutching her stomach, she leaned forward in pain, only to look up and see the pressed black uniform of an SS officer.

Tears stung her eyes. She wanted to lie on the ground and weep. Fruma... Gitel... She cried out like an animal that had been shot by a hunter and left to die in pain. She wanted to run after them, to end all of this misery, but she must not. Someday she would leave this place and go home to Eidel. For Eidel, she must fight to live.

The line to the left moved quickly, and Zofia lost sight of her friends within minutes. *I am alone.* None of the women who stood in line with Zofia were elderly or carried babies. Most of those had died during the trip. Those that did not were chosen to go left. The men were all of working age, and there were no children. Those had all been filtered out. Only the young and strong remained.

The others moved in the line, headed quickly toward extermination. Once the smell of the bodies from the pits reached them, the prisoners knew they were assigned to Hell. When the realization set in, some male prisoners resisted and were clubbed down by the Nazi guards, taken to the barbed-wire fence, and shot.

This seemed too much for a young girl with fiery curls that flowed down her back, and she became gripped by panic. She began screaming and ran out of the line, heading full force toward the barbed wire.

Two Nazi officers stood within hearing distance from where Zofia was.

"Shoot her," the older man said concerning the redhead.

The younger one, a slight man in his early thirties, looked at him blankly.

"Shoot her, I said."

From where she stood, Zofia could see his hands trembling as he took aim. He fired a shot at the girl but missed. The older guard turned to a lesser guard. "Bring that little slut here, schnell."

Two guards pulled the girl by her arms and dropped her in front of the SS officers. Her red hair spilled like blood around her.

"That Juden slut isn't worth another bullet. Beat her to death. Make an example of her for the rest of these trollops so they don't get any brilliant ideas of escaping," the one in charge ordered. The other SS officer looked at him, bewildered, as if in disbelief. "Are you a weakling—a coward?"

The younger man shook his head. "No. Of course not."

"You are a soldier in Hitler's army. Your duty is to save the German race. Now act like it."

The SS officer set his chin, nodded his head, but did not look at the girl as he raised his club.

In the line to the left, Fruma and Gitel held hands.

Over the loudspeaker came a male voice. It said, "Fold your clothes and put them into a pile before you enter the showers. Remember where you put them so that you can find them again when you come back out."

"You see, if they meant to kill us, then they wouldn't tell us to remember where we put our clothing," Gitel said.

Fruma smiled a wry, sad smile and patted Gitel's hand. "We are together, and that's all that matters."

"Do you think they mean to kill us?" Gitel asked.

"Of course not," Fruma said, her voice soft and comforting. "Of course not, my love." Again, she smiled at Gitel and touched her cheek. Then Fruma looked ahead of her at all the people in line, all the people who would never return from the showers, to find those neat little piles of clothing. Fruma had no illusions. She knew where she and Gitel were headed, but at least they were going together.

CHAPTER FORTY-SEVEN

"MANFRED, YOU DID WHAT WAS NECESSARY," Joseph Goebbels said.

"My wife is taking it hard."

"He was a traitor to the Fatherland. She should realize how fortunate she is that I was able to help you both, or you both would have been severely disciplined. All of you, your mother-in-law included, might have been sent to a camp."

"Yes, I know, and I am grateful to you."

They sat in Dr. Goebbels's office, looking over the busy street.

"I am afraid that there is another part to this tragedy. You are to be transferred out of this office. The orders come from higher up and must be carried out."

"Transferred? I thought I was doing a good job."

"Yes, but this mess with your father-in-law has made you suspect. The Party demands that you prove yourself further."

"Where am I going?"

"To a camp, I'm sorry to say. It's nasty business there. You are going to be the *Arbeitsführer* at Treblinka."

"The work boss? Why? I have no experience with such things. Don't these workers work out in the sun all day? I suppose I would have to be with them, driving them forward through force."

"Yes, I am afraid so. Don't try to refuse this, Manfred. I tell you as a friend. You must take this assignment. And you must do an excellent job. Show no weakness, no mercy. Constantly reaffirm your loyalty to the Party and the Fatherland."

"Dr. Goebbels, I am not a physical man."

"I realize this, but you must follow orders. We all must. It is the only way to keep the Reich strong."

"Where is this camp Treblinka?"

"It is in Poland."

"Poland? Where am I to live?"

"You and your family will be given a residence near the camp. You may take a prisoner or two as servants to help you around the house."

Manfred sighed. He put his hands on his temples.

"If I refuse?"

"You must not. I strongly recommend that you do as you are told."

"I trust you, Doctor. You have been a friend and a mentor to me. I will do as they ask, although I will miss it here. When am I leaving?"

"The end of next week. You will not report to work here anymore. Take the two weeks and settle your affairs. Pack and prepare for your new position."

Manfred's face dropped. He would never return to the office of the Ministry of Enlightenment and Propaganda. He would never sit in his office or have lunch with Joseph Goebbels again. There would be no more exciting parties to attend where he was a part of something bigger, a part of the new Germany. He was headed to some camp in Poland, where he had to herd Jews and other monsters like cattle. Dr. Henkener had done this to him.

"Keep in touch, Manfred," Joseph Goebbels said as he stood up, opening the door to his office, indicating that the meeting was over.

Manfred felt as if his entire world had just crumbled. He walked back to his office, dazed. He collected his things, a picture from his wedding, another of Christa holding Katja, and then the one where he stood beside Goebbels as Hitler shook his hand.

An *Arbeitsführer*, the work boss. What could that entail? Nothing good. Manfred imagined himself standing out in the hot sun or rain, ordering a group of wretched prisoners smelling of sweat. Worse yet, he would sweat in his uniform, filthy like a pig. No more would he enjoy lunches with Joseph or parties with high officials. No, he was to be a part of the nasty Final Solution, that dirty business of blood and dead bodies.

Again, he was angry with his father-in-law, but his anger was always overshadowed by the sound that filled his ears at the frightening moment when he fired the shot that ended the man's life. At night, in dreams that were so vivid they woke him up with a start, he heard that ringing in his ears and saw Dr. Henkener fall, again and again, into a pool of blood. These dreams were so real that he felt the cold steel of the pistol in his right hand, his hand trembling, and he smelled the acrid scent of gunpowder. He always awoke shaken.

Since the day of the execution, his mother-in-law had moved in. No one had consulted him or asked his permission. One day she was there, under his protection. If not, he assumed the old woman would probably be taken by the Gestapo. The Nazis would presume that she knew of her husband's treason and had taken part in it in some way.

From the first night following that fateful day, Manfred slept in the guest room alone. Gone were the nights wrapped in Christa's arms, the afterglow of their love flowing over him. Christa had not spoken to him. He couldn't blame her. She'd seen what he'd done with her own eyes. Those eyes accused him. So, he did not look at her, could not look at her.

Manfred still loved his wife with all his heart, but the guilt she brought out in him made him sick to his stomach to the point of an uncontrollably loose bowel. So, to avoid confrontation, he stayed in his room. But soon, he would be forced to talk to her. He must tell her that they were to leave for Poland.

Three days after his last day at the Ministry of Enlightenment and Propaganda, Manfred went into the living room to speak to his wife. She sat on the sofa, her mother beside her, both wearing black, looking lost. Christa held the baby, who sucked noisily on a bottle.

Both women looked up with accusing blue eyes to see him enter.

"Christa, I must speak with you."

"Go ahead." She looked back down at the baby. She did not meet his eyes. It was as if the very sight of him sickened her.

"Alone, please."

Christa glanced over at her mother. "Mama, I am sorry. May I speak to Manfred alone for a moment?"

Heidi got up. Manfred watched her walk to the bedroom she now shared with his wife. The sweet bedroom, the double bed, where so much love had once been made as he and Christa had entangled their bodies and souls in the darkness. How he had once loved that room and waited anxiously all day to lie in that bed beside the woman he adored. Frau Henkener had aged in the last few days. It seemed that she'd lost her will to live. He hoped she would stay in Berlin. If she did, perhaps there would be a chance, in time, to regain what he and Christa had once shared.

Before he sat down, he looked at the top of Christa's head. Such lovely blonde hair, uncombed… His heart hurt to see her grief.

"Christa, I've been let go from my job. Well, not exactly let go. I've been reassigned. I am being sent to Poland to work at a camp." His voice was soft, apologetic.

The baby hiccupped. Christa put the bottle down on the coffee table. She lifted Katja to her shoulder and began to pat the child's back.

"She's getting too old for the bottle," Christa said. "I will miss it when she stops taking it. I love the way her little face looks as she suckles, almost like she is an angel in Heaven."

"Christa, did you hear me? We have to pack up the house. We are to leave for Poland in a week and a half. These are my orders."

"Orders. Yes, orders. I heard," she said. Then she glanced out the picture window. "You see that old oak tree across the street? I will miss that tree." Her voice sounded far away like she'd lost touch with reality. It scared him. "At the beginning of our marriage, I used to wait for you to return home from work, and when I did, I'd look out the window, and there would be that tree."

He saw the tears begin to form in her eyes. He wanted to go to her, to take her in his arms and explain again and again until he could reach her, make her understand. He wanted to tell her he hated the orders but had no choice. He wanted to apologize for what he'd done to say he loved her. He stood up, his legs shaking and his body trembling. But before he could move toward her, she rose and stepped away from him, regaining her grip on reality and the moment at hand.

"I'll tell Mama. We'll be ready to go."

Christa left the room, the baby still cradled in her arms.

Manfred sunk back down onto the sofa. Tears fell from his eyes as he laid his head in his hands.

CHAPTER FORTY-EIGHT

The guard began hitting the redheaded girl with his club. She cried out, unnerving Zofia, who looked away. Bile rose in Zofia's throat, and she swallowed hard. If she vomited, that man might beat her, too.

Then an officer wearing the death head cap and black SS uniform walked over.

"Enough," he said to the guard, and then, addressing the girl, he barked, "Get back in line! Don't try this again. The next time will be your last time."

"Heil Hitler," the guard said to the SS officer, who looked drained from beating the girl.

"Heil Hitler," Manfred replied.

The soldier stopped beating the redhead and saluted. "Heil Hitler!"

The older guard approached Manfred. "Heil Hitler. You must be the new *Arbeitsführer*."

"Yes, my name is *Untersturmführer* Blau," Manfred said.

"Welcome to Hell," the SS officer said. "This is Treblinka."

Manfred looked around him. He saw the buildings that housed the barracks.

"What is that terrible smell?" Manfred asked.

"It's the crematory pits, just east of the camp. Have you not seen it yet?"

"No."

"It's constantly at work, burning night and day to dispose of all the bodies."

Manfred had heard about the gas chambers when he was working with Goebbels. But at that time, they seemed far away and unreal. Now he stood just yards away from the gassings. The ashes from the crematory pits fell like snowflakes into his hair and black uniform. These were the ashes of the dead and murdered. The very thought nauseated him.

"I am going to need one of these women to help me keep house. My wife is not feeling well," Manfred said. Christa had suffered some severe chest pains before they left. The doctor recommended bed rest.

"Pick one, your choice. To me, they are all the same: Jews, good for nothing." The older SS officer waved his hand, indicating the line of women.

Manfred looked at the group, a dirty, smelly bunch with matted hair and filthy clothes. He walked up and back, his heels clicking on the pavement until his eyes met Zofia's. Her dark eyes glistened with anger, defiant for sure but filled with life, and something else, a mystery—a dark, sensuous mystery. Interesting.

He had never really had much to do with Jews. Perhaps they were magical. It had been said that they sacrificed Aryan babies and drank the blood. Would little Katja be safe? Well, he had no choice but to choose one of them. After all, Christa was no longer keeping the house. Besides, he had never believed all that nonsense that he'd heard. Of course, if these silly Jews had any real power, they wouldn't be in the situation they were in, being led off to gas chambers and murdered like a herd of cattle. He looked at Zofia again. The very idea of this girl intrigued him. She was pretty. Even dirty and disheveled, she was pretty.

"Her. I'll take that one," Manfred said in German as he pointed to Zofia. She did not speak German and could not understand what he said. Manfred wrinkled his nose in disgust. “She stinks. Clean her up first, then send her to my house.”

“Yes, *Arbeitsführer*, it shall be taken care of for you.”

CHAPTER FORTY-NINE

The guard pushed Zofia to the head of the line where women and men were separated. The agonized screams that sounded like the very essence of Hell itself came from the direction where the left line of prisoners was taken. Zofia shuddered. Was that the sound of the prisoners dying in the gas chamber? Was that the sound of Fruma and Gitel?

The guard prodded her with his club to move. Why was she being singled out? The Nazi had pointed to her, indicating something, but what? Terror came over her in waves of panic.

"Take off your clothes," the guard said in German.

"I don't understand you," Zofia answered in Polish.

"Take them off now, *schnell.*" She knew the meaning of "schnell" but nothing else. She stared at him blankly.

He raised the club to strike her. The woman guard came forward.

"Hans, she doesn't understand German. She is a Pole from Warsaw."

"Greta, tell her to take her clothes off and get into the shower. The new *Arbeitsführer* has chosen her as his housekeeper."

"Take off your clothes and get into the shower," Greta, the

female guard, said in Polish and handed Zofia a bar of soap.

Zofia did as she was told, ashamed of her nakedness and filth and afraid of the shower. How could she be sure that this was not the shower that the woman had spoken about, the one that was gas instead of water? How could she be sure this was not the line to the death chamber?

She stood naked and shivering in a large room, waiting for the water or the gas. A dead silence came over the area. Others had heard the rumor, too. Someone wept softly, and the sound echoed. What would it feel like to die? Would it be painful? Would it be quick? It was only a few minutes, but it seemed like a lifetime before the nozzles began to spray water. Sighs of relief filled the room.

Zofia came out of the shower to find her shoes gone.

"You should have taken them with you," another prisoner said. How would she function without shoes? She looked around frantically, hoping to find them.

A guard came up behind her with a long iron rod. She pushed it into Zofia's back. Zofia jumped.

"Keep moving, *mach schnell*."

Zofia joined another line. Panicky and completely naked, she desperately tried to cover herself with her hands. At the end, a woman prisoner handed Zofia a striped green and brown dress made of rough cotton. She bent over and flipped it over her head. It hung like a rag, but she was glad to be covered. Now she had to join another line.

This time, she heard screaming as she got closer to the end. It unnerved her. What could be coming next?

She would have run, but there was nowhere to go. Gun-and club-wielding guards ushered her into the next room. The first thing Zofia saw was the floor, covered in hair of all colors and lengths, some curly, some wavy, some straight.

She edged out of the line just enough to see what happened at the front. Three chairs, each with prisoners seated in them. Behind the newly arrived stood other prisoners, who quickly shaved their hair, leaving them bald. Some cried, and others screamed, but the most unsettling were those who remained silent.

Zofia felt tears form in her eyes as she watched the locks of her full, wavy hair fall to the ground. The shaving took only a few moments. But as painful as it was to lose her hair, it felt wonderful to sit down. Her legs ached from standing.

Zofia was ushered into another line. This time, the group was ushered into the women's barracks. Long lines of cots stood in rows on a wooden floor. Each of the women searched for an open bed. Zofia found one at the end of the row near the wall, where she saw a black hairy spider crawling up toward the ceiling. She'd always had a terrible fear of spiders. Trembling, she tried to look for another cot, but nothing was open.

"Take that one," the girl across the row said. "If you don't find one, you'll end up on the floor, and that's worse." She was young, Zofia noticed.

"I'm Thelma," the girl said.

"Zofia."

"Welcome, I guess."

"Thanks. Is it as bad here as it looks?"

"Worse," the girl said and smiled. "But it could be even worse than it is. We could be on the other side."

"You mean the gas shower? Is that true, or is it a myth?" Zofia asked.

"It's true. I'm sorry to say it, but it is. My mother and father were both sent to the gas chamber."

"But how do you know? Maybe there is another work camp on the other side," Zofia said.

"I sometimes work in the forest, cutting wood for the crematory pits. We've had to unload the wood at the pits. Believe me, I know," Thelma said.

Zofia thought of Fruma and Gitel. They were probably already dead, their bodies on the way to be burned. It felt unreal that she would never see them again.

How could this be happening? It seemed like a nightmare, yet here she was in this terrible place. The musty smell of unwashed bodies and dirty bedding permeated the room. Zofia looked around her. She ran her hands over her shorn head. The tiny bristles of hair felt alien against her fingers.

Hopelessness began to creep in. The strength she'd been fighting to maintain slowly began to seep away. Her friends were gone forever. Dovid… He might be here, or he might be dead. Dear Gitel, with her warm, protective smile, and Fruma, the mother she never had. When she thought of Fruma, she wanted to cry out in anguish.

Her mind went back to the time they spent sewing side-by-side in the shop together. Fruma… She remembered how worried she'd been when she found out that she was pregnant. She'd been so afraid she would lose her job, but Fruma knew. She always knew, and she had her unique way of making things better.

Dear God, help poor Fruma. Could she really be dead already? Could that be possible? I must try not to think about this. I must try to think of Eidel. When this is all over, Eidel will need me. Eidel, my daughter, my child… God, please be with her, protect her, keep…

"You!" A guard pointed at Zofia. He spoke in German, but she understood by his facial expressions and hand gestures. "Follow me."

Zofia felt Thelma's worried eyes on her back as she followed the guard out of the barracks.

As they walked across the field, Zofia saw that there was a barbed wire fence separating the men's camp from the women's. She looked over, hoping to see Dovid but knowing she would not.

The guard noticed she'd slowed down and edged her side with his rifle butt. She looked forward and moved faster.

When they walked up to the exit, the guard explained something to the watchman in German, and they were allowed out of the gate.

Zofia followed the guard to a gate that opened to the entrance of a comfortable country house that sat back on a quarter of an acre of manicured lawn. As they got closer to the door, she saw an old woman peering out a picture window in the living room, her face deeply lined. Her hand fisted under her chin and had purple veins that protruded from the thin, pale skin.

They walked up three steps to a thick, wooden door painted

black, with a swastika in the center. The guard rang the bell, and they waited.

Zofia stared at the sign of the Nazi Party and shuddered.

A man in a striped uniform and a shaved head opened the door.

"Go and get the *Arbeitsführer*'s wife," the guard said.

The man nodded and walked away.

Zofia and the guard stood, waiting. The woman with the pale skin watched them from her window seat, saying nothing. From where she stood, Zofia could hear a baby crying. The sound brought back memories of Eidel. She felt tears forming in her eyes and forced the memories from her mind.

Several minutes later, a pretty blonde walked into the room. She carried a toddler in her arms. As soon as the child saw Zofia, she smiled. Zofia felt her heart melt as she looked at the lovely little girl with blonde curls like her mother's.

The woman called out, and the male prisoner who had let them in entered.

"Can you translate for me?" Christa asked the prisoner.

"Yes," he said.

"My name is Christa Blau. My husband is the *Arbeitsführer*. You will be working here at our home to help us with the housework and with Katja."

The prisoner translated from German to Polish.

Zofia nodded.

"This is Katja." Christa indicated the little girl, who smiled again. "Do you have any experience with children?"

The butler translated.

"Yes, I do. I had a daughter of my own," she told Christa, reaching over to touch the tender baby's cheek. "Hello, Katja. My name is Zofia," she said, pointing to herself, smiling.

The baby laughed. It broke the ice, and then the two women laughed, too.

"You may leave us," Christa told the guard. "She will work out just fine."

Christa showed Zofia around the house, accompanied by the male prisoner who translated her explanation of the tasks. She looked at Zofia's bare feet. "Well, if you are working in this house, you must have shoes." The prisoner translated, and Christa motioned them to follow her to her bedroom. "Your feet look just about my size," Christa said and retrieved a pair of brown shoes from her closet and two pairs of socks from her dresser. The prisoner translated, and Zofia was shocked, considering what she'd already witnessed at the camp.

She told Zofia that she was not well. She had been ill and needed help with her daily workload. As she walked, her blonde curls bounced. There was something good and kind about this woman. She was not cruel like the others that Zofia had encountered. She appeared to have a heart.

It seemed to Zofia that all would be well until the *Arbeitsführer* arrived home. Zofia could feel the tension in the air as soon as the door opened, and he entered the house. She kept her head down and did not meet his eyes, but she watched him when he looked the other way.

He was a slender man, proud in his uniform. He demanded respect as he walked through the house, barking orders at the prisoner who served as their butler. She wondered if the *Arbeitsführer's* overbearing manner had anything to do with his small stature. Perhaps he needed to prove his manhood. He was abrupt with his wife and worse with his mother-in-law.

She remembered him distinctly. He'd been the one who'd stopped the guard from clubbing the redheaded girl and then kicked her in the ribs and walked away. Why did he spare her life? He was a contradiction, this Nazi. Because he spoke in German, Zofia could not understand what he said, just his tone of voice, which made her shiver. *There appeared there was no contradiction in him now.*

At the end of the day, a guard from the camp came to take Zofia back to the barracks. Soon after her arrival, she was required to attend roll call. The prisoners stood in line as their names were called. Then, the dead were accounted for, their bodies carried out by other prisoners, and placed at the end of the line to be counted and removed from the next roll call. Then the prisoners lined up for dinner.

"Here is your spoon and your bowl," a guard said to Zofia in broken Polish. "If you lose them, you won't get another."

When she got to the front of the line, she saw a huge steel pot filled with soup. One of the prisoners poured the contents of a single ladle into her bowl and gave her a small piece of bread. Then she sat at a long table beside several other prisoners to eat.

The soup was nothing more than water with a small piece of potato and a bean or two. She was so hungry that when she saw the dead fly at the bottom of her soup, she continued to eat anyway, gagging a little. One of the other prisoners noticed Zofia's expression.

"Don't worry, you'll get used to it. There are insects in the soup all the time."

"I can't believe I am so hungry that I don't care," Zofia said. "I wonder what I am becoming."

"You just got here. Wait. It gets worse," the other woman said. "By the way, my name is Marsha. My bunk is just a few away from yours. I noticed you when you came in."

"My name is Zofia."

"Dora said that one of the guards took you to the *Arbeitsführer's* house. He is new, but already he is a terror."

"I was taken to his house to help his wife. She is sick, and they have a little girl."

"I have not seen his home, and I know nothing about his home life, but he is cruel and quick to administer a beating."

"And so, I've been told. When he came home today, he seemed to be a difficult man, even with his family."

"So, what can we do? Nothing. I just try to stay out of his way."

"What kind of work do you do?"

"Sometimes I cut wood for the crematory fires, sometimes I help carry dead bodies to the pits, other times I work in the stone quarries."

"That's hard work for women."

"Yes, but the Nazis don't care. If one of us dies, then they replace us with another one. The trains keep coming, with more and more prisoners. It is very hard, heavy work. It is so hot in the summer that I feel like I will die of heatstroke. Then the winter is so cold that we pray for the heat of summer. Still, we try to stay alive another day."

"What did you do before you came here?"

"Me? I was very good with numbers. I worked at the bank."

"A woman who worked at a bank. That's very impressive."

"Yes, I suppose," Marsha laughed. She was a tall girl with soft, brown hair and eyes the color of maple syrup. "On the side, I kept the books for the local businesses. And you? What did you do?"

"I was a seamstress."

"I suppose you made lovely gowns."

"Yes, I did."

"It's good to remember, and it is not so good," Marsha sighed. "My heart breaks when I think about how things used to be and what has become of us now."

"I know. You're right. Sometimes I feel as if my heart is breaking for all I have lost. Sometimes, I want to die, too. But it isn't that easy."

"No, it's strange. No matter how harsh things are, the will to live is strong, and it forces you to go on."

"That's true, but if that were all of it, then I could see giving up. But for me, there is more." There was something about this girl with the amber eyes and a sweet smile that made Zofia feel the need to confide in her. "I have a daughter. Somewhere out in the world, far away from this terrible place, I have a child. Then, as long as my child is living, I have the need to fight to go on."

"I never had children. My husband and I were only married for two months before they arrested him. He was a lawyer and refused to stop practicing when the Nazis took over. Besides, he was far too outspoken against Hitler. At first, I thought that he was arrested because he caused so much trouble. Would you believe I went to the authorities, begging for his release? Do you know what happened? They arrested me, too. What a fool I was. I thought they would be fair." She laughed a harsh laugh, looked out into the distance, and shook her head.

"Get up, let's go," one of the guards said as he walked around, gathering the prisoners into a line. "Back to the barracks, *schnell*."

"Do you understand German?" Zofia asked as they hurried into the line.

"Some. The longer you're here, the more you will understand."

"Quiet, no talking. March. Let's go."

Zofia lay upon her cot. It smelled musty, but she was so tired that she fell into a deep sleep within minutes.

Most days were spent taking care of Katja and keeping the house clean for the Blaus. The longer Zofia worked at the home of the *Arbeitsführer*, the more she became aware of the tension between Manfred and his wife.

Christa was ill and very weak. She grew tired easily, while her mother seemed mentally incompetent. Often, the older woman would go off talking to herself as she gazed out the picture window.

The little girl, Katja, followed Zofia from room to room as she cleaned, sometimes begging to be picked up or played with. Zofia didn't mind. She loved the gentle, innocent child, forgiving her that her father was a monster, which he proved at the quarries, time and again, so Marsha had told her.

When Manfred was not home, Christa offered Zofia food and drink, which she gratefully partook of, splitting what was given to her, eating half, and bringing the other back to Marsha, who had become a dear friend.

As she worked for the Blaus, Zofia learned to speak German, and Christa learned to speak Polish, making communication with Christa easier. But when Zofia and the baby were alone, she always spoke in Polish, not realizing that little Katja was learning.

One morning following roll call, as Zofia waited for the guard to escort her to the home of the Blaus, she heard the voice of the *Arbeitsführer*. He spoke quickly, making his words difficult to understand, but his tone was angry. Then she heard a gunshot and moved closer to see what had happened. One of the women, whom she had met briefly but did not really know personally, lay in a pool of blood at Manfred Blau's feet. She saw him kick her and then walk in the other direction. The guards forced two prisoners, using rifle butts in their ribs, to move the body out of the way.

Once it was done, the women began their daily march to the quarries and the forests. Zofia tried not to look at the body, but she couldn't help herself. The young woman lay dead, eyes open, with a track of blood leading to a large pool. The dark blood and the terror of what she just saw made her gag. Zofia could not stop dry heaving, even as the guard approached to take her to the Blaus' home.

"Let's go. March. *Schnell.*"

Why did everything have to be done fast? "*Schnell!*" was the first German word she learned.

Now she feared Manfred even more. Once she'd seen his cruelty firsthand and knew how heartless he could be, her fear of him grew so strong that she tried to avoid being in his presence. Some nights he returned late, and she was relieved to be gone back to the barracks before he entered the house. But when he came home, and she was still there, Zofia noticed him always watching her.

She heard arguments and raised voices coming from the living room between Manfred and Christa. Although she could not understand everything they said, she heard the yelling and the slaps, followed by Christa heart-wrenching weeping. Once the weeping began, Manfred walked out and went into another room, slamming the door. This same situation occurred at least twice weekly, and always on the following day, Christa would have a black eye or a bruised cheek. Zofia said nothing, but she knew Manfred hit his wife.

Once, Zofia arrived early in the morning, and Manfred was already gone, but Christa sat at the kitchen table, her eyes swollen and her nose wrapped in white bandages. Katja played on the floor with a stuffed fabric doll. When the child saw Zofia, the child's chubby arms reached up.

"Up," Katja said in Polish. Zofia lifted the girl.

"Please, take her out of here," Christa said in broken Polish and German.

"Yes, ma'am." Zofia was beginning to establish a good understanding that enabled her to communicate with her German employer.

As Zofia swept the floor, Katja pretended to sweep, too, toddling around on her short legs. Zofia's heart grew with love for this little girl, who had begun to call her "Mama." Zofia was afraid that Christa would hear Katja referring to her as mother and become angry, but Christa's illness seemed to be getting worse, and she spent most days in bed.

The grandmother never left her window seat. At night, she slept on the same sofa where she sat all day. Before Zofia returned to the barracks, she would deliver a meal to the older woman and then lay out the sheets and blankets for her to sleep. All the while, Christa's mother continued to stare out the window, never acknowledging Zofia standing right beside her.

Once a day, Zofia helped her to change her clothes and sometimes even to bathe. When the fights ensued between Manfred and Christa, the old woman sang softly to herself. Zofia tried to pity her. Instead, she was a little jealous that Christa's mother had lost her mind, so she knew nothing of the pain around her.

When Zofia left at night, Katja would cry and reach her arms out as if to say, "Please take me with you," so Zofia began to feed the child earlier and put her to bed before she left.

Winter was on its way. There was no heat or fire in the barracks.

With each passing day, the weather grew colder. Zofia shivered in her bunk with just a thin woolen blanket for cover. Every night, when everyone seemed asleep, Marsha crept into Zofia's bed. She brought her blanket, and the two girls put the two blankets on top of each other, making one thick cover. Then Zofia gave Marsha the food she had brought for her.

The two women huddled beside each other to keep warm. They told fairy tales that they remembered from their childhoods. Sometimes, they sang songs and even giggled over memories. Marsha reminisced about her husband and her wedding day, telling Zofia about the dress she'd worn and the wonderful meal that had been served. She even told Zofia about the boy she dated and slept with before she'd met her true *bashert,* soulmate.

Zofia told Marsha about Katja and how much the child reminded her of Eidel. They both agreed on how kind Christa was to give Zofia the extra food. But Zofia bit her lower lip, shaking her head in despair when she spoke of Fruma and Gitel, her dear friends, and Dovid, the gentle boy whose only crime was loving her. Sometimes Zofia allowed herself the indulgence of tears, her slender body rocking while Marsha held her.

One cold night, after Marsha gobbled the thick crust of bread Zofia had brought, they lay shivering under their two blankets.

"What is he like at home?" Marsha asked one night.

"The *Arbeitsführer*?"

"Of course. Who else?"

"I don't know him, really, but I hear him fighting with his wife all the time. He beats her."

"That's not surprising. He's very cruel. I think he hates women. I'm terrified of him."

"I know. So am I. Once in a while, he comes home before I leave to come back to the camp, and he looks at me."

"Looks at you, how?"

"I'm not sure. He looks at me with a strange longing, a hungry look, like he wants to sleep with me."

"Oh no!"

"So far, he has done nothing that I could say was unacceptable. He leaves me alone. Most of my fear of him is from how I see him treat others. I just hope he never touches me in that way."

"Yes, so do I. Oh, my friend, what a terrible place this is. We are in constant fear of everything."

"I know. The terror is the hardest part. Often, I think it is harder than dying."

"It's like dying every day, every minute."

"At least we have each other."

"Yes, we do." Marsha was silent for a moment. She smoothed Zofia's hair out of her eyes. "Have you ever thought about what we might be doing if Hitler had never taken over?"

"I try not to. The yearning is too painful. For me, the only thing that I allow myself to think about is Eidel. When I leave here, I will go and find my child."

"And that keeps you going?"

"Yes."

Ice and snow covered the ground as Zofia walked to the Blaus' home. Although of thick cotton, her uniform did nothing to shield her from the cold. One morning, when Zofia arrived, she found Christa in bed. She knocked softly on the door.

"Can I bring you anything?" Zofia asked.

"Some tea, *bitte*."

"Yes, ma'am. Would you like some bread and jam with it?"

Christa did not understand. So, Zofia held an imaginary piece of bread and spread it with an imaginary knife. Then she cocked her head and waited for the answer.

"No, thank you." Christa shook her head. "I'm not hungry."

Christa looked at Zofia. Her skin was red from the cold.

"Oh dear, look at you. Do you walk outside all the way from the camp without a coat? How stupid of me. Of course, you do. You have no coat," Christa suddenly realized. She was talking more to herself than to Zofia.

"Here." Christa got up from her bed. She went to her closet and removed a thick blue-gray wool coat. "This should fit you." Christa held it up to Zofia. "It looks like it should be about the right size."

Zofia looked at Christa, unsure of what she wanted.

"Here, try this on," Christa said as she helped Zofia to fit her arms into the coat. "Perfect fit. This is for you. It is a gift from me," Christa said, pointing to Zofia and then to the coat.

"For me?" Zofia hugged the warm garment to her body. First shoes, now a coat! Then she took Christa's slender hand and put it to her lips. "Thank you. God bless you." Zofia fell to her knees. She felt the tears fall upon her face as she still held the thin-skinned hand lined with purple veins, just like her mother's.

A coat! A coat! How wonderful to be warm. That night, Zofia and Marsha put the coat on top of the blankets where they slept. It felt like Heaven. Both women held tight to the coat, even in sleep. Zofia knew better than to ever let the coat out of her sight. Shoes, hidden food, and anything at all that could make life even a little more tolerable were at constant risk of being stolen. The guard escorted Zofia to the Blaus' residence each morning and asked Christa if Zofia had stolen the coat.

Christa told him it was a gift, then scowled and demanded that he leave.

As the months passed, Zofia became almost fluent in German. She understood most of what was said to her. As time passed, Christa found Zofia to be a friend to confide in. Manfred still kept watch on Zofia. His eyes, hungry with desire, unnerved her, but he did nothing.

One morning, just as the weather was beginning to break, Zofia straightened the living room. She noticed that Christa's mother had laid her head down in an unnatural position. It was only an hour since Heidi Henkener finished her breakfast, and Zofia assumed she'd fallen asleep while gazing out the window. So, Zofia took a blanket to lay it across the old woman's body. But when she did, Zofia realized that Heidi had passed away. Quietly, while watching the birds fly from tree to tree, the flowers just beginning to bud. Mother Earth embracing another spring, Heidi had left the confines of a cruel world and risen with the angels to meet her husband.

The old woman had already turned cold.

Zofia hung her head. It would fall upon her to tell Christa the bad news. She walked slowly into the bedroom, where Christa was lying under a thin cotton quilt.

"Ma'am?"

Christa turned to her. "What is it, Zofia?" Her left eye was filled with blood and surrounded by a purple and yellow bruise.

"Ma'am, I'm sorry to have to tell you this, but your mother has passed away."

"What? Are you sure?"

Christa got out of bed. She walked stiffly into the living room. When she saw her mother, Christa fell to her knees and took her mother's cold hand into her own.

"Mama. Oh, Mama, how am I going to go on without you?"

She wept.

Zofia stood there, not knowing what to say or do, until Katja came racing into the room, a doll in her arms.

"My dolly sick. Make better. You be doctor," Katja said in her broken baby language.

"Shhh. Quiet, your mama is having a hard time right now. Come with me. We'll go to your room and take care of your doll. All right?"

Katja nodded and put her tiny hand into Zofia's.

The guard did not come to the camp for several days to take Zofia to the Blaus' home. Instead, she was shuffled out to work in the quarries with the other prisoners. All day she carried stone. Manfred was there. She saw him and wished she could ask him why she'd been taken away from the house, from Katja, who she missed terribly, but she dared not speak to him.

"You, over there," Manfred said to a woman who was probably thirty, but hard work had made her look at least twice her age. She slumped over and moved slowly as she carried heavy piles of rocks. "You're too slow. I think you are trying to avoid working. Let me show you what happens when someone avoids work."

He pulled her up by the back of her dress. She was so thin she was almost weightless. Then he called all the prisoners over.

"Here, we have a lazy woman. That is not allowed. Laziness must be punished." Manfred slapped the prisoner across her face. One of the others, a girl of about twelve, winced.

"That is her daughter," Marsha whispered to Zofia.

"Oh, so you think I am wrong to punish this woman? Well, let's see… Would you rather I punish you?" Manfred said to the young girl, who looked around in terror.

"Please," the mother said. "I am the one who was lazy. I am the one who was wrong. Please let her be. Punish me, not her. I beg you."

"Oh, she must be your friend…"

"Come here, friend…" Manfred said. Zofia saw the cruelty glittering in his eyes, and she shivered.

"So, who should take the punishment? Shall we make a game of this?" he asked.

"Would you like to take the punishment for your friend?"

"She is my mother. Please, *Arbeitsführer*. Please let her be."

"Your mother? That explains everything. Women and their mothers are a disgusting lot." He smiled. "Well, I have an idea, Mother… Watch this. I'll bet you won't be lazy anymore." Manfred pulled the gun from his waist. He held fixed on the daughter's head.

"Please, have mercy," the older woman cried out. She ran to her daughter and lay on top of her. "Please. It is my fault…"

With his black leather boot, Manfred kicked the mother out of the way and then fired a shot. The daughter's brains splattered on the ground and the mother's face. The older woman screamed in agony. She wept. Loud, heart-wrenching cries filled the air.

"Shut up," Manfred said. "Shut up, right now."

But the woman could not be silent. No one dared go to her to comfort her, lest they be next.

Manfred seemed somehow frightened by the wailing. With his gun still in hand, he turned and fired into the mother's head.

Zofia's throat was dry. She felt as if she might collapse.

"Don't look. Just turn away. Go back to work and work quickly," Marsha whispered to Zofia.

It was several days before the guard returned to escort Zofia back to the home of the Blaus. After the rigorous, hot days of working in the quarries, she was relieved to see him. She had begun to fear that she would never return to the house again.

Zofia arrived to find Christa in bed, her skin white and thinned like parchment. Although she'd always been frail, losing her mother seemed to age her even further. Her once-golden curls had thinned and now lay like straw on the pillow. The room was dark except for a narrow ray of light that seeped through the curtains.

"Good morning, ma'am. Can I get you anything?" Zofia asked, keeping her voice soft.

"No, thank you," Christa said, barely above a whisper.

"Where were you?" Katja asked, angry and accusing. She'd been lying beside her mother.

"I couldn't come," Zofia said.

She picked the child up into her arms and put her face into the baby's soft hair, taking in the sweet smell of her.

"I'm mad at you," Katja pouted.

"I'm sorry," Zofia said. "Forgive me, and I promise we will play a game."

Katja smiled and hugged Zofia's neck. "What kind of game?"

"It's a surprise. First, you should eat some breakfast."

"Do I have to?"

"Yes, you do if you want to play."

"All right…" Katja said, reluctantly agreeing.

"Thank you, Zofia. I'm so glad you're here. I need to rest," Christa said in a raspy voice.

"I'll take her out of here and close the door."

"Thank you so much." Christa turned on her side as Zofia took Katja out of the room.

When Katja had finished her breakfast, Zofia peeked into Christa's room to see if her employer was all right. Christa lay facing the door, her eyes wide open.

"Ma'am, can I get you anything?"

"No, nothing."

"Yes, ma'am." Zofia turned to leave.

"I'm so tired of all of this," Christa began to speak. Although the room was dark and Zofia could only see shadows, she could tell by Christa's voice that she was crying. "I'm not well, and sometimes I feel that it is all just too much for me, this camp, with its murder and torture.

"I am married to a man I don't even know. Worse yet, I am so weak. I have no fight left. Soon I will die, and what will happen to poor Katja? Manfred has changed so much since we were married. I cannot trust him to care for a child when I am gone. He is far too angry and has turned vicious and cruel. My life is a terrible mess," Christa said.

Zofia did not answer. If she could, she would promise this woman who had been kind to her that she would care for the child. But as the last few days proved, the decision was not hers. So, all Zofia could do was stand silently in the doorway and listen.

"Zofia, where is your mother? Where is your family from?"

"My mother is dead. I have no living relatives," Zofia said, but she thought of Eidel.

"I am sorry. I am so sorry for you."

Zofia realized now that Christa was somewhat aware of the goings-on at the camp. She longed to tell her about Fruma, Gitel, and even Eidel, but she could not take the risk. If Christa turned on her, Zofia would be sent back, or worse. It was best just to stand there and listen.

Finally, that afternoon, Christa agreed to try to eat some tea and dry toast, which Zofia brought to her. She nibbled a bit and then lay down and fell asleep. Zofia took the tray and covered the woman. She wondered how she could feel so sorry for someone else, even in her own misery.

Christa was asleep when Manfred arrived early from work. Zofia had just given Katja her afternoon meal and put her down for a nap.

When the door creaked open, Zofia turned quickly. A shiver ran up her neck. It was the *Arbeitsführer*.

"Hello," he said, his voice civil, almost warm.

She cast her eyes down. "Good afternoon, sir," Zofia answered.

"You look quite lovely today," Manfred said.

Zofia did not answer.

"You aren't afraid of me, are you?"

She shook her head.

"Well, good, although you would do well to maintain a healthy respect if you understand what I mean. So, then…" he said, smiling. "Come to my office. I have something to talk to you about."

Zofia followed him, wishing somehow that she might escape.

He sat behind his desk and motioned to her to take the seat opposite him.

"Do you like it here? Working in my home?" He smiled.

"Yes, *Arbeitsführer*."

"You realize, of course, that I could send you back to the quarries anytime."

"Yes, *Arbeitsführer*."

"Speak up. I can't hear you."

"Yes, *Arbeitsführer*." She cleared her throat and tried to speak louder.

"I am a very powerful man. Your very life lies within my hands. So, in a way, to you, that makes me God."

She kept her head down.

"What do you have to say to that?"

"Yes, *Arbeitsführer*."

"Well, I would like to keep you here working in my home. My daughter likes you, and you provide much-needed help for my invalid wife."

"Thank you, sir."

"However, I expect more of you. This job you have, it is a very comfortable job, with plenty of food. I know my wife feeds you well. I realize she gives you more than you deserve, but I don't care. However, there is something you can do for me."

"Yes, *Arbeitsführer*."

"Come here," he said. She did not move. "Come on…" he said, his voice suddenly gentle in a frightening way.

Zofia got up. Her legs felt as if they were about to buckle underneath her. She gasped for breath.

"Don't be so scared. I won't hurt you," Manfred said.

She walked over.

"Closer," he said.

She moved closer.

He put his hand under her dress. She recoiled.

"*Ech*, don't do that. You must pretend you want me. You must convince me of it. Do you understand? I don't like to feel as if I repulse you. I get enough of that from Christa."

"Yes, *Arbeitsführer*."

He pulled the blinds shut. The room was in total darkness.

"Say it," he said. "Say I want you! You are a powerful man!"

"I want you, *Arbeitsführer*. You are a powerful man."

"Use my name. Call me Manfred. Tell me that I am a good husband. Say that you love me."

"I love you, Manfred. You are a good husband."

"Tell me more, Christa. Tell me that you are happy you married me and want me all the time. Making love to me is your greatest joy."

"I am happy I married you. I want you all the time. You bring me joy," Zofia said. Her knees gave way, and she had to grip the desk to keep from falling to the floor. She wanted to run away from the hands that searched under her uniform, touching, gently groping, fondling, and prying, his fingers finding her most private places. *Stop!* she cried out in her mind. Tears trickled down her face.

"More. Tell me, Christa. Do you love me? Do my fingers bring you pleasure?"

She nodded.

"Answer me!"

"Yes, *Arbeitsführer*."

"You ruined it. Manfred, call me Manfred."

"Yes, Manfred. Yes."

"Get down on your knees."

Zofia did as he told her to do. He unbuttoned his pants and undid the zipper.

"Touch me."

She placed her hand on his erect penis.

"Your hands are cold. Take me into your mouth," Manfred commanded.

Zofia thought she might vomit as she put her lips around him. She felt herself gag and hoped he did not realize it.

"Christa," Manfred said. "I love you. I am sorry. You forgive me, don't you? I have always loved you. You are my life."

Zofia could not move.

"Suck me harder! Make me believe you like it!"

Zofia gagged, but she continued while Manfred ran his hands through the short tufts of hair that had grown back on her head.

Finally, it was over. She wanted to vomit the slimy snot into the wastebasket but dared not. Instead, she forced herself to swallow. Uncontrollably, she gagged loud and hard.

"I forgive you this time. Don't gag again."

She nodded.

"Remember, next time, you will tell me how you have forgiven me. You will tell me you understand why I had to do what I did."

Zofia had no idea what Manfred was talking about, and she dared not ask, but she nodded her head.

"You may go now."

The rest of the day, Manfred stayed in his study.

When Katja awoke from her nap, she came dashing out of her bedroom and ran to Zofia, who was still shaken by the afternoon's events.

"Snack?" Katja asked.

"Yes, sweetie, let me get you a snack."

When the guard arrived to escort Zofia back to the camp, she was relieved to leave.

That evening, when Zofia stood at roll call, her shoulders were slumped. Even though she was hungry, she could not eat her dinner. Marsha watched her friend with a keen eye.

"Something is wrong. What is it?"

"Nothing," Zofia said.

"Can I have your food if you are not going to eat it?" one of the other prisoners asked.

Zofia handed her the bowl of soup.

Marsha brought her blanket that night and curled up on Zofia's cot.

"You've been so distant today. Please talk to me."

"Christa is very ill. I am afraid that soon I will be sent back to the camp permanently."

"I find that doubtful. Even if she dies, they will need you to care for the child."

"Perhaps. I hate to think she might die."

"You care for her?" Marsha asked.

"I do. She is kind to me. As you know, she is good enough to give me extra food and a warm coat. She is not a bad person, just an ordinary woman caught in a terrible situation."

"She is still a German, married to a Nazi. That makes her a Nazi."

"I don't believe that."

"Don't you, Zofia? Deep in your heart, don't you?"

CHAPTER FIFTY

It became a pattern. Zofia dreaded the daily fondling, prodding, poking, and darkness. She hated Manfred. The sound of his voice made her want to spit.

"Tell me," he said.

"I love you, Manfred." Pretend you are not here, she told herself. Pretend this is not happening to you.

"And?"

"I forgive you. Everything that happened was never your fault. There is no one else for me. There never has been."

"Christa," he said as Zofia took him into her mouth, her knees aching as she knelt on the hardwood floor.

After several months, Zofia was able to detach from her body. She did not feel his hands, nor the slime of his desire, run down her throat.

Then one afternoon, he wanted more.

"Leave the light on," he said. "Take off your dress."

She did as he asked, never looking into his eyes.

"You hate me, don't you?" he asked.

She did not answer.

"Does any of this please you?"

She did not answer.

"Tell me. I want to know the truth. Does any of this give you pleasure? I promise. I will not be angry at your answer."

"No, it does not. I wish you would stop." She could not believe she'd said that.

He nodded. "And what do you think of me? Come on, I want the truth. I want to know what it is about me that offends you."

She knew he drank. She'd cleared away the empty bottles. Could he be drunk?

"Please, tell me."

He seemed almost tender, almost begging.

"You are cruel. You flaunt your power on the women in the camp, on your wife, and on me. I am afraid of you."

"Hmmm," he said. "Afraid of me…"

Manfred got up and pushed her out of the way. He walked around the office for several minutes, pacing like a panther.

"I'm a horrible man, Zofia," he said, and then he took a swig from a bottle of whiskey that sat on the shelf.

Without warning, he walked over to Zofia and threw her onto the floor. Her head hit the ground with a thud. Then he stared into her eyes.

"You're afraid of me? I don't want you to be afraid. I want you terrified. You and every other woman will learn to respect me if you know what's good for you. I am sick and tired of women. Sick and tired, do you hear me?"

He took his gun from the side of his waist.

"You see this?"

Zofia lay naked on the floor, trembling.

"Answer me when I talk to you!"

She nodded. "Yes."

"Spread your legs."

She gazed at him, dumbfounded.

"Do as I say, or I will shoot you dead. I can, you know. I have no one to answer to. You will be swept away like the piece of trash that you are. No one will care or take notice of your death."

She spread her legs. "No, please." Her mind raced. She was sure he planned to enter her.

Instead, he took the gun and shoved the barrel inside of her.

Zofia could not disengage from her body. She felt the cold steel inside her most private place. Tears fell freely from her eyes and ran off her cheeks onto the floor.

"I beg you, please have pity, *Arbeitsführer*. Please..." She felt her legs quaking with fear. "I beg you, please..."

He knelt over her. She was so terrified that she felt she might urinate on his gun. That, she knew, would make him angry. He jabbed the weapon harder into her body. She cried out in pain and horror.

"You see, what can I do to you if I want to? I can do this any time I want to. I can pull the trigger and send a bullet right up inside of what makes you a woman. Women!" he screamed. His body was shaking, and his face was red with rage and alcohol.

"I beg you, Manfred," she said.

Perhaps it was the sound of his name. He removed the gun, stood up, and placed it on his desk.

"Get up, please. Put your dress on and leave me. Quickly!"

She complied before he changed his mind.

It was almost a week before Manfred bothered Zofia in a sexual manner again.

"Come into my office," he said one afternoon in early autumn.

She had almost allowed herself to believe that he was done with her. She'd hoped and prayed it was true.

"I wanted to apologize for my behavior," he said.

She nodded, knowing she could not trust him.

"We will begin our game again. However, you must not show me any more disrespect. Do you understand?"

"Yes, *Arbeitsführer*," she said, feeling the sweat run down her back.

And so, he began the daily ritual again. Zofia remained silent and just complied with his wishes, disengaging from her body, feeling nothing. At least he'd never used his pistol in that horrible way again.

"I've decided that you will not go back to the camp anymore,"

Manfred said. "You will sleep in the basement and be available for me whenever I want you."

She felt the bile rise in her throat and swallowed hard.

"*Arbeitsführer,*" she said, the words croaking out. "May I please ask a favor? Please..."

"A favor? You are already receiving a favor. You will sleep in a bed, in a clean room. You have enough food. What more could you want? Look at your peers. They would give anything to be in your position. And you have a favor to request. Hmmm..." he said, walking around her. "All right, I am feeling generous today. Go ahead and ask me. Perhaps I will indulge you."

"*Arbeitsführer*, please, I have a friend at the camp. I want to go and tell her that I am not going to be returning. I also would like to give her my coat so that she will be warm."

"Generous of you. Sometimes you Jews amaze me with your human-like qualities. You want to make a gift to your friend." He walked around her, nodding. "Oh, very well. I suppose it would be all right. When the guard arrives this afternoon, I'll have him take you to the barracks. You can spend ten minutes with your friend, and then you are to return."

"Thank you, thank you, *Arbeitsführer*." She bowed her head, hoping that he would not see that she had started crying.

As Manfred promised, the guard waited outside the barracks. Zofia had ten minutes to explain.

"I will not be back. I brought you my coat. Keep it safe. You will need it for the winter," Zofia said to Marsha.

Both women were crying. Zofia hugged her friend. She was glad she'd never told Marsha what the *Arbeitsführer* did to her. It would only cause her more worry.

"Be safe. I will miss you so much."

"I will miss you, too."

"I don't know how I will go on without you," Marsha said.

"But you must because the war will be over soon, and soon we will be free. I will find you again, my friend. We will sip tea at an outdoor café under an umbrella and watch the people walk by."

Marsha hugged Zofia harder.

"Don't stop fighting. Please, don't give up," Zofia said.

"You, too, keep fighting. Stay alive," Marsha said.

The guard entered. "Time is up. Come on, let's go—*mach schnell.*"

Zofia got up and followed the guard to the door. She turned and looked back. The two women's eyes met.

"Goodbye," Marsha said as the guard pushed Zofia out.

Except for memories of Eidel and time spent with Katja, Zofia had lost all emotion. When Manfred touched her, she felt blessed that she could no longer even feel the heat of his hand. She missed Marsha but forced thoughts of a friend from her mind.

Zofia had been given a room in the basement of the Blau residence. She'd never seen it before the day she moved in. Overhead, a single bulb dimly lit the area to reveal a cot with real sheets and a pillow. Two wool blankets lay folded at the foot of the bed. Adjacent to the room, Zofia saw a bathroom with a toilet, a small sink, and a shower. The walls had been painted gray to complement the gray concrete floor. It was safe. It was clean and far more comfortable than the barracks. Still, she would miss her friend. Manfred had constant access to her here, but so did little Katja. She wondered how it was possible to love a child so much and hate the father that created her.

As the seasons came and went, Christa grew weaker. Her eyelids, nails, and lips turned blue as a robin's egg, indicating that the heart condition she was born with had resurfaced.

On the morning of Katja's fourth birthday, Christa asked Zofia if she could try to bake a cake.

"Have you ever done any baking?"

"A little. I will try to make something nice for Katja."

"You care for Katja a great deal, don't you?" Christa asked. She sat up in bed, her back propped up against the pillows.

"Yes, ma'am, I do."

"Sit down, Zofia." Christa patted the bed. "Here, sit beside me. There is something that I must tell you."

Zofia ran her hand over the blanket, smoothing it over Christa, then sat down.

"I have never told anyone this. I feel that I must tell you. But as long as I am alive, you must promise to keep this a secret. Can you promise? I don't know why, Zofia, but I trust you and you to keep your word."

"I promise."

"Zofia, my condition is getting worse. I suppose you can see that. I am not sure I will survive the winter, so you must know. You must be aware of what I am about to tell you."

"Go on, please," Zofia said.

Christa took Zofia's hand. Zofia felt how cold Christa was.

"You are so cold. Would you like another blanket?"

"No, I must tell you…"

"I'm sorry. Yes, you must. Go on," Zofia said, squeezing Christa's hand gently.

Christa sighed, taking a deep breath. Then she began. "Katja is not my daughter, not by blood, anyway. Neither is she Manfred's. Katja is adopted. She was born in the Institute for the Lebensborn. Do you know what that is?"

"I've heard of it. Isn't it a breeding hospital for Aryan women?"

"Yes, it is. It is a place where children are bred to build Germany's new Aryan race, and then they are adopted by Aryan couples. Manfred and I had to be screened before we were allowed to take the baby," Christa said. She coughed a little, and then she reached beneath the sheets. "Here, I have been waiting to show you this."

Christa handed a few papers to Zofia. Zofia looked at them, bewildered.

"I'm sorry, they are in German. I can't read them," Zofia said.

"They are Katja's birth and christening papers from the home for the Lebensborn. It was called Steinhöring. It was in Munich. I wanted to tell you because I am not well, and if I should die… Well, a day will come when she will want to know the truth. I am hoping, God willing, that you will be there to tell her."

Zofia folded the documents and handed them back to Christa.

"I will do my best for Katja. You know that. She is an innocent child. But you must not think about dying. You must try to get well."

"I am not going to get well, Zofia. It's just a matter of time. It could be a week, or it could be five years. I don't know. Nobody knows. For a long time, my illness was under control. I almost believed I would live a long life... but then..." Again, Christa coughed. "Zofia, you have been very kind to me, and you don't know how often I've felt terribly sorry that all of this happened with the Jews at the hand of the Nazis.

"However, there is one good thing that came from all of this. And I suppose I am selfish, but I am glad to have had the opportunity to know you. You are a strong, kind woman, and without you and your help, I don't know what would have become of Katja and me."

"Thank you. It has been so long since I've felt appreciated in any way. I know all that is happening here at the camp is not your fault."

"Oh, Zofia, I feel so guilty. Not that there is anything I can do, but when I was younger, I just didn't realize it. I never realized. I was excited by the music, the flags, the marching, and Hitler's speeches. I had no idea. I am so ashamed. You have been my rock. You've held me when I was vomiting and never asked for anything. In my heart, I believe that it is because you are a good person, not because you are a prisoner. To me, you were never a prisoner. You have always been a friend."

Zofia smiled and moved the hair out of Christa's eyes.

"Oh, Zofia, there is so much you don't know, so much I am forbidden to tell you," Christa said. "When I adopted Katja, I wanted a child more than anything. I was young and strong, and believe it or not, Manfred and I were very much in love.

"He wasn't the same man he is today. You see, something happened, something terrible. He changed. He was seduced by the power of the Party. This man who I live with is not the man I married. I suppose the death of that love sucked the very life out of me." Christa's voice broke.

Zofia cast her eyes down. She knew that Christa was crying.

"You see, I was a young girl when I first met Manfred. He was an important man in the Party. It impressed me so much. Of course, then, I didn't know what it meant to be a Nazi. I had no idea. I was taken in by the glamor. You see, Manfred worked for Goebbels at the time. When I met him, he looked so handsome and important in his uniform. I was ignorant.

"I didn't think about the Jews or anyone else. I only thought of the moment. Forgive me. Oh, Zofia, forgive me. He took me to parties with all the top officials. I even met Hitler. Yes, it was all glitter in those days. But as they say, all that glitters is not gold, and that, my friend, is true."

Christa stopped for a moment. She labored for breath to continue. "I knew nothing of the cruelty that the Nazis stood for. I suppose I could have known if I'd looked more deeply. But I didn't want to know. I wanted to enjoy the good life. My father, God rest his soul, he knew. I had no ill feelings toward Jews or anyone else. I suppose what I am trying to say is that I am sorry, Zofia. I am sorry for how my people have treated you and yours." She was sobbing.

Zofia nodded.

"Please, be there for my child. I know I have been unable to do much to help you, but I've done what I could. Katja loves you. She thinks of you as a mother. Manfred hardly has time for her, so once I am gone, he will keep you here to care for her. Please care for her."

"I will. I do love her," Zofia said.

"I know you do, and that is why I am counting on you."

Zofia saw Christa's struggle to breathe and how difficult and taxing it was for her to talk.

"Shhh, now get some sleep, and I will bake the cake. All right?" Zofia moved the pillows and helped Christa to lie down.

"Yes, but you will not forget your promise?"

"I will not forget."

"I trust you, Zofia."

Zofia went to the kitchen and began to measure the flour and sugar. Katja squatted, playing quietly on a blanket that Zofia had spread on the floor. Zofia watched her and thought of Eidel. Once, she, too, had trusted the safety of her precious child to another woman. With God's help, Helen cared for Eidel how she would care for Katja.

"Mama?" Katja said.

"Yes," Zofia said.

"My dolly is going to be a Jew, just like you."

Zofia felt the hair on her neck stand at attention. She bent down beside the little girl, hugged her, and smiled.

"Katja, you must never say that to your father, alright?"

"Why not?"

"Because I asked you not to. Will you do that for me, please?" Zofia gently squeezed Katja and kissed her cheek.

"All right. It will be our secret."

"Yes, our secret," Zofia sighed.

Three days prior, Zofia had been cleaning the house when Manfred and several of his coworkers were in his study having a drink. She'd overheard them talking. From their conversation, she gathered that Nazi confidence in Hitler's ability to win the war against the Allies was waning after a decisive loss to the Soviets at the Battle of Stalingrad and the failure to crush the British Royal Air Force at the Battle of Britain.

The British had resumed their bombing attacks on Berlin again with a vengeance, and the Soviets gathered their armies to mount an offensive from the east. And then there were the Americans, the wild card—if the pacifists failed to keep the U.S. out of the war, there could be a new influx of fighting men and equipment to reinforce the battle-weary European Allies.

They spoke quickly, and she was not fluent enough in German to follow everything they said. They complained that Hitler had made a mistake by dividing his army and fighting on two fronts at the same time. The SS officers feared that the Allies were closing in on Germany, and there was great concern that the Fatherland might lose the war.

Quietly as she went about her tasks, Zofia prayed that it was true, that the Allies were on their way, coming to the rescue. How near were they? How soon might this nightmare end? Just the thought of such a miracle made her toes tingle with anticipation. To be free again. To find Eidel and hold her again. Could it be true? Dare she allow herself to believe? For so long, Zofia had wiped all emotion from her heart for fear of another disappointment. But she could not help but feel joyous as she listened to the worries of the SS officers.

Now standing in the kitchen, her mind went back to that conversation she'd overheard. If the camps were liberated, she must leave Katja or take her if Christa could grant such a thing. It would be difficult to leave Katja behind. She loved the child. Zofia glanced at the little girl with the golden curls and marveled again at how much she looked like Christa. With the new information that Christa had just given her, it was hard to believe that Christa was not Katja's birth mother.

It would be a difficult decision to leave Katja, but when the time came, and she was able, God willing, she would leave this terrible place. She would run as fast as she could to find Eidel. Eidel, the child of her blood, waited somewhere in the world for her mother's touch.

That evening, Zofia had served Manfred and Katja their dinner and brought a bowl of soup to Christa in bed. Afterward, she helped Christa out of bed and into the living room. Zofia placed her arms under Christa's and helped her into the plush chair next to the sofa. Then she brought out the cake adorned with candles. Katja squealed with delight, melting Zofia's heart.

Manfred watched Zofia with an intense eye. She could not fully read his expression, only that he fixated his threatening gaze upon her. Perhaps he worried that she might reveal the secrets of his desire for her to his wife. Perhaps he worried about breaking the Nuremberg laws by spilling his seed into her unacceptable womb. When her eyes accidentally met his, his cold, heartless glares made her shiver, knowing he had the power to send her back to the barracks or, worse, to the gas chamber.

A thin layer of frost covered the windows. It would be cold in the barracks, and she would be hungry again. Part of her wanted to be exiled and longed to be away from him, yet another side did not want to leave Katja. Still, another part of her wished for death, yet she was afraid to die.

"Help me, Mama," Katja yelled as she tried to blow out the candles.

Zofia felt a chill run down her back. She cast a quick glance in Manfred's direction. But before he could realize that Katja had called her 'Mama,' Christa stepped in.

"Katja, let Zofia help you," Christa said, "Can you pick her up for me, please, and help her to blow out the candles?"

"Yes, ma'am," Zofia said, lifting Katja to stand on the chair so she would be high enough to reach the cake. Zofia held the little girl's waist, so she would not fall. Katja leaned over.

"Now make a wish," Christa said to Katja.

Katja squeezed her eyes shut. "Ready!" she called out in her baby voice.

"All right, then. Blow out the candles." Christa smiled.

With all her strength, Katja blew and blew while Zofia held her tight.

Finally, all the candles were extinguished, and tiny trickles of smoke drifted up from the cake. Katja smiled, turning to kiss Zofia on the cheek. The little girl was proud of her accomplishment.

"Good job," Manfred offered, sipping a snifter of brandy.

"I love you, Mama," Katja said, but she was looking at Zofia, not Christa.

Zofia smiled at the child, and then her eyes darted to Manfred, hoping he would not take offense and punish her. He seemed unaware. She bit her lower lip.

"Can you cut the cake, please, Zofia?" Christa asked.

"Yes, ma'am."

Zofia took the cake back into the kitchen and cut it into pieces. She delivered the servings on Christa's China plates.

"Mama, you have some, too," Katja said.

"I am," Christa answered.

"No. You too, Mama," Katja said, pointing at Zofia.

"That is not your mother. That is a servant. She does not eat here in our dining room with us," Manfred said harshly.

Katja began to cry. Zofia longed to pick her up and comfort her, but the look on Manfred's face unnerved her.

"Go to the basement. Your job here is done for today," he said curtly.

Zofia turned and left. As she descended the stairs, she heard Katja crying, "I want my mama! I want my mama!"

Dear God, please soften Manfred's heart. Please don't let him hurt the baby or take this out on Christa or me.

Zofia sank onto her bed. "And please, God," she whispered aloud, "let the Allies come quickly."

CHAPTER FIFTY-ONE

The summer of 1943 was exceptionally hot. Fortunately for Zofia, heat rises, and the basement where she slept remained the coolest part of the house. Christa's health seemed to be taking a turn for the better. Due to Zofia's insistence, Christa agreed to allow Zofia to take her outside, where she sat under a tree for an hour each day.

Zofia brought Katja and stayed with Christa in case she should need anything. The child loved to play outside. Zofia taught her how to make necklaces out of dandelions, and although she could not quite grasp the hand coordination, Katja loved to run through the grass, collecting the weeds. Then she would sit beside Zofia, her face determined as she attempted to make the tiny connecting holes in the stems.

"You're getting better at this every day," Zofia said.

Katja giggled, and Christa leaned back to let the sun caress her face.

"I'm glad you convinced me to come outside, Zofia. I needed the sunshine."

"I'm glad you're feeling better. Your color is much better."

"I was very pale."

"Yes, you were quite pale. I was worried about you."

"Zofia, sometimes I think you might be an angel. How can you not hate me for all that you have been through?"

"Because I realize that you had nothing to do with it. In many ways, you are a victim, too." Zofia watched Christa lean back and lie down in the cool grass. She longed to tell her what she endured from Manfred's physical advances, but she could not. Not because she thought that Christa would turn on her and take her husband's side, but because Zofia realized that Christa also endured pain at Manfred's hand.

And yet, he loved her. Every time he forced himself upon Zofia, it was Christa that he yearned for, and Christa's name he called out. Something had happened, something terrible. She wished she could ask but felt that she might be overstepping her bounds. So, Zofia accepted her life, the bad with the good. Even with all that Manfred subjected her to, she knew she still had a better situation than those people who were at the camp.

Sometimes she thought of Marsha in spite of her efforts to wipe the pain of losing her friends from her mind. She hoped that Marsha was still alive and had found someone to share her burden with, another friend.

"Blow the fuzz off this one for me," Katja said, handing Zofia a fuzzy, gray dandelion and interrupting Zofia's thoughts.

"You would like me to do it? Or would you like me to help you to do it?"

"You help me." Katja handed Zofia the weed with a soft, furry top.

"All right, now get ready."

"I'm ready!" Katja said, laughing.

"Blow as hard as you can."

Katja blew, and Zofia helped. Then, as the fluff floated away in the breeze, Katja crumbled into Zofia's arms, laughing.

She needs me. She needs me so much, Zofia thought.

At noon, the sun had risen high in the sky, and the heat bore down upon them.

"I'm tired," Christa said. "Shall we go inside?"

"If you would like. Yes, let's go in."

Zofia prepared a light afternoon meal of bread and cheese.

"It is so hot in here," Christa said.

Zofia increased the speed of the fan. "Does that help?" she asked, bringing Christa a wet cloth to put on her head.

"A little," Christa answered. "It is cooler in the basement than up here. I'd love to go downstairs and lie down in your bed until the sun sets, but I am afraid Manfred wouldn't care for the idea."

Zofia said nothing. The thought of poor Christa lying on her bed, the very place where the awful things happened with Manfred, made her feel disgusted. She was glad that Christa had decided not to sleep in her bed.

That night, like most others, when it got late enough for the darkness to cover the earth, Manfred came downstairs.

"I have a special treat for you," he said. "I brought you some chocolate. That's very generous of me. You realize chocolate is hard to come by."

"Yes, thank you." She took the candy.

"You have become quite special to me, like a good, loyal pet."

Zofia did not answer. She placed the candy on the small table beside her bed.

"Do you pity me?" he asked, looking away.

Trick questions. Nazis always asked trick questions. She smelled the alcohol on his breath.

"My wife hates me. Do you know that?"

She didn't answer or dare to meet his eyes.

"I love her. I've always loved her, and I always will. But I want to take this moment to tell you something. I will never say this again, so you must listen closely."

His words slurred together, assuring her he was drunk.

"You have been a comfort to me. I know that you take good care of Christa and the baby. This means a great deal to me. I also want to say that I feel bad about what I must do to you. But sadly, I cannot seem to stop. I will try to go for several days without coming to you, but it is almost like a drug. I must see you. We must play our game of pretend. Do you understand?"

He took a flask from his pocket and put it to his lips.

She didn't answer.

"I have some bad news for you. Your friend died today. You should be happy that you are nowhere near those barracks. We have had a nasty outbreak of typhus. Those who were infected had to be eliminated to stop the spread of the disease, a messy business, to be sure."

She felt the bile rise in her throat. Marsha had died, sick and alone, while she ate well and slept in a comfortable bed. Even though she came to the home of the *Arbeitsführer* as a prisoner and not of her own choice, she still felt overwhelming guilt.

"I am tired, too tired for our game tonight. So, I suppose you are pleased to be rid of me. Ahhh, well, tomorrow I will make up for it. Sleep well, Zofia. Sorry about the news, but your friend has surely gone to a better place."

She listened to his heels click on the wooden stairs as he ascended back to the main floor.

Once she was alone, Zofia allowed herself the luxury of tears. She cried into her pillow, remembering all the people she'd loved and lost, Marsha, Dovid, Fruma, Gitel, and her parents. They were all gone now. How easy it would be to join them. All she needed to do was take a kitchen knife and run it across the blue vein in her arm.

Then it would be over, but what about Eidel? Eidel was still alive. And for Eidel, she must continue to live. Then she thought about Katja. What would become of the child if she were to end her life? Poor, innocent baby… She had not asked to be brought into this terrible Nazi-ruled world. She had not asked to be bred to be a perfect Aryan child. Katja, although they'd bred her to have golden hair and eyes the color of the sky, and they tried to teach her to hate, even in her youth, she defied them. Instead, she grew into a child with a heart as big as a lion's, filled with love. She was not a child of the Nazis but a child of God.

Zofia had come this far. She would not quit now. The Allies were coming. They must be coming. *Dear God, please let it be soon. I don't have the strength to hold out much longer.*

Relieved to be left alone, Zofia fell into a fitful sleep filled with vivid, frightening dreams. At three-forty-five in the morning, she heard a commotion coming from upstairs. She wasn't sure if she was awake or asleep and dreaming.

There were running footsteps on the floor above her. Manfred bellowed orders in German, and Christa answered in a tearful voice. Another fight? At this time of night? Then Zofia heard the door slam. She smelled the thick, heavy smoke of a nearby fire. Perhaps the house was burning. If it was, she must go upstairs and get outside. But dare she risk going upstairs? What if Manfred was there? She had no idea who slammed the door or why. Would Christa not come and tell her if there was a fire? The smoke grew thicker with each passing moment, and Zofia felt her lungs burning and spasming. She must take the risk and go upstairs.

Gingerly, she opened the door to the basement. There was no sound, but the lights in the house were all on. She tiptoed to Christa's room. As she did, she looked in on Katja to see that the baby was still asleep. Turning the corner in the hallway, Zofia peeked in the doorway of Christa's bedroom.

"Ma'am, are you alright? I'm sorry. I heard a lot of noise, and it's very smoky here."

"Yes, I'm fine. Come, sit down," Christa said, patting the edge of her bed. "There has been an uprising in the camp. One of the buildings has been set on fire. Manfred went there to try to set things in order. However, I am terrified. I am so afraid the prisoners will come here and set fire to the house. If they do, we won't be able to get out. But Manfred insisted that we stay here and wait for him."

Zofia nodded. An uprising? A part of her heart swelled with pride. The prisoners had finally begun to fight back. If they were to die, at least they'd not go to their deaths like lambs to the slaughter. Well, good for them! But still, she did not want to see Katja and Christa killed in the wake of their anger. She had so many mixed emotions.

"Ma'am, may I be so bold as to make a suggestion?" Zofia asked.

"Of course, Zofia."

"Let's go outside into the forest nearby. We can watch and wait to see when his car returns and then come back. It is cooler in the forest, and we will be safe until things settle down. Besides, I am afraid that the smoky air is hard on Katja, and you, as well."

"There are wild creatures in the forest. I am afraid for Katja."

"I know. So am I. However, if we stay here and the house is raided, who knows what will happen?"

Christa took Zofia's hand. "You will help me, please? I am weak and tired."

"Yes, of course. I will help you."

"Then yes, you are right, Zofia. Hurry, go and get the baby. Try not to scare her." Christa said.

When they walked outside, Zofia looked across the yard to see orange flames leaping in a fiery dance inside the camp. From where they stood, she could hear the shouts of the prisoners and the guards. The booming of loud gunfire assaulted their ears, and Katja began to cry.

"Shhh, it's all right. Shhh," Zofia said.

"Up," Katja said, tears still covering her face as she raised her arms.

Something exploded, and the sound shook the trees. Katja screamed in terror.

Zofia lifted the little girl into her arms.

Katja snuggled into Zofia's chest, weeping softly as Zofia carried her. With her other hand, Zofia wrapped her arm around Christa, helping her to walk. The ground shook beneath them as the two women and the little girl headed into the dark woods.

"I'm scared," Katja said, her voice trembling. "Mama, I am so scared."

"No, don't be afraid. This is going to be an adventure," Zofia whispered into Katja's ear as she hugged the baby tighter. Katja was getting heavier, and it was hard to hold her with one hand. But despite the pain in her shoulder, Zofia continued until she felt they were a safe distance from the conflict.

It did prove to be cooler in the forest. They could smell the smoke, but it was diluted and not as hard to breathe. The three sat down. Zofia propped Christa against a tree and then did the same for herself. Katja, usually curious about everything, sat still and quietly. She did not try to wander. Instead, she stayed close to the two women, who listened to the hooting of owls combined with the mysterious sounds of the forest at night and the distant uproar of the rebellion.

Katja laid her head on Zofia's lap. Zofia patted her back as the child curled up and fell asleep. Neither of the two women slept during the dark of night. They watched the sunrise in silence.

Zofia longed for freedom, not only for herself but also for all the others who suffered in the camp, but her heart was conflicted. She couldn't care less what happened to Manfred. Whatever ill befell him was well-deserved. However, Katja and Christa had never hurt her or anyone else, and she couldn't bear to think of what might happen to them should the prisoners have taken charge once the morning light came flickering through the trees.

Christa had begun to nod off as dawn broke, but Zofia stayed wide awake. She considered running away. This was her chance. She could be free of this nightmare at last. But it came at a high price: the possible sacrifice of an innocent child whom she had come to cherish and who called her "Mama." Her limbs ached to run. They trembled with the desire to stretch and dash deeper into the overgrown trees. She was sure that even if Christa awoke, she would not give her away. In fact, although Christa needed Zofia, Zofia knew she would turn a blind eye, let her get away, and then pray for her safety.

And that was why Zofia never left.

Sometime later that afternoon, stillness settled over the camp. Both Christa and Katja were awake now. Katja was hungry and continually asked for food.

"We have to go back," Christa said. "Do you think it's safe yet?"

"I don't know."

"Mama, I'm hungry," Katja said again, tugging at the hem of Zofia's uniform.

"I know, little sunshine, I know. You will have something to eat very soon." Zofia had taken to calling Katja 'little sunshine.'

This would quiet Katja for a few minutes, and then she would remind Zofia of her hunger again.

"We have to take our chances and go back," Christa said. "Do you agree?"

"Yes. We have no food," Zofia said. She stood up and brushed the branches and dirt off her clothes. Then she helped Christa to her feet, gathered Katja into her arms, and they headed back to the house.

Everything was just as they'd left it. Manfred had not returned since the previous night. Zofia secretly hoped he might have been killed in the uprising. She hoped that all the Nazis had been murdered during the night. That would make everything easier if only the prisoners didn't raid the house. She would care for Christa and Katja. They would stay in the house. And as soon as it was safe, Zofia would find Eidel and bring her back to live with the other two. Zofia would explain to Christa. She was sure Christa would understand.

But that was a daydream. The door opened, and Manfred entered. His eyes were bloodshot and wild with fear and exhaustion. His clothing reeked of smoke, and his hair stood on end and was disheveled.

"The prisoners went mad. They destroyed the entire camp. It's in shambles. They were wild and dangerous. It's been a terrible night. I'm waiting for orders from my superior officers."

"Are you alright?" Christa's skin was pale, and her eyes were puffy from lack of sleep. "Is it safe for us to stay here?"

"For now, I think so. I'm tired. I'm going to bed." He took a flask out of his pocket and took a swig.

Christa looked over at Zofia with worried eyes.

"Hungry," Katja said.

"May I give her something to eat?"

"Of course, and please have something yourself. I have to lie down. I am feeling terribly weak," Christa said.

CHAPTER FIFTY-TWO

On August 18 and 19, 1943, in a bold attempt to resist the treatment they'd endured, the prisoners at Treblinka, emaciated, disease-ridden, and weak, staged an uprising. Following this most unexpected display of force, most inmates who had not escaped were transferred to Sobibor (a death camp), where they were executed. Approximately twenty to thirty brave souls remained at Treblinka. They, too, were murdered. Then, in October 1943, the Nazis shut Treblinka down forever. The camp was completely dismantled ahead of the Soviet advance, and a farmhouse was built on the site to hide the evidence of the genocide.

CHAPTER FIFTY-THREE

In the weeks that followed, Zofia sensed the tension in the house. Manfred did not come to her at night, and she was glad he didn't. However, she was afraid she might be sent back to the barracks.

At night, while she was in the basement, she could hear raised voices coming from upstairs. Although she could not make out what they were saying, Zofia knew that frequent arguments broke out between Christa and Manfred, where she heard her name mentioned. She could not hear the entire conversation. It unnerved her. What were they planning? She wanted to ask Christa but was afraid to overstep her bounds. Christa had been kind to her, but she must never forget that she was little more than a slave and could be returned to the camp or worse.

It had been weeks since they'd sat outside under the tree.

"Ma'am, would you like to get some fresh air?" Zofia asked one morning in late October. The weather had cooled, and she thought it would be good for Christa.

"Sit down, Zofia."

Zofia sat on the edge of the bed. Katja came rushing in.

"Play with me, Mama," Katja handed Zofia a doll.

"In a minute, little sunshine, I am talking to your mother right now."

"Up."

Zofia picked Katja up and propped her on her lap.

"I should not be telling you this. If Manfred knew, he would never forgive me. But you have always been helpful to me, and so I must give you some advanced notice. What I am about to tell you is top-secret."

Zofia felt the hairs prickle on the back of her neck, and she shivered.

"Zofia, we are leaving here, Manfred, Katja, and I. The camp is being destroyed. That is probably a very good thing. However, I will miss you terribly. I cannot take you with me. I've begged. Believe me, I have begged. Manfred wanted to have you transported to another camp. I pleaded with him not to. He has finally agreed. Instead, we are just going to move in the middle of the night. If you stay here at the house, the other Nazi officers will come and find you. They will send you to another concentration camp.

"However, since this house is off the campgrounds, on the night we leave, you could easily slip into the forest unnoticed. Take some food with you and go. Get as far away from here as you can. I wish I could offer you more, but I cannot. I have no more to offer. When this is all over, please try to come to find Katja and me. She will need you."

Katja reached up and played with the hair that Zofia had regrown. Her tiny fingers curled into the dark locks.

Zofia looked at the baby, then back at Christa.

"She will be all right, at least for now. I pray that my health won't give out until you can take her. I know you will miss her. But things have taken a bad turn, and we must go. Manfred insists. Again, please promise me that you will try to find Katja when the war is over. She will need you."

Zofia's head was reeling. She felt slightly dizzy. "I don't know. What about her father?"

"Promise me you will try to find her."

"I promise. I will do my best. I don't know what the future brings."

"Oh, Zofia, nor do I."

"When should I leave?"

"We are going tonight. Listen closely after it gets dark. As soon as you hear we are gone, take what you can and run. No one should come to the house until morning."

"Yes, ma'am. Thank you for helping me."

"Zofia, if circumstances had been different, we might have been two friends having lunch at each other's homes, but the Nazis, the war, and my husband made things the way they are. All we can do is try to cope with what has been given to us."

Zofia held Katja a little tighter. She closed her eyes and inhaled Katja's baby scent. Tears threatened, but she did not cry. Zofia nodded her head.

"God be with you, Zofia. Please… Don't forget us."

That night, Zofia listened. She heard the movement upstairs. Katja was crying, calling out for her mama. She wanted to go to the child, to comfort her, but she could not. There were footsteps on the floor above her, whispers in the darkness, and then silence.

Zofia waited for almost half an hour to be sure that the Blaus were gone. Then she ran up the stairs, gathered as much food as she could, and wrapped it in a towel. She took the largest of the flasks from the cabinet, filled it with water, and added a large butcher knife from the drawer to the things she would take with her.

Next, she ran to the bedroom where she had cared for Christa these last few years. Christa had left several dresses and undergarments. Zofia quickly changed her clothes, abandoning the camp uniform. Her hair had grown back to touching her shoulders, so the telltale sign of the shaved head would not give her away. Still, she took a scarf from Christa's drawer to cover her hair. Now she would look like any other Polish woman, and no one would suspect she was an escaped Jew.

Zofia gazed into the mirror. It had been a long time since she studied her appearance. She'd grown older since the days of life with Fruma and Gitel. Fine lines had begun to form around her eyes, eyes that had seen far too much misery. Her dark, curly hair fell about her face. Her figure was slender. All in all, she was not unattractive. In fact, some might even call her pretty. She sighed. Once, long ago, being beautiful seemed to be the most important thing in the world to her. How little all of that mattered now…

As she passed through the kitchen, she took another hunk of bread and began eating. Then she stepped out of the house, never looked back, and headed as quickly as she could, going forward into the unknown.

Darkness hovered over her, but the moon shed just enough light for her to find her way. And quietly, like a shadow in the night, Zofia left the home of the *Arbeitsführer* and disappeared into the darkness on the way into the forest.

Her heart was heavy with a jumble of emotions. She was free, and for the longest time, it had been her dream to be away from the camp, away from the horrible *Arbeitsführer* at last, to be free. But she was also on her own, in the dark, in the forest. From now on, she must fend for herself. She must take great care not to be captured, for if she was, there was no telling where she might end up. Zofia knew that she had been lucky to be sent to work in the home of the *Arbeitsführer*, even with all she had to endure. She had seen enough of the camp to know what could have happened if she had not been chosen as a house servant. She'd spent those first months in the barracks with the dirt, starvation, and disease before Manfred had decided she should stay at the house.

If she had remained at the camp, she would probably have gotten typhoid when the epidemic broke out. Christa had allowed her to bathe, and she'd been so grateful to be clean. But she knew that her fellow Jews were much less fortunate. Should she be captured, she would know their fate firsthand.

The forest buzzed with life. A wolf howled in the distance, and a night bird cawed. The hooting of an owl came from above her. The thick odor of vegetation mixed with flowers surrounded her. *Dear God, help Katja and Christa. Watch over them.* She half-walked, half-ran through the forest, the brush sometimes scraping against her legs until she was well into the thick, protective blanket of trees.

Then, once she was sure she was far away from the house and the camp, Zofia sat down. A small rodent scampered across the ground, startling her.

Taking a deep breath, Zofia leaned her head against the rough bark of an oak tree and closed her eyes. *Katja.* The tiny face appeared in her mind. Soon, she would start asking for Zofia. Katja, her only sunshine since she'd come to this place. Where were they taking her? Would she be safe? Why do I care? So many Jewish babies have suffered. Why should I care for this spoiled little Aryan girl? This child who has never known pain or loss… Why, why do I care? But she did care. With her whole heart, she cared. Katja was an innocent victim, too, although she did not know it.

The child had been bred like a puppy to be what the Nazis wanted her to be, a blonde-haired, blue-eyed Aryan. They'd decided before Katja was born that she would grow up to hate the Jews, but they'd not counted upon Zofia. Katja, with her tiny fingers in Zofia's curls. Her innocent giggles when Zofia tickled her chubby little tummy. The way she sat, her face serious, eyes glowing, as Zofia told her a fairy tale in Polish. Would the little girl even remember her? Probably not. She was far too young to remember.

Zofia looked up at the sky filled with stars. A full moon winked at her. She pulled her knees up to her chest. So much loss… Everyone and everything she'd ever loved had been taken from her. Yes, I am alive but alone, except for Eidel, my Eidel. I must find her. Then she realized that she must stay far away from Eidel, at least for now. If she showed up in Eidel's life, she would endanger her baby, Helen, her family, and herself. Right now, Eidel was safe. She must not threaten that safety in any way, even if she longed to see her more than anything in the world. Eidel… At least, Eidel was safe.

The unfamiliar noises of the forest frightened her, keeping her awake through the night. She could not help but remember the night she'd spent under the umbrella of the trees, holding little Katja as she watched the smoke rise from the camp in the distance.

There was no doubt in her mind. She would miss that little girl; someday, if it were safe, she'd find a way back to the child.

As she wrapped her arms around herself, Zofia's thoughts drifted to Fruma, Gitel, and Marsha. She'd tried for so long to suppress her feelings of sadness and loss. It was hard to believe they were all dead. And Dovid? What of Dovid? She'd never been in love with him, but in a way, she'd loved him. His only crime had been falling in love with her. It was best not to let the guilt consume her. If she did, she might just lay her tired head down in the cool grass and sleep until she died. She was so tired, so exhausted, so utterly spent. No, she must find the strength to go on. Soon, this would all end. Soon, it would be safe to go to Eidel.

When the sun peeked through the trees, Zofia stood up. Her head ached, and her throat was parched. She must look for water. It took a moment to stretch the stiffness from her back and legs after a night lying on the hard ground.

Zofia looked around her, assessing the situation. Where she stood, the trees had grown so thick it would take an effort to find a path through them. She had no idea which way to go, which way was north or south, not that it mattered to her. All she knew was that she must find water to survive. For hours, she walked, pushing her way through the brush, but found no pond or stream. Rays of hot sun filtered through the trees, and the heat of the day mixed with a lack of sleep caused her to feel exhausted again. She rationed the food and water she'd brought from the house, but it would not last very long.

It took almost a week of wandering in the woods for Zofia to exhaust her food and water supply. She could hear her stomach grumbling, and from time to time, pain shot through her belly, doubling her over. It became hard to swallow because her mouth was as dry as a sandy beach. She grew even more tired and listless. A dull ache persisted behind her eyes, and she found it difficult to move when the sun was high in the sky. *I am dying. I'm dying of thirst and lack of food*, she thought. But she was too tired to care.

Sometimes her legs cramped up until she could not straighten them, causing her to fall to the ground. As hard as she could, she massaged the tender skin until it subsided. Still, the relentless sun trickled through the trees and found her. It washed over her with life-sapping heat.

She was drained and too tired to keep walking. Zofia sat down under the shade of a tree. Her mind drifted again. This time, she remembered dancing with Dovid. He'd hummed a waltz, and the two of them danced in the small, dark room where he lived. *Traa laa, traa laa.* She could see it in her mind's eye. *Gentle Dovid. Traa laa, traa laa… If I die, I will see everyone I've lost. Eidel will be all right. She won't even remember me. Traa laa. Dovid's hand at the small of her back. His other one holding hers…*

Her tongue felt thick, like a giant snake, filling her throat and choking her. She tried to swallow but couldn't and laid her head against the tree and closed her eyes.

She felt a tiny drop and then another. God knew where she was. He was not ready for her to come to Him, not just yet. Then a light rain trickled down from the sky. It filtered through the trees and covered the ground. The sound of the drops hitting the earth was the most exquisite sound she had ever heard.

Zofia opened her flask to refill her water supply. The raindrops caressed her skin, and she lay down where she saw a large opening in the trees that would allow lots of water. She opened her mouth wide, and scrumptious tiny bits of water found their way to her tongue. Relief came over her, and she laughed aloud. She lay there long after the rain stopped, looking up at the sky.

Along the west side of her vision, she caught sight of a rainbow. It shone brightly against a sunlit background. The loveliness of it took her by surprise, and she was suddenly aware of all the beauty surrounding her. She took in the green of the forest, the flowers that grew wild, spreading their sweet perfume, the crisp ice-blue sky with its sugar clouds, and a sense of well-being settled over her as if God were watching.

From where she lay, she observed a spider spinning a web in a tree across the path. It worked diligently to build its future. Once, she'd feared spiders. Today she would learn from that spider. She, too, would work hard and build a future, and soon, very soon, she would reunite with her daughter. If God had meant for her to die, she would have died. This short rain was a sign that she had much more to do in this life. Zofia closed her eyes, and a relaxed smile came over her face. Then exhaustion overcame her, and she drifted off to sleep.

CHAPTER FIFTY-FOUR

Zofia awoke with a start to find two burly, unshaven men standing over her, one shirtless and the other wearing a Nazi uniform with all the adornments removed. *Deserters.* Her mind, still cloudy with sleep, raced at the thought of danger. *Would they rape and kill her? Quite possibly. Why not? There was no one around for miles, and even if there were, she was a Jew. They could do as they wished.* She scampered to get up, but her legs gave way with fear, and she fell back to the ground. Her heart thumped so loudly that she was sure they could hear it. Then one of them spoke.

"Zofia? Is that you?" he asked.

She did not recognize him.

"It's me, Isaac Zuckerman. We went to school together in Warsaw. It's not surprising that you don't recognize me. It was many years ago, and I've certainly aged."

Isaac? She faintly recalled a chubby little boy, weak and shy, bearing no resemblance to the man standing in front of her now. This man was bold and unafraid, muscles swelling across his bare chest. He'd grown tall, and the golden curls his mother had kept short in his youth were now long, framing his face. Hunger and hard work had chiseled his features, leaving him with a strong jaw and high cheekbones. He smiled at her and his luminous brown eyes glowed.

"I certainly remember you. How could something like a Nazi takeover have made you even prettier than I remember? You tell me. How did that happen?" he asked and laughed.

She looked away, embarrassed by his froward comment.

"Sorry if I embarrassed you. I'm only trying to help you to relax."

She nodded.

"You have been hiding out in the forest?"

"Yes. Are you?"

"Yes, there is an entire group of us, a band of Hitler's escapees," he smiled. "We have learned how to survive in the wild. Can you believe it? Would you like to come and meet the others?" Again, he smiled at her, a warm, welcoming smile.

She nodded.

"By the way, this is my friend, Shlomie. He is a Jew, too. I guess the Nazi uniform probably threw you off. He took it off a dead officer before he left Treblinka. That officer had been his tormentor for years. Then there was an uprising, and Shlomie killed him. As a trophy, he took the uniform. Right, Shlomie?"

"Yes, right. Nice to meet you, Zofia."

"I was at Treblinka, too."

"We never saw each other because you were on the women's side."

"Yes, I know. But I was also chosen to work at the home of the *Arbeitsführer*."

"That son of a bitch! Manfred Blau, right?" Shlomie asked.

"Yes, right."

"Once, I saw him kill a man by castrating him. The pleasure I saw on his face when he cut the man made me sick. He's a real deviate. Maybe he is a latent homosexual."

She turned away, feeling the bile rise in her throat and wishing he would change the subject.

"It's too bad I didn't see him during the uprising. I would have returned the favor by doing the same to him," Shlomie said.

"Enough of this talk. It's upsetting. We've just found Zofia. Why don't we try to make her feel welcome? Come on, Shlomie. Let's try to take our focus off of the Nazis, at least for a little while. All right? What do you say, Zofia? Would you like that?"

"Yes, good idea," Zofia said.

"Come, follow me. I'll bet you're hungry. We have food," Isaac said as he helped Zofia to her feet.

At first, she was a little wobbly.

"Steady there," Isaac said, taking her arm. "I'll help you." Isaac slipped his strong, muscular arm under hers and guided Zofia forward.

Isaac led her through a thick growth of trees to a house that had been built out of logs. There was no glass in the windows, just open space, but it offered some shelter from the elements.

"Did you build this?"

"We all built it together. For now, it's home. With the help of God, we will be here and be safe until the war ends. I don't know if you have heard the good news, but Germany is falling. We had a guest the other day, a Jew passing by on his way to find his family in Russia. He told us he'd heard this over the BBC on the radio. He said that soon the Allies will come marching in, and the war will be over."

"From your mouth to God's ears," Shlomie said. "It should only happen soon."

Zofia smiled at them. "I'm glad you found me. I was beginning to feel like I was going to go crazy wandering the forest alone with nothing but my thoughts and memories."

"The memories are the hardest part," Shlomie said. "I avoid them whenever possible."

Isaac knocked on the door to the little cabin. "It's Isaac and Shlomie."

"Itzik, is that you?"

"Yes," Isaac said, turning to Zofia, "'Itzik' is my Yiddish name. I thought I should explain."

"I like it, Itzik."

He blushed as he opened the door. Inside the cottage was a

single, unfurnished room. Horse blankets lay strewn about the floor. In the corner, two rifles stood against a wall, and a small pile of handguns and ammunition lay beneath them. Three women and four men other than Isaac and Shlomie were scattered around the room.

"So, who is this?" one of the women asked. She appeared to be around thirty, a pretty woman, tall and slender, with dark hair caught in a braid down her back. Her skin was tan against her bright blue eyes.

"Sarah, this is Zofia. I've known her since we were children. She went to school with me in Warsaw."

"Hello, Zofia."

Zofia nodded to Sarah.

"Shlomie and I found her in the forest. I think she might be hungry."

"Yes, I would think so," Sarah said, watching Isaac. She seemed uncomfortable with how he looked at Zofia, and Zofia wondered if the two were lovers.

"Here, sit down." Sarah motioned to a blanket that was curled up on the dirt floor.

Zofia sat down.

"Let me introduce you to everyone," Isaac said. "You've already met Shlomie and Sarah. Sarah is like a sister to me. You're really going to like her." Isaac smiled at Sarah. Zofia saw Sarah return the smile, only to have it fade from her face quickly. "This is Rivka, and that is her sister, Esther."

Zofia nodded.

"Over here are Moishe and Ben. They are friends who escaped from Soldau, and this is Aaron."

"Nice to meet all of you," Zofia said.

"Itzik, I can understand your kindness and generosity, but we hardly have enough food for us. I mean, yes, we can offer her a meal. But I think after she has finished, your friend should go on her way," Sarah said. She handed Zofia an apple and a piece of matzo which had been made from stolen flour, mixed with water, and then cooked on a stone over an open fire.

"We were all in her position once. How can we even think of turning her away? Seriously, Sarah, sometimes you surprise me. I refuse to even listen to that. Zofia stays," Isaac said.

"I agree with Isaac," Shlomie said.

"Let's take a vote?" Ben offered.

"Fair enough," Isaac nodded.

"All in favor of Zofia staying here, raise your hands," Ben said. Everyone except Sarah raised their hands.

"It's decided. If you want to stay, you are welcome here," Ben said.

Zofia smiled. "Thank you." She felt the tears tickle her eyes. Bowing her head, she whispered, "Thank you."

"Think nothing of it," Isaac said. "It is as it should be, Jews helping other Jews, isn't that right, Shlomie?"

"Of course it is," Shlomie smiled. "I'm going out to dig up the bag of vegetables. Can you help me, Isaac?"

"Yes, of course."

"Dig up vegetables?" Zofia asked.

"Yes," Isaac smiled. "We've learned to plant them on the ground in these burlap bags that we found in one of the barns we raided. In fact, it was Shlomie's idea. He's a scientist, you know. Anyway, we plant them during the winter so that they stay fresh. When we dig them up again, sometimes during the winter when the ground is not too hard or at the beginning of summer, they are perfect. That way, if we can get it during the summer or autumn when it is most plentiful, we have a small hoard of food to carry us through."

"That's brilliant," Zofia said.

"Thank you," Shlomie said, grinning from ear to ear. "It works, anyway."

CHAPTER FIFTY-FIVE

Over the next several days, Zofia learned the stories of her companions. They'd all been in camps except for Isaac. When the Germans began rounding up Jews for deportation, his father insisted that he live with a Gentile family. They'd taken him for a price, and for a while, all was well. But one of the neighbors turned them in, and the entire family was arrested, along with Isaac.

As they were herded into the back of a large, open truck filled with people, Isaac grabbed the gun from the guard. Then he hit the guard across the face with the pistol and ran. As he raced across the street and through the crowds, he could hear gunshots behind him. He just kept running and never looked back.

"God was with me," Isaac said, "and I also believe the ghosts of my parents were with me as my angels. Bullets were flying all around me, but somehow, I was not hit."

"Where did you go?"

"I hid in abandoned buildings. At night I made my way out of the city until I reached the forests."

"Then?"

"Then I had to survive on my wits. I stole food from local farms at night when I could. Sometimes, I didn't eat. The winters were the worst. They still are, even for all of us here in the cabin."

"I'm sure. I assume food is scarcer and the cold… Well… Where did you sleep?"

"Barns, mostly tool sheds, or a cellar, sometimes. I met some very kind people along the way, too. They sheltered me for a night or gave me a heel of bread. It helped. I couldn't expect them to let me stay. If they were caught hiding a Jew, they would risk death. But the amazing thing is that there were people who were kind and brave enough to take that risk."

"You were lucky to have found the rest of these Jews here."

"Yes, I was, and I cherish their friendship. Together, things are much easier than when I was alone."

Shlomie walked over. He placed the bag of vegetables on the table. "Now I am going outside to gather berries. Either of you want to come along and help?"

"Yes, of course," Zofia said.

"Why don't you stay here and help me clean the guns?" Sarah said to Isaac. "The picking of a few berries doesn't take an army."

Isaac looked disappointed. "Yes, all right."

Zofia and Shlomie walked through the forest. "Now here, let me show you which ones we can eat and which we can't." Shlomie showed Zofia what was edible and what was poisonous.

"You learned all of this?"

"I was going to major in science. I planned to find cures for diseases if I had been allowed to attend college. I had big plans. But now, I am just happy that I know a little about botany. It helps the group. I make medicines when I can, too."

"You live on the plants for the most part?"

"No, we live on whatever we can get. We steal a little food from a local farm. Sometimes people are kind, and they give us food.

"Isaac came to us one day while we were sleeping on the ground. He had an ax in his hand, so we built this cabin together. He has learned to fashion a bow and arrow, and he hunts. We never use our ammunition for hunting because we might need it to fight if the Germans ever found us."

"A bow and arrow? Really? I remember Isaac as being this shy little boy."

"Yes, well, the Nazis have managed to change all of us. I've learned to fish with my bare hands. Can you imagine? There was a time when I was afraid of water. Now I swim like I was born to be an Olympic swimmer."

"You are right about that. The Nazis really changed my life, too," Zofia said.

"You want to talk about it?"

"No, and yes. I just can't. It hurts too much to talk about the losses."

"Yes, I know. I lost my parents, my sisters, and my fiancée."

She nodded. They walked in silence for a while, gathering berries and green plants.

"Shlomie?"

"Yes…?"

"Isaac and Sarah, are they a couple?"

"She would like them to be. He is distant. It's strange. I mean, Isaac is one of the kindest people I know, but he is hard to get close to. He keeps his distance from all of us. I guess it is his way of surviving."

"That makes sense. If you never let yourself love anyone or anything, you can't get hurt. Still, you're right. He is very nice."

"Yes, he is, and you're probably right. I think that is the reason he doesn't allow anyone too close. He keeps to himself and goes out alone to hunt. He is generous and always shares his kill with the group. I think that a part of him died when he had to leave his family and then when he had to come out into the forests."

"Does he talk to you?"

"A little, not much. You are going to see that here in our little group, nobody pries. Every one of us has a past that is unpleasant. People we loved, gone, disappeared, dead. We share what we choose to share, but no one asks questions."

"Can I ask you a question?"

"Yes, if you would like." He had been kneeling over a green leafy plant. He stopped and looked up.

"You were in Treblinka, yes?"

"Yes." Shlomie nodded, looking up at her.

"Did you know a man named Dovid Greenspan? He was from Warsaw?"

"Yes, I knew him."

"You did?" She felt her heart jump in her chest.

"Is he… alive?"

"No, I'm sorry. The *Arbeitsführer* shot him. I saw it with my own eyes."

"Dovid?" She sat down on the ground. It was too hard to take this news standing up.

"Yes."

"He was a friend of mine."

"Your boyfriend?"

"Yes, and no. Just someone I once knew." She felt her heart sink. Dovid. Poor Dovid. Fruma… Gitel… Dovid.

"I'm sorry."

"You knew the *Arbeitsführer*?" she asked.

"Manfred Blau?"

"Yes, Manfred Blau."

"Oh yes, I knew him. He was a sadist. A horrible man, one of the worst. He hated the men and had some sort of sexual problem with them. I am not sure what it was. He did terrible things to the men: castrated them, tortured them. It was horrible."

"I knew him, too. But he wasn't a homosexual. You mentioned that before, but he wasn't… I assure you."

Shlomie nodded. "I believe you. And I'm sorry for your suffering. I guess that is all I can say."

"Yes, and I feel the same about yours."

"You like Isaac, don't you?"

She shrugged.

"I can tell. He is a difficult man, a loner. I wouldn't want to see you get hurt."

"I don't think I like him in that way. I am just impressed with how he has grown into such a strong and capable man."

Shlomie nodded his head. "All the women have a special place in their hearts for Isaac. I wish I knew why." Zofia thought she saw a longing in his gaze when he looked at her.

CHAPTER FIFTY-SIX

As THE WINTER cold descended upon the forest, the men took wooden slat covers made of tree branches that they'd built and began to cover the windows.

"It gets a little dark and depressing here during the winter. Still, we must remember that we are the fortunate ones. We are still alive," Shlomie told Zofia as he hoisted a large square of wood slat over the window. Isaac came and held the heavy wood while Shlomie hammered nails into the corners.

"Where did you fellows get all of these tools?" Zofia asked, looking at the axe and the hammers, the nails.

"Stolen," Isaac said, smiling.

"From whom?" she asked. She watched Isaac closely. His smile was infectious.

"Local farms, mostly. We took the guns off of dead Nazis."

"I'm impressed."

"As well you should be. We have set up a palace for you here, my lady," Isaac said.

She laughed.

"I'm sorry to say that the winter will be rough. We don't always have enough to eat, but we are lucky. It's true. At least we are alive and not in camps," Shlomie said.

"At least we are together," Sarah said, walking over to Isaac.

"Yes, and of course, ladies, I will do what I can to see to it that you do not starve. In fact, I will take my trusty bow and arrow and catch you both your own rabbit. How does that sound?"

"Oh, Isaac, you are always being silly," Sarah said.

"What good is life if we can't stay happy?"

"He never takes anything seriously," Sarah said, shaking her head.

"No, I don't take anything seriously, not after all I have seen. I live for the moment, and right at this very moment, I am happy. I am surrounded by my friends. There is a kettle outside with a nice stew simmering. What more could a man ask for?"

"Love?" Sarah asked.

"Love, yes. It is the greatest gift. It can make all darkness light," Shlomie said.

"That it can, but it can also make you very vulnerable. That's something that none of us can afford right now," Isaac said.

"I would take the risk. I would be willing to pay the price," Shlomie said.

"You're such a romantic," Isaac laughed.

"Have you ever loved anyone?" Sarah asked, her glare directed at Isaac.

"My family, but if you mean romantically, no. I didn't have a chance. I was too young to think of those things when all this started," Isaac said.

Once they finished covering the windows, the four friends sat down to eat a small meal of matzo and apples.

"After eating, I am going outside to chop wood. Would you like to help me, Shlomie?" Isaac asked.

Shlomie nodded.

"I'd like to help too," Zofia said.

"You and Sarah can gather the wood and put it into piles. That would be very helpful."

"Of course. I would be happy to," Sarah said, taking a bite of apple.

Isaac was shirtless, his back tanned from the sun, rippled with muscles, and glistening with sweat as he lifted the axe. Zofia could not help but feel a tingle when she looked at him. His golden hair and dark eyes were like the pictures of the Greek gods she'd seen in books long ago when she was still in school.

For a second, she remembered Mr. Taylor. What a fool she'd been to fall for him and quit school because of her embarrassment. If only she'd realized that he wasn't worth the effort. Then again, if she'd never quit school, she would never have been blessed with the friendship of Fruma and Gitel, two people she would remember for the rest of her life.

Shlomie was thinner than Isaac. It was obvious to Zofia that the heavy labor was harder for him, but Shlomie chopped wood beside Isaac, who made it look effortless. In fact, Isaac amazed her.

The overweight little Jewish son of the baker had grown into a man who seemed able to overcome almost every obstacle. He hunted, usually returning with a rabbit or bird. Sometimes he and Shlomie fished. Shlomie would bring back a catch or two, but Isaac always came back with a big smile and a pile of fish in his hands.

Occasionally at night, the men raided the neighboring farms. They took as little as possible, just enough to survive, hoping the farmers would not notice the food missing. It was easy to find apple trees with rotting fruit that had fallen to the ground. They cleared the ground, collecting the apples in buckets they'd stolen.

In the summer, at night, they walked for miles until they were far enough from the cabin to feel safe. Then they dug up potatoes, carrying them back to bury them near the cabin for the lean winter months. Several times in the fall during their hunt for potatoes, they found corn growing along the edge of the forest, which they took and hoarded.

One night, Isaac walked almost ten miles to steal extra horse blankets. He had explained before he left that he did not want to take them from the barns nearby lest they come in search of the thieves.

All night, Zofia lay awake, listening and wondering if he'd been caught. Nobody else seemed concerned, and she wondered how often he did this. But no matter how hard she tried, she could not sleep. Her mind raced with frightening possibilities.

By the time Zofia heard Isaac's footsteps outside the cabin, the sun had begun to rise. She lay squeezing her eyes shut, pretending to be asleep, not wanting him to know how worried she had been about him.

The door flew open. With her eyes cracked just a little, she watched him lay a huge pile of horse blankets in the corner of the room. He turned quickly to catch her watching him. A broad smile came over his face, and for the first time, Zofia noticed that Isaac had dimples.

"Good morning to you, princess," he teased. "Your humble servant was out securing your needs for the winter."

"Yes, I can see that. Thank you. I'm sure that everyone here thanks you," she said.

She sat up, and he sat down beside her.

"Come on, laugh a little. It doesn't hurt."

She smiled.

"There you go. You look even prettier when you smile."

"Oh Isaac, aren't you ever serious?"

"You want me to be serious, huh?"

"Yes, sometimes I do."

"All right, then. Winter is on its way, and I have to make use of the time I have now, while the weather is still good, to be sure we have enough food and blankets to keep us all from freezing or starving to death."

Zofia thought about the coat that Christa had given her long ago. She wished she had it now.

"What about making fires? We gathered all that wood. Won't that help?" Zofia asked.

"Yes, of course, it will, but then again, fires send smoke signals, and we have to be careful. We can't make them too big. In fact, they cannot be much bigger than the ones we use for cooking."

"It is going to be rough," Zofia said. She felt the heat of his body next to hers. He smelled fresh, like the air outside, mingled with a little perspiration. She inhaled deeply, not realizing that she had.

Isaac saw her face and laughed. "I guess I must smell terrible after that walk last night. I'm going to the pond this afternoon to take a bath."

She looked away.

"And by the way, I brought you a present."

She turned her head to meet his eyes.

"Oh?"

"It's not much, but I thought you might like it. Here." He took a bar of plain brown soap out of his pocket. "Of course, it's not diamonds, but considering our present situation, it was the best I could do. Anyway, when I saw this soap in one of the barns, I thought you might like to have it."

Soap was a luxury, and even though it had been used probably on a farm animal, Zofia was genuinely touched. "You thought of me?"

"Actually, yes, I did. The whole time I was gone." He put the soap into her hand.

"Thank you, Isaac. This is very kind of you."

He shrugged. "Like I said, it was the best I could do."

"Well, it was very nice of you to bring me anything," she smiled.

Sarah stirred where she lay across the room, and Zofia realized that she was awake and listening.

"Nothing for me, Isaac?" Sarah asked.

"I brought blankets for everyone," he answered.

She nodded, her face scrunched in disappointment. Then she stood up, stretching. "Well, you should eat something. You've been out walking all night."

The rest of the group began to awaken.

"We have some corn meal left from last week. I am going to make some porridge. If you want it, help yourself," Sarah said, not looking directly at Isaac. She filled the kettle with water, then tossed a handful of meal into the pot. With her back straight and her head high, she walked outside.

Zofia watched Sarah. She felt bad because Sarah's feelings for Isaac were obvious to everyone. Zofia did not want to come between them. And yet, when he talked to her in his cavalier style, she looked into Isaac's eyes. It was as if they were living a normal life, not stuck in a cabin in the forest hiding from the Nazis. He made her feel good and light, sometimes even giddy.

Over the next several weeks, everyone did what they could to build the stockpile for the winter. They worked hard well into the night while the weather was warm enough to do so. For now, they had water, but once the stream froze, they would have to melt the snow over a low fire.

"I hate the winters," Shlomie said.

"There is nothing we can do. We must make the best of what we have. I will hunt as much as I can."

"Yes, but sometimes the snow gets so high that you cannot even walk."

"I'll manage," Isaac said.

"I'm a little scared," Zofia said.

"Don't be. I'll do what I can. I've learned to ice fish. That should help, too. We'll get by just fine." He smiled.

She smiled back, a little nervous.

CHAPTER FIFTY-SEVEN

THE WINTER WAS BRUTAL. It came on with a blast of frozen air and gusty winds, carrying enough snow to reach the middle of Zofia's calf. The group of survivors stayed in the cabin, all except for Isaac, who insisted on going out to hunt. He was fortunate enough to catch a rabbit, and Shlomie skinned it. It was cold and difficult to make a fire, but the group watched as Isaac built a small one and cooked the meat.

Once the sun went down, it was even colder. Zofia shivered on the bare ground inside the cabin. The blankets helped, but she never seemed to feel warm. On an exceptionally cold night, Isaac offered her one of his blankets.

"But everyone has three. If you give me one of yours, you'll freeze," Zofia said.

"I'll be all right. I'm warm-blooded." Isaac smiled and laid the blanket on top of her.

It did help. She felt warmer. But as she watched Isaac trembling from the cold, her heart broke. Zofia looked over at the others. Rivka and Esther were huddled and sharing their blankets, and so were Moishe and Ben.

"Isaac, would you like to come in and share all of our blankets together? It would be a good way for both of us to stay warm." It was a bold statement, Zofia knew, and she was glad that it was dark because she knew that her face had turned red. But after all, it was bitter cold, and she meant nothing by it other than that it would help to keep them both warm.

He cleared his throat.

She waited in silence. The room was small. She knew that Sarah and Shlomie had heard her. No one said a word.

"Yes," Isaac said in a soft voice. "That would probably be a good idea."

"You will be a gentleman?"

"Zofia, I would never be anything else."

Clumsily, Isaac slid under the blankets beside Zofia. It felt uncomfortable to be so close to him. Still, the warmth of another body and the additional blankets provided enough heat to keep her from shivering. At first, they lay side-by-side without speaking. But somewhere before the break of dawn, Zofia drifted off to sleep. She awoke to find Isaac asleep beside her. He'd kept his word. He was a gentleman.

Sarah couldn't bear to look at Zofia, but when their eyes met, Zofia saw the hurt and disdain on Sarah's face. She wanted to apologize, but nothing had happened. There was nothing to apologize for, perhaps just the stirring that had begun in her heart.

Everyone had been right. It was true that food was scarcer in the winter. In fact, the group was close to starvation. Isaac tried to hunt daily but brought back very little. The streams had frozen, so the men took the axe they'd stolen and went out to break the ice.

Zofia waited with the other women, shivering as they sat against the cabin wall. Esther had begun coughing. Her small, slender body hacked until she lay down, exhausted. Zofia noticed a bloody cloth that Esther had been spitting into was filled with blood-tainted mucus.

She watched the two young girls, and her heart broke with sadness. It was doubtful that Esther would live much longer. If the Nazis had never taken power, these two young women would be attending parties, school, and dances. Instead, they were struggling for survival. Zofia felt a sense of overwhelming sadness as she watched Rivka pat Esther's back lovingly.

It was almost dark when the men returned, their beards and eyelashes coated with tiny icicles. Their bodies shook with the cold, but Isaac held up a few small fish.

"It was a success!" Isaac said, a smile breaking on his wind-burned face and his voice cracking with cold.

"Yes, we almost froze to death, but we have some food anyway," Ben said as he sank to the floor and pulled an extra blanket over his shoulders.

Isaac began to cut the fish. The snow was so thick, covering a layer of ice, that it prevented them from making a fire.

"We will have to eat this raw," Isaac said, slicing the fish thin. Then he burst out laughing. "Zofia, you should see your face."

"I've never eaten raw fish," Zofia said.

"Come over here. Let me give you a piece."

She walked over to him. He held a sliver of slimy white flesh in his hand. Even though she was starving, her stomach lurched a little.

"I don't know if I can eat that."

"Trust me?" Isaac asked, smiling.

Zofia nodded.

"Open your mouth."

She did as he instructed.

He put the sliver of fish in her mouth. At first, she gagged.

"Think of the wonderful smells when my mother baked bread. Do you remember how they filled the streets?"

She nodded. Her mind began to embrace the memory.

"Everyone for miles around rushed in to buy it as soon as the bread started to bake because of the smell. Remember?"

She nodded, and he put another piece of raw fish into her mouth.

"And the cookies… Ah, do you remember the cookies? The ones with the apricot jam? And the strudel? The raisin and vinegar strudel…"

"Yes, I do," she said. She'd swallowed the fish.

"Come on, open up your mouth," Isaac said, speaking to her as if she were a little girl.

Zofia opened her mouth, and Isaac put another piece of fish inside.

This time, she swallowed.

"Think of other food while you are eating this. It will help." Isaac smiled. Then he put another piece of fish into her mouth.

She gagged.

"Challah, think of thick, braided challah on Friday morning for the Shabbat," he said.

She nodded, trying to picture the soft, crusty, hot bread straight out of the oven.

When she'd finished eating a few thick pieces of the fish, Zofia looked into Isaac's smiling eyes. "I want to thank you," she said.

"No need," he answered.

"You helped me to get that down."

"I know. It was hard for me at first, too, but the mind is very strong. You can make yourself believe that what you are eating is something else."

"It worked."

"I'm glad. I will do what I can to help you anytime you need it," Isaac said. Their eyes locked. The warmth she saw in his deep-brown eyes melted her heart.

Everyone tried to keep moving as much as possible to avoid freezing to death. They walked in circles around the cabin with blankets wrapped around their shoulders, watching as their breath turned the air white.

"I know this is hard for you. It's true that the winters are rough, but if we can survive, we'll be all right once spring comes. You have to think that spring is just around the corner," Isaac said. His beard had grown thick.

"You look like a rabbi," she teased him.

"Do I?"

"No, you look more like a caveman."

He laughed, "Now that I can believe."

Shlomie watched them, and she saw the loneliness in his eyes. If only she could divide herself and become two people, one for Shlomie and one for Isaac.

"As terrible as the snow is, it is beautiful. Don't you agree?" Isaac asked, pulling her attention back to him.

She gazed out the window. It was like a wonderland she'd read about in fairy tales long ago—so long ago, in another lifetime.

"Yes, it's beautiful. Like a fairy tale, except if you remember, there is always an evil force in fairy tales."

"Well, we certainly aren't lacking there. We have a whole group that is an evil force. In fact, an entire country, Germany. Now there is one evil force. They top any monsters in any fairy tales I ever heard," he said.

"Do you believe that all Germans are bad?"

"I do."

"They aren't. I promise you this. I've known some very wonderful Germans who aren't Nazis at all."

"I don't believe it."

"You should believe it. I would never lie to you, Isaac."

"But look what they have done to us. If they were decent people, why wouldn't they stand up to Hitler and stop his madness?"

"Maybe they were afraid? Maybe they were victims, too."

"Perhaps." He nodded.

"Without even taking much time to think about it, I know at least two wonderful women who are both non-Jews. One is Polish, and the other is German. Neither of them were Nazis."

"I wouldn't trust either one."

"I've had to trust both of them with my life and each of them with something precious to me."

"Do you want to talk about it?"

"No, I can't, not yet." She thought about Eidel and Katja.

"Someday you will tell me?"

"Yes, someday." There was a spark, a light in Isaac's eyes that made him different from any man she'd ever known. How could he stay so optimistic against the odds they faced every day? But he did. Yes, someday, she would tell him.

The following morning, Esther was dead. Rivka wept silently as the men carried the body of the beautiful young girl out of the cabin and deeper into the forest. No one mentioned it, but everyone knew the ground was too hard to bury her. Esther would be eaten by wild animals that were also trying to survive the winter.

CHAPTER FIFTY-EIGHT

"AUSCHWITZ!" Manfred exclaimed, spitting it out as though it were a curse. "Another filthy camp full of filthy Jews. I thought that when we left Treblinka, I would be sent home to Berlin. We've been here now for five months! Will this black mark that your father put on my name never be erased? How long, Christa? How long must I pay for his crimes?"

Christa lay in bed with Katja curled up beside her. The sound of her labored breathing filled the room.

"You have no answer? I tried to telephone Goebbels. He was in a meeting with Otto Dietrich, that good for nothing. Do you remember him?"

"No. I'm sorry, I don't."

"He was a bastard. Anyway, the secretary promised Joseph would return my call, but he hasn't. I've been waiting all day. Do you know why he hasn't? I'll tell you why. It is because I am considered bad news. To befriend me is to join the traitors, and of course, Joseph wants no part of that. Why would he?"

Christa shrugged, too weak to answer, too weak to endure another argument. Christa was recovering from a recent heart attack. She'd spent the previous two weeks in a hospital connected to tubes, worried because she'd been forced to leave Katja in Manfred's care.

Katja was too young to tell Christa what had happened while she was away. However, since Christa returned home, she'd noticed that Katja was quiet when Manfred entered a room, and she seemed to make an effort to stay out of his way. Christa was afraid that Manfred had been physically violent with the child. It was so easy for him to lose his temper. When Manfred called Katja's name, whether for dinner or otherwise, she trembled and hid under the sheets in her mother's bed.

"Look at you. You've become an invalid. I am ashamed that my wife is a sickly weakling. As if things are not bad enough." Manfred stomped around the room, speaking more to himself than to Christa.

"I'm sorry, Manfred, for everything," Christa said, wishing Zofia was there. She trusted Zofia and cared for her. If Zofia were here, Christa would devise a plan for her to take Katja and run away. It was just a matter of time before Germany would be forced to surrender. When she was born, the doctors had said she would not live long. For a long time, she'd refused to believe them. Now she knew it was true. Her life would be cut short, and who would care for her child? She could not trust Manfred. Oh, Zofia, Zofia, where are you?

"This house is a filthy mess. I'll have to get another Jewess to help you around here. I hate having them in the house for so many damned reasons. You realize that they cannot be trusted. They steal, they lie… But still, we need one. Somebody has to do your work." Manfred left the room in a huff.

Christa looked away and gazed out the window. So long ago, she'd loved this man with all her heart. It was hard to believe that Manfred was the same man she'd married. What had he become? Where was the shy, gentle lover she'd fallen in love with? Gone—power hungry—and gone forever. Tears trickled down her face.

"Mommy, don't cry. Please don't cry," Katja said. Since Zofia left Katja, she had started to call her "Mother." It made her heart ache every time she heard the word. Oh, how she had once longed to hear that very word. Now she felt as if she'd made a mistake, taking a child she would never live to raise.

"I'm all right." Christa managed a smile and ran her hand over Katja's head. "Why don't you go and get your baby doll, and we can give her a bottle? I'll bet she's hungry. I can tell."

"I think you're right. I'll be right back. It is time for her dinner."

"Yes, it is…" Christa said, using all the effort she could muster to lift her body to sit up in bed. Even though she was tired, she would play with Katja. The child had no one else.

The phone rang. Christa saw Katja jump at the loud sound. Something has terrified her. Oh, Manfred, what did you do? Did you hit this little girl in my absence? Please, God, let it not be true.

Katja returned with her doll tucked under her arm.

"You were right, Mama. She told me she was very hungry."

"Well, let's not keep her waiting, then. Let's feed her."

About half an hour later, Manfred brought bread, cheese, and fruit to Christa and Katja on a tray, along with a tall decanter of water. He set it down in front of his wife.

"I'm sorry. I don't mean to be so harsh with you," Manfred said.

"Thank you for bringing our dinner," Christa answered, tears filling her eyes again. Sometimes, Manfred would do something kind, and it would touch her so deeply. Katja curled into her mother's side.

"I have excellent news. Goebbels called," Manfred said.

"Oh? What did he say?"

"He wants me to come to Berlin. There is to be a meeting in Hitler's bunker. I am invited. Maybe this curse is lifting. Maybe I will finally be forgiven. I am elated right now."

"When must you leave?"

"Next week. I will have a Jewess here to help you with everything. I'll see to it before I leave."

CHAPTER FIFTY-NINE

THE NEW WOMAN Manfred found to take Zofia's place turned out to be nothing like Zofia. She was pretty enough, and he thought she would make a fine substitute for his needs, but Manfred could see that she just didn't have the compassion for the child or his wife that Zofia had shown. In fact, if he'd had time before his trip to Berlin, he would have sent her off to the gas chamber and gotten another one. But he was in a hurry. His mind focused on Berlin and the meeting.

Manfred packed carefully. In the morning, he'd be on his way. Perhaps this would be the road back to the life he'd cherished. What wouldn't he give to be away from the camps? The smells of blood, feces, sickness, vomit, and death haunted him. The looks on the faces of the prisoners tormented him at night, robbing him of his much-needed rest. Often he'd awaken feeling that he was face-to-face with God and forced to answer for his actions, his body bathed in sweat.

But as much as he loathed the prisoners and all they stood for, he'd come to enjoy the power and thrived on the knowledge that he was God to the poor souls who worked under his command.

He felt like Caesar in a raised box in the Coliseum in Rome, with all eyes upon him, waiting for a thumbs-up or thumbs-down signal. At any time, he might choose to end their lives. Or, should he feel benevolent, he might hand them a crust of bread. It was all in his hands. Ultimately, whether they lived or died depended upon little more than his mood. Sometimes the depth of his power could send him into ecstasy.

In other instances, all the decisions forced upon him were nothing but annoyances. It was a strange mixture of emotions, of that, he was certain.

"Behave yourself," Manfred told the Jewess as he carried his luggage to the door. "If I return and my wife has any complaints about you, I will see to it that you are made to be very sorry. A guard will watch your every move, so I suggest you do as you're told. Do you understand me?"

The young woman nodded her head.

Manfred lifted her chin, squeezing tightly to make his point. "Answer me when I talk to you." His voice was soft and controlled, but the underlying threat was very present.

"Yes, *Arbeitsführer*, I understand," she said.

"Good, then we should have no problems."

Manfred peered into Christa's room. The sun had just begun to rise. Christa lay in bed with Katja, her arms wrapped around the child. Manfred gazed at the little one. How pretty she'd grown to be, her blonde curls lying across Christa's arm, her thumb in her mouth. She was such a beautiful child.

Christa, on the other hand, was withering away. Manfred felt a pain in his chest as he looked at his wife. Once, they'd been happy. Once, they'd been so in love. He wanted to go to her and leave her with a tender kiss, but something inside of him would not allow him to. He stood for several moments gazing at the woman who still, somehow, after all they'd been through, held his heart in her hand. If only he could tell her. But he could not let her know. Why? He could not forgive her father. He could not forgive her.

There were no clear-cut answers, only a million questions. If, no, not if, when she died, he knew he would be devastated. And yet, she had no idea. Somewhere, he'd lost himself.

Manfred hung his head, lifted his suitcase, and headed outside, where the driver awaited.

CHAPTER SIXTY

Three days later, Manfred was on his way to meet with Goebbels at a pub a few blocks away from the office of the Ministry of Enlightenment and Propaganda. Although he had a car at his disposal, Manfred chose to walk. He needed the time to sort out his thoughts.

As he meandered down the familiar streets, the emptiness that constantly plagued him felt like a black hole growing deeper in the pit of his chest. Even though Christa was still his life and the only woman he'd ever loved, he could not find a way to forgive her.

He resented her father and the fact that she'd taken his side. It had swallowed their marriage, leaving nothing but an empty shell. If only visions of her father's execution didn't come to mind whenever he looked at her. If only he could take her in his arms the way he used to and tell her how much she meant to him. "Christa, Christa… It was all for you," he found himself speaking aloud.

"Everything was for you, and now I am buried. I've tasted power, and once I did, it became an addiction I could not live without. It was wonderful to find acceptance. I'd never had that as a boy, but Goebbels gave that to me. I became someone. Someone important. Can't you see, Christa? Your father stole that from me, and now every day, I am fighting to regain what I've lost.

"Without the Party, I am nothing. I am no one. I am just the old Manfred: weak, helpless, pathetic—nothing more than a small, uncoordinated little boy in the back of the room at the meeting of the Hitler Jugend, hearing the others laugh at me when they chose their teams, always knowing I would never be chosen.

"You know, at night, sometimes I awaken, and I can still hear the laughter and teasing from the other children. Those boys, those naturally gifted athletes, would never have believed how far I've come. They would never have thought that Manfred Blau would be married to the beautiful and popular Christa Henkener. How I loved you, Christa. How I still do…"

Quickly, he took a handkerchief from his pocket and wiped his eyes. He thought it silly for him to be walking alone, talking to himself, and crying. He forced his shoulders back. He wore the uniform of the SS. He must look a fool to anyone watching.

Still, his mind drifted to his wife. At any time, it could all end. Christa was dying, and he could not save her. When he considered her death, pangs of anxiety cut like the blade of a knife at his insides. *I am going mad. I must get control of myself quickly.*

He took a deep breath, inhaling the fresh air. *I am so haunted. What if this meeting meant the end of his work for the Nazi Party?* Perhaps they intended to discharge him of his duties. One could never be sure where he stood or what the Nazis might do. The very idea terrified him. Had someone begun to realize that he was not the powerful man he pretended to be? Did they know he was a fake, that he was not really strong at all? In fact, every day he hid behind his uniform—every day.

The child… He thought about Katja. That child had never had the chance to touch his heart or to mean a great deal to him. It wasn't Katja's fault, but she'd arrived in their lives just as things had turned.

When he'd agreed to adopt a baby, it had been more for Christa and Himmler's approval than for his needs. Perhaps if things had gone differently, he might have come to care about the little girl.

But as it stood, she was little more than a burden, and he had to stifle the desire to hit her when she interrupted his thoughts or his work.

When Christa had been hospitalized after her heart attack, he'd been overwhelmed with worry and work, leaving him tense and unable to control himself. He'd beaten Katja and then felt terrible.

Manfred knew that his wife and child feared him, which saddened him in many ways. In fact, he knew that all the prisoners took great care to stay clear of his flare-ups of anger.

And then, there was that girl, that Jewess, Zofia. Those dark, brooding eyes of hers came to him in dreams, haunting and taunting him. She epitomized the guilt he felt for all he'd done to her people. But how could he feel so guilty yet still need the feeling of power that he held over the starving Jews who worked under him?

When he thought of them, the smell of dirt and disease they brought to mind and the look of their sunken eyes and emaciated bodies sickened him. He longed to be away from the camp, away from them. And yet, if he were, he would never have that god-like feeling that burned within him when he decided who would live and who would die—he was addicted to his emperor's thumb.

As he approached the tavern, he took a handkerchief from his back pocket and wiped the sweat from his brow.

"Manfred!" Joseph Goebbels called to him from the back of the room. "Come over here. It's been a very long time."

Manfred headed to the table where Goebbels sat.

"Heil Hitler."

"Heil Hitler," Goebbels said. "You've lost some weight, Manfred."

Manfred thought of how difficult the smells at the camp made it for him to eat.

"Yes, I have. You're looking well, sir," Manfred lied. Dr. Goebbels looked strained. He'd always been skeletally thin, but now his clothes hung on him.

"We have much to discuss, but not here. There are too many people around, and with times, as they are, you just cannot be sure who you can trust. Let me pay this check, and we can be on our way."

Dr. Goebbels paid the meal tab and motioned for Manfred to follow him.

"How have you been?" Goebbels asked as they walked.

"I've managed."

"Dirty business, those camps."

"Yes."

"Unfortunately, they are necessary if we are ever to achieve our goals of a perfect Aryan world."

Manfred nodded, but he wondered how Joseph Goebbels would feel in his position, how the Minister of Propaganda would cope with the daily doses of death and disease he'd been forced to put up with. It was a nasty business.

"Anyway, this meeting that we are going to attend is top-secret. You must never reveal anything that is said here to anyone. Do you understand?"

"Yes, Doctor."

"Good. It took a great deal of convincing on my part to secure your invitation. There is still great mistrust for you in the Party, but having saved the Führer's life once did tip the scales in your favor."

"You realize that I had nothing to do with that Jew business. It was my father-in-law. I had no idea."

"I know that. But the others…"

"Yes, and no matter how hard I work for the Party, they never seem convinced."

"Things have become rather ugly. Party members are constantly looking for reasons to turn on each other. Manfred, we are losing the war."

"I know." Even though he knew it, the reality of what Goebbels said hit him like a slap in the face. If Germany lost the war, what would become of him?

They walked in silence for several moments. An automobile honked as a driver yelled an obscenity out the window of his car at another driver who'd cut him off.

"This meeting is about the Party's plans for the future,"

Goebbels said. "There was a meeting a couple of years ago. I told you all about it. Distasteful stuff… Like the Final Solution. That was the beginning of what we must discuss today."

"The Final Solution has kept us busy."

"Yes. We must try to complete this mission as quickly as possible. How is the progress on exterminating the Jewish vermin?"

"We have increased the gassings. The ovens are working at full capacity. It has certainly increased the workload at the camp. The guards complain about their additional hours."

"A pity what happened at Treblinka," Goebbels said.

"It was the first time a labor camp had an uprising. We were forced to respond with a heavy hand. We all learned a lot from Treblinka. Now all the camps are more closely guarded," Manfred said.

"Of course, I heard. We were forced to close it down. It did not reflect well on you or the other officers in charge…losing control like that."

"Yes. I know. I am sorry." Manfred turned away. Another catastrophe he was to be blamed for.

"How is Auschwitz?"

"It's run well. I am in charge of work details. However, because of the elimination process, there are fewer and fewer prisoners available to work."

"Well, we must finish this Final Solution business before the end of the war."

"Is this what the meeting is about?" Manfred asked.

"No. That has already been decided. Enough talk on the street. We will talk more when we arrive at our destination." Goebbels seemed jumpy. He kept looking in all directions. Manfred worried that someone at this meeting might decide to rehash his father-in-law's treason.

It was dusk as the two men silently walked down the dimly lit street. The sun had left the sky and most of the light of day with it. Following Goebbels's lead, they turned down Wilhelmstrabe Street and into the garden of the Old Reich Chancellery Building. Manfred cast a side glance at Goebbels. He could not imagine why they had entered a garden at night. Goebbels did not look back. He walked to the back of the building. Manfred followed. Then Goebbels looked around him.

"Come," Goebbels said to Manfred. "Follow me."

They entered the back of the Old Reich Chancellery through a hidden door. A single light bulb lit the dark, damp room.

Manfred followed Goebbels down a long metal staircase, their heels clanking as they went. It seemed like an endless walk. Manfred was frightened. Even though he trusted Goebbels as much as he could trust anyone in the Party, he could not be sure that his demise was not at hand.

Twenty-eight feet below the garden of the old Reich building, they entered a series of rooms surrounded by thick concrete. The rooms were lit with lamps and well-furnished. Other Party members walked through the rooms, greeting each other and drinking schnapps. It was evidently a meeting and not his execution. Manfred had been worried, and he breathed a sigh of relief.

Hitler's secretary, a slender woman with dark, wavy hair, greeted them.

"Heil Hitler."

"Heil Hitler."

"Good evening, Dr. Goebbels. Would you gentlemen care for a drink?"

"Yes. Would you like a drink, Manfred?"

"Yes, that would be very nice," Manfred said. The alcohol would calm his nerves.

"This is my old friend Manfred Blau. Manfred, this is Traudl, our Führer's secretary."

"I recall your name. Didn't the Führer attend your wedding?" the secretary asked.

"Yes. You have quite a memory."

"I have to. It's my job." She smiled at him.

The woman took a decanter of carved crystal off the shelf. The crystal sparkled in the light where a large swastika had been etched on the side. She poured them both a drink.

"Make yourselves comfortable. The meeting will begin in a few minutes," she said as she handed them the glasses. "Right over there, in the Führer's Center Conference Room."

"Thank you, Traudl," Goebbels said.

"Very nice to finally meet you," Traudl said to Manfred.

"Likewise," Manfred smiled.

"Come. Let me introduce you to everyone."

"Heil Hitler. This is Dr. Theodor Morell, the Führer's personal physician," Dr. Goebbels said.

"Heil Hitler," said the doctor.

Manfred was taken aback by the smell of the filthy, obese pig of a man who had won the Führer's complete confidence with his most valuable asset—his health.

"Herr Doctor, I trust our beloved Führer is in good health under your care?" asked Manfred.

"Indeed, he is. He has the best medical care in the Reich!" he said, smiling at his own accomplishment.

Manfred couldn't help but be repulsed by this filthy pig. *What did the Führer see in him?*

"Are you attending the meeting, Herr Doctor?"

"Of course. I go everywhere our beloved Führer goes."

The Führer's Bunker's Center Conference Room held only twenty people at a time. Manfred concluded that this was but one of many meetings, the number limited by seating space. The room's walls were not furnished or painted but bare concrete resembling an underground basement. The room held a long table and some simple chairs. The usual trappings of a Nazi meeting place were absent, save a couple of Nazi flags on the wall. A familiar form approached.

"Heil Hitler," the man greeted.

"Heil Hitler. This is Dr. Clauberg, but of course, you already know one another," said Goebbels.

"Heil Hitler. Yes, Dr. Clauberg is doing some fascinating work with some of the subjects from Auschwitz. He has a very interesting project to tell you about, Dr. Goebbels," Manfred said.

"Yes, of course. I have been composing a museum of sorts. You see, once the Jews are extinct, there will be little left to show our people what we were forced to eliminate from the world. So I've put together a skeletal collection from Block Ten at Auschwitz. I have approximately one hundred and fifteen specimens. From the specimens, you can see for yourself why the Jews are an inferior race. If you are ever in the area, drop by. It's on display at the University of Strasbourg. Fascinating stuff, if I may say so myself."

"Sounds fascinating, indeed," Goebbels said.

"Yes. You see, the Jews have a different skull structure than the regular person. In fact, they are not like us in any way."

"I am aware of this, although I've never seen an actual comparison of skulls. Do you think this is what makes them so cunning and dangerous?" Goebbels asked.

"Possibly. They are that. Cunning and dangerous, I mean. They certainly cannot be trusted. I suppose the bottom line is that they are inferiors."

"For certain," Goebbels said.

Traudl entered the room. "The meeting is about to begin. Gentlemen, please, if you would, make your way into the study and be seated."

"We will talk later," Dr. Clauberg said.

About fifteen men were present, a few lower-ranking officers, like himself, but most notable was Dr. Josef Mengele, whom Manfred knew from Auschwitz, and *Reichsführer* Himmler. As Hitler's secretary clapped her hands to bring the meeting to order, the men took seats around the room. As Manfred took his seat at the table, he observed two ashtrays made from human pelvises with lit cigars in them.

"It was a feat for me to obtain permission for you to attend this meeting," Goebbels whispered as he leaned into Manfred.

Manfred turned to thank him, but before he could speak, the entire group rose up as the Führer entered the room.

"Heil Hitler." They raised their hands and voices in unison.

Hitler walked through the group and stood at the head of the table. He raised his hand in answer to the group.

"Thank you for attending. You may be seated." Hitler said, his voice calmer than usual when he addressed a crowd.

"I've gathered you here tonight because I am sad to say that there is a possibility that we may be facing some rough times ahead. I deeply regret this, but the Reich may lose the war."

A gasp came from somewhere at the back of the table.

"However, we must remain firm in our belief that we are the superior race and will rule the world. We may just need to restructure a bit."

A roar of applause followed.

"In the near future, we may be forced to flee Germany and regroup elsewhere, where we will rebuild. I've made agreements with several countries in South America that are willing to allow former SS officers to migrate there to restructure the Reich. Once the Reich is strong again, we will return and reclaim Germany."

There was another round of applause, less enthusiastic. The men glanced around the room, meeting each other's frightened gazes.

"I am afraid the world will not understand what we have done here. There is a good possibility that we may face prosecution.

"Therefore, I have discussed our predicament with several doctors who have proven themselves loyal to our cause and able and willing to reconstruct the faces of those who will be going to South America. Your hair will be made dark brown or black. Photographs will be kept as records of your original faces with photos of your newly constructed faces so that there is no confusion about your true identity when you arrive at your new homes. You will look like Jews and, therefore, pass easily as survivors of the camps.

"Only top SS officials who have been cleared for this work will have access to the original pictures and information, so your security will be safe. I have also begun having papers forged for you that will identify you as a Jewish refugee. Do not be offended. This, I feel, is the best way for us to hide. We will hide in plain sight! I am planning to join you. I will not have my face reconstructed until I am sure we cannot recover Germany at this time. Then I will do what must be done.

"Once you are relocated, you will receive a contact that will ask you to meet at a specific location. Remember these words, for they are the passcode, letting you know the contact is legitimate. This is the beginning of the message you will receive in South America: 'Won't you please join my wife and me for a glass of wine to celebrate our wedding anniversary?' It will be signed 'Julio,' a common name among our Spanish and Portuguese-speaking friends. This is your indication that the message has come from the Nazi organization.

"You will follow the instructions as to the time and place. Once you arrive, you will find that we are together once again. And then, we will begin to make plans to re-establish our control of our country. Is this understood?"

"*Jawohl, mein Führer*," the men answered.

"What we do, we must do for the preservation of the Fatherland," Hitler said.

"*Jawohl, mein Führer!*" The room vibrated with an echo.

"Close your mouth," Goebbels whispered to Manfred. "You look like you're trying to catch a fly."

Manfred glanced sideways at Goebbels. His face could not conceal the shock at what he'd just heard.

"You should see your expression," Goebbels said. "It's almost laughable."

"And you're not astonished?"

"I am, in a way, I suppose. But I've known for a while that we were losing the war. I was just waiting for our brilliant Führer to come up with a solution, a way for us to regain power. I think this is genius. Don't you?"

"Oh, yes."

"You don't sound convinced."

"I am stunned. I mean, it's a lot to absorb: South America, reconstructive surgery to make ourselves look like Jews. Overwhelming…"

"Yes, I suppose so. But at least, at my insistence, you have been selected to join us."

"I thank you for that." Manfred smiled. "I am grateful for all you've done for me, Dr. Goebbels."

"I know you are. I know you have always been." Goebbels

patted Manfred's shoulder. "Now, don't look so bleak. I am saddened, too. None of us wants to see Germany fall. And, of course, who would want to take on a Jewish appearance?

"However, we must carry on. We must make plans, just in case we should be left without any choice but to act and act quickly. I am going to set up an appointment for you with a qualified surgeon. His name is Dr. Schmidt. Then either he or I will send you further instructions, should it become necessary to put this plan into action."

"And you, Dr. Goebbels? What will you do?" Manfred asked, genuinely concerned.

"I am going to wait until the very last minute. Because of our close friendship, Hitler asked me to bring my family and join him here at the bunker. I suppose he will have arranged everything. I will follow his plan from there. I don't know for sure, but I am assuming we will be the last to be surgically altered. Then I suppose we will meet up with the rest of you in South America."

"South America? Where? Do you know?"

"I don't know for sure. Adolf has had a good reception from Argentina. Perhaps we will go there?"

"This is a lot to absorb. I will have to tell my wife."

"Hmmm, I don't know Manfred. Your wife… Her father… Can she be trusted?"

"Yes, she has no contact with anyone other than the child and me anymore. Her mother is dead, and she has no one else."

Goebbels nodded his head. "Don't tell her quite yet. I will let you know when the time is right. Wait until I contact you for further instructions."

"I'll wait until I receive clearance from you to inform her of everything," Manfred said.

"Yes, make sure that you do that."

CHAPTER SIXTY-ONE

When the cold became unbearable, the entire group began sleeping together, with all the blankets covering them to stay warm. Isaac slept beside Zofia. She'd come to rely on the warmth of his body next to hers, although there had been no sexual advances.

Often the entire group would lie on the frozen ground in the dark of night and reminisce about things they'd done before the Nazi takeover. Shlomie once told a story about how he'd won a science fair and traveled across Germany with a group of ten-year-old children to explain his project to other schoolchildren.

Sarah described how excited she was as her mother had curled her hair for her first dance. She went on to recapture the thrill she'd felt as she put on her new lavender dress. This was the first time she would dance with a boy. Each of them told a story. One night, as Sarah lay on the other side of Isaac, she cleared her throat.

"Isaac, tell us about your mother's bakery."

"Ahhh… Mama's bakery," Isaac said with a sigh. "The best bakery in town, by far. My mama could twist a challah in seconds and bake the most heavenly *hamantaschen*." *Crumbly, triangle-shaped cookies with a fruit filling.*

"I remember," Zofia said. "I used to go to pick up bread and cakes for my mother. Your mother was a fantastic baker."

"She was. I miss her. I miss my father, too." Isaac said as he reached over to find Zofia's hand. Once he found it, he took it into his own and squeezed gently. "You remember my parents?"

"Oh yes, Isaac. How could I forget? I even remember you. You were the little blond boy with the round face and the big smile, always eating bread with butter," she laughed. "I remember so many people from the old neighborhood. I often wonder what has become of them."

"Do you think we will find anyone we knew still alive after the war?" Shlomie asked.

"I don't know," Sarah said. "I am praying every day for my family."

"We should not dwell on this stuff from the past," Rivka said from across the room. "Talking about the bakery and family only makes us sad. Maybe we should sing."

"That's an idea," Zofia said.

First, they sang familiar Yiddish folk tunes.

"Does anyone know any American music?" Zofia asked.

"I do," Shlomie said. "I love it. I used to listen to it as often as I was able to. I loved the big bands."

"This song is not swing. It's American folk music. Do you happen to know the song 'You Are My Sunshine?'"

"I do. I know it in English."

"Yes, me, too. I learned it a long time ago when I was still in school."

Shlomie and Zofia began to sing, "You are my little Mary Sunshine, my only sunshine. You are my joy and my happiness," their voices, the only sound penetrating the frozen darkness.

They sang it through once, then again. The second time, the entire group joined in with the words they were able to recall.

"My little Mary Sunshine…" Zofia remembered Katja. She'd called her 'sunshine' and secretly sung that song to her at night when she put her to bed.

"You wake the stars; you stop the rain…"

My Eidel, my Katja, Fruma, Gitel, Dovid, Mama…

"Sweet Mary Sunshine, you are my sweet Mary Sunshine. You bring light to the dark and gray days."

She heard Isaac's deep voice struggling to remember the words. His hand still clasped Zofia's, and she squeezed a little tighter.

Little by little, the weather began to break. The icicles on the trees melted, and tiny sprouts of green pushed their way up through the thawing ground. Even though it was still chilly, Zofia insisted on bathing in the stream. The water had just thawed, and it shocked her naked body. But she took the soap Isaac had given her and scrubbed her skin and hair as quickly as she could. Then she dried herself with a blanket, dressed, and returned to the cabin.

"You smell like springtime itself," Shlomie said.

"Why, thank you. It feels wonderful to be clean."

"Yes, I am sure it does. I am going to the pond as soon as it gets a little warmer. Getting into the water in this weather is not for the faint of heart." He laughed.

"Well, I am going today," Isaac said.

Zofia smiled at him.

"Me too," Sarah said, glancing over at Isaac.

"Come for a walk with me, Zofia," Isaac said.

"I'd like that."

The birds had begun to return to the forest, and their songs filled the afternoon as the sun's orb was filtered, golden, through the trees.

"Did you know that before all this Nazi stuff began, I had a crush on you?"

"Really, Isaac, I never knew."

"You never paid much attention to me, but I remember watching you and your friend walk to school and thinking how pretty you were."

She laughed. "How pretty I was?"

"Yes, and how pretty you still are."

She blushed. "It's funny. We've slept beside each other for months. And yet, when I look into your eyes, here and now, in the light of day, I am shy."

"Me, too," he said. "I cannot court you the way that I would like to. Our lives don't permit it. If I could, I would ask you to dinner, maybe dancing as well, then to meet my family. But as it stands, I have no family left, and the dinner that we share, well, I must admit, isn't quite how I would like it to be, with wine and soft music. Instead, I am sorry to say that all I can offer you is the wild game and fish we share with the entire group. Still and all, I am incredibly attracted to you."

"Isaac... I don't know what to say."

"You have never been with a man?"

"If I told you that, I would be lying. Although I would like to lie to you, to tell you that I am a virgin. I guess the truth is I was a free spirit once."

"I understand."

"There were two men I chose to take as lovers, and then there were two I did not choose."

"You were raped?"

"I was forced by a Judenrat at Warsaw and the *Arbeitsführer* when I was at Treblinka."

"I'm sorry. I wish I could kill them both with my bare hands."

She shrugged. "I had it bad. Many others had it far worse. At least I am still alive."

He said nothing, but in his silence, she knew he felt helpless.

"I have not told anyone else this since I left the Warsaw Ghetto, but I must tell you."

"Tell me what?"

"Isaac," she sighed and turned to face him. "I have a child, a daughter. She is living with a non-Jewish family. Before the invasion began, the woman who took her for me was my friend. I had someone from the black market contact her while we were in the ghetto. She agreed to take Eidel into her home and pretend Eidel was her child. There was so much disease in the ghetto. I was afraid for my daughter, so I sent her away."

He smiled at her and touched her face, smoothing the lines of pain.

"Men want a woman who is pure. I am not pure. I met Eidel's

father when I was young and not very smart. I thought I was in love, but it turned out that I was just a fool. Then later, when I was living in the ghetto, I met a boy. He was kind and gentle, and although I was not in love with him, I learned to care for him deeply. We were both so lonely and afraid of what the future might hold that we grasped each other. I believe he was in love with me."

"You will search for him when the war is over?"

"He's dead. I was the cause of it. I will blame myself forever." Her voice choked in her throat.

"Do you want to tell me what happened?"

"If you want to know."

"I want to know everything about you."

And so, she told him about Koppel and Dovid, Fruma and Gitel, and most of all, Eidel.

"So, you see, I am not pure, not virginal, and probably not worthy of your affection."

"I love you, Zofia. Everyone makes mistakes. I just want you, just who you are. That's enough for me. Will you marry me?"

Could he really overlook my past and my brokenness? He is a good man, and he means what he says.

"Yes. I love you, too," she whispered, tears streaming down her eyes. "But there is no rabbi."

"And there is no marriage ceremony without one, but I'm sure God understands," Isaac said. "But someday, when there is a rabbi, I want us to have the ceremony."

"Yes. Do we tell the others? Sarah is in love with you, you know. She has had so much pain…"

"I know, and Shlomie is in love with you. The whole group is bitter and depressed about life itself. I think our joining will not be well received. Let's do this before God alone."

"I agree. But we Jews have a marriage ritual and don't have vows. We have no rabbi."

Isaac laughed. "We Jews say vows concerning everything. It is important that we include God in our union. We will make our own vows."

"Okay." Isaac took Zofia's hands and looked into her soul with his kind, gentle, loving eyes.

"Before the Lord God of Israel, I will be your husband, and I will cherish you with every breath that is in me and care for you always, as long as I live."

"Before God, wherever you go, I will go; wherever you live, I will live. Your people will be my people, and your God will be my God. Wherever you die, I will die, and that is where I will be buried," Zofia said with trembling lips, quoting a passage from the book of Ruth that she remembered as a child.

He put his arms around her. She allowed herself to fall into his embrace, to lose herself and her memories for a moment. His lips brushed hers. They were face-to-face, their eyes locked.

"I've never done this before. I've never made love to anyone," Isaac said.

She nodded.

He took her face in his hands and gently pressed his lips to hers. Tears came to her eyes, and she felt them fall upon her cheeks.

She had never felt this way before, not with Dovid, not with Don Taylor, not ever. Zofia wanted to protect Isaac like a mother, to lie with him as a lover, and to stand by his side no matter what they might face in the future.

He took his shirt off and lay it down on the ground. Then he sat and reached for her hand, pulling her down beside him, laying her head gently on his shirt. Zofia sighed, trembling. After what she'd endured with the *Arbeitsführer*, she was afraid she'd lost all sensations in her body. For so long, she'd forced the death of any feeling. She was wrong. Her body tingled and sang to the music that Isaac's body played. The warmth of skin against skin made her tremble and realize the need she'd suppressed for so long.

When it was over, he held her tightly in his arms, kissing the top of her head. She took a deep breath and marveled at how strange things were.

Zofia had feared that after the *Arbeitsführer*, she would never be able to enjoy the touch of a man again. After putting up with his repulsive groping, all the while forcing her mind to kill any sensations her body might be required to tolerate, she was sure that her ability to share love had died somewhere along the line, too. And then, a miracle happened. Zofia was blessed. She'd found true love. Every cell in her body responded, dancing with heightened ecstasy, tingling, and embracing the pleasure.

"How can I be so happy when I should be miserable?" he laughed, holding her gently in his strong arms.

She laughed, too. "I think love is like that. It makes you happy no matter what else is going on around you. You just can't help but smile."

"I can't help but smile," he repeated. "You are everything I want in this world."

"I am right here, and I will be right here."

"Someday, I will buy you a big house, and the three of us: you, Eidel, and I, will have an extraordinary future."

"Do you think you could learn to love a child that was not your own?"

"She is yours, and you are mine. That makes her mine, too. I'll adopt her if you allow me to, and I will love her as if she came from my loins," Isaac said.

She smiled, and she thought of Katja. She hated the Nazis, but she could never bring herself to blame the child. The poor child, who'd been bred by the SS to be what they thought to be ideal, had fooled them all by becoming a beautiful and loving little girl in spite of their efforts. Zofia believed that Christa was responsible for Katja's sweet nature. Although Zofia knew nothing of Katja's birth mother, the child had grown to be just like her adopted mother.

"Of course, I will allow you to adopt her." Zofia smiled at Isaac. How could she have failed to notice him when they were growing up, with his golden curls and amber-brown eyes?

They lay under the umbrella of an oak tree and watched a family of ants walk in a line along the bark. It was still slightly chilly, but neither wanted to return. They embraced, shivering slightly.

"Do you remember Lena, my friend?"

"Of course, the two of you were always together. But you were the prettier one."

Zofia smiled and tickled his side until he laughed.

"I wonder about her sometimes. I wonder how she is and if she is all right. I have so many memories. There were so many people that I think about in the old neighborhood," she said.

"Yes, I know what you mean. Do you remember Mr. Zeitlman, the shoemaker? He was so mean. He would yell at us as we walked home from school, 'Stay off the grass! Stay off! You and you, and you!' Remember? All the boys used to run over the small patch of grass outside his shop just to irritate him."

She laughed aloud. "I do remember him. He was an old grouch. Were you one of the boys who tormented him?"

"But of course. He set himself up for it. Every time we walked by—just walked by the front of his shop—he'd call out in that booming voice of his. 'Remember the grass!' So, of course, we would remember. We would remember to walk on his grass," he laughed.

"How about Frau Applebaum? Remember her? She could have been a news reporter. Every time I saw her, she would say, "So, Zofia, what have you got to tell me?" I'd cringe. That woman made it her business to know everybody and everything about them."

"Yes, crazy, old Frau Applebaum. What a gossip. She would come to the bakery, and I'd hear my mother groan. Then Mom would say, '*Oy vey*, here comes Frau Applebaum.'" He laughed. "She'd come in and stay for at least a half hour, questioning every customer who came in to buy. 'So what's new?' she would ask…and everyone knew she was just prying into their lives, looking for something interesting," he said, shaking his head.

"It's a little painful to remember, but it is also kind of wonderful. I suppose that's because I have you to reminisce with. What a blessing to have found you again, Isaac. We share so much because we were raised in the same neighborhood and remember all the same people. It's almost as if we can make-believe that everyone is still alive somewhere and we are only away on holiday. Sort of like when we return, everything will be normal as it once was, before Hitler," she said.

"I like to think that way, even though it is impossible that nothing has changed. We know it has, but it is good to remember. If we forget people, then they will really die. As long as we keep memories alive, they live in our memories," he said.

"Yes, you're right. A rabbi told me that when I attended a funeral years ago."

"It's true. But we must not dwell on the sadness. Instead, we should remember the good times and the funny things that happened. That way, the good memories are the ones that stay alive. Once this war is over, you and I will start over. We'll pick up the pieces of our lives and know we are blessed by God because we have survived, and we have each other." He smoothed her hair and continued to speak, "Then, when Hitler and his kind are nothing but a bad dream, we will bring Eidel home to live with us. Together, we'll rebuild."

"Have you ever thought about leaving Europe?" he asked.

"I've never given it much thought. Where would we go?"

"To Palestine. Of course, someday Palestine will be a Jewish state—Eretz Israel, the Zionists call it... Isn't that the dream of every Jew?" He ran his hand over his chin. "Palestine... Israel, a Jewish homeland, a land of our own. Can you imagine? A place where Jews can live in safety."

"Do you think it's possible? Do you think it could ever come true?" she asked. He looked over into her eyes. The sun had begun to move, and it was shining brightly into her eyes. She squinted up at him.

"I do. I believe the day will come when we have a land of our own." He nodded, squeezing her shoulder. "And if you were with me, I would go to Palestine to build Israel," he said.

She reached up and smoothed his wild curls. "Isaac, I will be with you," she said, smiling.

"I love you, Zofia."

"I love you too, very much," she said, her voice choking with emotion.

He leaned down and kissed her. Her entire being swelled with joy.

How can I be blessed to have such happiness when there are so many others suffering? But even guilt could not quell the bliss she felt in her heart.

CHAPTER SIXTY-TWO

As WINTER LOOSENED her grasp and the forest began to come alive with the spring, food became more plentiful. Isaac hunted, returning with rabbits or squirrels. The women gathered edible greens to stew over low fires. The dreaded winter had passed.

The mood Zofia and Isaac spread through the cabin was one of pure happiness. Nothing could stop the constant flow of romantic electricity.

"Here, taste this. It's a raspberry." Isaac put a small, hard, green ball into Zofia's mouth.

"It's bitter. It's not ripe," she laughed.

"Not yet, but guess what? I've found a bush, and it's filled with fruit. Soon I can feed you raspberries as sweet as the sugar in my mom's bakery."

She giggled.

"But of course, not as sweet as your smile," he said, touching her face.

Their eyes met, and she felt the current run through her body. Zofia had never been in love before. What she'd had with the teacher was little more than an adolescent crush. Dovid was a nice man, but her feelings for him were brought on by a need to deal with mutual loneliness.

She had never felt like this before. Isaac made her laugh and cry and bless everyone and everything on this earth all at once. Yes, she knew she was stuck in a cabin deep in the woods with limited food and resources for survival. Yes, she'd almost frozen to death this past winter. Yes, she'd lost her friends and family and missed them terribly. Yes, she had a daughter somewhere out in the world whom she longed to see. Yes, there was a little German girl whose well-being she worried about. And yes, she should have been miserable, but she'd never been happier in her life.

Ben and Moishe were annoyed.

"You walk around here like you're on a honeymoon. Quite frankly, it's getting on my nerves," Ben said.

Zofia looked over at the others and realized that perhaps their suffering was made worse by her joy.

"We could walk around here with sad faces, but why? We are the lucky ones, all of us. We are alive," Isaac said.

Sarah sunk down against the wall and sat on the floor. Zofia saw the look in her eyes and was saddened.

"I'm alone. I have no one left. I saw my parents murdered, shot right before my eyes. So what is there to be happy about? I am lucky, you say? Ha!" Sarah exclaimed.

"And I've been beaten to less than a man. I couldn't even defend my wife and two children. I watched as a guard forced them away into a line to a gas chamber. And what did I do? I stood there, too afraid to do anything. Now I am overcome with self-hatred," Ben said, spitting the words out of his mouth like venom.

"I was forced to bury my mother. I saw them shoot her, and they made me dig the hole," Moishe said, his eyes cold as glass.

"Stop this. Does it do you any good to wallow in self-pity?" Isaac said. "We have all lost someone. We have all lost a great deal. I don't know where my family is. I don't know if I will ever see them again. For all I know, they are all dead, and chances are they *are* dead. Now I have only their memories to keep close to my heart." He looked around at them, scanning the room, meeting each person's eyes before he continued. "But we are still alive… We have a chance for a future, a chance to rebuild and start again. If you want to honor those you loved and lost, honor them by honoring God's greatest gift: life."

"Easy for you to say, Isaac. You've found someone. You've managed to fall in love in the worst possible conditions. My hat is off to you. But for me, it is just another day filled with pain and memories," Shlomie said, and he got up and walked outside. The others followed, leaving Zofia and Isaac alone in the cabin.

"Isaac," Zofia said. "It makes me sad to see what has become of all of us."

"Yes, it does. But Zofia, I cannot be sad when I look at you and know God has blessed me."

She felt the tears forming in her eyes. He took her in his arms for several minutes, and they were lost in the warmth of each other's embrace.

CHAPTER SIXTY-THREE

In August 1944, Goebbels telephoned Manfred at his home.

"The time has come, Manfred. Would you like me to make arrangements with the surgeon?"

"Yes."

"Then you will be going south with the rest of our friends?" Goebbels chose his words carefully, revealing as little as possible over the phone.

"Yes."

"I will discuss the matter with the correct parties and get back to you as to the date of your appointment."

"I'll wait to hear. May I talk to my wife?"

"Yes, but explain that she must not discuss this with anyone else."

"Yes, Dr. Goebbels."

"I will be in touch, Manfred."

"Thank you, sir."

"Heil Hitler."

"Heil Hitler."

CHAPTER SIXTY-FOUR

Christa lay on her mattress, her skin white and thin as parchment paper against the cornflower blue of her lips and eyelids. Manfred's heart felt as if it were ripping apart as he looked at her, Katja's head resting on her stomach. Christa was dying.

The mother and daughter had fallen asleep together as Christa read to Katja from her book of fairy tales. The book had fallen to the floor. Manfred picked it up and held it to his chest for a moment.

Everything had gone so wrong, so terribly wrong. Tears welled in his eyes. Soon, the face he'd lived with all of his life would be gone, replaced by one that he had grown to hate, the face of a Jew. His hair would be dyed black, a big hook nose would beckon like a crooked finger, and frightening deep-set eyes would look back at him from the mirror, reminding him of the innocent lives he'd taken in the camps. His papers would reflect the name of a Jewish refugee. He would dress, act, and speak as a Jew. And to everyone who was not an elite member of the Party, he would be a Jew.

The plan was brilliant but nauseating too. Once the war ended, there would be displaced Jews everywhere. It would be easy to pose as one of them and to leave Germany, but the price, ah, the price.

Now he would wear a face he'd come to hate, and all of his power would be gone.

And yet, Hitler had said that he must do this for the Fatherland. So he must. Because of what he'd witnessed with his Nazi brothers, there was a spark of distrust. Were they possibly planning to murder all the lower-ranking officers to keep their secrets hidden? Manfred would not put it past them. He heard rumors that Goebbels, Himmler, Göring, Eichmann, and Mengele had not been scheduled for the surgery. Only the lesser officers had been registered for the procedure. Perhaps he would never awaken from the anesthesia. The thought was both frightening and comforting.

There was no doubt in his mind that the Allies would punish the Nazis for what they had done. How could they begin to understand, to see the bigger picture, a Germany ruled by a superior race? No, they would not see the big picture, the goal. Instead, all they would see were the piles of bodies and the ovens. They would see the gas chambers, and they would condemn the Third Reich forever.

The secrets of what had been taking place in Germany would circulate throughout the world. He felt a shiver run up his spine. If the operation didn't kill him, he might be caught by the Allies, which would most assuredly be worse. How did it feel to die? He'd witnessed so much death, yet he'd always pushed the questions from his mind. Would it be painful? Afterward, what would happen? Was there simply nothingness? Or was there a God? And if so, how would God feel about what he'd done?

Manfred felt clammy as he watched the Jewess prepare the evening meal. She stood in the kitchen across the hall from Christa's room. He had no desire for her. She was not as pretty as the one that worked for them at Treblinka, Zofia. Now that one was very attractive in that Jewish, evil way. But he had no desire for any woman right now. In fact, he doubted that his male apparatus would work properly.

The smell of the food wafting through the air sickened him. Soon, he must talk to Christa and explain everything. He glanced back at her lying asleep on the bed. If they were both to die, who would take the child? Did it matter? Did he even care for the little girl? Not really. That had never turned out the way that he'd thought it might. Once things went bad, it had never been the same as having his own flesh-and-blood child. The child was just a child living in his home. He could not find it in his heart to love her.

Christa stirred under his stare. Her eyes opened slowly. He was stunned, even now, by her delicate beauty.

"Manfred, what is it?"

"I must speak with you."

"Of course, sit down," she said as she moved her feet, making room at the end of the bed. The soft in and out of the child's breathing lent a quiet rhythm to the semi-darkened room as Manfred explained Hitler's plan.

CHAPTER SIXTY-FIVE

Zofia had not seen her menstrual blood for two months. She had been pregnant before and recognized the symptoms. It was hard to be unhappy, even though she knew she should be. Without a home to bring the child to, without any guarantee of a future, she should be miserable, but instead, she was filled with purpose, light, and joy.

A new life had formed within her. It was tiny right now, her tiny secret. A part of her and Isaac, a reflection of the love they shared. A gift from God, even in the darkest hour, here in the middle of the forest with the Allies coming from both sides, a small flicker of light had been ignited in her womb: a child, a dear life.

As Isaac slept on the floor in the cabin, she gazed at him and smiled. For the first time in her life, she knew what it meant to love another human being. It was the most rewarding, wonderful feeling imaginable. Nothing she'd ever known before could compare to the sheer bliss of it. When the war ended, they would be married. The child that grew within her body would be a brother or sister to her precious Eidel. Even though she'd been through Hell, she'd found Heaven, and Zofia felt truly blessed.

Her only concern was having enough food to ensure the baby would be healthy. This worried her. When she was pregnant with

Eidel, she'd had meat and milk, not a lot, but enough. Now she could never be sure of the food supply. Still, even with all the challenges, she could not help but smile. She carried Isaac's child, the seed of the man she loved. Her hand caressed her belly.

"Oh, little one, with God's help, you will be born into a world without Nazis. Your father and I will take you to Palestine, a land of our own, where you can be proud to be a Jew."

Isaac walked over and leaned down to kiss the top of Zofia's head.

"Who are you talking to?" he asked.

"No one, just myself."

"So this living in the forest has finally driven you mad?"

She laughed.

"Isaac?"

"Yes, love?"

"I'm going to have a baby."

He gasped. Then a big smile came over his face, and even though his eyes were filled with worry, he couldn't help but smile with joy.

"Zofia…" He was choked with emotion.

She saw tears run down his cheeks, and she was moved by the sight of this strong man, whom she'd come to love, made soft by his emotions.

"My wife," he whispered, caressing her belly, "my child. I will do whatever must be done to protect you both. I will make sure you are taken care of, no matter what it takes."

"I know that, Isaac. I've always known it," Zofia said.

CHAPTER SIXTY-SIX

Ben and Moishe had gone out to gather unripened fruit that had just blossomed on the nearby farmer's apple tree. They returned in less than an hour with a man injured and bleeding. They brought him back to the cabin. The yellow star on his armband told them that he was a Jew.

The man's head was covered in bloody bruises. The bones jutted out of his face, and his eyes were clearly frightened. His body shivered, although the weather was warm.

"He's lost a lot of blood," Moishe said.

Zofia looked at the hole torn into the man's shirt.

"He's been shot," Isaac said and rushed over to help.

The man trembled and pulled away.

"It's all right," Isaac whispered, his voice soft, gentle, and kind. "We're Jews, too. I am not going to hurt you."

The man's eyes were black pools of fear and pain. He stared at Isaac, but he didn't move. He allowed Isaac to open his shirt.

"The bullet passed through his upper right arm, missing the bone," Isaac said, his mouth twisted. "Zofia, would you please get me some water? I'll also need some rags."

Shlomie peered over Isaac's shoulder. "I'll make a poultice to draw out the infection starting to set in."

"Thank you, Shlomie," Isaac said, but inwardly very fearful for Zofia's safety.

Zofia got up without speaking, took the bucket to the pond, and filled it. When she returned, Isaac began cleaning the wound. From where Zofia stood across the room, she could see that thick, dark blood still oozed from the opening.

"They will be looking for me," the man said, his eyes wild, scanning the room. "I should leave here. I will put all of you in danger."

"Where did you come from?" Moishe asked.

"I had been hiding in barns, woods, wherever I could since the Nazis gathered all the Jews from my hometown in Plock. A farmer turned me in, and I was being moved to the camp in Soldau. I jumped from the truck, and the German soldier shot me as I ran away. I took to the woods and hid in a bear's den. Lucky for me, the bear wasn't home. I'm sure the Nazis will organize a manhunt."

Moishe looked from Sarah to Isaac and the others, alarmed. The Nazis were sure to find him, and if he were here, they would find them all.

"Isaac, maybe he's right. Maybe he should leave," Sarah said.

"We can't send him out of here in this condition. He will die."

"But if he stays, we will all die," Sarah answered.

"Sarah's right," Shlomie said.

"Yes, she very well may be right, but we cannot just throw him out," Isaac said. Then he looked over at Zofia and remembered the baby. Zofia knew him well enough to understand the dilemma that he faced. She saw the concern as it crossed his face.

"Isaac, I wouldn't hear of putting him out. We are all running away from the Nazis. We are all in the same position. He must stay. There is no other humane choice," Zofia said.

"If it were just me, I would have no qualms about you staying here, but I cannot put the others at risk," Isaac said, hanging his head.

The man nodded. "I understand."

"He'll die, Isaac," Zofia said. "If they don't find him and kill him, he'll die of infection or starve to death."

Isaac continued to clean the man's wound. "I think the fairest thing to do would be to take a vote." Isaac took a deep breath. Then he continued, "Does everyone agree?"

They all nodded.

"All in favor that he stays, raise your hands." Everyone except Sarah and Isaac raised their hands. Even Shlomie didn't have the heart to put him out.

"It looks like you will be staying with us," Isaac said. "What is your name?"

"Seff."

Isaac introduced the others as he continued to bandage Seff's arm.

"It looked worse than I thought. If we can avoid infection, you'll be all right."

"I thank you," Seff said. "I feel terrible about putting all of you in danger. But this might help. I have news. I was staying with a friend in the neighboring village for a while. She had a radio. At night, we tuned in to the BBC. Listen to this… Three months ago, the Allies landed in Normandy, France. From what I understand, it was a bloody battle. But they are here: the Americans, the Canadians, the British, they are here! God be with them! And praise God, Germany is losing the war against Russia, as well. Soon the Russians are marching toward Berlin. Any day now, if we can just hold out, this will all be over."

"From your mouth to God's ears," Shlomie said, taking a deep breath.

"Well, Germany is on the defensive. They are in bad shape. Hitler sent his ill-equipped men to face a winter in Russia, and Stalin beat the hell out of him." Seff smiled, even though the pain of his injuries still showed on his face.

"Yes, and the Russians are as cruel as the Germans," Ben said. "Maybe the Nazis are finally going to get a dose of their own medicine."

"So, as far as we are concerned, we can only hope that the

Western side gets to us first, the British and the Americans. You know the Brits have been bombing Berlin like crazy."

Isaac had finished his work on Seff's wounds. He took the bucket of water and emptied it outside the cabin door, and then he came to sit beside Zofia. He took her hand and raised it to his lips, kissing it gently.

"I know you don't want me here," Seff said to Isaac.

"It's not that I don't want you here. For myself, I would gladly keep you here and face the consequences. But this is Zofia, my wife. I cannot, and I will not put her in danger."

"They are not really married. Today, out of the blue, from nowhere, they've just decided that they are married," Sarah said.

"We are married before Almighty God, and Zofia is going to have a child, my child."

Sarah gasped. Shlomie turned pale.

"Isaac..." Zofia said.

"Everyone might as well know. It's just a matter of time before they will be able to see what is happening. I want them to know that you come first to me, Zofia, before everything, before my own life. That is why I am uncomfortable taking this poor man into our cabin. The Nazis are chasing him. We don't know if he has been followed. We are taking a big risk."

Shlomie cleared his throat. "That changes things greatly." He glared at Isaac. "How could you be so thoughtless? She will be ready to give birth in the middle of the winter, with no food... bitter cold. What were you thinking, Isaac? She will surely die." Shlomie got up, paced like a tiger in a cage, then slammed his fist into the wall.

"Yes, I know the baby will come in the winter. Believe me, I think about it constantly. But I won't let her die. I will provide food and warmth. She will survive, and so will our child."

"You are a selfish man," Shlomie said, glaring at Isaac. Then Shlomie walked over to where Isaac sat and kicked his leg.

Isaac rose and punched Shlomie in the stomach. Shlomie fell backward against the wall of the cabin, clutching his belly.

"Stop! Stop this right now," Zofia said, getting up and standing between them. "This won't solve a thing." She glanced back and forth between the two men, who were breathing heavily. "Seff will stay. He will heal and then decide if he wants to stay or move on. We will manage. If the Nazis are hunting him and they find us, then that is just our fate. But we cannot turn him away. He is a Jew, just like we are."

Isaac nodded in agreement.

Shlomie continued to glare at Isaac. "You stupid, selfish fool, how could you do this to Zofia? How?" he said under his breath, folding his arms across his chest. He fought to keep from crying.

CHAPTER SIXTY-SEVEN

Despite their disagreement, Shlomie was the best friend Isaac had ever had, and he regretted their fight. Isaac knew he was the stronger, more attractive, more capable, and, more importantly, the one Zofia had fallen in love with. For this, he felt he must make some concessions.

Later he would talk to Shlomie, and he would apologize. He took his bow and arrow and went outside to see if he might shoot a rabbit or a bird. He had become a good shot over the years he'd spent living in the forest. It was hard to imagine that the little boy with the double chins who sat on the wooden stool nibbling on cookies in the back of his parents' bakery was the same man he'd become. Well, he'd done what must be done to survive.

Isaac walked through the woods. His clothes were drenched with sweat in the heat of summer. The smells of the flowering plants and the songs of the birds surrounded him. God had surely created a beautiful world for man to live in. It was too bad there were people filled with greed and hatred to spoil it.

Above him, two bright-red birds took flight, following each other in an age-old mating dance. Isaac smiled. He couldn't help but think of Zofia with her lovely, black sausage curls caressing her back, her smile that lit up his world. Her eyes, those eyes…

When Isaac looked into Zofia's eyes, he saw God, the beauty of true love, but when he looked deeper, he knew she hid the pain of the terrible things she'd seen. Every part of him wanted nothing more than to shelter her from ever knowing any more tragedy. But would he be able to do this? He was a man, only one man, against an entire army of demons. How could he keep her safe? And now, she was pregnant, and yes, it was a true blessing, but he also felt that Shlomie was right. It was his fault.

The woman he loved would bring his child into the world in the dead of winter. Would she survive? Would the child survive? They must. He must be sure that they did. He saw a squirrel move up a tree and pulled the arrow back into his bow. Isaac sent the arrow flying through the air, but he missed. He was far too lost in thought to hunt. They needed the food, but he couldn't seem to focus.

Perhaps he would ask Shlomie to go fishing with him. That would be a good time to make peace, to apologize. Together they'd always been able to bring back something, even if it was only a few small fish. Yes, he would talk to Shlomie. The idea felt right.

Isaac found Shlomie gathering wood for a fire. He walked over to him.

"I'm sorry," Isaac said. "I'm sorry for what happened earlier."

Shlomie nodded, not meeting Isaac's eyes.

"We could use some meat. I went hunting today, but I didn't catch a thing. Would you like to go fishing?"

"I suppose," Shlomie said. "We could use the fish. Zofia needs meat and milk too."

"We will have to go to one of the farms and steal the milk from the cows for her," Isaac said. "I mean, I will have to go. You don't have to. It's not your responsibility."

"I want to go. We'll go together." Shlomie had never stopped loving Zofia, even though he knew she had given her heart to Isaac.

"Thank you, Shlomie. I appreciate everything."

"I know you do, and I know how much you love her."

"I do love her, Shlomie. I do."
"Yes, I know."
And so do you, Isaac thought.

CHAPTER SIXTY-EIGHT

Seff healed quickly and turned out to be an asset to the group. He was a fast learner. When Isaac showed him how to hunt with the bow and arrow, within a week, he was able to reach his target. He was not a complainer, and for that, Isaac was grateful. The more Isaac knew him, the more he found that he enjoyed Seff's company. This made him feel guilty for wanting to turn the man away.

But he still felt that Zofia was his most important concern, and the thought of putting her at risk still made him anxious. Zofia mattered more to Isaac than anything else. Everything he did, he did with Zofia's welfare first and foremost in his mind. When he went hunting or fishing, Isaac's thoughts were always to bring back enough for Zofia.

So far, she maintained her slender figure. The only time he could see any evidence of her pregnancy was when she was naked. And then, he was so struck by her beauty and this beautiful gift God had given him that he found it hard to catch his breath. Zofia... Even the thought of her brought a smile to his face. He let his mind drift for a moment to her long hair floating on her back, her skin the color of white roses.

"Thank you, God," he whispered to the earth and sky as he

walked through the forest alone, carrying his bow and arrow. This was his time for deep thought. This was his time for planning. Someday, as soon as this ended, he would find a way to build a wonderful life for his wife and child. If he had to work twenty-four hours a day, he would make sure they were comfortable. Isaac saw a large hare move in the grass. Quietly, he adjusted his bow and arrow, and then he shot. Zofia would have meat tonight.

Isaac returned, carrying the rabbit. When Zofia saw him, her eyes lit up like the evening stars as a smile broke across her face.

"You brought meat?"

"Yes. I had a good shot."

"That's great! Why don't we take a walk and see if we can find some carrots and onions to make a stew? Then there will be plenty for everyone."

"You mean the farm down the road?"

"Yes, we could walk there and gather some vegetables."

"It's risky during the day. I'd rather wait until night," Isaac said.

"But then, we can't make a stew tonight."

"I don't think it's a good idea to steal vegetables out in the open, Zofia."

"Well, I'm going. You can come with me or not. It's your choice."

He looked at her. She was so pretty and so stubborn. He shook his head. "I won't let you go without me. It's just too dangerous."

"Then you'd better get moving because I'm going." She smiled at him, and he felt as if a light from Heaven had come to light up this small cabin in the woods.

"You win. All right, let's go," he said and laughed at how easily she could sway him.

Zofia took the basket from the shelf Ben had built in the cabin just as Shlomie came in carrying two small fish.

"Where are you going?" Shlomie asked.

"Isaac and I are going to the farm down the road to gather some vegetables for a stew tonight. Isaac caught a rabbit."

"I'll come with you," Shlomie said.

Isaac leaned back and stretched. When Zofia and Shlomie had

walked outside, he took one of the guns from the small pile and put it into his pants pocket. He strapped his bow and arrow across his back. *I've become such a mountain man*, he thought.

Then he thought again of his life before, of his parents. "Oh, Mama, I miss you and Papa. I wish you could have known my Zofia. She is such a special girl. You would have loved her." He found himself talking aloud to no one. He smiled, and it was a sad smile. He missed them both.

If only things had been different. Right now, his mother would be helping to plan the wedding for him to marry Zofia. And Zofia would not be pregnant, that's for sure. He laughed a little aloud. He probably would not have touched her until their wedding night, when she would have worn a modest white gown, and he would have gingerly removed it. Of course, there would have been naysayers because of her previous pregnancy. In fact, if he were honest with himself, his mother would not have approved.

Ah, well, things have a way of working themselves out. It's God's will that we are together, and I am thankful for that. It is my greatest blessing in life, but I cannot help but miss my parents, even though I know that if you were both here, Zofia. I would have a more difficult time being together. There is good in bad and bad in good. Nothing is ever all black or white. Shaking his head, he went to join his friends.

Zofia kissed him full on the lips when Isaac approached her. The warmth of the sun shining on his face and the sweetness of her kiss made him smile.

"Come on, you two lovebirds, let's get going," Shlomie said.

"Are you sure you want to do this? This could be dangerous. I don't like to leave the forest until night," Isaac repeated, hoping Zofia would see reason.

"We will be quick," Zofia said.

Isaac nodded.

There was no sign of anyone when they approached the farm. Isaac stood guard, looking in all directions, his hand under his shirt, gripping his pistol, while the other two began to gather vegetables. A truck went by, and the three friends looked at each other with fright in their eyes, but the vehicle did not stop.

"I think we should go," Isaac said, a little annoyed that he'd allowed Zofia to convince him to do this perilous thing. He'd allowed her to put herself at risk. The truck could return or send others to come for them at any time. This was just plain foolishness.

"All right, Shlomie and I have gathered enough for now," Zofia said, her voice soft. She sensed that Isaac was on alert. His tone had been curt and caustic.

"Come on. Let's move swiftly," Isaac said.

The three friends darted away, heading back to the safety of the forest. Isaac thought they looked like three children walking home from school, except for their age, their tattered and dirty clothes, and, more importantly, their terrified expressions.

Zofia smiled at Isaac. It was a timid smile, but it always lit the fire in his heart. He couldn't stay angry with her. He wrapped his arm around hers and kissed the top of her hair. But he continued to be on edge and watching until they were deep in the woods.

It was almost a three-mile walk back to the cabin. But under the protection of the trees, Isaac's tension lifted, and he began to relax.

CHAPTER SIXTY-NINE

Zofia was giddy. She felt almost childlike walking through the sun-filtered trees with Isaac, the man who'd brought purpose to her life, and her best friend, Shlomie. True, it had been a scare when the truck chugged by, but it was only a farmer. The back of the truck was open and filled with hay.

Of course, there was a reason to be cautious, but she was tired of caution. It was summer, and she was in love. Zofia wanted to be careless, to be free, and to be young. Silly thoughts these were, especially with all the dangers that surrounded them. Isaac was right. They were so close to the end of this war. Any day, this could all be over. Why take any risks now? Play it safe. She shivered at the thought. Why had she wanted so desperately to take the chance of being caught? What was it in her that wanted to take that step over the edge? The joyous feelings of summer began to disappear, being replaced with self-reproach.

Zofia shuddered at her own stupid actions. Maybe it was a hormonal imbalance from the pregnancy, but she began to think of what could have happened. I am so lucky to be alive, to have Isaac, and all of our friends, to be safe. Tears sprung to her eyes. She would not take a risk like this again.

Isaac saw that Zofia was crying. He stopped and turned to take her in his arms.

"What is it, sweetheart?" he asked, confused. Just a few moments ago, she'd been laughing and squeezing his arm. He lifted her face so that her eyes could meet his. "You're crying." He wiped the tears from her cheek with his thumb. "Zofia?"

"I'm sorry. I put us all at risk. I am so sorry." She was sobbing.

"Women get very strange when they're pregnant," Shlomie said, "one minute happy, the next sad."

"Quiet, Shlomie," Isaac said. "Now, darling, talk to me," Isaac said, sitting down on a rock and pulling Zofia gently to sit on his knee. "Don't cry, please."

"I am really sorry. When I think of what could have happened… I don't know why I didn't think of it before we left. I am so confused, Isaac."

"Shhhh…" He patted her back like a baby and cradled her in his arms. "It's all right."

Shlomie shook his head. "I'm going back to the cabin. This is a little nauseating. I'll see you two lovebirds in a little while."

"Go," Isaac said, Zofia still emotional in his arms. He rocked her gently until she calmed down.

"I don't know what got into me," she said.

"It's all right. Nothing happened. We're all fine."

"Yes." She nodded and swallowed hard. "But we won't do that again." Why was she so irrational? She had never been this way when she was pregnant with Eidel. Yet, with Eidel, she'd been terribly sick. This time, at least, she'd not experienced that awful nausea. Every pregnancy must be different. Still, from now on, she must make a conscious effort to control her rash behavior.

"I agree. Let's not do that again," Isaac said as a small smile came across his face. He'd tried to tell her this in the first place. Now he was glad that she'd realized it on her own.

She started to cry.

"Shhhh… It's all right," he whispered into her ear.

"I love you so much, Isaac. You came into my life and made me realize so many things I'd never known before. I mean, there were other boyfriends and all. Once, I even thought I was in love, but I didn't know what love really was. I do now. You are my true *bashert*."

"And you are mine. Do you remember when you used to come to buy bread, and I would be sitting in the back of my mom's bakery?"

"I do remember. You were so fat."

"Yes, I was," he laughed. "I could never get enough of that warm bread with butter fresh from the oven." He wiped the tear from the side of her cheek. "But you know what? I'm going to tell you a secret."

"I love secrets." She smiled through her tears.

"I loved you even then. I would look out through the back door and watch you. I thought you were the prettiest girl in the whole world, at least in Warsaw, which was our whole world at the time."

She smiled, her eyes lighting up with the memory.

"We did believe that Warsaw was the entire world, didn't we? When I was a child, I could never have imagined all that had happened."

He nodded, watching a butterfly light on a yellow flower. Then he smoothed her hair with the palm of his hand.

"I knew you never noticed me when we were children, but I used to go to sleep at night wishing that somehow I would grow up to be handsome. And somehow, someway, God would bless me, and you would marry me. Of course, I hardly expected it to turn out the way that it did. Still, this may sound crazy, but even with all that we have gone through, I wouldn't change it because if things had been different, you would probably never have been mine. I would gladly suffer any pain in trade for the joy of having you as my wife."

She felt shivers run down her spine. Then she hugged him close to her. She felt his heart beat against her chest, through his shirt, and the tenderness of it brought fresh tears to her eyes.

"Oh, Isaac, you say the dearest things."

"Well, in a way, God granted my wish, even if he didn't make me handsome," Isaac said, winking.

"Oh, but you are handsome," Zofia said, taking a blond curl out of his eyes.

For a moment, their eyes locked. Then he gently put his hand on the back of her head, drew her toward him, and kissed her.

Their kiss was interrupted, and their peace was shattered by the sound of multiple gunshots from the direction of the cabin.

Shlomie ran toward the sound of the gunfire and arrived to see a truck with three German soldiers driving away from the cabin. He was shaking, his face flushed with angry red blotches, and perspiration ran down his forehead. He ran inside and was devastated by the sight. Isaac and Zofia arrived at the cabin, and Shlomie ran to them, out of breath, his face contorted with grief.

"They've been to the cabin. The Nazis have been here. Everyone is dead."

"What, Shlomie? Slow down," Isaac said. Zofia got off his lap, and Isaac stood. "What's going on?"

"I looked in the cabin." Shlomie's words caught with his ragged breath. "They are all dead—everyone—shot. Their bodies are all over the inside of the cabin. Sarah, Ben, Moishe, Rivka, Seff. All of them are dead. Dead, I tell you. It was horrible."

Isaac took a deep breath. "I'll bet they were looking for Seff." He glanced around him, instantly alert. "We must get away from here as far as possible. They are probably still somewhere nearby. But first, I have to go back and get the weapons."

Zofia looked into Isaac's eyes. "I'm scared."

"I know, darling. I know." He looked at Shlomie. "Watch her. Stay hid. You understand me?" Isaac said.

"Yes." Shlomie nodded.

"Isaac, please don't leave me."

"I will be right back. I have to go. We need the weapons."

"I want to go with you."

"No. I forbid it. Wait here. Please, Zofia, just this one time, do as I ask."

She saw how firm he was, and she nodded.

"Watch her, Shlomie."

Isaac ran through the opening in the trees toward the cabin. He kept turning back to watch the spot where he'd left Zofia to see if Shlomie had been followed. It looked safe. The Nazis must have thought that they got everyone. With God's help, they were long gone by now. Still, he must hurry. There was no telling what would come next. They could be waiting, or worse, they could have followed Shlomie, which would bring them to Zofia. But he doubted that. If they'd seen Shlomie, they would most likely have shot him on the spot.

Isaac's heart thundered in his chest as he approached the log cabin. He looked around quickly from his hiding place in the trees. Then he took a deep breath and entered. The bodies of his dearest companions, the only friends he'd known and come to love, lay strewn like rag dolls drowning in pools of their own blood. He wanted to cry out to God, "Why?" to scream, question, kick down the walls, kill a Nazi or two, or more, with his bare hands. He shook with rage. His face flushed with anger.

Stop looking. Stop thinking. There is no time for this. Find the guns and the food, and get back to Zofia. You can't do anything for these poor souls now. They have left this earth.

He went to the corner of the room where the group had kept the weapons. The entire area had been cleared out. He stared in disbelief at the empty dirt floor as a spider sprinted under the wall. The Nazis had taken the guns. All he had left to defend the three of them was the single gun he'd taken when he'd left and his bow and arrow.

Then Isaac raced to the tiny workstation where they had kept the food. There was nothing left. Even the rabbit he'd shot earlier that morning was gone. No vegetables, no rotting fruit, nothing. They took the blankets. All that the Nazis left in their wake were the dead bodies.

"I'm sorry, Ben," Isaac said aloud as he went to Ben's side. Quickly, he undressed him and took his clothes. Then he whispered a prayer for the dead, walked out of the cabin, and closed the door on that segment of his life forever.

CHAPTER SEVENTY

"Put these on," Isaac said to Zofia, handing her Ben's clothes. "You'll be able to move better in pants than in a skirt."

"They are all dead? All of them dead?" she asked, unable to keep the shock and horror from her voice.

Isaac nodded slowly.

She knew her face had gone pale. She'd felt the blood drain out of her earlier when Shlomie had told them what he saw. She knew by the look on Isaac's face that he was worried about her.

"It's all right, sweetheart," Isaac said, giving her an encouraging smile. "Come on, put them on."

"Ben's clothes," Shlomie said aloud, but mostly to himself.

Ben was the heaviest of the men except for Isaac. Isaac hoped that Ben's pants would be large enough when Zofia grew into her pregnancy.

She took the pile of clothing with a lump in her throat and went behind a tree. A few minutes later, she emerged wearing the pants and shirt. For some reason, Isaac had overlooked the large spot of blood on the shirt, and now it bothered him to see it on Zofia. However, he said nothing.

"You look adorable." He gave her a smile. *Be strong, Zofia,* he thought. It must be hard for her to wear the clothes she'd seen Ben wear all those months. If only he could take the strength from his own body and transfer it to her, he would gladly do so.

"Isaac, how are we ever going to survive the winter?" she asked.

"We'll manage. You'll see. Don't worry about anything. Just let me handle it all, all right?"

"Should we try to build another cabin?" Zofia asked.

"I don't think we have enough manpower," Shlomie answered, "and we don't have the ax. Isaac, did you look for the ax?"

"Yes, it was gone. All the weapons except a single gun and my bow and arrow are gone."

"Oh, Isaac, I think we're done for," Zofia said, and she sank to the ground, almost as if she could no longer find the strength to stand.

"Silly girl, we are not done for." He lifted her up into his arms. "Do you trust me? Have I ever lied to you?" Again, he tried to make light of things for her sake.

"Yes, and no."

"Yes, no, no, yes." He tried to laugh, hoping his laughter would sound sincere. He didn't want her to know the truth about how worried he actually was. "Trust me, please." He touched her face. She could see how hard he was trying to assure her, and for his sake, she mustered a small chuckle.

"There now, that's my girl," he said. "Now, let's begin walking."

"What direction?" Shlomie asked.

"I don't know. Let's try going west. From what Seff said, the Allies landed somewhere in France. They should be coming in from the west."

"And the Russians will come from the east," Shlomie said.

"Yes, but I think I would rather be rescued by the Americans and the Brits than by the Russians. I have heard that they are not too crazy about Jews."

"You are probably right. Let's go west," Shlomie said. Then he walked over to a thick-trunked maple tree and looked for the green moss. Once he spotted it, he indicated with his finger. "That's north, so this is the way we want to go."

"I realize that we are all saddened by what happened, but we should give thanks to God that we were not there at the cabin with them. We could be dead. We could all be lying on the floor of that cabin right now. But somehow, for some reason, God saw fit for us to be alive, so we are alive, here, and together. It is a blessing," Isaac said.

The other two nodded in agreement.

Again, Isaac smiled at Zofia. He took her hand in his and kissed it. Then he wrapped his arm around hers, and the three of them began to walk.

CHAPTER SEVENTY-ONE

"How long is the waiting list? How many months before I can expect to have this surgery done?" Manfred asked Dr. Schmidt.

"Everyone seems to want it, and all of you want it immediately, especially all the lower-ranking officers. I've committed to doing this, but I can only perform one, maybe two, per day. So we are looking at about a year."

"A whole year? I thought I was coming to have it done now, today."

"No, I sent for you to explain exactly what you should expect once I performed the surgery. How long the recovery will be, what kind of pain you will experience, and how striking the change will be when you see your new face."

"You called me all the way here to discuss this?"

"This is best not discussed on the telephone. It is top secret, as you know. Now please understand that what you are considering is a life-altering experience."

Manfred nodded. Then he listened for the next two hours as Dr. Schmidt explained the procedure. When he'd finished, Manfred asked if Goebbels, Hitler, or any others had made a reservation to be operated on.

"I'm sorry, but I am not at liberty to disclose that information, even to you," Dr. Schmidt said, stretching his arms.

"Now, once it is done, you will stay at our makeshift clinic until you have recovered sufficiently to travel. As soon as I remove your bandages, you will be on your way to South America."

"Where exactly will I be sent to in South America?"

"I don't know. I assume you won't be told until the last minute due to security issues. This is a tough time for us, Manfred, a tough time indeed. We must all do what we can to save the Reich, even if it means personal sacrifice."

Manfred nodded, taking a deep breath. The surgery would be painful and life-changing in every way. He would have to learn to live with his new face, the face of a Jew, his new name, the name of a Jew.

"Do you think there is any possibility that Germany will pull herself back up and recover?" Manfred asked the doctor, although he already knew the answer.

"We have already lost the war. We are just holding on now, but I don't know for how long," Dr. Schmidt said, lighting a cigarette. "Would you like one?"

Manfred shook his head. "No, thank you."

"This is going to be very bad for all of us. We are going to have a hell of a time once the Fatherland falls."

Manfred nodded. He saw the worry lines on the doctor's face.

"Do you think we will be able to get out of Germany in time?"

"I don't know. If you want the truth, I am afraid. The Americans are powerful and coming at us in full force. It's hard to say. However, I can tell you this: they won't understand what we have tried to do, and if we are captured, it will be a dark day for the Aryan race."

"Perhaps I should leave the country now, without having had the surgery…"

"I expect that the Americans or the Russians will find you. There are just too many prisoners still alive who've seen your face. They'll probably hunt you down."

Manfred nodded. He felt the anxiety rise in his chest. His heart skipped a beat, and the pain shot through him. What the doctor said was true. He'd earned the hatred of the prisoners he'd lorded over, and once the war was ended, if they were able, they were likely to retaliate. There was little choice left to him. He would arrange to have the operation.

CHAPTER SEVENTY-TWO

SURGERY TO ALTER Manfred's face, a new life in South America…it was overwhelming. Christa was too weak to cope with all that was coming at her. For just a moment, she closed her eyes, and her mind drifted to a ball she had attended with Manfred before things had gone wrong. Without thinking about where she was, she began to hum a waltz.

"Mama, are you all right?" Katja asked.

Christa had been lying in bed with Katja at her side, reading from a book of fairy tales.

"Yes, dear, I'm fine."

"You scared me. You were reading, and then all of a sudden, you just started singing, and your eyes were closed. It was very strange. Are you sure you are all right?" Katja squeezed Christa's arm.

Christa saw the alarm on Katja's little face, and she felt sorry to have caused it.

"Yes, I'm sorry. Something in the book must have jogged my memory," Christa said and hugged the little girl to her side. Christa felt the warmth of Katja beside her. What would become of this child when she died? Every day, she grew weaker. Every day, the child grew older. Sometimes, she believed she stayed alive purely out of love and concern for her little girl, who'd been her only glimpse of happiness for years. Could she trust Manfred to care for Katja?

He'd never really taken to her the way Christa had. She hated to reminisce about the man she had believed she'd married. It hurt far too much to remember the dreams they'd shared when they had gone to Munich to adopt a child. *Those were the days of light*, she thought. *Those were the golden days*.

If only she'd been able to keep Zofia with them when they left Treblinka… She'd begged Manfred, but he rejected the idea, becoming angry and refusing to discuss it further. However, she had insisted that he not send Zofia to the gas chamber. As weak as she'd been, she'd fought him on that point.

She knew what was going on at the camp. She'd heard the SS men talking. It sickened her, horrified her, that her husband was a part of all of it. She'd yelled and screamed with every ounce of energy she had in her broken body until he finally agreed. Zofia could go free. Christa had kissed his hand, thanking him. She couldn't bear the thought of Zofia's murder.

But if only Zofia were with her now, she would have cared for Katja. Christa knew she could trust Zofia. She had come to love her. She was a good woman. Sadly, fate had not favored Zofia. She had been born a Jew in Hitler's Germany, and for that reason, and that reason alone, she had suffered a terrible fate. Christa had done what she could to make Zofia's life better, but there was little that she could do. Sadly, Zofia had probably died by now or been captured and sent to another camp. The poor woman had been set free, but she had no place to go. Chances were good that the Gestapo had found her. Christa sighed.

Deep sadness and guilt came over her. She clutched her chest and thought of her father. How angry she'd been at him in the beginning. All he'd had to do was remain quiet about his opinions and follow the rules. That is what she'd told him. But he was not one to be intimidated, not the good doctor. He had told her many times that a man's character was his most prized possession, and he'd proved it. He'd died because he'd stood up for his beliefs. Her father had ruined her marriage, but she'd realized later that her father had been right. She might have found the courage to stand up and fight for Zofia if she'd been stronger and healthier. She wished she had.

CHAPTER SEVENTY-THREE

October 1944

The Royal Air Force, following a year and a half cessation during the Luftwaffe's attempt to crush them, resumed their bombing raids with a vengeance in March 1943, just before the crushing defeat of Hitler's 6th Army in Stalingrad. By the fall of 1944, few Germans no longer believed the Nazi propaganda of a thousand-year Reich.

The Nazis watched in horror as the Allies came crashing in on them from both the east and the west, their dreams of a thousand-year Reich bursting into flames right before their eyes as the bombs fell on Berlin. Hitler's pride kept him from admitting that he'd made a fatal error by invading Russia while the country was embroiled in a war with the British, but Manfred knew. He could see the writing on the wall.

It was only a matter of time before Stalin came marching into his beloved country with a vengeance. The previous summer, the Allies had landed on the shores of Normandy. Manfred had sat in his office at Auschwitz, Poland, glued to the radio, listening to the updates on the BBC on the bloody battle. He no longer believed what German radio was reporting. After all, he had been a propaganda officer, and more and more, he had convincing proof that the British BBC was reporting the facts and that German radio was feeding them the Party line. Germany had given it their all, but they were war-weary, and the Allies just kept coming.

America had joined with Great Britain, giving the SS officers even further cause for concern. Although they risked accusations of treason, many privately admitted to each other that they had lost faith in their great Führer. On the Russian Front, the soldiers starved and froze to death all winter at an alarming rate. Hitler had been so confident that Germany would take Russia as quickly as it had taken Poland that he sent his army east, unequipped and without sufficient food or warm clothing to face the devastating cold of the Russian winter.

CHAPTER SEVENTY-FOUR

EVEN NOW, several months after the event, Isaac refused to discuss what he'd seen that day in the cabin. Zofia didn't ask, but she knew it had affected him deeply. His usual optimism was clouded.

Winter had invaded the land, her frozen heart destroying all evidence of the previous summer's abundance.

Isaac, Zofia, and Shlomie found warmth in tool sheds and barns, but they never stayed more than a night, settling in after dark and leaving before the sun rose. They'd stolen winter coats along the way. Isaac had made sure that Zofia had the first one. But still, the cold and lack of food took their toll. Within two weeks of the onset of winter, Zofia turned weak and pale, and she had begun to bleed. She was sick to her stomach and vomiting. Isaac was terrified.

He said nothing but held her tenderly in his arms, blaming himself for her predicament. Zofia trembled, and her teeth chattered with the cold and blood loss.

"We have to stop running. I know it's a risk, but we must. The farm we passed this morning has a large tool shed. We'll settle there. With God's help, the farmer won't be going out to use his tools anytime soon," Isaac said. God, how he loved her. If only he could take her pain, he would gladly do it. Her suffering was worse to him than dying.

"It's risky," Shlomie said, shaking with cold.

"I don't care. We can't keep going. Zofia needs to rest."

Shlomie nodded. "It's true. Let's stop." He looked at Isaac accusingly out of the corner of his eye.

They hid in the forest across the road from the tool shed all day. Zofia lay in Isaac's arms. When night fell, he lifted and carried her like a baby, and the three entered the shed. Even inside, Zofia still shivered, and her skin had turned the color of chalk.

There was no light in the shed, no windows. Shlomie tripped over something but regained his balance without falling.

"It's better in here than outside, but it's still so damned cold," Isaac said, taking off his coat and laying it over Zofia, who was too weak to speak.

"There is nothing else we can do," Shlomie said. "At least we have some shelter."

Isaac nodded. "I wonder if there are any extra blankets in the barn."

"I wouldn't take them. That would only alert the farmer. In the morning, you and I will go to a neighboring farm and try to find some blankets," Shlomie said.

"I know it's a lot to ask, but why don't we take all three coats and put them over the three of us? If we huddle together, we will be warm," Isaac said.

"You're worried about Zofia?"

"Yes, of course I am. She's bleeding, and I'm very worried."

"You did this to her," Shlomie said. "How could you get her pregnant in the position we are in?"

"Shut up," Isaac said, angrier with himself than at Shlomie. "I'm sorry. You're right. I should never have done this. If she dies, I will never forgive myself." Isaac began to cry. *God, take me instead. I did this. It isn't her fault. It's mine. Please, take me instead. I am begging you.*

For several moments, the room was dark, cold, and silent, except for the sobbing that came from Isaac's tortured soul.

"It's all right. She'll be all right," Shlomie said. They could see his white breath as he spoke.

Zofia was drained. Her eyes were closed, but she could hear them. It was difficult to speak, but she knew that she must.

"Isaac…" Her voice was barely a whisper. "Isaac, my love, don't blame yourself. I wouldn't trade one minute of what we had. I am not sorry for what we did."

He leaned his body down beside her and took her into his arms. The tears still fell freely on his face, dripping onto hers.

"I love you." It was all he could say. "I'm sorry. I am so sorry." There was no way to change the past.

"I love you too, Isaac, and I am really not sorry."

All through the night, Isaac held Zofia, watching her sleep. In the morning, he breathed a sigh of relief as the sun burst like a bouquet of ribbons through the slats of wood in the shed to find she was still alive. Now, with the light, Isaac could see everything in the room. It was filled with useful tools, matches, and horse blankets. Isaac put the entire pile of blankets on top of Zofia. He took his coat and put it on. Then he strapped his bow and arrow to his back.

"You're going hunting?" Shlomie asked.

"Yes. Stay with her. I am going to see what I can find."

Several hours had passed before Isaac returned carrying a bird, a squirrel, and a bunch of soft brown apples. In his other hand, he held a steel bucket filled with water.

He put the apples down. "I took these from the farm down the way. I turned the bushel over. The farmer will think that the horse got to them. And I was blessed. I caught two animals for us."

Shlomie nodded. "Where did you get the water?"

"I walked to another farm and stole the horse's water."

"You must be tired."

Isaac shrugged. He was tired, exhausted, in fact. He'd not slept a wink the entire night. "How is she?" Isaac bent beside Zofia.

"She's weak."

Isaac nodded.

"I'm going to start a fire," Isaac said, spying a fifty-five-gallon oil drum, a small can of kerosene, and a saw.

"It's too dangerous. We can't start a fire inside a building. Are you crazy? The windows are all boarded up. We'll die in here."

"I'll knock the windows out. Look. There's an ax on the wall."

"No, this is madness," Shlomie said.

Zofia lay shaking on the ground, too weak to voice an opinion.

"Leave if you don't like it, but I am going to do it," Isaac said. "I'll be back. I'm going to gather some tree branches. Watch Zofia. I won't be long."

Isaac returned with a pile of branches. He laid them on the ground. Then he shivered as he sawed the top of the oil drum off. There was almost no oil left. He placed the branches inside and then poured a small amount of kerosene over them. Next, he took the ax and punched the windows out. A rush of frigid air flooded into the shed. Isaac took a match and lit the contents of the drum. Then he quickly opened the door. The fire began slowly, but quickly it caught, and the room began to grow warmer. Then he cleaned the fur and feathers from the animals he'd caught and began to roast them.

The smell of food filled the shed, and even Zofia was stirred by the odor. When the meat was cooked, Isaac tore off tiny pieces and put them into Zofia's mouth. The meat was dry and difficult to chew. She gagged. Seeing this, Isaac realized that she could not eat this without his help. He chewed tiny pieces of the fowl until they were soft and then put them into Zofia's mouth. She swallowed. He continued until she lay back and fell asleep. Every night as the sun set, Zofia could hear Isaac as he prayed in Hebrew on his knees beneath the moon. Once he'd finished the prayers, he begged God to spare Zofia, to take him instead.

Then in the morning, Isaac would go out to hunt. Some days he returned with nothing, but most days, he caught at least a small animal, enough to get them through. Shlomie offered to accompany Isaac to ice fishing, but Isaac wanted Shlomie to stay with Zofia.

As the winter broke, Zofia grew stronger, but she'd lost the baby. She knew it by the amount of blood she'd shed. But at least God had spared her life. Zofia was able to eat by herself now, and every day Isaac insisted that she walk around the shed for a while for exercise.

"We need to think about moving on. The farmer will be coming out to begin his planting work soon. We certainly want to be gone before then," Shlomie said.

"Yes, I know. I hate to move. Zofia is thriving here," Isaac said.

"Next week? I am not sure, but if my calculations are right, it is nearly the end of March. We are taking a big chance being here," Shlomie said. "I've been keeping a log to help me know what month we are in ever since I escaped from Treblinka."

"What year is it?" Isaac asked.

"If my calculations are correct, it's 1945."

CHAPTER SEVENTY-FIVE

Shlomie proved to be right. It was three days later that the man who owned the farm came to the shed. When the door opened, Zofia felt her heart would burst in her chest. Isaac immediately stood up, his hand on the pistol in his back pocket.

"What is this?" A man with weathered skin blotched with red looked at them, horrified. "Who are you? Jews?"

Shlomie nodded. Zofia got up and stood beside Isaac, who moved her away just enough to keep control of the situation.

"Jews? In my shed? How long have you been here?" The farmer didn't wait for an answer. "If you'd been caught, I would have been blamed. How dare you? How dare you? I'm going to inform the authorities today." The man's face grew red with anger. "You have put my family and me in danger, you filthy, miserable Jews. Don't you move!" He looked at their faces and then began to cry out, "Alex, Alex, come quick. There are Jews in the…"

Before he could continue, Isaac had pulled the gun and shot him in the head. Blood spurted all over the walls. Zofia gagged and turned away.

"Come. Let's go! Hurry!" Shlomie said.

Isaac stood stunned, looking at the gun. "I've killed a man. God, forgive me. I've committed the ultimate sin." His hands were shaking.

"Stop it, Isaac, come on. We can pray later. Right now, we have to get out of here. Zofia, are you all right to walk?" Shlomie shook Isaac's shoulder.

Zofia nodded, still in shock.

Isaac still stared at the gun. Shlomie slapped him hard across the face. "Come on! Let's go."

The slap brought Isaac back to reality.

The three ran from the shed, Isaac gripping Zofia's arm to help her. It was less than half a mile until the welcoming trees of the forest beckoned with protection. Once they'd ventured far away from the road, the three stopped to catch their breath.

"I killed a man back there," Isaac said.

"You had no choice." Zofia touched his arm tenderly.

"I took the life of another human being."

"If you hadn't, we would be on our way to a camp right now. Isaac, you've never been in a camp, thank God. You have no idea what goes on there. Just be glad we've made it through the winter. You did what you had to do. Enough said," Shlomie asserted.

Isaac prayed every night, asking God's forgiveness. Zofia listened as he knelt, singing the Hebrew prayers. He refused to make love to her out of fear of another pregnancy. But they lay in each other's arms, rubbing each other's backs tenderly, kissing, caressing, and touching. The passion between them burned constantly, and they longed to allow it to consume them, but Isaac fought the need with all the strength he could muster. Zofia meant too much to him to put her at risk again.

One night, as Isaac prayed under the full moon, Shlomie called out from where he was seated against the side of a tree. A light drizzle had begun to fall.

"*Bar Mitzvah*, boy, enough already. You're getting on my nerves."

Isaac paid no attention. Instead, he continued to chant in Hebrew.

"You can be the *Bar Mitzvah* boy. You didn't suffer, and you've never been in a camp. What do you know about what it means to be a Jew?"

"Shlomie, please," Zofia said.

Isaac finished and came to sit beside Zofia, taking her hand. "I'd appreciate it if you would mind your own business, Shlomie."

"There is no God. If there was God, He abandoned us when Adolf Hitler came into power." Shlomie crossed his arms over his chest.

"You're entitled to believe anything you'd like."

"Look at our people, look at us, and you still believe there is a God?"

"I do. I believe every time I look at the sky and see the stars, every time I catch a fish that feeds us. We survived the winters against great odds. Who do you think was helping us? But most of all, I know there is a God every time I look at Zofia."

"Echh, I think we survived by sheer luck. Of course, you believe. You're like a schoolboy in love. I don't know why I bother to talk intelligently with you."

"Shlomie, that's not fair. Isaac is entitled to his religion," Zofia said.

"It's not so much religion for me. It's God. I don't believe that any one religion is better or worse than another. For that matter, religion itself isn't even important. I believe that each man knows what God expects of him," said Isaac.

"Oh, and what is that? And how did our entire race of people fail God so badly that we ended up under Hitler's thumb, marching off to death camps? You tell me, smart boy. You have all the answers."

"I don't have all the answers. I wish I did. But I will tell you this. I believe that God expects us to stand by him and to know that he is there for us."

"Was he there for the poor souls as they walked into the gas chambers at Treblinka? I watched them, Isaac. I saw it with my own eyes," Shlomie said. "I dug the pits they used to burn the bodies, then cut the firewood to fuel the pyres. I saw the heaps of bodies waiting to be burned and smelled them later. I saw little children tortured. Why was that, Isaac? Why did God allow that?"

"I don't know, Shlomie, I don't have the answers. I can't tell you. All I know is that I believe, and I don't think God was responsible for what happened in Treblinka. It was the Nazis."

"Ech, isn't your God stronger than Hitler?"

"Yes, and he must have a reason for allowing this to happen. I don't know the reason. Maybe someday I will, but I don't know it now. I only know that there is a God, and He is here with us in this forest. Regardless of what we have lost, we three are blessed because we are alive."

"Please, let's try to get along. I realize that it's difficult because we are together all the time. But we have to try to make the best of it, alright? This arguing and fighting is not good for any of us," Zofia said.

Both men nodded.

"Then we are all in agreement?" She smiled.

CHAPTER SEVENTY-SIX

In the morning, Isaac took his bow and arrow and went out to hunt. He needed the time alone. Sometimes, it seemed as if he had to exercise all the self-control he had not to beat the hell out of Shlomie. Obviously, Shlomie harbored feelings of jealousy. He'd been in love with Zofia too, but she'd chosen Isaac, and now he continually found reasons to pick on everything Isaac said or did.

The sun broke through the trees in mid-April. The weather was still cool but not nearly as bad as it had been a month earlier. Isaac was lost in thought. He wished that he could make love to Zofia. He yearned to feel her body pressed against his own, to feel the heat of her breath on his neck. How he loved her with every beat of his heart.

A large, black bird flapped its wings as it flew above him. Isaac looked up. When he looked back down, four German soldiers stood in front of him with their guns drawn.

CHAPTER SEVENTY-SEVEN

ALL WAS LOST. The beloved Fatherland stood on the brink of disaster. Manfred's head ached, and he'd vomited several times over the past week as the news circulated among the remaining party members. Manfred had fled Auschwitz before the Allies arrived with his family when he got the call that it was time for his surgery.

Stalin's troops had marched into his beloved but bombed-out Berlin. Manfred was in the back of a car on his way to the secret operating theater, where he would meet the doctor and go forward with his cosmetic surgery. News spread fast amongst the Party members. Manfred had been told that when the Russians descended upon Berlin without pity, the only German forces left to meet them were old men and little boys. The battle that ensued was catastrophic for Germany. From what Manfred had ascertained, they'd raped the women and murdered them, too.

German citizens were taking their lives by the thousands to avoid an uncertain future without the leadership of their precious Führer. Although Hitler had made a speech to the German people telling them they must never surrender and fight to the end, he had gone down into his bunker with his longtime lover and newly wedded wife, Eva Braun, and the two had committed suicide.

Worse, he had lost his best and only friend, Dr. Goebbels. Not only had Goebbels gone to the bunker and killed himself, but he'd also killed his entire family.

Manfred wondered if perhaps Hitler and Goebbels had escaped to South America. Perhaps they'd been surgically altered and planned to reconnect with the others but decided to keep this plan secret. With Hitler and Goebbels, anything was possible. Cyanide pills had been distributed among the SS officers, giving them the option of suicide, rather than a trial, if they were captured. The idea of suicide terrified Manfred. He cringed when he thought of death and what judgment might await him if there, by some chance, was a God. Although he tried to put the fear of his demise out of his mind, it continually haunted him.

Now he had less than twenty-four hours before his surgery was to be performed, and then his face would be altered forever. He'd been warned to be careful on his way to the hidden bunker where the doctor worked diligently on his fellow SS officers.

Manfred must be cautious and sure that he'd not been followed. If he were captured, he knew he could expect to be hanged. If he were followed, he would expose the entire operation. With a heavy heart at the thought of losing his friend, Dr. Goebbels, and terror mixed with anxiety shooting through him, he, Christa, and their little girl headed toward the secret clinic forty kilometers north of Berlin.

Katja laid her head on her mother's lap. With her thumb in her mouth, she tried to sleep. Christa did not speak. It was one in the morning, and an eerie darkness surrounded them, relieved only by the need to dodge a pothole in the road caused by bombs.

In less than a week, they would be on a plane headed to a foreign land. Manfred had no desire to be in Argentina. In fact, he still longed for the days when he lived in Berlin and worked with Dr. Goebbels. It was hard to believe that the Führer and the Goebbels were dead. Who was going to rebuild all of this once they got to South America? He wanted to believe that Hitler and Goebbels were not dead and that all of this was part of the plan.

It was just a secretary, a name he didn't even recognize, who'd called to inform him that he must leave immediately to have his surgery performed. Perhaps Hitler suspected that the phones were tapped, and the information of his death was given to him to confuse the enemy. His mind raced. It was entirely possible that Hitler and Goebbels had already undergone their face-changing operation and were now living under new identities.

Manfred could only hope that once he arrived at the underground hospital, Dr. Schmidt would tell him that his friends were alive and on their way to South America or already there waiting for him.

Nearly two hours later, they arrived at the clinic.

The vehicle in which they rode killed its lights as it slowly moved down the road, turning into the park. Even in the darkness, Manfred could see the rubble everywhere due to the bombings. The driver pulled the car over and let them out according to the instructions Manfred had given him as to where he must go to find the underground hospital.

"Thank you, Rolph. You've been a good friend all these years. Best of luck to you," Manfred said to his driver. "Heil Hitler."

"Heil Hitler, and best of luck to you too, sir."

"Come, sweetheart," Christa said, waking Katja. "We are going on an adventure."

"I'm scared, Mama," Katja said, her thumb still in her mouth.

"Hurry. Let's get moving," Manfred said.

"Shhh, it's all right," Christa whispered, taking Katja's hand. They walked, hiding in the shadows of the trees and buildings, Katja crying softly until they arrived at a small building in the back of the park.

Manfred found the trapdoor in the ground behind the bathroom, just where he'd been told it would be. With some effort, he moved the thick patches of grass that had been placed over the opening. Then he pulled the door and descended into the underground hospital. It was dark except for candlelight.

Katja began to cry softly.

"Shhhh, it's all right… It's all right," Christa whispered as they went down a narrow iron ladder.

Katja slipped and almost fell. Manfred moaned, annoyed.

"Watch the child, Christa," he said.

Manfred reached the bottom. Then he helped Katja and Christa down the ladder.

The three of them walked through the silent hall until they reached a room where several oil lamps were lit. But instead of Dr. Schmidt, they were greeted instead by a squad of U.S. Army soldiers.

"Hello, Manfred Blau, we've been waiting for you," one of the soldiers said. "Your buddy, Doc Schmidt? We already arrested him. After a few minutes of coaxing, he told us to expect you."

"You are Americans? Or Russians? Or British?" Manfred stammered.

"Americans. And you, Mr. Nazi concentration camp torture man, are in a hell of a lot of trouble," the American said, taking a puff of his cigarette, throwing it on the ground, and stamping it out with his foot.

Manfred stared at him in disbelief. The flame in the oil lamp grew larger.

"Manfred Blau," the American soldier said, taking a pair of handcuffs and placing them on Manfred's hands while another soldier held him at gunpoint. "You are under arrest for crimes against humanity."

CHAPTER SEVENTY-EIGHT

Isaac did not return that afternoon or that evening to the little campsite where he'd left Zofia and Shlomie. Zofia kept watching for him to appear through the trees, wearing his big smile, carrying a kill he'd made for dinner that night. But as time passed, she began to panic. Darkness began its descent upon the forest, bringing with it the dreadful fear of disaster.

"Shlomie, Isaac is never gone this long when he goes out hunting. Something is not right."

"I hope he wasn't shot or caught by the Germans."

Zofia was already pacing the forest floor in panic.

"Oh, dear God, no. Not my Isaac!" she cried, reaching her arms up to the sky. "Please, God, please send him back to me."

Shlomie had been sitting with his back against a tree. He, too, had begun to fear the worst. He walked over and hugged Zofia. "He'll be all right. It's Isaac. He's strong, the strongest man I know. He'll be back soon." But he didn't believe it himself. Isaac never stayed away for an entire day without telling them he planned to be gone for a long time.

All through the night, Zofia sat awake, trembling with fear.

"I have to go and see if I can find him," she said.

"Go in the morning. You can't see anything at night. It's too dark. Stay here with me, and as soon as the sun comes up, I'll go with you," Shlomie said.

Zofia waited for dawn, barely able to contain her nerves. As each hour passed, she grew more alarmed. What could have happened? Was he killed? Would she and Shlomie even find his body in the morning? Was he hurt and alone in the darkness? She wrapped her arms around herself. "Isaac," she whispered, "I love you. Wherever you are, I hope you can hear me." Tears streamed down her face, and she rocked back and forth until, finally, the light of the morning broke through the darkness.

Shlomie had not slept, either. He'd sat through the night without speaking, not knowing what to say. Now he got up and took her hand to help her to her feet.

"Come, we'll go together and find Isaac," he said.

All day, they searched. First, they walked in one direction and then another. Next, they went back to the original area where they'd set up camp to see if he had returned, but there was no sign of him.

Every day for a week, they continued to look for Isaac. Zofia began to lose heart. She could not eat or sleep. Shlomie went fishing and brought back two small fish, but she shook her head when he cooked them over an open fire and offered them to her.

"If something has happened to him, then you must accept it. You have no control over this. Zofia, so many people have lost so much. You can't just stop living now. You can't just give up. There must be someone waiting for you once the war is over… Your parents, perhaps?" Shlomie said, trying to offer some comfort.

"No, my parents are dead," Zofia said. "But there is someone, my daughter, my Eidel. She will need me."

"Yes. For her sake, you must try to stay alive."

Zofia nodded, her heart heavy with grief and a darker sadness than she'd known. There was no doubt Zofia had suffered a loss, a terrible loss, but no loss matched this one. She wanted to die, longed just to give up and die. But she'd come so far, and soon, she would be reunited with Eidel, who needed her mother.

At first, the food would not go down her throat, and much of it was regurgitated, but little by little, Zofia began to eat small amounts, chewing slowly, and with every bite, she thought of her child.

The weather grew warmer as the days passed into weeks. Zofia and Shlomie were crossing the road to steal strawberries from a neighboring farm one afternoon. Since Isaac had disappeared, Zofia had become less cautious. Just then, an army truck came barreling down the dirt road. Shlomie and Zofia were paralyzed with fear until they looked further. Hanging on the side of the truck was a sight that made them both gasp: the red, white, and blue American flag. Americans! The Allies were here! Right here, in front of them, right this minute, right now!

Shlomie cried out to the soldiers, waving his arms in the air. The Americans pulled over and stopped the truck.

"Help us… Please, help us… We are Jews running away from the Nazis," Zofia said in the little English she'd learned from Don Taylor, and both she and Shlomie ran toward the truck.

A tall, handsome, athletically built man in his early twenties wearing the uniform of the American army jumped with ease off the back of the vehicle.

"We are Americans," he said. "The war is over. The Germans surrendered last week. Come on, get in. We'll take you to a refugee camp with a hospital where you can get yourself some food and medical care."

Shlomie turned to Zofia. She translated what the man had said, and he began to cry. She patted his arm, stunned. The Americans had arrived!

The American extended his hand to help Zofia into the truck, then again to Shlomie.

As the vehicle rocked along the dirt road, Zofia thought of Isaac. She would have given her life to have him sitting in the back of this army truck, safe and alive. It all seemed like a dream. She folded her hands together in her lap and squeezed, trying to grasp the reality of it.

"Where are we? What country are we in?" Zofia asked. They'd walked so far and for so many months.

"You're in Germany. We are about ten miles south of Eberswalde, and we're headed to Berlin," one of the soldiers answered. She turned to Shlomie and gave him the news. "Don't worry. I will translate everything for you."

"I am lucky to have learned English. It will make things much easier when dealing with the Americans," she said to Shlomie. "Don't worry."

As they drove through Berlin, they were surrounded by bombed-out buildings. Russian troops filled the streets, as well as American and British troops.

They arrived at a large makeshift camp. A few Red Cross trucks sat parked, surrounding a tented area. Nurses in white uniforms scurried about, carrying food and medicine. Men and women in concentration camp uniforms wandered aimlessly or sat against the walls of the buildings. Even though the camp had been liberated and the prisoners set free, many survivors had no place to go, no families, no friends, no homes. The Red Cross set up hospitals for the sick or injured inside what once was the Nazi officers' quarters, but there were so many people in dire need that caring for all of them was a constant struggle, and many waited in line for help.

Zofia looked around. She saw a group of dirty and half-naked men sitting against a building, with their rib cages so pronounced that they protruded from their bodies. Their arms and legs were so skinny that they were the size of a normal wrist. Dead bodies lay in corners, covered with masses of flies, their numbers increasing daily. The stench of death, urine, and feces hung like a cloud of misery over the area.

At the front of the tent stood a folding table with two chairs occupied by two volunteers. One was a survivor, the other a Red Cross worker. A long line of people waiting for help had circled the tent. The American soldier who had brought Shlomie and Zofia to the camp pointed to the line of people.

"You ought to get into that line right there. That's where you gotta go to find out if any of your family members have come in and registered at this camp. They have a list of folks come lookin' for their families. Maybe someone you know came through here already." The well-fed American soldier looked at Zofia with compassion.

Zofia's heart leaped. Could Isaac be on that list? Was it possible he might be alive and searching for her? Oh, dear God, anything could be possible.

"You might want to get something to eat first. The line looks pretty damned long," the soldier said. Zofia saw the sympathy in his eyes. She knew she was dirty and painfully thin.

"Thank you," she said. "Thank you so much for bringing us here to this camp."

Shlomie nodded. "Yes, thank you." He knew that much English.

"We've seen some terrible things comin' over here to Europe, the likes of which I ain't never seen before in my life." With a slight twang to his voice, one of the other soldiers said, "We liberated one of them concentration camps. Was the first ones in after the Nazis tucked their tails between their legs and ran. Well, I'll tell you, I ain't never seen nothin' like it. If I live for a hundred years, them horrible sights will stay in my mind." He shook his head and looked as if he might vomit.

The other soldier jumped off the truck, lifted Zofia by the waist, put her down on the ground, and helped Shlomie off the truck.

"There's food right over there," he indicated with his hand.

"Thank you again," Zofia said.

The soldier nodded, got back into the truck, and the truck pulled away.

"Let's get something to eat," Shlomie said.

"I can't eat. I have to get in line first to see if Isaac has been here. Maybe he has put his name on the list."

"You can do it afterward."

"No, you go ahead. I have to do it now."

"How about if I bring you something, and you can eat while you wait in line?" Shlomie offered.

"Oh yes, that would be wonderful. Thank you, Shlomie."

"I'll go and get in line for food. You get in line over here. As soon as I get something to eat, I'll find you and bring it to you."

Hours passed while Zofia stood in line. It seemed as if there might be a million lost and frantic people searching for loved ones, hoping that, somehow, someone they knew had survived. Refugees continued to pour into the camp every hour, it seemed, and the lines continued to grow. The smell of unwashed bodies and perspiration mingled with the smell of desperation as people cried out in anguish when they learned that their loved ones had not registered or, worse, were listed as dead.

It took Shlomie over three hours to return with a hunk of bread and a bowl of soup for Zofia. She ate it while they stood in line, Shlomie beside her, the two of them waiting to find out if there had been any news of Isaac. The lists constantly grew: one list of those who'd been displaced, and the other a list of the murdered. Because of the ever-growing crowds, it was hard to maintain organization. So many people returned to the line, day after day, in case a loved one had been found since the last time they'd checked.

Finally, it was almost eight that evening when Zofia came to the front of the line and stood before the two women who'd been working all day looking up names. She could see that they were weary, ready to retire for the night. This made her doubt how thoroughly they would check the endless lists of papers.

"Who are you looking for?" the woman asked.

"Zuckerman, Isaac. Isaac Zuckerman," Zofia's voice cracked.

"Let's see what we have."

"Please, may I look too?" Zofia asked.

"Sure," the woman said, her accent clearly American. She handed Zofia a pile of papers.

Zofia scanned the lists of names. For the most part, they were written in English, making them difficult for her to read. Still, she had to try. Sadly, she recognized the word 'deceased' even in English, written over and over again next to most of the names.

"I'm sorry. I don't see any Isaac Zuckerman. You can feel free to check back tomorrow."

Zofia nodded, defeated. She turned to walk away, and then she got an idea.

"Miss?" Zofia asked.

"Yes," the American volunteer answered.

"Can I help you here at this desk? I can read in Polish, and also a little bit of English. Perhaps I can help with the language when you have Polish refugees come through this line," Zofia said.

"We are not paid."

"That's all right. I want to help, and who knows? My Isaac may come through here to register."

"Yes, it's very possible that he might. If you want to help, you are welcome to. We are closing this booth for the night in a few minutes. Come in the morning, if you would like. We could certainly use the extra manpower. I warn you, though. It's demanding and heartbreaking work."

"I'll be here," Zofia said.

The next morning, Zofia was waiting at the table before the Americans started work. She also added many names to the *deceased list* from her eyewitness accounts.

CHAPTER SEVENTY-NINE

ZOFIA WORKED TIRELESSLY. She put her heart and soul into helping, with a determination and understanding for the survivors that the Americans and the British could not match. They tried but could not comprehend the horrors forced upon these people. Zofia knew them firsthand.

She rose early to begin work and did not rest until well after sundown. She ate at the registration table, not leaving to take a break. This gave her purpose, and more importantly, it gave her hope. She planned to continue volunteering, but first, she must find a ride to Warsaw. It was time to go to Eidel.

"Please," Zofia said to the young nurse, Marion, who worked with the Red Cross, and who'd been kind and befriended her. "If you know anyone who is going to Warsaw, I must go there. Not to stay, but to see someone."

"Oh, honey, I doubt anyone you knew is still in Warsaw. I'm so sorry to have to tell you that."

"No, you are wrong. She is there. It is my daughter. She was living as a Gentile with a Gentile family. They were protecting her, caring for her, God bless them, until I could return."

"Hmmm, that does make a difference. She just might be there in

Warsaw. Let me see if any of the fellas are going that way. If they are, you could go along with them."

"I would like to find Eidel and then bring her back here with me. I want to stay here at the camp and do what I can to help others find their lost loved ones for a while, anyway, until all of this is settled. Maybe with God's help, my Isaac will show up."

The nurse nodded. The humanity Zofia saw in Marion's eyes made her look away. It was hard to face such kindness without tears.

"Very well, give me a day or two, and I'll find you a soldier headed that way, and we'll see if we can't get you a ride back here with your daughter when you're all done in Warsaw. It's about a six-hour trip, so they will probably leave early and arrive here late." Marion smiled and winked, and then she walked away.

"Next," Zofia said aloud. She was speaking to the people waiting in line. A boy of fifteen, covered in filth, wearing a ragged, torn, striped uniform, walked forward.

"Please, ma'am," he said in broken English. "I look for my parents. Their names are Gretchen and Hymie Mikelsky. Also, can you please add my name to the list of people searching for their families? My name is Yankel Mikelsky." Tears threatened to fall from his eyes. "You can help, please?"

"You speak Polish?" Zofia asked in Polish.

"Yes," he answered. "I am good at speaking Polish. I am born in Lodz."

Zofia nodded, answering in Polish. "I'll do what I can. Let me check the lists." She began to scan for the Mikelskys.

CHAPTER EIGHTY

The following week Marion, the nurse, with her pressed white uniform, blonde finger waves, and perky little hat, approached Zofia as she sat at her table. "I've got great news. Two of the fellas are going to the border of Poland next week. They'll be there for a few days, and then they'll be heading back here. That would be a perfect opportunity for you to go and get your little girl." Marion had a lovely smile with perfect white teeth. Her eyes twinkled like stars.

"Oh, that's wonderful news, Miss Marion. I am so happy. I will finally see my Eidel. I cannot thank you enough for arranging this for me," Zofia said in broken English.

"Would you like to bring your boyfriend along with you?"

"My boyfriend?" Zofia looked at her, confused. "Oh, you mean Shlomie. He is not my boyfriend, just a very good friend. But yes, if possible, I would like him to accompany me, and thank you so much. It is so kind of you to do all this for me."

"I can arrange for you to get as far as the border. But from there, you'll have to deal with the Soviets. However, I've talked to the JDC. They've promised to help you to get in. They've promised to do what they can. But here is a little money for you, just in case you need to bribe the soldiers at the border to let you in."

"You are an angel."

"Zofia, you have been such a help to us that this is the least I can do. The fellas are going on Thursday."

"Just tell me where I should go to find these men and what I should do, and I will be there on Thursday," Zofia said.

"I'll get you all the info." The young American nurse squeezed Zofia's shoulder. "I wish you the best in finding your little girl. I'm glad I can be of a little assistance, anyway."

"Oh yes, you are a great help."

Zofia's heart leaped with anticipation. It was difficult for her to concentrate. All she could think of was Eidel. She'd waited for so long and through so much. She'd dreamed, hoped, and prayed for her child. Now, within days, Eidel would be in her arms. She asked one of the other volunteers to watch the desk for a few minutes. Zofia had told someone, someone who knew her, someone who would understand. She ran to find Shlomie.

He sat under a tree, reading a book. Before she approached him, she watched from across the path, smiling at how peaceful he looked. Of course, she knew his inner demons continued to haunt him and probably would forever, as her own demons would walk with her for the rest of her life. It was part of surviving this, a part every survivor would have to learn to accept. Shlomie missed his loved ones and told her as much. Worse, although they only discussed it briefly, both felt tremendous guilt at having survived while so many others had perished.

"Shlomie!" Zofia called out. He looked up from his book and smiled. "I have to talk to you."

"Yes, of course. Please come and sit down." He patted the ground.

She sat beside him.

"One of the American nurses has arranged for me to go to Warsaw next week to find Eidel and bring her back here. Would you be willing to go with me?"

He took her hand in his. "Of course, I will go with you, Zofia. I wouldn't let you do this alone." His eyes showed genuine concern.

"What is it, Shlomie? Why do you look so troubled all of a sudden?"

"Zofia, I don't think you have given this meeting with Eidel a great deal of thought."

"I have. I have thought of it every minute of every day. Eidel has kept me alive." Her voice cracked.

He squeezed her hand and then patted it. "Yes, I know that. But Zofia, you realize that when you last saw her, Eidel was just a baby. She isn't going to know you. It will be hard for her just to get up and leave her family, the family she has come to know and love, and go with you. Zofia, to Eidel, you are a stranger."

Zofia stared blankly ahead, considering. Shlomie was right. How could she not have realized this? What was she thinking? She would rather die than hurt Eidel. And yet, that was just what she was about to do. Still, how could she not go back and see Helen and Eidel, see how Eidel reacted? Maybe, just maybe, Shlomie was wrong. Not trying to find her child was unthinkable. She must go. She must see for herself.

Maybe Eidel had been a burden on Helen's family, and Helen might be glad that Zofia had finally come to claim her. But what if Helen was attached to the child? Zofia's presence would serve to break up a family. Would it be better for Eidel if she grew up with Helen and her husband? Was it better if Eidel never knew her mother? If she did not return, Helen would assume she had died, and their lives would go on. But what if Helen was only hanging on and waiting for Zofia's return? What if she'd told Eidel about her mother? Zofia was filled with questions without answers.

"Oh, Shlomie, what am I going to do? I don't know what to do."

"Give it some serious thought. If you decide to go to Warsaw, I will be there at your side to help you."

"I must go, Shlomie. I must know how Eidel is doing. I must know if she is alive—if Helen is alive. When I get there and see things for myself, I will know better what to do."

Zofia was silent during the entire long and tedious ride to

Poland. She sat in the back of the open army truck beside Shlomie, her slender shoulders hunched in worry. He held her hand as they moved along with the rhythm of the bumpy road. At about one o'clock in the afternoon, they arrived at the border of Poland.

"You two are on your own from here."

"We're heading back the day after tomorrow. Now don't you be late 'cause we can't be waitin' on you.," an American soldier with gold stripes on his shoulder told them.

"Yes, thank you. We will be here on time," Zofia said.

"I hope we can get in," Shlomie said.

"Let me go and talk to the guards. I'll mention the arrangements that were made by the JDC for us."

"No. I don't know how they will act. It could be dangerous. I'll do it. You wait here."

Zofia watched from across the street. Her nerves were strung as tightly as a rubber band. What if they were turned away? What if they'd come all this way only to be sent back? A shiver ran up her spine.

She watched the gestures between Shlomie and the Soviets. Both of their hands moved this way and that as they spoke. Zofia could hardly breathe. Finally, after what seemed like a long time but was only a few minutes, the guard took the cash and nodded. Then Shlomie turned and motioned to Zofia to come. She followed him as they entered the Soviet-occupied country. They walked for a while, then took a train into the city. With a heavy heart, Zofia looked around her. It was hard to believe just how badly her beloved Warsaw had been ripped to shreds during the war. When Zofia was in the ghetto, she heard people talk about how bad things had gotten for the Polish in Warsaw. It was common knowledge that the Nazis hated the Poles, making their lives miserable.

But even as terrible as it was for the citizens of Warsaw, everyone in the ghetto agreed that the living conditions of the Polish were not nearly as horrific as the life of the Jews. She'd known all of that. But until now, seeing the burned-out buildings, she hadn't realized how much destruction had been inflicted upon the city. The city had been brought to ruins. It frightened her. An electric shock of fear raced through her. It was unthinkable, but was Eidel all right? Was Helen still alive?

However, even though Zofia was shaken by the destruction, her old memories of life in Warsaw began to tap softly at the back of her mind. Zofia and Shlomie, both silent, began to walk down the old streets so familiar to Zofia. The streets she'd taken to school, strolling beside Lena, young, carefree, and giggling. The same roads she'd meandered along with Fruma and Gitel, talking as they pushed Eidel in her buggy to the park.

Zofia felt a chill run down her spine as she passed the old bakery where Isaac's mother had once sold her bread and hamantaschen, so long ago, so many ghosts… Now the bakery was a general store owned by a man with a Gentile name. Zofia sighed. *Isaac, my love and friend, how I miss you and wish you were beside me.*

Zofia let out a small cry of pain and then looked at Shlomie. "Ever since that man, Karl Abendstern, took Eidel out of the ghetto and to Helen's house in the middle of the night, a day did not go by when I did not think of her. Sometimes, I wanted to die. I wanted to kill myself and end the misery, but I thought, 'My Eidel needs me,' so I fought back the urge to give up. And now that this is all over, I can't believe how afraid I am to see her. How afraid I am of what lies ahead."

"You knew Karl Abendstern?" asked Shlomie.

"Yes."

"He was the one who gave his life by giving covering fire while some of us escaped to the woods during the Warsaw Uprising, but I was captured later and sent to Treblinka," Shlomie told her.

"Karl's dead?"

"Yes."

One more person that helped me has died, she thought as she made her way toward Helen's apartment.

The apartment building where Helen lived was just as Zofia remembered it. Somehow, it had gone through the war untouched. Except for a subtle difference, a small change that no one would notice unless, of course, they were looking for it as Zofia was. As her eyes scanned the bells and mailboxes inside the door, Zofia saw there were no Jewish names of occupants. It was as if Jews had never lived in Poland at all.

They stood in the lobby. Helen would have to press the buzzer to let them into the building.

Zofia could hardly steady her finger to ring the bell under the name "Dobinski." Her hand was trembling so hard that she needed to use her other hand to hold it firmly enough. She pressed the small gray button.

"Yes…?" It was Helen's voice. A voice so far away, so far in the past, that Zofia felt her heart pounding in her ears.

"Helen."

"This is Helen."

"Helen," her voice croaked, barely a whisper. "Helen, it's Zofia."

There was a long hesitation. Then the buzzer rang, and Shlomie pulled the door to the apartment building open. Zofia could not breathe deeply. She could only inhale shallow breaths. It was as if her lungs had shrunk and would not allow the intake. Her legs felt like jelly. She was afraid they might collapse beneath her. She was only a few steps away from Eidel after all this time and after all she'd endured. If she was still alive. *God, please let her be alive.* Eidel was here, right here in this building.

"The apartment number is 302. We have to walk up three flights," Shlomie said.

Zofia nodded.

"You remember this place?"

Zofia nodded again, unable to speak. It was strange that even with all the miles she'd walked and all the hills she'd climbed in the forest, these three flights of stairs seemed like the highest mountain in the world.

When they reached the third floor, Zofia gasped for breath, smoothed her hair, and knocked.

An older, less lighthearted, and far-less beautiful Helen opened the door. The war had taken its toll on the gorgeous blonde who'd had such a kind and gentle heart.

"Zofia?" Helen hugged her. "Thank God you are alive."

Zofia watched as tears filled Helen's eyes. But she could not cry. She could not speak.

"Eidel is here," Helen said. "I am sorry, Zofia, I had to rename her. It was for her own safety."

Zofia nodded her head, her heart beating like a drum. Eidel was alive! She was alive!

"You want to see her?"

"Yes."

"Ela, come here. I have someone who wants to meet you," Helen called, and then she turned to Zofia. "She just got up from her nap."

Ela came into the room. "Yes, Mama?" She smiled at Helen and tucked herself under Helen's arm, shy in the presence of strangers.

"This is Zofia."

"Hello, ma'am. It's nice to meet you."

"Hello, Ela." Zofia almost choked on the words. The child was beautiful. She resembled a young Helen in many ways, more in her mannerisms than in her physical appearance. She wore a golden cross around her neck.

"Ela, why don't you go to your room and play now?"

"Yes, ma'am."

"When I am finished talking with my friends, I will call you, and then we can make supper together."

"I want to bake. Can we bake tonight?"

"Perhaps. I have some flour and sugar, so we will see. All right then, run along now."

Ela smiled up at Helen, and then she looked at Zofia. "Will you be staying for supper, Miss Zofia? We would love to have you, wouldn't we, Mama?"

Helen nodded. "Of course, we would." Helen's eyes were pleading as she watched Zofia's face. She didn't want to lose the child she'd come to love, this little girl who had become her own, especially after her son died of influenza the previous year. But Zofia was her real mother, and she was Helen's friend. Had the time really come to say goodbye?

Zofia studied the slender five-year-old girl with the golden-brown curls cascading down her back, who answered the name "Ela."

Eidel, my Eidel. This child was not Eidel. Eidel was a baby wrapped in a blanket who'd been ripped out of her life almost four years ago. The lovely young girl who stood before her now was Helen's daughter. As she watched them together, she saw the affection and love between them. Helen's arm around Eidel's neck, the smile they shared. Helen was her mother; she'd raised her. Shlomie was right. Zofia was no more than a stranger.

"I don't think so but thank you for the invitation."

Helen cleared her throat. "Go upstairs to your room and play. Mama and Zofia need to talk." Helen kissed the top of Ela's head.

"Yes, Mama," Ela said and went upstairs.

"I don't know how to tell her. It is going to be hard. I mean, she has no idea. She believes I am her mother. It was safer for her not to know. I was afraid if she knew the truth, it might slip out when she was talking to someone. I couldn't take the risk, Zofia." Helen hesitated for a moment. "Do you plan to take her with you today?"

Zofia suddenly realized that Helen's son was not there. "Helen, where is your son?"

Helen began to cry. "He's dead, his father, too."

Zofia considered that Helen had risked her life to save her Eidel, and now, if Eidel were gone, she would have no one. Helen was the only mother Eidel had ever known. Eidel would never understand, and it would kill Helen.

"No," Zofia said. "No. I am not going to take her today."

Helen breathed a sigh of relief.

"She loves you. You are the only mother she has ever known. Do you want to keep her?" Zofia asked, turning away, hoping Helen would say no, but knowing she would not.

"More than anything in the world, but I understand that you are her mother and."

"I am not going to take her away from here, Helen. Let her live her life believing that you are her mother and that this is her home. She has grown up to believe this. To tell her the truth now would only hurt and confuse her."

"Are you sure? Are you sure this is what you want?"

"Yes, I'm very sure. I love her. But sometimes, love is about sacrifice. This is what is best for my Eidel." It felt as if a hole had opened in her heart, another hole, one that would never close.

"I love her, too. She is all I have now. She is my life. I will always be good to her," Helen said.

"I know that, and God bless you for all you have done and all the risks you have taken for us."

"You are welcome to come back to see her anytime."

"I will not be back, Helen. It is best that I leave here and never return. But from the bottom of my heart, I thank you for everything."

"Zofia, are you sure? Are you sure this is what you want?"

Zofia nodded. Her skin had broken out into red blotches from nerves. She got up to leave, and Shlomie followed, out the door, down the three flights of stairs, and out into the streets of Warsaw.

They walked silently to the truck, where they waited for the soldiers, without speaking, for almost a half hour before the Americans returned.

The entire ride back to Germany, Zofia gazed at the landscape with unseeing eyes. She knew she'd done what was right for Eidel; that was all that was important. If only Isaac was here. If only she could feel the strength of his arm around her. Shlomie reached over and took her hand.

"Zofia," he whispered. Then she wiped the tears she didn't even realize had covered her face. "I'm sorry that things turned out this way."

"I know, Shlomie. So am I."

"But you did what was best for your daughter."

"Oh, Shlomie, I have lost so much, and the pain in my heart is so deep."

"Zofia, I know that you are in pain. But you must realize that we have all suffered great loss. Life goes on. It must." He squeezed her hand.

"I have nothing left, no reason to go on living," Zofia said in Polish.

The two American soldiers that sat in the back of the open truck were quiet, watching with serious expressions on their young faces. From their expressions, they must have understood the language.

"You have me," Shlomie said, his voice unsure, almost pleading.

"Yes, I have you, my dearest friend." Zofia managed a smile for him.

For a few minutes, no one spoke. Then Shlomie cleared his throat.

"Marry me, Zofia. I will make you a good husband. I will work hard to take care of you. We will have children. You will have more children, and I promise I will do everything to give you a good life."

She looked into his eyes. They shined as if they'd been coated with oil. She could look deep into them and see the depth of his emotion.

"Shlomie. Oh, Shlomie…" She reached up and touched his face. "I am sorry. You are a dear friend, and you always have been, but I can't. I can't marry you. Isaac is my husband, and unless I know for sure he is dead, then I can't and won't marry anyone. But even if Isaac was dead, I could not marry you."

His eyes glassed over. "I hate to see you hurt, and believe me, Shlomie, I love you. But not in that way or how a wife should love her husband. I love you like a brother, like a precious brother, and it wouldn't be fair to you. You deserve better. You're a wonderful person, one of the kindest people I know, the smartest, too. You deserve to find someone who will love you with all her heart; believe me, this woman you are searching for is out there. You just have to find her. Shlomie, you deserve to have what Isaac and I have."

"And what do you deserve, Zofia?"

"I don't know anymore. I've had great happiness in my life. I think, for me, if I don't find Isaac alive, those days are over."

"Let me try. At least, just let me try to make you happy. Give me a chance. You've never really given me a chance."

"Oh, Shlomie…" She reached up and ran her hand down his cheek. "I am so tired of fighting, of trying…"

"Please?" he asked.

She swallowed hard. His eyes looked so hopeful that she could not answer.

"Zofia, think it over. I know I am asking a lot. But you and I have been through so much together. In time, you will forget Isaac. If not, at least you will learn to go on without him. Maybe you could even come to love me. Please, don't say a thing. Just think it over."

CHAPTER EIGHTY-ONE

ZOFIA THREW herself into her work. At least, she might feel useful if she could help others in some way. Shlomie remained at her side, hoping that time would change her mind about marrying him. She'd fought so hard to go on living, and now it seemed as if she'd fought for nothing.

The endless lines of displaced persons in desperate need were the only thing that forced her to keep going. Most of them still wore the tattered striped uniform they'd worn in the camps. One after another, they came to the front of her line, their eyes hopeful and their faces thin and tortured.

Most of the time, she had no luck finding the seekers' loved ones on the list of names, so all she could do was add their names to the endless list of those who searched. However, on rare occasions, there would be a connection. Two people who'd been separated would find each other again. When this happened, the look of gratitude on the faces of the people was enough to keep her going. Day in and day out, she sat at that table scanning the lists over and over again.

One afternoon as the sun beat down on her, she called out, "Next in line, please," as she always did.

A woman approached, dressed in a dove-gray suit with a cream-colored blouse. At her neck, she wore a brooch of gold and pearls. Her dark hair was caught up in a twist and pinned tightly.

"Hello," she said in Polish. "My name is Bernadette Holland. I am an attorney. Are you Zofia Weiss?"

"That was my maiden name. I am Zofia Weiss Zuckerman, now."

"Did you know a man called Manfred Blau? He was the *Arbeitsführer* at Treblinka."

"I knew him," Zofia said, looking away, not wanting to remember.

"I need to speak with you. Can we go somewhere?"

"Yes, we can take a walk. Let me ask someone to watch the table."

Zofia walked beside the beautiful attorney and listened.

"Manfred Blau has been arrested for crimes against humanity. He is to be tried in Nuremberg. We desperately need witnesses. If we don't have any witnesses, he could get away with everything he did. We need your help, Miss Weiss. Would you be willing to testify against him?"

She thought for a moment, remembering Manfred and all he'd done to her. The thought of seeing him again made her sick to her stomach. Still, the thought of him walking away without punishment for all he'd done to her and everyone else made her feel even worse.

"Yes, I will do it, and my friend, Shlomie, he knew him, too. Perhaps you would like to speak with him?"

"Yes, I would," the attorney said.

Zofia introduced Miss Holland to Shlomie. She explained what she needed from him.

Shlomie agreed to testify.

That night after dinner, Shlomie and Zofia talked about the trial to come.

"The thought of seeing him again makes me sick," Zofia said.

"Yes, I know, but we must. He must be made to pay for what he did."

"I am ready to put all of this behind me, Shlomie. I am ready to leave this camp, find a place to live, and find a job. I want to begin my life over. After the trial, I am going away from here. I am going to try to forget."

"Have you given any further thought to my proposal of marriage?" He was wringing his hands.

"Shlomie, I can't marry you. I told you before. Nothing has changed. I am married to Isaac and will not marry until I know if he is alive or dead. I will not marry. Even if Isaac was dead, I could not marry you. I care for you very much, but I don't love you in that way, not in the way that you deserve to be loved."

"This is what you want? You are sure this is your decision?"

"Yes. I am sorry," she said.

He nodded, keeping his eyes shifted away from hers.

"Perhaps it is best if I leave this camp now. It will help you to heal if we are separated. I will not see you again until the trial."

"Are you sure, Zofia? Where will you go?"

"I will go and begin again. My friend, my dear friend, Fruma, taught me a trade. I will find a job. I will work. I will live and save money. As soon as I can, I will leave here and go to Palestine."

"You still have that dream?"

"Oh yes, there will be a Jewish state. You mark my words, Shlomie. There will be a homeland for the Jewish people, a place where we are safe, a new Israel. And when I can find a way, I am going."

"A promised land, yes? Well, I hope so, Zofia. I hope so, for your sake."

"It will come to pass, Shlomie, you'll see. I only wish Isaac were here to see it," she sighed.

He nodded, unconvinced.

CHAPTER EIGHTY-TWO

For Zofia, the time to leave had come. It was time to begin living a normal life. Zofia talked to Marion, explaining that she must quit her volunteer work with the Red Cross and start over. Marion was disappointed but understood her need to go. She insisted that Zofia take some money to help her get settled. Zofia reluctantly agreed.

"An American attorney, a woman, will come looking for me. I will forward an address where I can be reached as soon as I find a place to live. Will you see to it that she receives the information?" Zofia asked.

"Of course," Marion replied.

It was almost dawn when Zofia gazed down at Shlomie sleeping on his cot, his breathing steady and even. Only in sleep did he ever look at peace. She leaned over him and gently kissed his forehead. He stirred but did not awaken.

Zofia took a brief moment to take in his memory. She would miss him. They had spent the equivalent of a lifetime together. But after the love she'd shared with Isaac, she knew that the love she felt for Shlomie was not enough to sustain a marriage, even if Isaac was gone forever. Zofia looked down at Shlomie one final time. A tear formed in the corner of her eye. Then she turned and walked through the camp and out the gate into the real world. It was time.

Thank God for Marion. She'd given Zofia enough money to find a small flat in the basement of a burned-out apartment building. There was no work for a seamstress, not even a good one. But Zofia was a quick learner and willing to do anything, so she secured a job baking at a local bakery within a few days.

She swept and washed the floor on her hands and knees. She cleaned toilets and scrubbed pots and pans. Her day began at two a.m. and ended at five in the afternoon. It was hard work, but she had plenty to eat and a safe place to sleep at night. The smell of bread made her think of Isaac when he was just a child, sitting in the back of his mother's bakery, a bittersweet memory. Isaac was the one true love of her life.

Zofia sent word to Marion with her address, and three days later, Miss Holland came to the shop where she worked.

"I will see that you have a paid, round-trip train ticket to Nuremberg from here."

"I am afraid to go. I will lose my job if I take time off of work."

"I will give you enough money to hold you over until you can find another position when you return.

"But there are so few jobs available."

Miss Holland looked at Zofia. She needed her testimony. Without her testimony, another war criminal might go free.

"Perhaps I can help you find work in England. Do you have any skills?" Miss Holland asked.

"Yes, I am a seamstress. I can make beautiful wedding gowns. I can do embroidery…"

"That is very good." Bernadette Holland bit her lower lip in thought. "I think I can help you. I have friends in England who should be able to give you a job. Just please, show up at the trial."

"Miss Holland, I am a poor woman. Please, this job is all I have right now. Are you sure that you can help me? If I leave here, I am going to be in trouble. I will have no money and no place to live."

"I give you my word. I will help you."

"Then I will be there. I trust you, Miss Holland."

"And I will keep my promise."

The weeks passed, and finally, it was the night before Zofia was to leave for Nuremberg. When she told her employer she must take a leave of absence, she was discharged, just as she expected.

Her nerves were on edge. By the end of the week, she would be face-to-face with Manfred and all of her memories. Zofia wondered if she was crazy for agreeing to do this. She'd lost her job on a promise, and now she was headed to Nuremberg and back into the nightmare of Manfred Blau, a terror she'd escaped from. And yet, she agreed with Shlomie. The *Arbeitsführer* must pay for what he'd done. If no one stood up against him, then he might go free.

CHAPTER EIGHTY-THREE

When the war ended and the Allies liberated the concentration camps, what they found sent a cry of horror echoing around the world. Heaps of dead bodies, piles of human ashes, lampshades of human skin, pillows stuffed with human hair, huge gas chambers built to kill people in large quantities, and massive ovens to burn the bodies. The prisoners that were still alive were emaciated to the point of being walking corpses.

Some soldiers cried while others vomited, but they all witnessed what everyone had been trying to ignore. Now the nations who, during the war, closed their doors to the helpless people who begged them to let them in while trying to escape Hitler's tyranny would demand vengeance. They insisted that the Nazis pay for their crimes against humanity.

It was decided that there would be a trial. A tribunal consisting of the Soviets, the French, the British, and the Americans would be created. This tribunal would be called "The International Military Tribunal." They would stand in judgment of the war criminals.

Due to the destruction from the bombings Germany incurred during the war, very few courthouses remained intact. However, the courthouse in Nuremberg, known as the Palace of Justice, was in perfect condition. This was ironic because it was in Nuremberg that Hitler had put his laws of racial purity, which stripped the "lesser humans" of their human rights, into effect.

It was decided that there should be three sets of trials. The first would be for major war criminals. The second would be for doctors, lawyers, and judges, and the third was for the *Einsatzgruppen*, also known as the death squads. These were murderers who had killed the so-called "inferior" civilians in large numbers.

Twelve trials took place in Nuremberg, conducted by the International Military Tribunal. On October 11, 1946, the first set of trials ended, and verdicts of the twenty-two accused Nazi leaders were handed down. Eleven of those leaders received the death penalty; three were given life imprisonment; four received prison sentences of ten to twenty years, and three were acquitted.

Sadly, Hitler was never brought to justice. Instead, as the Soviet army began to advance on Berlin, Hitler and his newly wedded wife, Eva Braun, went down into the underground bunker and committed suicide. It is rumored that the cyanide capsules were tested on Hitler's beloved German Shepherd, Blondi, to be sure they were effective. The dog died almost instantly. Eva Braun took a cyanide capsule, and Hitler blew his brains out with a pistol. Dr. Goebbels took Hitler and his new wife's bodies outside the bunker, covered them with gasoline, and set them on fire, offering one last *Heil Hitler* salute.

With his Führer dead, Dr. Goebbels chose to kill himself, his wife, and his children rather than face trial. Heinrich Himmler took a cyanide capsule while being examined by a British doctor and died within seconds. Hermann Göring took cyanide on the day he was to be hanged.

Still, many Nazis managed to conceal their identities and escape to Europe or South America. Some were never found. Others, like Adolf Eichmann, were pursued by *Mossad*, the Israeli secret service. Mossad eventually found Eichmann living in South America. They captured and brought him to Israel, where he was tried and hanged at Ramleh Prison in 1962.

Most Nazis who were tried, convicted and sentenced to prison terms at Nuremberg never served their entire sentences. Most were released early.

CHAPTER EIGHTY-FOUR

NUREMBERG, GERMANY
JANUARY 5, 1946

THE PROSECUTING attorney's opening statement:

> Mr. Justice Jackson:
>
> May it please, Your Honors: The privilege of opening the first trial in history for crimes against the peace of the world imposes a grave responsibility. The wrongs, which we seek to condemn and punish, have been so calculated, so malignant, and so devastating that civilization cannot tolerate their being ignored because it cannot survive their being repeated. That four great nations, flushed with victory, stung with injury, stay the hand of vengeance, and voluntarily submit their captive enemies to the judgment of the law is one of the most significant tributes that Power has ever paid to Reason...

Zofia, dressed in a simple black shift, sat alone in the back of the overcrowded courtroom. She held a small handbag on her lap, the leather handle of which she could not stop twisting. It was difficult to breathe here in this courtroom, once again amongst the persecutors of her race. Shlomie was not there. He never came. She knew it was because he would rather not face her, and she understood his feelings.

A long table where the representatives of the tribunal were seated stood at the front of the room. A guard escorted each defendant into the courtroom to be tried individually. Zofia watched in horror as the witnesses told their stories, and the perpetrators defended their actions.

For three days, she heard unnerving testimony, until finally, on the fourth day, Manfred was brought into the courtroom, his hands cuffed, his face lined with worry. It had been years since she'd last seen him, but fear shot through her like a hot iron blade as he cast his troubled eyes over the courtroom—Manfred, the *Arbeitsführer*. Now she must tell the world about the terrible humiliations she suffered at his hand. Nausea bubbled in her stomach as she remembered his hands on her body, his drunken words, and the foul smell of his breath on her face as he demanded.

Her thoughts were interrupted.

"Zofia Weiss Zuckerman." The prosecuting attorney called her name. She felt the sweat forming in her armpits and on her forehead. If she could, she would run away, out the door and into the fresh air. But for the sake of those who'd died, and could not be here to speak for themselves, she must do this. Zofia stood up and smoothed her dress, and then she took a deep breath, feeling all eyes upon her as she walked to the witness chair at the front of the room.

"Do you promise to tell the truth, the whole truth, so help you, God?"

"I do."

"Is your name Zofia Weiss Zuckerman?"

"Yes."

"Were you a prisoner at the Treblinka Concentration Camp?"

"Yes."

Zofia looked around the room, and her eyes caught those of Christa Blau, who sat beside her little girl Katja. Christa had been good to her. For Christa's sake, Zofia wanted to leave the witness stand, to stop what she had started, but she could not. She must speak for those who would forever be silent. Zofia did not look in Christa's direction again until she'd finished telling her entire story.

Zofia told the court everything she'd seen and endured because of Manfred Blau. There were gasps of horror from the audience, and although she didn't even realize it, tears ran down her cheeks. But she continued until she'd spoken her piece and told her entire story. Then Manfred's lawyer cross-examined her, trying to make her seem like a liar, but the defense attorney was ineffective. Everyone, the audience, the attorneys, and the Tribunal knew Zofia spoke the truth.

"Wasn't Frau Blau very kind to you, *Frau* Zuckerman?" Manfred's lawyer tried another tactic.

"Yes, she was always kind to me."

"And didn't she try to help you in every way?"

"She did, but *Frau* Blau is not on trial here. I was told that this was to be the trial of the *Arbeitsführer* Manfred Blau. He is the one that is accused of crimes against humanity. Is that not correct?"

"I will ask the questions, Frau Zuckerman."

But in the end, Zofia's testimony stood strong and was very damaging to Manfred.

When she was excused from the witness box, Zofia left the courtroom. Outside in the hall, Miss Holland awaited.

"Would you like to come back for the sentencing?"

"No, I've done my part. There is nothing more I can do. I want to put all of this behind me," Zofia said.

"I can understand. I will arrange train fare for you to England."

"You are going to keep your promise?"

"Of course. Did you doubt me?"

"A little, maybe, but I am very grateful."

"Give me a couple of days? I will arrange everything."

"Yes, of course. Then I should stay at the hotel?"

"At the hotel, yes. I will pay the bill. You needn't worry about that."

"That's very kind. Thank you. I'll wait to hear from you," Zofia said.

CHAPTER EIGHTY-FIVE

THAT NIGHT, Zofia brought a hunk of bread and cheese back to her hotel room. Then she took a hot bath and washed her hair. It was over at last. She would carry the memories forever, but at least she would never see Manfred again.

She sat gazing out the window at the city of Nuremberg. The destruction from the bombings surrounded her. England had suffered a similar fate, and she knew that she would face the same bombed-out reminders when she got there, but at least, she would be far from Germany and Poland.

As she sat, lost in thought, the phone rang. Zofia trembled. Who could that be? The loud buzzing unnerved her. It might be one of the Nazis coming after her for testifying. A shiver climbed down Zofia's neck. *But what if it is Miss Holland with information on my departure to England? Perhaps she has already secured tickets?* Brrrrrrrrrrrrng! It rang again. *I must answer.*

"Hello."

"Zofia?" It was a familiar female voice. "Zofia?"

"Christa?"

"Yes, it's me. I need to speak with you."

"Christa. I am sorry. I never wanted to hurt you, but I had to testify. It was not against you…"

"I know that, Zofia. I don't blame you. I heard you on the stand today. I know now what Manfred did to you, and from the bottom of my heart, I am sorry."

"Please, don't blame yourself."

"I must see you, Zofia. Will you let me come to you at the hotel?" Christa asked.

Zofia trusted Christa, but this could be a trick. She was afraid, unsure. Still, she must oblige.

"How did you find me?"

"This was the closest hotel to the courtroom. I called and asked for you, and by the grace of God, I've found you."

Zofia was silent for a moment.

"Yes, come," Zofia said.

"Now? Is now all right?"

"Now is a good time," Zofia said.

CHAPTER EIGHTY-SIX

Zofia dressed in a simple housedress and pinned up her wet hair. For the half-hour until Christa arrived, she agonized about whether she'd made a mistake. What if a group of former Nazis appeared and took her or killed her?

Nevertheless, she could not believe that Christa would ever do anything to hurt her. Still, she'd given very damaging testimony against Manfred. Would Christa trick her out of vengeance for her husband? She refused to believe Christa would act that way, but who knew? Blood was thicker than water, wasn't it? That was what her mother had always said. A woman will stand behind her husband, no matter what.

There was a knock at the door.

Zofia jumped to her feet and opened it. Christa stood, looking down at the ground.

"May I come in?"

"Of course."

Zofia indicated the chair by the window for Christa to sit in, and then Zofia sat on the bed.

"You look well," Christa said.

"I'm doing all right."

"I heard your name is Zuckerman now?"

"I married Isaac Zuckerman, but I don't know if he survived the war."

"I hope he did, for your sake. I wish you every blessing."

"Thank you." Zofia breathed a sigh of relief.

"Zofia, I've not come here to make small talk. I have something important I must discuss with you."

Zofia nodded.

"Do you remember my little girl, my Katja?"

"Yes, of course. She was in the courtroom today. It was hard for me to say all of those things I had to say with the child listening."

"I know. That was why Manfred insisted that I bring her. He was hoping it would deter the witnesses from making their testimony. I must admit yours was shocking to me. I never knew what he was doing to you."

"I knew that you didn't know, and I am sorry. It must have hurt you today."

"It did, but that's not why I am here. I am here because I am dying. As you know, I've been sick for a long time. I could linger for another five years, or I could die tomorrow. The problem is that I keep getting weaker and can't care for Katja anymore."

Zofia tilted her head and studied Christa. "Yes, I know you are ill, and I'm sorry."

"It's all right. I've known that I must take some action. I've known it for a while. I couldn't trust Manfred with Katja, and now that he will probably be convicted, it isn't even an option. In a way, this trial was a godsend to me.

"I wanted to find you, and it is because of this trial that I have. Zofia, I want to ask you..." Christa took a deep breath and took Zofia's hand. "I want to ask you to take Katja. I saw you with her when you lived with us. I believe you care for her. Although she may have forgotten, once you are together again, she will remember that she loves you."

"I never expected this..." Zofia turned away and looked out the window. "I don't know..."

"Please, Zofia. I beg you. I know you will love Katja, and I know you believe in your heart that what happened was no fault of hers. She is just a child. You would never blame or punish her for what you went through. I know you too well."

"No, I would never do that. It is not her fault."

"Do you remember what I told you about her birth mother and the Lebensborn?"

"I remember."

"Katja is a victim, too. She was taken from her rightful family. She will probably never know her birth mother."

"Yes, I realize that."

"Here…" With trembling fingers, Christa fished several papers out of her purse and handed them to Zofia. "These are the documents of Katja's birth. They are from the Lebensborn. Katja's real mother's name is Helga Haswell. I don't know anything about her, but someday you might choose to tell Katja everything. I will leave that decision up to you. That is, of course, if you agree to take her."

"I don't know…" Zofia said, suddenly remembering the tender and loving child she'd once sung to sleep. "You're sure this is what you want, Christa?"

"I am sure. I am begging you, Zofia."

Zofia looked into Christa's eyes. Then she nodded. "I will take her."

"May I bring her here tonight?"

"No, I need the night to sort everything out in my mind. I will meet you in front of the courthouse in the morning. Try to talk to her tonight and explain what you are about to do to help ease the transition for her. Then I will take her from there."

"God bless you, Zofia. We will be outside the courthouse in the morning waiting for you."

Zofia nodded.

Christa took her hand and kissed it. "God bless you, Zofia."

"I will take good care of Katja."

"I know that. And Zofia, I am sorry for all that you went through. I wish I could have done more."

"Christa, you always did right by me. Put your mind at ease. You don't have to worry about Katja."

"I always knew that if I could find you again, I could count on you."

CHAPTER EIGHTY-SEVEN

As she turned the corner to the street leading to the courthouse, Zofia saw Katja standing beside Christa. Katja held Christa's hand. She wore a blue velvet dress, and her golden curls glistened, illuminated by the bright sunlight.

"Zofia, over here," Christa called out.

"Hello, Katja."

"Good morning, ma'am. My mother says I must go with you."

"Yes, that is right." Zofia smiled.

"Mama?" Katja said, suddenly a little shaken.

"It's all right, Katja. This is Zofia. You will be going away with her for a while. Now be a good girl and do as Mama tells you."

Zofia took the child's hand. "Do you remember me?"

The little girl shrugged, unsure.

Christa silently slipped away. Katja turned to see her go and cried out, "Mama! Mama!" But Christa did not turn around. Instead, she disappeared around the corner.

Katja began to cry in panic.

"It's all right, sunshine. It's going to be just fine." Zofia said, smoothing her hair.

"I'm scared. I don't know you."

"I knew you when you were little. Perhaps you might remember me singing this song to you?" Zofia began to sing softly. "You are my sweet Mary Sunshine, my Mary Sunshine…" Zofia's eyes filled with tears. "You wake the stars at night and bring light to the dark and gray days." Zofia's mind drifted back to the night she lay beside Isaac on the floor of the little log cabin in the woods when she and Shlomie had sung this song.

Zofia bent until she was eye-to-eye with Katja. "Do you remember?"

"I remember. I think I remember," Katja said. "Sing some more."

Zofia lifted Katja into her arms, her arms that had been empty for so long. "You are my Mary Sunshine, my sweet, sweet sunshine…" she whispered into Katja's ear as she took in the sweet, childlike fragrance. Then she hugged her tightly. "Don't be afraid, little one. I will be here for you from now on."

Katja smiled, but the tears still stained her face. "Where are my mama and papa?"

"They had to go away for a while. I am going to be your mama for now."

Katja began to sob again. "I want my mother."

"Shhh, I know. I know." Zofia felt the papers from the Lebensborn inside her bra, stabbing into her flesh. This poor child had no idea who her real mother was. Someday, Zofia would help her find out, but not today. Today and from this day forward, she would comfort and love her as her own.

Zofia rocked Katja in her arms. Katja moaned, but Zofia continued to rock her, smoothing her hair from her forehead and kissing her cheek. Finally, the child put her thumb in her mouth and grew quiet.

"Come, let's go home," Zofia said, putting Katja down on her feet.

"What shall I call you?" Katja asked.

"What would you like to call me?"

"May I call you Mama? Can someone have more than one?"

"You are a very special girl. You can have as many Mamas as you'd like."

"I would like to call you Mama," Katja said, wiping her eyes and nose with the sleeve of her sweater.

"Very well, then." Zofia managed a smile. "I have an idea. How would you like to take a walk in the park? I've heard there is a lovely park right down the street." Zofia had seen an entrance to a park not far from the hotel where she was staying.

"Yes, I would! Do you think there might be a playground? Do you think there will be ducks? I love to watch the ducks," Katja said.

The mention of the park brought a nice distraction. Zofia was glad she'd thought about it. Katja seemed excited.

Zofia smiled. "I don't know, but why don't we go there and find out?"

Katja nodded. They walked together in silence. As they turned the corner, Katja tripped on a piece of stone that had fallen on the cobblestone walk from one of the bombed-out buildings. Before the child could fall, Zofia caught her.

"Are you all right?"

"Yes, but my ankle hurts a little."

"Why don't you hold my hand? That way, I can keep you steady if you lose your balance?"

"No, thank you," Katja said.

"Please, do it for me? I could fall over one of these big rocks, and then who would be there to help? If I am holding your hand, that will keep me from falling, too. We can steady each other."

"Really? I would be helping you?"

"Yes, you would. You don't realize how much you really would," Zofia said, her heart aching.

"Then, of course, I will take your hand." Katja smiled. "You should have said so."

"You're right. I should have."

A vendor cart stood at the open gate in front of the park. The old woman was selling cookies and sausages.

"Are you hungry?" Zofia asked.

Katja shrugged.

"Don't be shy." Zofia nudged her. "How about a cookie?"

Katja nodded her head enthusiastically.

After she had bought the treat, Zofia handed the little girl her cookie wrapped in white paper.

"Thank you."

"You're very welcome," Zofia smiled.

The two ducked through the canopy gate entrance and into the park. Then hand-in-hand, they walked along a narrow sidewalk through an overgrown garden of lush grass and thick, green trees sprinkled with flowers and weeds in vibrant shades of purple, pink, and yellow. Obviously, there had not been much manicuring lately, but the result was magnificent. Occasionally, they saw a tree that had fallen due to the bombing. Still, the park was like a Garden of Eden, filled with God's natural abundance.

"Look, there is a bridge. Is that the ocean?" Katja asked, pointing to a sunlit body of water beneath an iron bridge that had somehow been spared by the bombs that had destroyed so many buildings.

"No, sunshine, it's not the ocean. It's just a pond," Zofia said, looking at the water.

"Isn't it pretty? I think I see ducks swimming in there."

"Yes, it is very pretty, and I think you're right. There are ducks in the water. Do you like it here?"

"I do like it, but it kind of frightens me too. That bridge looks like the bridge in a story my mother once read to me. It was a story about a mean troll that ate billy goats who crossed his bridge. Do you think there are mean trolls hiding underneath?"

"No, I don't think so. Would you like to walk up onto the bridge?"

"No, I'm scared."

"You can't see the ducks very well from here, now, can you? I'll tell you what. I promise you that you will be safe. I will keep you safe. Put your trust in me, all right?" Zofia knelt down until her eyes were level with the child's and squeezed Katja's hand. "When I was a little girl," Zofia said, "we used to go to *shul* on *Yom Kippur.* That is a very important Jewish holiday, and on that day, our rabbi used to say this prayer. It was called 'The Narrow Bridge.' Would you like to hear it?"

"Yes."

"All right then, now you must listen closely, and I will tell you." Zofia smiled. Katja returned the smile. "Are you ready?"

Katja nodded.

Zofia nodded back. Then she began, her voice soft and soothing.

> *"The world in which we live can be a narrow bridge. The most important thing is not to fear. Keep moving straight ahead, and your heart will be led by God. Don't waste your day in dread. Help is near.*
>
> *A narrow bridge, a narrow bridge, but every step across will lead you home.*
>
> *So many things have changed. Nothing near the same. Is it the way you thought it would be? Hang on every hope. I climb the burning rope. Suspended free, I float, look up and see.*
>
> *A narrow bridge, a narrow bridge, but every step across will lead you home."*

"I don't understand what it means, but I like how it sounds," Katja said.

"Well, it means don't be afraid. God is with you, my little sunshine."

"I don't know much about God, but my papa used to say that Jews were bad, and you said this was a Jewish prayer."

"Well, I am a Jew. Am I a bad person?"

"No, I don't think so."

"Katja, you are very young. Keep your mind free, and you will learn a lot in the years to come," Zofia said, kissing Katja's forehead. "Now, do you trust me enough to climb the bridge holding my hand?"

Katja nodded, her eyes clear and bright with faith. Zofia felt tears form in her own eyes. From this day forward, Katja would be her own child. She would love her and raise her to be a good person. She would do everything in her power to erase any evil planted in this innocent child's mind by the Nazis. And most of all, she would take this vulnerable little person and protect her with her life if need be. Zofia bent down, took Katja in her arms, and hugged her warmly as she vowed this to herself.

They walked across the bridge hand-in-hand, stopping in the middle to look across the pond that appeared golden from the light of the sun.

"We are going to England, leaving tomorrow. It will be a great adventure." Then Zofia continued speaking, more to herself than to Katja, "and, in the future, we will have another, even greater adventure, God willing. Someday, I cannot tell you when, but someday, a ship will leave for Palestine. This is a very special place. You and I will be on that ship. We will go together. There is nothing left for us here, little one. Our lives will begin again in Eretz Israel… the Promised Land."

Katja squeezed her hand. "I'm not afraid anymore."

Zofia bent down and hugged the little girl, kissing the top of her golden hair.

CHAPTER EIGHTY-EIGHT

BEFORE THE WAR ENDED, Britain had promised that the land of Palestine would be awarded to the Jewish people. The Zionists held fast to that dream throughout the entire war. This was to be the long-awaited Jewish homeland. Now that the war was over, Great Britain was not sure it wanted to keep its promise.

After their liberation from the Nazi terrors, Jewish refugees worked, saved, and waited, in hopes of embarking on the voyage that would carry them far away from Europe and all the memories they wanted to leave behind—far away, to Palestine, the Promised Land.

On July 11, 1947, a ship christened *Exodus* departed from a port near Marseille, France. Aboard this ship destined for Palestine, 4,515 immigrants sailed with hope in their hearts; 655 of the passengers were children. They were on their way to Palestine, where Jews could live without fear. The Promised Land.

Watching this ship sail into the open sea, one would believe this was the end of the Jewish struggle. They would be wrong. This was only the beginning.

CHAPTER EIGHTY-NINE

On a hot morning on July 11, 1947, with the sun beating relentlessly on their heads, Zofia held Katja's hand at the dock in Site, France, near Marseilles. Zofia watched Katja look around excitedly and wished she still had enough innocence to feel some of that awe. All she knew was that she was leaving Europe forever and, with it, the bitter memories of the Nazis and the war.

The English were not pleased about surrendering the land they promised to the Jews, and Zofia expected that there would be problems ahead. She gazed at the boat, a massive vessel with the word "Exodus" shining in black letters on her side. There had been much speculation among her friends about whether this boat would be allowed to cross the seas to Palestine or somehow be diverted back to dreaded German soil. The passage had cost her everything she'd saved, but it was worth the risk for Zofia. Through discussions about Palestine with Isaac, she'd come to yearn for a Jewish homeland. They'd talked about it often, and it was a dream that they shared. Now she would embark upon that dream with a precious child who was just as much a victim of Hitler's madness as she had been. A child not of her body, but a child she had come to love completely.

The lines to board the vessel were long. Everyone stood waiting, holding their papers and any belongings they had. All around her, Zofia heard the buzz of conversations. In each one, she heard words like "the Promised Land, a place of safety, a home for our people, a Jewish homeland at last, where our children can grow up without fear…"

The crowded line of hopeful, tattered, and broken refugees moved forward. A light sun shower fell from the sky.

"Finally, the end of our suffering," someone said.

"Perhaps we will finally have a land where we can live in safety, a place to call our home," a man said to another man who wore a tall, black hat.

"Yes, we have surely waited a long time, and *oy*, how we have suffered for this. But now, praise God, we are on our way to Palestine, to the Promised Land," a woman answered the man with the black hat, tears covering her bony cheeks.

The Promised Land. Yes, soon, all of them would board the boat called the Exodus and be on their way to Palestine, a land the English had promised them. A dream had come true, at long last. A dream that had kept so many alive during the horrors they endured in the concentration camps. Surely, the Jews had suffered enough. Surely, their suffering would end now as they boarded the vessel soon to sail out into the ocean, out of Europe, and away from the memories of all that had happened there. Soon, all of that would be behind them.

Soon, they would step aboard the boat and never look back. Soon. If only it had been that easy, if only… But the Jews, although they didn't know it at the time, the Chosen People, had a long road ahead: a road filled with challenges, danger, lies and false promises, unseen enemies, and a fight for a dream that would cost them dearly, and continue to cost them forever. But they would go forward to a barren desert on the other side of the world. From the dry, unproductive land, they would find a way to produce fertile soil capable of growing food. Here they would strive to build a homeland, a homeland for Jews, a place where Jews could turn if the world ever turned its back on them again, a place they would one-day call "Israel."

A sailor strolled by with a tiny puppy. The dog barked, and Katja turned around. Then Katja loosened her grip on Zofia's hand and ran out of line to see the little golden dog.

"Come back, Katja!" Zofia cried out. "I cannot go after you. We will lose our place in line."

Katja caught up with the man. She played with the dog and giggled as the little mutt licked her hand. There were too many people and too much chaos at the port that day for Zofia to allow Katja out of her sight. She left her place in the line to go after the child.

Zofia ran, pushing the crowds out of her way until she reached Katja.

"Look, Mama, isn't she a beautiful puppy? Can I have one when we get to Palestine, please?"

"Katja, I don't know. I don't know what things will be like when we get to Palestine. If it's possible, I will get you a dog. For right now, you must not leave my side under any circumstances. We talked about this last night. It would be far too easy for you to get lost here or on the boat, and anything could happen. Do you understand me?" Zofia reprimanded Katja, her voice harsher than she would have liked due to her nerves at almost losing sight of the child at the crowded port.

Katja looked up at Zofia, her lower lip puffed out. Her feelings were hurt, and she began to sob.

"I'm sorry, sunshine. Don't cry. I'm sorry that I yelled at you. I know you only wanted to see the dog, but please, you must not leave my side. You are far too precious to me. I don't want to lose you… All right? Promise me."

Katja nodded.

"Now, give me your hand. We will have to go to the end of the line. We've lost our place."

Zofia and Katja walked past the crowds waiting to board the *Exodus*. The smell of sweat permeated the air.

"Zofia!" a voice rang out from within the line of tattered refugees. "Zofia!" It was a voice she recognized, one she could not mistake. The bright rays of the sun on that crystal-blue day stung her eyes as she surveyed the crowd in search of the voice that called for her, the one who knew her by name.

And then her breath caught, her lungs tightened, and her hand went to her throat. She was shocked with recognition as she looked right into the eyes of a very familiar face. Zofia felt dizzy as if she might faint. Her heart beat too fast. Could she believe her eyes, or were they deceiving her, blinded by the sun's rays?

"Zofia…"

"Oh my God, it's you," she said. Zofia could hardly catch her breath. "You're here?" she said, knowing it sounded foolish, but she could not believe her eyes. "Is it really you?" The words caught in her throat.

"Yes, it's me…"

AUTHORS NOTE

I always enjoy hearing from my readers, and your thoughts about my work are very important to me. If you enjoyed my novel, please consider telling your friends and posting a short review on Amazon. Word of mouth is an author's best friend.

Also, it would be my honor to have you join my mailing list. As my gift to you for joining, you will receive 3 **free** short stories and my USA Today award-winning novella complimentary in your email! To sign up, just go to my website at www.RobertaKagan.com

I send blessings to each and every one of you,

Roberta

Email: roberta@robertakagan.com

ABOUT THE AUTHOR

I wanted to take a moment to introduce myself. My name is Roberta, and I am an author of Historical Fiction, mainly based on World War 2 and the Holocaust. While I never discount the horrors of the Holocaust and the Nazis, my novels are constantly inspired by love, kindness, and the small special moments that make life worth living.

I always knew I wanted to reach people through art when I was younger. I just always thought I would be an actress. That dream died in my late 20's, after many attempts and failures. For the next several years, I tried so many different professions. I worked as a hairstylist and a wedding coordinator, amongst many other jobs. But I was never satisfied. Finally, in my 50's, I worked for a hospital on the PBX board. Every day I would drive to work, I would dread clocking in. I would count the hours until I clocked out. And, the next day, I would do it all over again. I couldn't see a way out, but I prayed, and I prayed, and then I prayed some more. Until one morning at 4 am, I woke up with a voice in my head, and you might know that voice as Detrick. He told me to write his story, and together we sat at the computer; we wrote the novel that is now known as All My Love, Detrick. I now have over 30 books published, and I have had the honor of being a USA Today Best-Selling Author. I have met such incredible people in this industry, and I am so blessed to be meeting you.

I tell this story a lot. And a lot of people think I am crazy, but it is true. I always found solace in books growing up but didn't start writing until I was in my late 50s. I try to tell this story to as many people as possible to inspire them. No matter where you are in your life, remember there is always a flicker of light no matter how dark it seems.

I send you many blessings, and I hope you enjoy my novels. They are all written with love.

Roberta

MORE BOOKS BY ROBERTA KAGAN

AVAILABLE ON AMAZON

Margot's Secret Series

The Secret They Hid

An Innocent Child

The Blood Sisters Series

The Pact

My Sister's Betrayal

When Forever Ends

The Auschwitz Twins Series

The Children's Dream

Mengele's Apprentice

The Auschwitz Twins

Jews, The Third Reich, and a Web of Secrets

My Son's Secret

The Stolen Child

A Web of Secrets

A Jewish Family Saga

Not In America

They Never Saw It Coming

When The Dust Settled

The Syndrome That Saved Us

A Holocaust Story Series

The Smallest Crack

The Darkest Canyon

Millions Of Pebbles

Sarah and Solomon

All My Love, Detrick Series

All My Love, Detrick

You Are My Sunshine

The Promised Land

To Be An Israeli

Forever My Homeland

Michal's Destiny Series

Michal's Destiny

A Family Shattered

Watch Over My Child

Another Breath, Another Sunrise

Eidel's Story Series

And . . . Who Is The Real Mother?

Secrets Revealed

New Life, New Land

Another Generation

The Wrath of Eden Series

The Wrath Of Eden

The Angels Song

Stand Alone Novels

One Last Hope

A Flicker Of Light

The Heart Of A Gypsy